Now no one would ever recognise her as Geraldine Frances...

She touched one high cheekbone with her fingertips, feeling the living skin. It frightened her sometimes to look into the mirror and see this unfamiliar mask, but she had to suppress that fear. This was what she had wanted, this porcelain perfection of feature...this almost unreal beauty....

No matter how hard she tried to forget, to tell herself that she was now a beautiful, desirable woman, her old inhibitions wouldn't let go, grimly reinforcing the refrain that pounded over and over again through her mind. Words it would surely take many lifetimes to obliterate, words that she felt were carved upon her soul.

Charles's words, cruel and condemning, bitter and hurtful...the words he had used to describe her to another woman.

Penny Jordan is married and lives in a beautiful fourteenth-century house in rural Cheshire, England. The *New York Times* bestselling author of *Power Play*, Penny has more than sixty novels to her name, with a staggering 30 million copies of her books in print.

Penny Jordan

Silver

HARLEQUIN BOOKS

TORONTO·NEW YORK·LONDON
AMSTERDAM·PARIS·SYDNEY·HAMBURG
STOCKHOLM·ATHENS·TOKYO·MILAN

First published in Great Britain
in 1989
by Worldwide Books

ISBN 0-373-97120-6

First Harlequin North American paperback edition 1990

PART ONE
Silver

CHAPTER ONE

THERE were just the two of them in the ski-lift. The avalanche warning issued that morning by the Swiss Federal Avalanche Institute was keeping the other skiers away from these dangerous off-piste slopes.

In Gstaad Silver had overheard a group of guides mourning the loss of income the avalanche threat would bring.

Since the British heir to the throne had come so close to death on off-piste snow at Klosters, the authorities had clamped down heavily on guides foolish enough to allow the persuasion of their clients to overrule their own better judgement.

She, though, had no need of a guide. Neither, it seemed, did he. She recognised him. In his twenties and thirties he had been famous as an amateur racing driver, and it seemed he had never lost that need for the exhilarating thrill of speed. Especially when that thrill went hand in glove with death.

She knew he was watching her, and she knew why. In her mind's eye she re-created an image of herself, tall and slender, wearing a cerise ski-suit, the kind that speed-skiers wore. It moulded her body, revealing high, taut breasts that owed nothing to silicone injections or indeed any other artifice. She had a narrow ribcage and waist, flaring out to feminine hips and long, long legs. It was a body which could have been that of an athlete, but which, in her, was softened into voluptuous femininity.

Her head was covered with a snug-fitting hood, and her profile as she stared silently down into the valley would have made a poet cry for the inability of mere words to convey the perfect, haunting quality of her features.

As he looked at her, Guido Bartoli wondered what it would be like to make love to her, here, high above the mountains where the air sang crystal-clear and the snow cracked ominously under its own weight. He mused that if he were to make love to her, and if she were to scream her pleasure noisily into the silence, as he liked his women to do, it would undoubtedly bring about the avalanches that were threatened. Life, death, love—the eternal triangle. He dwelt for several cynical and pleasurable moments on the possible consequences of his mental meanderings.

To be destroyed in that moment of ecstasy by the displeasure of nature at having her virgin world of silence splintered. It would be a fitting way for him to die... But for her... He looked at her again.

Deep in her eyes was that fierce, hungry look he remembered from his own youth. No, she was not yet ready to join him in mutual destruction.

He was forty-two years old, a wealthy, good-looking man whose company was still much sought after in bed and out of it. He felt the familiar clutch of excitement tighten his muscles as he watched her.

She knew he was looking at her, but she didn't betray it. He liked that. It showed style. He wondered who she was. Most of the regular Gstaad crowd were known to him. This woman wasn't. Neither was she someone it would be easy to overlook.

She puzzled him—intrigued him—some sixth sense telling him that there was a dichotomy about her, a mysteriousness, that in itself was a challenge.

He spoke to her, softly, so as not to arouse the wrath of the snow. In English first, since her pale skin made him think she must have Celtic origins, and then, when that got no response, in French, and finally in Italian, half a dozen ruefully apologetic words that drew no response other than a coolly enigmatic look that for some reason made him feel slight chagrin. She had eyes like those of a young hawk he had once tamed: wild and feral; dangerous both to herself and others; green eyes that threw back the reflection of the trees edging the snowfields.

The lift stopped. He had to step past her to get off. She stood back from him and apologised.

In Russian.

The shock of it made him stand and stare at her. Russian, for God's sake! Just who the hell was she?

He stood watching her as the lift swung her upwards. Silver permitted herself a small smile. She'd heard about Guido Bartoli and wondered if they'd meet. He was an Italian count with a very Catholic marriage and a reputation for treating his mistresses with extreme generosity, as indeed he could afford to—but his wealth wasn't what interested Silver. She had contemplated using him for the final test and then had changed her mind, but it was a good omen that they should have met, and by accident, today of all days.

She stretched luxuriously, breathing in the cold, sharp mountain air. The threat of the storm and its attendant danger exhilarated her. She felt a fierce surge of pleasure and power run through her body—a body lithe with exercise and careful honing. A body that matched the beauty of her face.

She touched her skin and frowned slightly, reaching for her goggles. She mustn't let euphoria make her take a stupid risk . . . *Calculated* risks, now, they were a different thing altogether. Calculated risks were designed to test her progress, her readiness for a task which she had never deceived herself would be anything other than hard. She pulled on her goggles, her eyes focusing on the horizon. Green eyes with a touch of grey, that changed colour so that people who looked at her often weren't sure what colour they really were.

It had started to snow, and the peaks above her had disappeared.

No matter...she shrugged the thought of danger aside as the lift shuddered to a halt and she got off. The only passenger...the only skier foolhardy enough to come up so high, to risk the danger of off-piste skiing. But it wasn't on a mere whim that she was risking her life on this, one of Gstaad's most dangerous runs. It was a very definite purpose that had brought her here. The final test, bar one...

But first the run... and then... and then the ultimate barrier must be breached. For until it was...

A fine, delicate shudder ran through her. Closing her eyes, she arched back her throat and looked upwards, an expression of rapt, fierce anticipation carving the perfect structure of her face...an expression that was almost ecstatic as her body quickened with feverish excitement, her eyes behind her goggles glittering cold as the ice- and snow-covered mountain.

She smiled to herself as she recalled the look of chagrin in Guido Bartoli's eyes when he'd realised she was not going to respond to his flirting. It had amused her to address him in Russian. She had a facility for learning languages and was equally fluent in Italian, French and a number more. A legacy from her father, who had...

But no, she was not going to think of the past...not today. She had lived with it as her closest companion for the last two years, and today she was going to step away from it.

Guido had been right about one thing, though. She was Celtic in origin, heiress to a fortune so staggeringly large that even her trustees weren't quite sure exactly what she was worth.

And not just heiress to a fortune, but heiress to an ancient title as well, carrying a family name that echoed with over a thousand years of history. Her ancestors had been Celtic princes when Egypt had ruled the known world. They had been princes long before the Romans had discovered the misty shores of the land of the Angles, their names written on every page of history that followed that invasion. They had also had a facility for picking a winning side, and their English titles had added weight and wealth to their hereditary Irish lineage.

She was the last of her line, and her father had reared the girl who was the only child fate had seen fit to bestow on him as the son he had never had.

She stood ready at the top of the slope, poised, alert, the adrenalin flowing through her veins like a powerful drug. The day; her life; eternity itself lay spread out before her like the village below, offered up to her as a sacrifice, as she in turn offered up herself... To live or to die...the decision was not hers. Who but the fates knew on which side they would weigh the scales? A higher power, if such an authority existed, must see into her soul and know what she planned; reared by a father who had been insistent on a sporting code of ethics that no longer existed, she had felt it only fair to give that power a chance to intervene. If it chose not to do so...

She bent her knees, her body fluid and ready, waiting until the falling snow thickened, driven by the wind, and then she dug her poles into the fresh snow and laughed out loud, throwing herself forward into the ferocity of the storm.

If she was good enough, if her skill matched her self-confidence, she would survive; if it didn't, she would die, her body broken and her beauty destroyed.

The final test...but not the final hurdle. That still remained...and she knew enough about her own make-up to recognise what this ski-run was all about...the final psyching up for the barrier through which she must pass if she was going to go on and achieve her ultimate goal.

Snowy trees flashed past, blurred by her speed and the impact of the storm, and she felt the siren song of all she had done and would do sing in her blood.

This was her first taste of the narcotic of absolute self-confidence, but it would not be her last.

* * *

The chalet was small and utilitarian, unlike her own. Hers was a luxuriously equipped hideaway owned by a Saudi Arabian prince who had been persuaded to allow her to hire it for an unspecified amount of time. Its sole appeal for Silver was its inaccessibility. The over-whelming richness of its décor, the ostentation of its size and splendour, irritated her to the point of distaste. It was as though someone had tried to create the fabled luxury of a rich nomadic sheikh's tent within the totally unsuitable framework of a wooden chalet.

This one, though, was everything that such a building should be. Neat and four-square, with a balcony on the upper floor and a large glass window for viewing the mountain. Smoke curled slowly from the chimney, but she didn't hesitate as she used the key she had purloined to let herself in.

She was still wearing the cerise ski-suit. The chalet wasn't far from where she had finished her run. Another piece of careful planning. To the rear of the property lay the garage and drive, cleared of snow for access to the narrow road that linked the remote cluster of chalets, of which it was one, with Gstaad.

She let herself in and closed the door behind her. The entrance hall was plain and yet welcoming in a way in which the large, imposing, marble-flagged hallway to her rented chalet was not.

This one had a natural wood floor covered with a rag-rug. The floor was highly polished, and Silver smiled grimly as she stepped on the rug and discovered that it had been very carefully stuck to the floor.

As she opened the inner door she saw that several other rugs covered the polished floor in the main living-room of the chalet, their textures different, so that anyone walking on them would realise even blindfolded which way they were walking. One row led to the sofa, in front of the stove, another to the small kitchen, and the third to the stairs that rose up in one corner of the room.

She didn't linger in the living-room, despite the tempting warmth of the log-fuelled stove, but instead crossed it and went upstairs.

The chalet had two bedrooms, both with their own bathroom, and, outside, a passage linked the chalet to the garage and sauna.

She knew all this without having to look. She had done her research well, and in all honesty it hadn't been difficult. Annie had been all too easy to milk of information. She was so ridiculously proud of Jake and all that he had done—all too ready to sing his praises to anyone who was ready to listen.

Silver wondered idly whether, when Annie visited him up here, they shared one bed or whether she slept alone. Nothing she had ever said had indicated that they were lovers—just the opposite—and Silver knew that Annie still loved her dead husband, but...

Halfway up the stairs she paused, wondering what it would be like to make love with a blind man. Would it give a woman an added thrill of excitement to know that he must learn her by touch, taste and scent alone, and therefore employ those senses to make up for his lack of sight—or would she feel repulsed by the knowledge that those dark blue eyes could see nothing other than the blackness of permanent darkness?

At the top of the stairs she wondered if he had made love to many women since losing his sight, and then she shrugged the thought aside, heading first for his bathroom, where she stripped off her clothes and stood beneath the hot sting of the shower until her skin glowed.

Then, wrapped in a huge, fluffy white towel, she went into his bedroom, noting approvingly that the simple furniture was exactly right for the chalet, that the two paintings on the wall had been chosen with taste and a good eye for colour, and that the sheets on the bed were pure cotton and freshly laundered.

For a man who was currently virtually unemployable, and who had apparently no money of his own to fall back on, he lived very well. Very well indeed, even if the chalet did belong to one of Annie's wealthy patients.

Silver wasn't deceived by the chalet's apparent simplicity. Such a blending of colours and fabrics, so much use of materials that were natural rather than synthetic, so much attention to detail, right down to the pure and very expensive soap in the bathroom, not to mention the Hockneys on the wall downstairs—all whispered discreetly, to those with the properly attuned ear, of wealth and privilege. And more than that: of knowing just how such things should be done...and when, and by whom...

The chalet wasn't representative of Jake's taste, though; how could it be? It wasn't his. What kind of tastes would he have, a man who spent his life with the very roughest kind of people—those who dealt in drugs—and who was in Switzerland to recover from the effects of the bomb blast which had tragically destroyed his sight.

She unstrapped the plain gold watch which had been her father's last birthday present to her, along with the details of the various secret trust funds he had set up for her and the deeds to the Irish castle which had been in the family long before William the Bastard had ever set his covetous eyes on Harold's England.

She had loved her father. Now he was dead—a hunting accident, one of those appalling, unthinkable accidents that should surely never have happened to such a keen and excellent sportsman, a rider admired for his ability and skill.

No accident, of course, but her father had been too wealthy, too important, had had his fingers in far too many pies that no one wanted stirring for too much fuss to be made, and, besides, only she knew the truth. A quiet announcement...the death of the Earl of Rothwell, Lord Wesford, James, William, Geraint...and so on... All his titles and dignities...all his names: family names, each showing an affiliation for the various causes her family had espoused over the years. James for the

Stuarts, William for the Hanovers, Geraint, a derivation from the family's French titles.

She still missed him. Her father had had a brain which had allowed him to build a modest inheritance, counted merely in the odd million or so, into a multi-billion-pound empire. There wasn't an innovation or a discovery he hadn't been aware of and involved in—secretly, subtly... he had not been a man who ever courted publicity.

He had also been a first-rate sportsman. He had had everything to live for, mourned his friends at the funeral. What a tragic waste that he should die. And she had moved among those mourners, blundering, overweight, unable to imagine the enormity of her loss, for once unaware of the amused and contemptuous looks people gave her, the raised eyebrows and unkind comments...the incredulity that a man like her father should have produced a child like her.

But that was all behind her now. This wasn't the time to dwell on the past, other than to acknowledge what it had given her. Now she had to concentrate on the future...a future she could only be fit for if... She tensed, hearing a car drive up to the chalet. It had to be Jake. The taxi that collected him from the hospital would have picked him up at three, as it always did. Now it was almost four.

She wondered how long it would take him to find her. Not too long, surely? She had deliberately worn a particularly strong scent. She wondered if he would recognise it. She didn't normally wear it during the daytime, and to the best of her recollection there had only been one evening occasion on which she had met him. That had been Annie's birthday, when she had booked a table for her friend at Gstaad's most exclusive eating spot, only to have her refuse, uncomfortably explaining that she had already agreed to have dinner with Jake.

Silver smiled to herself as she remembered how Jake had stood there and looked at her... Strange to think he was blind. No one looking at him and not knowing it would ever realise. He had somehow or other perfected a trick of looking directly at people that made it seem as though he could actually focus on them.

He hadn't invited *her* to join them, simply smiled at her in that grim-lipped, scornful way of his that made it so abundantly clear what he thought of her. Rich bitch...spoiled playgirl...shallow...useless...predatory...she hugged to herself with glee the words he had not voiced but nevertheless felt, enjoying them, and the joke of it was that he had no idea that it was for *that*— because of his so obvious contempt and disdain—that she had picked him above the others she had contemplated approaching. His blindness only gave the situation an added piquancy.

It was a pity he knew so much about her. She had been angry when she'd discovered how much Annie had told him, but in the long run it was probably for the best. It would make any explanations so much less tedious and messy. And there would have had to be explanations, no matter whom she had chosen.

The car drove away and the door to the chalet opened. She had left the bedroom door open, but she still couldn't hear him moving. She had noticed that about him before: that silent, menacing tread that Annie had once told her was a legacy of his early army training.

Annie had never told her why he had left the army and joined the special anti-drugs squad of carefully chosen operatives, working alone and in secret, reporting only to their superior in Whitehall. Whatever the reason, it was unimportant as far as *her* plans were concerned.

'What are you doing here, Silver?'

Silver was glad he wasn't able to see her as her eyes widened fractionally. She hadn't heard him come upstairs, and the sight of him standing in the doorway, looking directly at her, made her muscles clench.

She forced her body to relax, curling her mouth in the lazy, teasing smile she had been practising, knowing that it would be reflected in her voice.

'Why don't you come over here and find out?'

She made no comment on the fact that he had recognised her. It simply confirmed her view that she had chosen correctly...made the right decision.

She watched as the mobile eyebrows rose. It was odd, after all he had been through, that his black hair should remain untinged by any grey at all, while she...

'Silver, I'm not in the mood to play games. Simply say what you've come to say and then get on your way.'

No compromise there, simply a harsh, flat statement that indicated very clearly what he thought of her. That was good...

'I want you to be my lover,' she told him equably. She had been practising this for over a week now, mentally rehearsing every question he would ask and every answer she would give, and now, with all the poise she could muster, which was considerable, she added coolly, 'Or rather, should I say, I want *you* to teach *me* how to make love to a man so that he won't be able to resist me?'

She smiled as she caught the betraying indrawn breath. Much as Annie knew about her, there was one thing she did not know.

'You see, Jake,' she went on, taking firm hold of her advantage, 'I *need* that expertise, and I need it very badly.'

'What the hell kind of game is this?' he asked her angrily, and she knew that she had broken through the tough armour of his self-assurance because he swore at her, something she had never heard him do before. An odd conceit in a man who lived the way he did.

'No game,' she assured him smoothly. 'Annie's told you a lot about me, hasn't she? About why I'm here? About what I intend to do...?'

She saw from his face that she was right, and went on as though he had invited her to do so.

'Unfortunately, there's one major stumbling block. As a virgin, I'm afraid that I rather lack the—er—expertise necessary for my plans . . .'

'A virgin . . . ?'

She gave him a cold smile which showed in her voice as she bit off the words. 'Amazed? You needn't be. As my ex-fiancé once commented, a woman as ugly as me in both face and body is hardly likely to attract lovers. Of course,' she added pleasantly, '*you* can't see me . . . and I understand that physically you *might* find it impossible to become my lover, but I'm sure if you were to imagine I were someone else . . .'

Now she had broken through his guard.

'My God,' he swore, 'what kind of woman are you?'

'The kind who generally gets what she wants and pays generously for it,' she told him sweetly.

'Pay?'

For the first time in the months she had known him she saw him make an awkward movement. He stepped forward automatically, as though he intended to reach out, grab hold of her, and inflict a physical punishment on her; but she had deliberately moved the chair from beside the bed to the open doorway, and as he walked into it he tensed and swore savagely under his breath. Her father would have described what she had done as cheating. She tried not to admit that knowledge. She couldn't afford that kind of weakness . . . not now . . . not ever again.

'Please don't be foolish about this, Jake,' she said with composure. 'Obviously I should wish to pay for the skills you can teach me, just as I would pay for any other commodity.'

'Just the way you paid for your new face,' he jeered unkindly, but she didn't wince. Why should she? Once she had been sensitive, vulnerable, easily hurt by others, but not any more.

'At least *I* have a genuine reason for being here,' she told him sardonically, unable to resist the temptation to punish him just a little. She saw that her barb had found its mark. He tensed momentarily, his whole stance betraying wariness, and then it was gone and he had himself under control.

'Well, you've come to the wrong man, Silver,' he told her curtly. 'I don't need your money. Now get the hell out of my bed before I throw you out...'

Now she had him cornered, and the fierce thrill of triumph that ran through her was visible in the brilliant glitter of her eyes.

'You're lying, Jake,' she countered softly, and then, before he could speak, added coolly, 'I *could* allow you to continue to lie to me, but I don't have that kind of time to waste. You see, I happened to be standing outside Annie's sitting-room when you were telling her how desperately you did need money.'

What she hadn't heard was why. Annie, it seemed, knew far more about Jake than she was prepared to admit. It had been obvious to Silver from the quality of their conversation that they were two people who knew one another well—as friends, not as lovers—and, intrigued as she was by the mystery that seemed to enshroud Jake, she was pretty sure that his presence at the clinic had nothing at all to do with any supposed reaction to his surgery, as Annie had originally intimated to her in the days when she'd had far too much to accomplish herself to worry about other people's affairs.

Lost in her own thoughts, Silver took several seconds to become alive to the deep aura of menace emanating from Jake. It washed over her in an icy cold blast, activating her own instinct for self-preservation.

'What you want the money for, what you do with it—that's your concern and not mine, but don't waste both our time by lying about not needing it,' she told him, ignoring his anger.

She waited, feeling the tension ease out of her body a little as the menace evaporated.

'Hasn't anyone ever told you that it's dangerous to listen outside other people's doors?' he asked her.

Silver shrugged the question aside and said firmly, 'I'm prepared to pay you a million pounds——'

She didn't get any further; Jake interrupted her with a smothered curse.

'God! If it's just your virginity you want to lose, you could lose it for free any night of the week just by picking up someone——'

'It isn't,' she interrupted him flatly. 'If you'd listened to what I said originally, you'd realise that. My virginity isn't of any importance. I simply mentioned it to illustrate why I need the expertise you can teach me. It isn't pleasure I want from you, Jake. It's simply knowledge. A crash course in what turns a man on, in what sends him out of his mind with desire... In what makes him forget everything else in the driving need to possess one particular woman.'

'Go and buy yourself a sex manual,' he jeered. 'It will come much cheaper than a million pounds.'

But Silver could see where the tiny betraying nerve pulsed in his jaw as his mouth compressed, and she felt a corresponding savage kick of triumph in her own stomach. She was going to win... whether he knew it or not, she was going to win.

She didn't make the mistake of letting him sense her triumph. He might be blind, but his other senses, already honed by the years he had spent staying alive in one after another of the world's danger zones, had been hardened by the accident, compulsively perfected by what Annie had once, in an unguarded moment, described to her as the strongest will she had ever come across. His perception was a hundred times greater than that of the majority of sighted human beings.

'I'll give you twenty-four hours to think over my proposition,' she told him coolly. 'After that, the deal's off.'

As she spoke, her voice was cold and brisk, formidably like that of her father, a man who had singlehandedly run one of the world's most successful private business empires. It had none of the deliberate sensuality she had injected into it before. She was a clever woman, who for the first time in her life was learning to direct that intelligence into promoting for herself a false image—which in time she was determined would *become* herself—and she had already learned the power of projecting conflicting messages. She did it now, contrasting the frozen chill of her voice with the deliberately erotic movements of her body. She slipped off the bed and walked slowly up to and then past him, holding herself tall, using her powerful imagination to create the role she needed.

She was a high priestess of an ancient religion, sure of her strength and her power, knowing that her body was one of her strongest tools, unconcerned by her nudity. Her hair rippled down her back, a silver cloud, her skin warmed by the room's heat.

She didn't touch him—that would have been a beginner's mistake—but she walked close enough to him to be quite sure he would be aware of her nudity...of her body, with its woman's scents and allure.

Annie had told her that he was generally an abstemious man who didn't indulge in any of life's pleasures greedily. It was an admission Silver had rather trapped the other woman into giving.

A dulcet comment about the anomaly of the fact that he was a man in his early thirties apparently without any intimate relationship in his life had provoked Annie into defending him, and had also elicited the information that he had once been married and that his wife was now dead.

Silver had sensed that Annie was torn between protecting Jake's privacy and telling her more. She had been curious to know how his wife had died, but not curious enough to push Annie too hard.

She had other ways of finding out all there could possibly be to find out about him if she so chose…there were those admirable men of business in Switzerland who had looked after her father's affairs so discreetly and who now looked after hers. But Jake Fitton's past held no interest for her, and neither did his future. She had a use for him, that was all—a use that, once finished, would cease to be of any importance.

He let her walk past him without moving, looking stoically towards the window as though unaware of the tormenting, warm human presence of her.

Her clothes were in his bathroom. She opened the door, wondering what she would have done if he had given way and reached for her.

She didn't like admitting that she could make mistakes, and *had* he reached for her she would have had to acknowledge that she had made one.

She didn't want a man who wanted her, who felt desire for her…just as she didn't want to know anything about Jake other than the fact that he suited her requirements admirably and that he disliked her enough to ensure that their relationship did not cross any of the barriers she intended to set around it.

Yes, he was ideal for her purpose, this cold, angry, embittered human being who looked at her with those hawk's eyes that couldn't see her, but that still held bitterness and dislike. She approved of that. She understood it and could relate to it. She needed him, and she meant to coerce him into submitting to that need.

CHAPTER TWO

SILVER waited out the twenty-four hours in her chalet. The oil sheikh had installed a jacuzzi in a specially built extension that was raised on pillars some thirty feet above the ground.

The room was circular, one third of its wall-space taken up by specially treated glass that allowed those inside to look out, but no one to look in. From the jacuzzi the view of the mountains was spectacular.

Low divans followed the curve of the glass wall, heaped with priceless rugs and silk cushions. The jacuzzi was large enough to hold an entire rugby team, and sometimes, when she relaxed in it, Silver wondered about the women who had shared it with the sheikh.

Had they enjoyed the experience? He was fifty-odd years old and fat, with heavy jowls and small, greedy eyes. His hands flashed with jewels and his beard smelled of perfume.

Silver had rented the chalet through an intermediary who had been instructed to describe her as a very wealthy middle-aged widow. She had not wanted any unheralded visits from the chalet's owner while she was in residence, something which she had heard on the grapevine had happened to a beautiful, amoral socialite she knew, who had described the event with a shudder of distaste.

The socialite's companion, a sleek, too pretty nineteen-year-old boy with homosexual tendencies, had laughed maliciously and taunted, 'Oh, come on, you must have been tempted. They say he's a very generous lover, and gives uncut stones as a mark of his appreciation. The more appreciative he is, the higher the carat of the

23

diamond.' And he had looked pointedly at the brilliantly cut stone she had been wearing on her finger.

Everyone had laughed until she had told him tartly, 'This, my dear one, is a fake. He also punishes those who don't please him by knocking them around or passing them on to his bodyguards.'

Silver had no real fears that he would arrive unexpectedly. She moved languidly in the warm water and then got out. The twenty-four hours were almost up, and she had heard nothing from Jake.

She dried herself, standing carelessly in front of the huge window, enjoying the room's heat. A jungle of plants covered the back wall, turning the room into a luxurious green cavern of tropical indolence, an erotic contrast to the crisp sharpness of the snow outside.

Before she dressed she smoothed body lotion into her skin; it had the same expensive perfume as her scent. It left her skin velvet-soft and with the same lustrous gleam as expensive heavy satin.

Jake had another two hours. After that she would start packing for her return trip.

The phone rang, and she dropped the silk underwear she had just picked up, reaching for the receiver, subduing the wild dance of elation that sang through her blood.

'Silver?'

It wasn't Jake. She forced down her disappointment.

'Annie. How are you?'

'Fine. Can you make it for dinner on Friday? It will only be a fairly informal affair. Some old friends are passing through. Jake will be there...'

'Does he know you've invited me?' Silver questioned her, wondering if this was a skilful ploy of Jake's to evade her time-limit and yet accept her terms at the same time.

'He doesn't even know yet that I'm going to invite *him*,' Annie told her.

'Mm...Friday...I'm afraid I won't be able to make it. I won't be here.'

There was a short silence, and then Annie queried almost sharply, 'So you're going through with it, then? I understand why you feel the way you do, but is it really wise? Wouldn't it be better to simply leave things as they are? To put the past behind you?'

'No,' Silver told her with emotionless economy. They had been through this so many times before, ever since in that moment of weakness she had confessed to Annie how important it was to her that she reach the goal she had set herself—an impossible goal, some might claim; an unhealthy, even dangerous goal, others might say...especially Annie...especially if she knew the full truth. There were certain things that Silver had kept back from her, certain truths which she had suppressed because even now she could hardly accept them herself.

To have learned that the man she loved had not only betrayed her but was also involved in her father's death, and in supplying drugs to other members of the wealthy and élite circles he moved in, had devastated her.

No, these were not things that could be told to anyone. Charles had boasted to her that he was beyond the reach of the law, that he had powerful friends who would protect him...well, she was going to show him that, though he might think himself invincible, he was vulnerable just as she had been vulnerable...just as her father had been vulnerable. She was going to bring him down...to destroy him...to...

'Silver, think!' Annie cautioned her. 'If you do succeed, what then—what afterwards?'

'I don't care about afterwards,' Silver told her truthfully.

In her cluttered, untidy office, Annie stared at the calendar on the wall. It depicted a paradisiacal Indian Ocean island, all pale yellow sands, emerald seas and waving palm trees. If she was truthful, she had never felt happy about doing Silver's operation; that was why she had

abandoned the lucrative field of cosmetic surgery in the
first place. The puritan in her had balked at what she
was doing... And yet there had been something about
Silver that had called out to her for help... something
in her very desolation and determination that she hadn't
been able to resist. She had felt an awareness of the extent
of her suffering, of her need... she, who had thought
herself armoured against emotionalism, just hadn't been
able to refuse to help her.

And then, of course, there had been the money.

Five million pounds to help finance her clinic here in
Switzerland... her very special clinic where she used her
skills to treat the victims of human violence and destruc-
tiveness, mending ruined faces and bodies torn, ripped
apart... destroyed by human cruelty.

All her skill, though, hadn't been enough to save Tom.

As always, the memory of her husband weakened her,
pain sweeping through her, blotting out the environment of her hospital with its orderly, sane demands on
her, taking her to another place... another life and the
man she had shared them with.

It was no good remembering Tom. He was never going
to come back, never going to bound into their flat,
sweeping her off her feet and into bed. She trembled,
remembering how it had been between the two of them,
and knowing that it was as much because of that...
because of all she had shared with Tom that Silver would
never have... that she had finally been persuaded to carry
out the operations which had given Silver her new face.

'Be careful,' she said quietly. 'Be very careful, Silver...'

Silver smiled mirthlessly as she replaced the receiver.
She had no need of Annie's warning. She knew full well
the enormity of the task she had set herself, but it would
be accomplished, and without Jake Fitton's help if
necessary. There were other men.

*   *   *

But none quite as ideal, she acknowledged bitterly twelve hours later, standing on the platform waiting for the local train which would take her to Innsbruck. She was travelling light, the same way she had arrived: one piece of hand luggage, into which she had managed to pack everything she had brought with her.

In Paris she would buy new clothes, clothes for the woman she had made herself into. For the woman Annie had made her into, she amended grimly. She had no illusions about herself. Outwardly she now bore the physical attributes of a beautiful woman. The ability to reflect those physical attributes inwardly, to project the reality of being that woman—that task lay with *her*. She had the determination to do it . . . the motivation . . . she had the intelligence. And the skill? Only time would tell.

She now possessed the physical body and face of a beautiful woman; in Paris she would clothe that body as it needed to be clothed if she was to attract Charles's attention and ensnare him. She knew exactly what kind of woman appealed to him. How he liked initially to be challenged, even dominated by the woman he desired . . . It was only later that his own true character surfaced and he began to need to inflict cruelty and humiliation on his lovers . . . to subjugate them . . .

She had learned a good deal about the real Charles since her father's death . . . about the Charles who hid behind the mask of almost godlike physical beauty . . . behind the appeal of his tall, broad-shouldered body and his golden, deceitful face.

Yes, in Paris she would buy clothes: clothes from Valentino and Armani, from Chanel and Yves St Laurent, clothes from those designers who knew all about how subtly to emphasise a woman's sexuality without making a parody of it.

And from Paris she would go to London. To a new life . . . a new identity. Everything was arranged: the exclusive apartment that whispered sleekly of old money . . . the letters that would allow her to enter

Charles's milieu as an accepted member of that exclusive and very small world.

Everything was planned, right down to the smallest detail.

A frown touched her forehead as she acknowledged the one major obstacle still confronting her. She now had to find someone to take Jake Fitton's place. Someone dispensable... someone who would give her what she wanted... what she had to have if her plan was to succeed.

Damn Jake Fitton. She had known he would be difficult to persuade, had known it instinctively, a gut-deep reaction rather than any logic. After all, by his own admission he needed the money... and she had counted on his needing that money too much to refuse her.

That she should have miscalculated so badly and so early on in her planning was more worrying than she wanted to admit. It spoke of an underlying lack of facts; of having made an emotional rather than a clinical decision; of having made the kind of basic error her father would have derided. He had taught her to play chess, he had taught her to gamble for the highest stakes, and he had taught her to run his business affairs, which were now hers... and she had thought she had learned those lessons well. She had thought there was nothing anyone could teach her about man's basic greed and vulnerability; now she was having to rethink the assessments she had made... to backtrack... to look for an alternative route by which she could reach her ultimate goal.

The train arrived. She got on board without looking back, swaying easily down the carriage, knowing that people were watching her, but remaining outwardly oblivious to their interest.

She sat down and removed a magazine from her bag, coolly snubbing the attempts of the man seated opposite her to engage her in conversation.

Maybe in Paris she would find a man. She told herself it was stupid to allow herself to get so worked up over Jake's refusal of her proposition, that there was no point in dwelling on what was after all a very minor matter, but it remained there like a small shadow, clouding her mood, growing as the miles passed. The fact that he had rejected her as a woman didn't bother her... After all, she reasoned mirthlessly, that was something she was used to.

No, it was her own miscalculation that worried her... her own failure to correctly judge the situation, guess what his reactions would be. It showed a grave lack of judgement—a lack of judgement she could not afford. And only now did she admit that she had chosen Jake Fitton as much because he was such a challenge as because of his suitability for the role. It was that small piece of vanity that had been her downfall, and now she was furious with herself too for putting her whole plan into jeopardy simply for the unnecessary and trivial pleasure of putting Jake down, of forcing him to acknowledge her superiority.

His thinly veiled contempt of her had rankled after all... and that was a weakness she could not afford to have. After all, before she was finished, there would be people who felt far more than mere contempt for her...

She closed her eyes and leaned back in her seat, ruthlessly regimenting her thoughts, forcing herself to admit her own stupidity...

The train rattled into Innsbruck.

She was spending the night in a hotel before flying out in the morning. A porter caught sight of her and hurried towards her beaming, only to grimace when he saw she had no luggage. She walked out into the sharp winter sunlight, looking for a taxi. A car drew up alongside her, the rear door opened and from inside it Jake Fitton said quietly, 'Two million pounds.'

She wanted to refuse, to tell him that it was too late, that the deal was off. The words trembled on her tongue, but she fought them back. She couldn't afford to give in to emotionalism now.

Instead she smiled and said coldly, 'You put a high price on yourself, Jake. I hope you're worth it.' And then she slid into the car beside him, closing the door and settling herself into her seat while he instructed the driver.

He was taking her back to his chalet, she realised, listening. Two million pounds. Well, she could afford it—easily! She closed her eyes again; her heart was thumping frantically. Until this moment she hadn't wanted to admit to herself how important it was that it was this man who completed the final hurdle for her...that his acceptance of her terms had a symbolism that was very important to her. Far more important than the man himself.

On the drive back to Gstaad he addressed no comment to her, and she was skilled enough to make none of her own.

She had been brought up by a father whose realisation, eight years after her birth, that she would be the only child he could ever have had led him to pour into her all that he himself had learned in his determination to make her a fitting heir to his name and possessions. Car journeys, for her, were always a reminder of those times when she had sat beside him in the back of the Bentleys he had always chosen over the more status-laden Rolls-Royces, listening while he talked, answering while he questioned. So Jake's silence was an added burden.

She wondered if such silence was habitual to him, or if he was deliberately trying to unnerve her. Apart from that afternoon in his chalet, she had never really been alone with him, having always encountered him only in Annie's company.

On those occasions he and Annie had talked as old friends did. There had been silences, generated when he'd become aware that she was there, a silent third, an interloper on their intimacy, and then it had been Annie who had talked, sensing the atmosphere between them and trying her best to disperse it.

The road twisted and turned, offering superb views that were not designed for the nauseous or nervy. In Gstaad they had to stop to allow returning skiers to cross the road. Silver recognised Guido Bartoli among them. Even now it was not too late to change her mind.

The skiers cleared, and the car pulled away smoothly.

'Second thoughts?' Jake said quietly beside her, focusing on her as though he could see her.

She had known from the moment she met him that he was dangerous, ruthless—a merciless foe—but such enmity demanded a degree of involvement, of intimacy even, that would not enter their relationship.

Allowing only polite coldness to inform her face and voice, she said quietly, 'Two million pounds is a lot of money.'

He smiled at her, a curling, taunting smile that said what they both knew: that her second thoughts had nothing to do with money.

As she looked away from him, Silver wondered why, when, since he was blind, she was completely free to look at him, to study and assess him, she found it so difficult to do so.

Where did it come from, this innate distaste for breaching his privacy even when she knew he would be unaware of it?

It was true that he was conspicuously formidable, hardened by life into something almost indestructible. You could see that in him by just looking at him, by seeing how he reacted to his blindness, how he accepted it and adapted to it, daring it to imprison him.

They had reached the chalet. Silver fumbled for the door-handle and got out, waiting for Jake to join her. He stopped to say something to the driver and then walked across to her, finding her unerringly.

He unlocked the chalet door, telling her calmly, 'Just as a matter of interest, I've had the locks changed.'

Silver followed him inside. The stove was burning warmly, and from the kitchen came the mouth-watering aroma of something cooking.

'I thought it might be as well if you moved in here for the duration of your...tuition. I've allocated you a bedroom—second on the left. It doesn't have a private bathroom, but there is a shower. Since I'm sure neither of us wants to draw this out any longer than necessary, I suggest we make a start this evening. Since you specifically mentioned that seduction was your prime objective, I have to assume that where the non-sexual aspects of such a role are concerned you require no enlightenment.'

He paused, as calmly polite as a lecturer addressing a student, which of course she was.

Silver inclined her own head and replied evenly, 'Your assumptions are correct.'

'Mm...you sound confident, but a confident woman wouldn't have worn that perfume you were wearing the other day. It's too strong...too obvious. Unless, of course, your prey has a particular penchant for it.'

Silver almost gasped at his astuteness. He was so close to having guessed exactly why she had chosen that particular perfume. The perfumer who had mixed it for her had disapproved.

'Tuberoses are not really for you,' he had told her critically, but she had ignored his advice, insisting that he made the strong, heavy scent.

'I'm sure I don't need to say this, and you must forgive me for being crass, but since the object of this exercise is not to seduce *me* I'd prefer you not to use it...'

It took her several seconds to assimilate the subtle insult. When she did she was tempted to retaliate, but she forced herself to say mildly, 'It costs a thousand pounds an ounce. In view of your extortionate fee, every little I can save is a bonus.'

He didn't smile, but simply gave her a level, assessing look which she withstood only by reminding herself that he could not actually see her.

'Next point—clothes. Since you are ultimately to play the seductress, I have no doubt you will probably want to dress for the part. Again, I would caution you against overstatement. I personally find nothing particularly erotic about a woman who has obviously dressed herself with sex in mind. However, the discovery that a woman dressed in jeans and a sweatshirt, with her face free of make-up, is wearing silk satin underwear...now, that...'

Silver was tempted to lie and say that she was allergic to silk, but controlled the childish impulse, saying curtly, 'I'd like to go up to my room and unpack.'

He shrugged, looking at her impatiently.

'In a moment. There are still some points we have to discuss. The first, and I should have thought one of the most important as far as you are concerned, is that I have a clean bill of health, at least as far as any sexually transmitted diseases are concerned.

'The second is that I have assumed that you will have taken the necessary precautions to ensure that no pregnancy occurs.'

'I have,' agreed Silver coldly.

'Good. Now, since I'm hungry, we may as well start the first lesson now. You can leave your unpacking until later. Right now, try imagining that you've invited your prospective victim round for a meal. During the course of this meal you intend to make him sexually aware of you and also of your availability. How would you accomplish that?'

Silver felt her heart thumping just a little bit too fast. This was what she wanted, but now that it was here... She tried to blank out of her mind Jake as a person and instead use her imagination to create the scenario he had just described.

She closed her eyes, summoning concentration, asking him a little huskily, 'Two questions...'

She opened her eyes. He seemed to be watching her.

'One: how long have we known one another? Two: what is our existing relationship? Do we work together, or...?'

'We've met twice before,' he told her immediately. 'The first time a mutual acquaintance invited us both to dinner. The second was at a cocktail party when you discovered that my existing lover has gone to spend a fortnight with her parents. This invitation for dinner was given on the pretext of your having been asked to keep an eye on me, so to speak, by my lover.'

Silver gave him a sharp look spiked with dislike.

'What's wrong?' he asked her evenly. 'Don't you like the character I've cast for you?'

She digested his silky-voiced comments in silence. Annie had obviously told him a great deal. Too much. 'I have no feelings at all about her. I was just wondering why you accepted the invitation.' She wasn't going to let him guess at her disquiet. He was trained to play on people's weaknesses. For all she knew, he might simply be assessing...guessing... He smiled at her then, a mocking, warning smile that made her muscles lock.

'Ah, now that's for me to know and you to gamble on, isn't it?' he told her softly. 'After all, surely that's what this is all about—knowing your victim's vulnerabilities? You've got five minutes and then we begin. I've arrived at your front door and you've let me in.'

She closed her eyes, blotting out both the man and her surroundings; the latter was easy to do, the former surprisingly difficult. She tried to superimpose on his granite-tough features another man's smoother, younger face and to hold on to that vision. She waited until she had only seconds left before saying softly, 'Jake...you've made it. Marvellous,' and wondered if he'd notice her subtle and deliberate betrayal of the fact that she had doubted that he would arrive. 'Come on in and make yourself at home. Dinner won't be long... It won't be anything very special either, I'm afraid.' She mimicked the warm gurgle of laughter she had once heard an acquaintance use to devastating effect. She had a good ear and was adept at reproducing intonations and nuances. 'I was running late at the gallery and only had time to rush into my local delicatessen on the way back, but then I did warn you that I was no cook, didn't I?'

She gave a slow, warm smile that promised that she was far more accomplished in other areas, which she hoped was carried through into her voice, because Jake could certainly never see the smile.

'What should I do with my coat?'

The interruption was unexpected, as was the way Jake feigned uncertainty, looking back over his shoulder as though searching for a hallway.

'Here...let me take it.'

Silver knew she was several seconds late in picking up her cue. She also had an odd reluctance to approach him and take the jacket he was slipping off.

'It's freezing outside, isn't it?' she improvised wildly, thrown off-key by his unexpected participation. And then, remembering something a friend had once told her, she added quickly, 'I've lit a fire in the sitting-room. Come on through.'

She still hadn't taken his coat and he checked her abruptly, saying briefly, 'Adequate, Silver, but not good. The fire was good, but you failed to make good use of the opportunity I gave you when I asked what I should do with my coat, and the suggestion that something more exciting than dinner might be on offer was very precious...some might even say tacky. We'll go through it again, only this time we'll reverse the roles. Still, at least you didn't pretend I'd arrived early and caught you in the middle of getting changed,' he said drily. 'I suppose that's something. Now listen...'

Speaking as though he were she, he turned to her, matching the smile she had used.

'First, before he even sets a foot inside the door, you'll have prepared a mental dossier on him: what he likes and doesn't like, his weaknesses and strong points. Let's say this particular victim is an up-and-coming producer of television documentaries with a slant towards the political. You just happen to number among your acquaintances a politician you know he's been keen to meet. And if you don't, I'm sure you'll be able to find a way to make sure that you do.

'You open the door. He's on edge, not sure what the evening's going to hold. He's aware of the signals you've been sending out, enjoyed the prelude to flirtation, but is now getting cold feet, wondering if the evening is going to end up heavy and problematical.

'You surprise him, get him off guard. You pull a pretty regretful face and tell him you've been trapped into joining some old friends for dinner, but that he's included in the invitation. He breathes relief. The pair of you leave for the kind of venue you know is going to impress him. Your tame politician is already there. You introduce them and discreetly pretend not to notice how impressed he is.

'At a suitable opportunity, whenever the politician's gone to the bar or whatever, you tell the victim how marvellous he's being, helping you to entertain your father's brother's cousin's dull friend. If you've done your homework well, you can even get the politician to dangle some tempting bait in front of him, by praising his work and suggesting that the two of them get together.

'Already your victim is disarmed. He's totally forgotten that he wasn't sure he wanted to have dinner with you.

'As soon as dinner's over, you start getting a little on edge. You look at your watch...make it subtly obvious that your attention isn't really on your victim. He'll feel the withdrawal symptoms like a blast of Arctic air. You announce hesitantly that you really must leave. On the way home he asks you if something's wrong. You hesitate and then admit to man-trouble. You're expecting a phone-call or whatever. He then starts thinking he's mis-understood the entire situation and suffers the conse-quent challenge to his ego. When you invite him in for a drink, he's only too eager to accept and offer you his ''brotherly'' advice——'

'Oh, come on,' Silver interrupted him acidly. 'That wouldn't deceive a five-year-old. It's so obvious.'

'Never underestimate the efficacy of the obvious. That is why it is obvious, after all.'

'This is ridiculous,' Silver told him sharply. 'I haven't come here to play these kind of games. What I require you to instruct me in is sexual technique. That's all.'

'If that's the way you want it.'

He shrugged and seemed completely unaffected by her outburst. Silver, on the other hand, was flushed and angry. Did he think her such a fool that she hadn't got the intelligence or the ability to be able to coax her prey into her carefully baited trap? She had seen others do it often enough.

'I'm hungry,' she said, aggressively now. 'Do I get any dinner, or is that an optional extra?'

There was a small silence. She could feel him as-sessing her, and she cursed herself for so nearly losing her temper. He was probing her for her weaknesses as deliberately and cold-bloodedly as she had searched for his.

'Board and lodging is inclusive,' he told her unemotionally.

Over dinner neither of them spoke, Silver because she was still too angry, as much with herself as with him. *His* silence, she suspected, had a more dangerous and manipulative motive.

She didn't offer to help afterwards as he loaded the dishwasher and deftly restored the kitchen to pristine order.

He hadn't offered her anything to drink during dinner, or had anything himself, and he didn't offer her any-

thing now, saying briskly as he walked back into the
room, 'Well, we'd better make a start, hadn't we? We'll
take all the opening stages as accomplished. Your victim
has reached the stage where he's ready to contemplate
wanting to make love to you.'

She was sitting in one of the chairs in front of the
fire, and as he came towards her he told her drily, 'In
order to facilitate matters, it might be advisable if I show
you what's possible, preferable—and desirable.'

He sat down on the sofa and added, 'Come and sit
here,' and when she would have sat next to him said
firmly, 'No, not there... Here on the floor.'

Silver shot him a suspicious glance, but his face was
perfectly grave and composed, as controlled and
emotionless as though he were quite simply a lecturer
instructing a rather dull pupil.

As she knelt ungraciously at his feet, he told her wryly,
'In the harems of the East, the concubines used to be
taught to wriggle snakelike upwards from the foot of the
bed, adoring their master's person with their hands and
lips as they went.'

Silver was glad that he couldn't see the betraying wave
of colour that burned her skin. With great difficulty she
managed to stop her colour from fluctuating.

'Not that I'm suggesting you do the same thing, at
least not at this stage, but it's a point worth remembering. Now, sit in front of me, resting your back against
my legs.'

Silver did as he instructed, sitting ramrod-straight as
she stared into the fire.

'Now, when I speak to you, instead of turning round
to look at me you can tilt your head back so that, were
I able to see, what I would see would be the undoubtedly
tempting line of your exposed throat... your breasts...
very temptingly within easy reach of my hand... thus.'

She wasn't prepared for the brief, clinical touch of his
hand, and her body flinched at the contact until she

willed it into acquiescence. 'I could, if I wished, lean down to kiss you, or, more probably, reach down to pull you up over my body, like so.'

His hands fitted easily beneath her armpits, and although she was so tall he turned her easily, so that for a brief, startling moment of time her face was pressed against his hard thigh. Then he was drawing her upwards, as though she were as fluid as a piece of silk.

'At this stage if I were physically aroused you would be aware of it, and if I weren't . . . Well, there are several options open to you, depending upon how much time you have and how far the relationship has already advanced.

'If it's still in its early stages and you think I'm drawing you up to kiss you, like so . . .'

He lifted her easily so that she was virtually draped across his body. One hand in the hollow of her back pressed her torso against his; the other found her nape and locked smoothly in her hair, his mouth cold and clinical on hers.

She wondered a little unkindly if he closed his eyes when he kissed her or if his perpetual darkness rendered it unnecessary.

Her own had closed instinctively, more to blot out the sight of him than to focus her awareness on his mouth, which was just as well, she acknowledged grimly, because there was certainly nothing provocative or erotic in its distant possession.

His eyes weren't closed, but his lids were lowered so that his dark irises glittered between them. She lay totally unmoving against him, not wanting to remember how she had felt when Charles had kissed her—how joyously, frantically grateful she had been that he loved and wanted her; how eager to respond . . . to please . . .

'You're not concentrating.' The harsh criticism jolted her out of her memories, her body tensing in dislike before she could stop it.

'You're supposed to be learning how to arouse a man to desire, not wallowing in self-pitiful memories,' he derided her.

She stifled her rage that he should so easily have followed her thoughts.

'Now listen and remember. You've gained an advantage—physical contact. Now you've got to make the most of it . . . turn a tentative embrace into an erotic enticement.' When she said nothing, he muttered under his breath, 'My God, what the hell happened to you when they were handing out good old-fashioned feminine instinct?'

She could have told him that she had never been encouraged to develop her femininity; that her father had treated her as the son he could never have; that plain women, ugly women, as she had heard herself described, were not given many opportunities to develop such instincts. But instead she folded her mouth into a hard line and reminded him coldly, 'If I *had* those kinds of instincts, I wouldn't need you to teach me, would I?'

He was still holding her, but there was nothing intimate about it, apart from the proximity of their bodies, his own all hard, solid, unyielding muscle, unprepared to accommodate her more vulnerable softness, so that leaning into him and being held there hurt her breasts. She tried to ease her discomfort by moving away, but the weight of his hand on her back wouldn't allow her to put any space between them, and all she could do was move slightly sideways.

'Let go of me,' she complained. 'I can hardly breathe.'

She felt his chest expand as he suddenly took a deep breath and she winced at the uncomfortable pressure against her breasts.

'You can feel that, can you?' he asked her.

'Yes.'

'Well, that's a start, at least. Now this time, when I kiss you, I want you to move your body against mine. Here,' he told her, the hand in her hair sliding unerringly to her waist and then upwards to the curve of her breast, touching her briefly before moving away. 'And here...' His other hand left the hollow of her back and traced the curve of her hip.

'As rhythmically as you can manage. I trust I don't have to tell you what kind of rhythm,' he added under his breath, and Silver was glad that he couldn't see the fierce flood of angry colour that burned her face. She wanted to wrench herself away from him and tell him that she would find someone else to help her, but the stubborn streak of hardiness that had enabled her to survive so much wouldn't let her. There was far more than mere pride at stake here.

'Now, just in case you haven't already realised it, the object of this exercise is to transform what is on my part merely a light kiss into... Well, let's see what you *can* turn it into, shall we?'

She hated him... Hated the cold, dismissive way he spoke to her, the way he touched her...the way he made no effort to hide his dislike and contempt. But she needed him too much to show her feelings, and so she waited as his hands moved back to her body and he held her as he had done before, pressing the same cold mouth to her own.

Instinctively she froze, while her mind screamed its impatience with her body's ineptness and she forced her unwilling muscles to obey her mental commands, moving her body against his, trying to imagine that he was Charles, and that this situation was real.

It was harder than she had thought, her body made clumsy and bashful by the unresponsiveness of his. It was like trying to soften iron, she decided angrily, knowing even before his mouth left hers that she had failed to impress him.

It was a shock to open her eyes and find his boring into her, as though he really could see her. Her heart jerked uncomfortably and she pulled away from him, saying bitterly, 'Is all this really necessary?'

'You seemed to think so... Look, I'll show you how it should be done and then we'll give it another try. Now concentrate,' he instructed her, taking hold of her, ignoring her body's tense rejection as he manoeuvred her ungently on to the sofa and then kept her there with the weight of his body.

'Now,' he said grimly against her mouth, 'this is what should happen.'

This time his mouth was just as clinical, but it moved slowly and subtly on hers, matching the slow tempo of his body, the subtle rotation of his hips pressing her deeper into the sofa, the movement of his chest against her breasts, his hands in her hair, as he deliberately increased the rhythm, enforcing their erotic cycles on her body. He held her head between his hands so that she couldn't evade his mouth, making a thousand unknown pulses leap under her skin, making her breasts swell and harden and her belly turn weak. The rhythm quickened, changed and became more forceful, and then, shockingly, stopped.

'This is what I meant when I told you to move your body against mine,' she heard him saying calmly in her ear. 'If he's attracted to you, it should turn him on. Now it's your turn.'

He levered himself away from her briskly, leaving her to stare up at him. She felt too shocked to move, her pride bruised by the inescapable knowledge of the effect he had had on her. She shuddered as she sat up, wondering why on earth she felt so weak.

As she looked at him, sitting relaxed and composed at the other end of the sofa, she knew there was simply no way she could do to him what he had just done to her.

He must have read her mind, she suspected, because suddenly his voice changed, softening slightly.

'Forget about me. Just try imagining that I'm someone else—this all-important man that all this is for.'

The palms of her hands had gone damp. She was more scared than she had ever been in her life, even when Annie had explained to her just what the surgery she had wanted would involve...how painful it would be...how potentially dangerous. She didn't want to touch him...didn't want to experience his amusement and contempt when she failed to match the effortless sensuality he had just shown her. Was it just experience that brought such skill, or was there more to it than that? Did you have to be born with a facility for it? If so... If so, her plan was doomed, and she wasn't going to allow that to happen.

Taking a deep breath, she got up.

'We'll take it from the top this time, when you're sitting on the floor.'

Obediently she sat at his feet, closing her eyes and willing herself to believe that she wasn't here in this chalet, but in the library at Rothwell, that it wasn't Jake's body behind her, but Charles's. She breathed slowly and deeply, trying to relax, trying to capture the evocative scent of old leather and wood that permeated the high-ceilinged room. Trying to imagine the heat of the fire, the guttering of the candles on the desk behind the old leather chesterfield, the feel of Charles's hands on her hands as he reached for her and twisted her round in his arms, drawing her up over his thighs.

She tried to imagine she was water, amorphous and fluid, flowing against him; her hands touched his chest, feeling the hardness of muscle that unexpectedly flexed beneath her palms. Again the touch of that cold mouth; for a second her concentration wavered and her nails dug into his shoulders as she tensed, but then she pushed Jake's image to one side and fought to superimpose over it that of Charles.

The kiss was warm and teasing, as Charles's had been, but instead of accepting it shyly and awkwardly she remembered what Jake had taught her. She was a powerful, seductive woman, and he was her victim. She murmured softly beneath the cold mouth and slid her fingers into his hair, frowning momentarily, conscious of its texture and thickness, knowing by some form of osmosis that Charles's fair, fine hair would never feel like this, vibrant with male energy. For a moment her confidence faltered, the image of Charles she was fighting to fix behind the closed eyelids fracturing and the pieces reassembling into Jake's face. She shivered and suppressed the image, telling herself fiercely that this wasn't Jake, it was Charles... Charles, and that this was her chance to take hold of her own fate and shape it... form it. This was her chance to start exacting payment, and to do that she must seduce him away from other loyalties... other loves.

She moved her body sinuously, ignoring the unresponsive muscle and tissue that was Jake, letting her movements whisper promises of pleasure, trying to re-create the rhythms Jake had shown her, forcing her mouth to soften and linger coaxingly on the implacable, shuttered lips that refused to give her any encouragement.

When Jake took hold of her shoulders and held her away she stared at him, waiting for his judgement. This time her body had not reacted the way it had when he had kissed her, for which she was profoundly grateful. That was a complication she didn't need or want. Nor did she want to remember that, despite all she had felt for Charles, he had never drawn that involuntary, unstoppable feeling from her.

'You're beginning to get the idea,' Jake told her.

Beginning... Silver glared at him, conscious of a fierce stab of disappointment. What had she expected? she derided herself. Lavish praise? She suppressed her chagrin and said as lightly as she could, 'I see. And how long will it be, do you suppose, before I've absorbed it to your satisfaction?'

'Who knows, but until you have we don't go any further.'

As though he heard the angry protests locked in her throat, he said evenly, 'What do you want from this, Silver? You told me you wanted to be able to seduce a man to the point where he'd virtually kill to have you. Judging on your present performance, you wouldn't even be a good lay; you'd be forgotten even before the bed had gone cold,' he told her brutally, and although the words cut into her ego like thin whip-strokes she knew he was telling the truth.

'Now ... we'll do it again, and remember, a seductress doesn't necessarily love the man, but she does love herself and her power over him, and because of *that* she enjoys what she's doing. She loves making him ache and burn ... making him want ...'

An hour later, her throat burning with suppressed tears of rage, her pride cut to rags and her temper burning through her like vitriol, Silver pulled back from Jake's restraining hands and gritted, 'Don't tell me ... I know ... try again. Tell me something, Jake. What exactly do I have to do to get a pass mark?'

He wouldn't release her, and a flash of caution warned her against trying to overcome his physical strength. She reminded herself that there was nothing personal in this; that it was idiocy to let her dislike for him prejudice her progress. After all, she had chosen him.

'I should have thought that was obvious,' he told her. He was beginning to sound terse, and his mouth snapped shut with uncompromising hardness. She had known all along that he wasn't a man who would suffer incompetence easily, and now he was proving it to her. 'When you can arouse *me*, you'll get your pass.'

Arouse him? She couldn't stop the shudder jolting through her as she snatched her hands away from his shoulders.

'We're talking about a physical reaction, nothing more,' he told her drily, correctly reading her reaction. 'A physical reaction to deliberate provocation. It isn't impossible. It isn't easy, either... I don't like you, and I certainly don't want you,' he told her frankly, 'but until you can draw that involuntary physical response from my flesh, we don't go any further. There wouldn't be any point.' He gave her a hard look which made her catch her breath until she remembered that he couldn't actually see her.

'Now, let's try it again, and this time remember: the sooner you get it right, the sooner we can move on to the next stage, and ultimately the sooner you and I can go our separate ways.'

It should have been all the encouragement she needed, but it had exactly the opposite effect. She became unbearably conscious of herself and of him, and totally unable to superimpose Charles's image on to his features, no matter how tightly she tried to close her eyes and use her imagination. Her movements became clumsy, her body tense and awkward.

After three humiliating attempts to recapture her earlier burgeoning skill had failed, she was tempted to call the whole thing off.

She was too demoralised even to hide from him how she felt, pushing her hair back off her hot face as she protested angrily, 'It's no use. I'll never get it right...'

She expected him to agree with her and was surprised when he remained silent, until she remembered that, for all his contempt, he would stand to lose two million pounds if she backed out now.

'We'll have a break,' he told her equably at last, adding, 'Think of it as mind over matter, Silver. The physical skills alone aren't enough. You have to be confident of success...to *know* you have the power to arouse me...to *know* that you can make me want you. Without that mental strength, no matter what I teach you, you won't succeed. The outward skills can only facilitate the effectiveness of the inner ones. Which is perhaps why they say seductresses are born and not made.'

It infuriated her that, after she had faced so much, endured so much, she was failing at this last obstacle ... surely the most simple of them all?

'I'm tired,' she told him pettishly. 'I'm going to bed.'

She waited for him to stop her, to make some cynical and mocking retort, and when he didn't she walked stiff-backed over to the stairs and then up them.

A month of Jake's time was what she had bought. Four short weeks of his time and his tuition. So why should it suddenly seem as though those short weeks were going to prove a lifetime of endurance and punishment?

CHAPTER THREE

HER bedroom was simply furnished. Rag-rugs on the polished floorboards, a large double bed with bolster pillows and two huge quilts, a solid-looking chest of drawers in an unvarnished bleached wood that felt smooth and worn to the touch, and a wardrobe to match. The small shower-room was as basic and frugally furnished as the bedroom, but there was a rightness about the plain white sanitaryware that was pleasing to the eye.

Silver showered, dismissing her longing to soak her tense muscles in a hot bath, and then moisturised her face completely. Annie had warned her that for some time to come her skin would be vulnerable. When she had finished she brushed her hair vigorously, her mouth curling into a crooked smile.

When she'd walked into Annie's clinic her hair had been russet-brown. It was the shock of the series of operations she had put herself through that had turned it almost pure white.

The mirror gave back to her a perfect reflection. She studied it clinically, trying to see it as others would see it...as Charles would see it. Flawless skin...she had always had that before, though no one had ever really noticed. An elegant, straight nose; not for her the cutesy girlish bobs favoured by starlets. High cheekbones slanting under widely spaced eyes, small ears, a delicate jawline, a full mouth. That too had already been hers, although in the heavy, plain setting of her old face its fullness had appeared almost grotesque.

Standing naked in front of the mirror, Silver studied her body. No surgery had been needed here. Just diet and exercise—almost an entire year of it before this svelte, high-breasted figure had emerged from the smothering layers of fat.

Now she had a narrow ribcage and a tiny waist, curving hips and long, long legs.

She looked back into the past, seeing her reflection not as it was now, but as it had been then. She had started overeating as a teenager, partly in compensation for her own deep-seated insecurities, partly out of the guilt induced within her by her aunt.

The awareness that her beloved father, much as he'd loved her, would have preferred her to be a son wasn't something which had grown on her slowly, but had been cruelly forced upon her by her cousin.

She shivered, remembering with devastating clarity the day her cousin had relentlessly and cruelly explained to her that for her father there could never be a son... someone who would carry on the family name, its titles and burdens... That she, as a daughter, could never inherit them, and that it was through her that her father had contracted the childhood disease which had led to his inability to father any more children.

Charles would inherit... Charles would become the fourteenth Earl of Rothwell on her father's death... Charles, who if she was lucky might condescend to marry her. And so her insecurity had begun, her awareness of her lack of worthiness to be both her father's only child and Charles's wife... and with it her obesity.

How assiduously and malevolently her aunt had nurtured those insecurities. She could see it all so clearly now... as she had not been able to do then.

And Charles... how cleverly Charles had used his mother's manipulation of her, charming her one moment, spurning her the next... offering her compassion and caring one day and replacing it with coldness and disdain another. And so it had gone on, the constant see-sawing of her emotions, so that her lack of self-worth and her vulnerability had grown at the same pace as her dependence on Charles.

She had totally believed her aunt when the latter had told her that it was her father's wish that she marry Charles, never dreaming that she might have lied, and so she had grown through her teens adoring her Adonis-like cousin...loving him...wanting him...to such an extent that, when her father had finally begun to appear antagonistic toward Charles, when he had tried to caution her, she had refused to listen, believing herself to be deeply in love with her cousin.

It had been the only thing they had ever quarrelled about... Silver bit her lip, wondering whether, if he were alive now, her father would recognise anything of the daughter he had known in her, or would pass her by in the street as one of her godmothers had done in Gstaad last week.

She had loved her father so much; and she had indirectly been responsible for his death. She shivered suddenly. It wasn't just a desire to make Charles pay for the hurt he had inflicted on her in rejecting her that was making her put herself through this...this self-torture. Motivating her just as strongly was her deep-rooted belief that justice must be done, that Charles must pay for the crime she knew he had committed. Charles had murdered her father, and, what was more, he had murdered him because he had known that her father stood between him and Rothwell, that the information her father had about Charles would ensure that she broke her engagement to him; and so Charles had killed him. How safe and secure he must feel now... As far as Charles was concerned, both of them were dead, her father and then apparently her. But she was going to rise again from the dead...not as the girl everyone thought had committed suicide, the plain and ugly Geraldine Frances—but as Silver. And she was going to teach him what it meant to love someone, to desire them and to believe those feelings were returned, and then to face rejection.

But, over and above that, she was going to take away from Charles everything he thought he had gained by murdering her father. For that, any sacrifice, any self-torment could be endured.

Now no one would ever recognise her as Geraldine Frances...

She touched one high cheekbone with her fingertips, feeling the living skin. It frightened her sometimes to look into the mirror and see this unfamiliar mask, but she had to suppress that fear. This was what she had wanted, this porcelain perfection of feature...this almost unreal beauty...

She had been frightened this evening as well, when she'd realised how very easily she could fail this last test.

She shivered and pulled on her pyjamas. Cream satin, the fabric severely cut, almost masculinely so, flowed over her body, changing subtly so that it no longer appeared severe, but instead became subtly erotic. She had bought the pyjamas because she felt she was too tall for frilly feminine nightwear, and because she knew that the ancient flannelette nightwear she had worn since she was a teenager, comfortable though it was, could no longer be a part of her life.

Now, as she walked into her bedroom and the coolness of the satin stroked her skin, she remembered what Jake had said to her about wearing silk underwear beneath a pair of jeans and her body tensed angrily.

There had been a point this evening when she had been tempted to accuse him of deliberately drawing out her torture, but then she had remembered his cold distaste when she had first put her proposition to him and she had held back the bitter words, knowing that, no matter how much he disliked her, it wouldn't make any sense for him to spend any longer with her than was necessary. And anyway, he had been right, she acknowledged drearily.

No matter how hard she tried to forget them, to tell herself that she was now a beautiful, desirable woman, her old inhibitions wouldn't let go, grimly reinforcing the judgement of his hard, unyielding body, until the rhythm she was trying so desperately to maintain became the beat of painful music to the refrain that pounded over and over again through her mind. Words it would surely take many lifetimes to obliterate, words which she felt were carved upon her soul.

Charles's words, cruel and condemning, bitter and hurtful...the words he had used to describe her to another woman.

She got into bed and lay there, knowing that she wasn't going to be able to sleep.

She had been there just over half an hour when Jake knocked on her door and called her name, loud enough for her to hear, but not so loud that it would have woken her had she been asleep.

She was tempted to pretend that she was, but she stifled the pettish instinct, getting up instead and padding over to the door to open it.

'What do you want?' she asked him ungraciously.

He smiled mirthlessly. 'Still sulking? *You* might be able to afford to waste your time, but I can't.'

She turned her back on him and said curtly, 'Save the lecture for tomorrow, would you, Jake? I want to go to sleep.'

'And you shall. But not yet...'

She looked at him and read the inflexible purpose in the hard bones of his face. She should have anticipated this, and she berated herself mentally for believing that he would allow her to overrule him.

There were two courses open to her now: she could stand her ground and risk having him call the whole thing off, or she could give in.

Great as her desire was to defy him, she couldn't let their personality clash come between her and the course she had set for herself.

He was looking at her, and despite his blindness the blue eyes were alive with intelligent awareness. That panicked her. She wanted to turn away from him so that he couldn't look at her, even though she knew it was impossible for him to see her.

'I'll come back downstairs,' she said woodenly.

'A very wise decision.' He held open the door, waiting for her. She wanted to protest that she would have to get dressed, and then thought of the intimacies she would have to endure before she was free and gave a faint sigh, preceding him through the door.

The stove was still burning, and she was glad of its warmth. The settee stood in front of her, an implacable reminder of her failure. She thought bitterly that she would never again feel quite the same about that particular piece of furniture.

'Now,' Jake instructed her coldly, 'this time, try to use your intelligence. *Think* about what you're doing... about the image you're projecting. We haven't been lovers yet, but all the signs are that we will be. The scene is set. It's up to you to make the most of the opportunity I'm giving you. Remember, when I walk away from you tonight you want me to lie awake remembering the feel of you, the scent of you, aching for you. You want me to forget every other woman I've ever held...'

Silver shivered, bitterly aware of how very skilled he was, of how he was using his voice and his imagination, of how he was forcing her to confront her own failure and fears.

She wanted to scream at him that it was no use, that she couldn't do it, but her stubbornness wouldn't let her. She had come too far, sacrificed too much.

As she stood there, curling her fingers into tight, hard balls of tension, he said coolly, 'Stop trying to think of me as him. That immediately sets up barriers you can't overcome. He's too important to you. Try instead to imagine me simply as man... all mankind... not a person with characteristics you may or may not like, but merely a symbol of maleness to your femaleness.'

She wanted to tell him that he was wrong about
Charles, but she suspected he would know that he wasn't,
so instead she closed her eyes and willed herself to blank
out his features, to see him simply as a body, a set of
reflexes which she had to activate.

Into the darkness, he added, 'If it's the basic pattern
of movements that worries you, try improvising slightly.
Let your instincts guide you and not your brain.'

What instincts? she longed to demand bitterly. Haven't
you realised yet that I don't *have* those kinds of instincts? If I did I wouldn't need you! But she knew that
to lose her temper would achieve nothing. He wasn't responsible for the past; he was nothing in her life, simply
a cipher... a necessary staging post through which she
must pass on her self-selected route.

She breathed deeply and evenly, steadying her nerves,
and then went over to him, dropping into the now familiar position. He reached for her, and she saw the frown
touch his forehead as his fingers slid over satin, but he
made no comment, simply disengaging one hand and
then the other, so that he could slide his hands up her
bare arms beneath the sleeves of her pyjama jacket.

She stiffened instinctively as her body touched his,
forgetting for a moment the purpose of his touch—she
hadn't realised how different it would feel to lie against
him without the constricting layers of clothes—and then
she forced herself to ignore her own reactions and to
concentrate instead on his. If she could feel his body so
much more intensely through the satin of her pyjamas,
then surely he must be correspondingly aware of hers:
of the sleek, subtle movement of the fluid fabric as it
flowed over her skin. That was what she should be like,
she told herself: fluid, amorphous, clinging, silken, inviting his touch, teasing him with her very lack of substance; making him aware of her every subtle movement.

Her hands were on his chest and, as she willed her
flesh and bones to mould themselves to his, she smoothed
her palms over his shirt-front, levering her torso away

from him, the better to allow her hips to sink into him. Think of it as a dance, she told herself, a subtle, dangerous dance which only one of us can control, and as she moved her hips a small, forgotten memory came back to her, a laughing conversation she had overheard between two girls at a party, and she broke the cold dominion of his kiss with the soft pressure of her mouth, mimicking the slow movement of her hips, her mouth open and moist.

Unexpectedly, his throat muscles clenched and then his fingers circled her wrist as though he was going to push her away.

She felt anger and disappointment, bitterness at yet another failure followed by a savage determination to force some reaction for him. She pulled her wrist free and held his face in her hands the way he had done hers, driven by her need to prove to him what she could do, opening her mouth on his, flattening her torso against him, moving her whole body against him, willing him to react, to give her the words of praise she so desperately craved, and when he didn't she used her teeth sharply against his bottom lip, caught up in a fierce, furious rage of resentment, her hands leaving his face to curl into bitter fists which she beat frantically against his shoulders as she spat furiously, 'It's no good! I can't do it. I'll *never* be able to do it.' Tears of temper and failure burned her throat and eyes.

He fended her off easily, holding her away from him and then shaking her firmly to silence her, saying calmly, 'That's enough. And you're wrong.'

It didn't penetrate at first, and then, when it did, she went rigid. 'Wrong?' She stared at his face, looking for signs of deception, of pity, but there were none. 'Why didn't you say something, then, instead of letting me...?'

'I was about to,' he told her, extremely drily. 'But you didn't seem to want to listen.'

She was almost afraid to believe it. She watched him suspiciously, half afraid he was just playing a cruel joke on her.

'I'm not lying to you,' he told her calmly, reading her mind, easing her on to the sofa beside him and then reaching for her hand.

When he placed it against his body and she realised why she tried to pull away, but he wouldn't let her.

'Stop that,' he told her curtly. 'You're going to have to do far more than touch a man with such shrinking reluctance if you're going to play the seductress.'

She had known, of course, only somehow, contemplating the intimacies she would have to endure, the skills she would have to learn, hadn't seemed quite the same as it did now, with her hand forced to lie against the hard pulse that betrayed his arousal.

'Now,' he told her quietly as he released her hand, 'having got this far, we might as well make full use of what you've achieved. To arouse a man is easy,' he told her, ignoring her angry muttered protest. Easy, was it? *She* didn't think so. 'To sustain that arousal, and then to turn mere arousal into desire, and desire into obsession, is something else. So you've aroused your victim, shown him that you're capable of exciting his desire. Now you've got to show him how much you want that desire. You've got to flatter him into thinking he's the only man to arouse you to that intensity of desire...'

'Can't I just tell him that?' Silver demanded truculently.

'You can...and in fact you should, but not at this stage; we'll get round to that later. For now you just concentrate on convincing him that he's the ultimate in macho virility.'

He waited for a few seconds, and then said crisply, 'Think, Silver. You've got what you wanted. He's aroused but he's vulnerable; the true seductress knows that men don't like feeling vulnerable. Now you've got to restore his pride. You've got to convince him that you're vulnerable. Think,' he reiterated impatiently. 'Think of what you'd want him to do if you did actually want him.'

His words rang warning bells in her brain.

'I'm the one seducing him, not the other way round,' she reminded him coldly.

'Yes, and one of the most effective means of seduction is to appear seduced oneself. It's a simple, basic precept. You arouse him; you pretend to be aroused in turn; you apologise and tell him that you don't normally react like that. His ego loves the flattery, and immediately, because of your apparent desire for him, you become more desirable to him.

'I presume you don't know how to simulate desire. Hence your truculence? It isn't that difficult...' His voice was extremely dry. 'All you have to do is to kiss me as you were doing before...' She was glad he couldn't see her face.

'While you're doing it, you can take hold of my hand and put it on your breast, or, if I'm already touching you there, you can press yourself against me and make some pretty little moaning sounds. If you can manage to tremble as well, that's even better. If I don't take the hint then and start undressing you, you can whisper in my ear how much you'd like to have my mouth against your breast. Think you can manage any of that?'

The question trapped her. She wanted to hurl a denial at him, and yet she sensed that he was deliberately testing her...seeing how serious, how committed she was to the course she had chosen. If she backed out now, she would only have it all to go through again with someone else. At least Jake couldn't see her. At least he was clinical and detached from her...even in his arousal.

She thought of all the answers she could give him and opted for the one that was honest.

'I don't know,' she told him.

'Well, shall we see if we can find out?'

She paused, nodded, and then realised that he couldn't
see her and said brusquely, 'Yes.'

'Right, then, let's give it a try.'

She was becoming more adept at summoning up her
will-power and focusing her concentration. Perhaps the
enforced constant repetition had something to do with
it as well, she reflected, acknowledging as she moved
towards him how familiar the sensation of Jake's body
against her own had become.

She kissed him as he had told her to, telling herself it
was only like climbing a mountain, or skiing down a
dangerous slope. It was only another goal she had to
reach. She moved, surprised by how easily her muscles
slipped into the provocative rhythm, flesh against flesh,
muscle against muscle, her softness against his hardness,
part and counterpart, two skilfully designed compo-
nents that, once put together...and then she realised
that the reason her body was moving so easily and
fluently was that Jake's was moving with it, helping
her...encouraging her.

It was the first time he had done anything other than
remain like solid stone, and she felt the same thrill she
had that day on the ski-slopes: that surge of knowledge
that she would win, that nothing could stand in her way.

Jake was helping her, not so much in accolade to her
burgeoning skill, but in a silent acknowledgement that
she would succeed...a subtle carrot dangled after the
painful sting of the stick.

He broke the kiss and said against her mouth, 'Stop
daydreaming, Silver... My hand, remember?'

She had been so carried away by her own euphoria
that she had forgotten. And now her mood was broken.
Her body tensed. She felt awkward and uncertain, but
she knew that Jake wouldn't allow her to back out. If
she flunked it this time he would make her go over it
again and again until she got it, just as he had done
earlier, and so she made her body relax, trying to en-
visage it as fluid satin as she had done before, trying to

imagine it as settling smoothly over Jake's body, remembering that it was her task to arouse him as she closed her eyes and kissed him, curling her fingers round his wrist as she lifted his hand to her breast.

Charles had never touched her body, and she had learned why. He had found her too repulsive. Just for a second she saw herself as she had been then: ungainly, overweight, insecure, and painfully shy.

She was none of these things now. She had a body now that was sleek and streamlined, her flesh smooth and silky.

She now had the kind of body that any man would want to touch.

As she registered the contact of Jake's hand on her body, long, lean fingers splayed out across her satin pyjama jacket, radiating heat through the fabric and on to her skin, she wondered if she would ever totally manage to vanquish the past and the woman she had been then.

Against her ear Jake's voice warned, 'Remember, you're supposed to want this. You're supposed to be making me feel I'm driving you wild.'

Driving her wild. He was—wild with anger and tension and insecurity and a dozen or more other negative emotions she thought she had already put behind her.

There was no pressure in the touch of his hand, no more intimacy or awareness than if he had simply been touching her arm to help her across a street.

But *she* was aware of him; aware of the heat and alienness of him where his hand covered her; aware of the softness of her own body, of the curve of her breasts and the sensitivity of her nipples where the satin touched them.

She shuddered as she felt Jake's chest expand with impatience.

'Don't think about me,' he commanded her harshly, withdrawing his hand. 'Don't think about me...don't think about anyone; think only of yourself, of what

you're projecting...of what *you* want to achieve. You're
so goal-orientated; think of this as a goal you have to
achieve, let your senses monitor the degree of your
success or lack of it ... Let them tell you how the man
touching you is feeling. Desire is a very sensitive emotion;
only by understanding that will you be able to truly
control and manipulate a man's sexual reaction to you.'

Silver had stopped listening to him; he was pressing
her too hard, demanding too much of her too soon, and
she thought she knew the reason why. He was so anxious
to be rid of her and get his money that he was trying to
set a pace it was impossible for her to match.

'Listen to me, damn you!' he swore at her suddenly.

Suddenly her control snapped.

'I'm not like you,' she told him angrily. 'I'm not so
used to casual sexual intimacy that it doesn't matter to
me who...'

She gasped with pain as his fingers bit deeply into the
soft flesh of her upper arms.

'You know nothing about me,' he told her tersely.
'Nothing. If you've changed your mind and want to
bring this whole thing to an end, then say so, and stop
trying to manufacture an excuse.' His mouth twisted and
he released her, adding unexpectedly, 'And, for your information, I do not use and never have used sex indis-
criminately. Nor have I ever used it as a weapon,' he
told her devastatingly. 'What is it you really want from
this man, Silver? You told Annie you wanted revenge——'

Her mouth tightening, Silver interrupted angrily, 'She
had no right to tell you that.'

'She was concerned about you. Annie's like that. She
can't stop herself from caring, from becoming involved.
A human weakness I doubt you'd understand.'

Almost she told him, and then she stopped herself just
in time, sensing the cleverly baited trap. It would be
madness to allow this man to know too much about
her...to witness her vulnerabilities.

'Why?' he probed, ignoring her tension. 'Why all this...?' His hand touched her face fleetingly.

'I have my reasons,' she told him freezingly.

'A woman spurned,' he mocked. 'What really motivates you, do you know? Anger...hatred...love...?'

Silver shuddered, the fine hairs on her arms rising warningly. He was too aware, too sensitive in some way to her most private thoughts and feelings. It was almost as though he himself knew what it was to be driven... to be possessed...obsessed almost. And as for that last softly spoken challenge... Please God she no longer felt any love for Charles. Hatred, anger, yes... she needed them just as much as she needed her driving hunger for retribution...

'What is it exactly you hope to achieve?' Jake pressed, and then added, 'Oh, I know what your physical goal is, but what satisfaction do you expect to gain from achieving it?'

Silver almost wished she hadn't allowed him to see that shudder of sensation which had made him take his hands from her body. In its own way this was an almost equally painful form of torture—this probing into her mind, her feelings. Physically, at least most of the time, she could hide her reactions from him, but mentally, emotionally...he was far too good at finding her weak points and playing on them.

Holding up her head, she said coolly, 'The Chinese have a saying: "There is nothing so amusing as to see an enemy fall from a high roof." I intend to make sure Charles falls from a very high roof indeed.'

'You intend to see that he *falls*...or do you mean that you intend to make sure he does, by giving him a push? Be careful,' he warned her firmly. 'The Chinese have another saying: "He who seeks revenge must dig two graves"...' He paused deliberately, and Silver had the uncanny sensation of feeling her resolve waver. It was like discovering that what she had thought to be absolutely solid ground had suddenly turned to something treacherous, without substance, and she fought against it in panic almost as though she was in fact losing her balance and being sucked into something dangerous and unstable.

'Oh, and by the way,' Jake told her softly, 'you got your quotation wrong. In actual fact it goes: ''There is nothing so amusing as to see a friend fall from a high roof.'' A very cynical race, the Chinese, but perhaps the mistake was Freudian in origin and you aren't sure whether he is your enemy or your friend. Is it revenge you want, Silver, or is it something else?'

'What are you trying to say?' she demanded, fighting back her panic. This was worse, much worse than the physical intimacy which had sent her flying headlong down this perilous path.

'I'm just trying to warn you about the pitfalls you're going to encounter...'

She laughed then, a too high, too sharp sound that grated warningly against her own ears, betraying her panic and her fear; and if her laughter betrayed those emotions to her, how much more must it betray to Jake's far more astute ears?

'Why?' she demanded acidly. 'I've hired you to teach me about seduction, Jake, not morality. Anyway, what makes you such an expert? You don't know how I feel or why...'

'Wrong.'

He said it so blandly, so emotionlessly that it was a few seconds before she realised just what the word meant.

She blinked, and then focused on him. His face was stern in repose, unyielding, his mouth controlled, everything about him so diametrically opposed to all that the word cloaked that she thought for a moment that he was lying to her.

'I know exactly what motivates you, Silver, exactly what you're feeling, and I can tell you this: you're going to have to be far more resolute, far more determined, far more single-minded if you want to succeed. Revenge, just like any other human emotion, is a two-edged sword, as dangerous to the person who wields it as the person it is wielded against. This man you're so determined to destroy...do you really think he's going to calmly allow you to destroy him...that he won't try to destroy you in turn?'

'I'm not a fool, Jake.'

'No, you're a spoilt and wealthy young woman, who obviously believes that her wealth can buy her anything and everything she wants,' he responded equably.

The unfairness of his allegation momentarily robbed Silver of her ability to retaliate.

'You're wrong,' she told him emotionally, forgetting the warnings she had already given herself about lowering her defences with him. 'I may be rich, but as for being spoilt... Materially, perhaps, but emotionally... apart from my father, I doubt that anyone has ever given a thought to my emotional needs...love——'

'Love?' Jake interrupted, taunting her. 'I thought it was revenge you wanted.'

'It is!' She realised that her hands were balled into fists and that her temper was dangerously close to breaching her self-control. Taking a steadying breath, she demanded less emotively, 'What are you trying to do, Jake?'

There was a small pause and then he said quietly, 'What I'm trying to do is to make you face up to reality. You think you're invulnerable, but you're not...you're far too easily swayed by your emotions.'

'I've had enough of this,' she told him abruptly. She turned away from him dismissively, but he forestalled her, taking hold of her in a grip she couldn't break.

'No,' he told her quietly, 'that isn't the way it's done, sulking like a child when things don't go as you want them to. You've got to learn to make your own weaknesses work for you...to use them and to conceal them— and conceal them well—but first you've got to learn to recognise and acknowledge them. Now, if you've got over your little tantrum, we'll start again.'

He felt the tiny shudder that rippled across her skin and was momentarily caught off guard by an unexpected twist of fellow feeling, of sympathy almost... sympathy for this woman...

Moralising, he taunted himself. Was what she was doing so very different from what he himself was doing? Both of them were motivated by the same need... but that was the only similarity between them. She wanted to hurt and destroy a man who had rejected her, while he... As he felt the floodgates to his memories tremble beneath the force of his own pain he clamped back on his thoughts...

He had come so close to achieving his goal, only to discover that while he turned his back his entire world had been destroyed. Now he sought vengeance against those who had wrought that destruction. One of the men was dead already, murdered by a rival drug baron, in a bomb blast before Jake could intervene. Two of the others were in American gaols, awaiting sentence. It was the fourth and so far unknown member of the quartet, who had been responsible for the destruction of the one person who had mattered to him, whom he now sought... All he knew was that the man was based in London, but where and who he was were things he still needed to discover, and the only way he *was* going to discover them was with Silver's money, which was why...

Which was why he could not afford to allow himself the luxury of feeling anything for her... especially not sympathy.

'Now, if you're ready, we'll start again,' he told her curtly.

That betraying shudder had left her feeling cold and afraid.

It seemed to Silver that it was a long, long time before she heard Jake saying coolly, 'That's better, but there's still a lot of mileage left for improvement. Remember, you're seducing me while allowing me to think you're out of your mind with wanting me. Try and co-ordinate everything now,' he instructed her. 'Here.' He tapped her bottom briefly. 'And here.' He repeated the brief instructive gesture alongside her ribcage. 'Another little theatrical shudder, a soft moan or two, and then we'll call it quits for tonight.'

Silver wondered what he'd say if she told him the truth—that the shudder hadn't been faked and that it hadn't been caused by desire. She thanked God he couldn't read minds.

She felt physically and mentally exhausted, drained of the desire to do anything other than match his exacting standards as quickly as she could so that she could be released from this purgatory to go back to bed.

She moved automatically, mentally registering surprise at how easy the rhythm was now becoming. He moved against her, helping her. He was probably as eager to get the whole thing over as she was herself. She didn't kiss him; it was too much of an effort to concentrate on everything else. She wasn't sure she could manage to fake a shudder, and tried thinking about walking barefoot on ice or something equally shiver-inducing, but Jake's free hand touched the base of her spine, pressing her against his body and moving her so that as she automatically moved her hips in the rhythm he had taught her she felt his arousal, and the shudder she had been fighting for came naturally. Like a perfectly synchronised pattern of actions, his hand tightened fractionally on her breast, his thumb rubbing over the nipple so that her throat-muscles contracted in shock, and without even knowing she was doing it she produced the requisite moan...of protest, not desire...but that didn't seem to matter because Jake turned his head and said into her ear, 'Good, that's better.' And then to her shock he nipped ungently at her soft earlobe and transferred his hand from her spine to her nape, covering her mouth with his own. When she stiffened, he didn't release her, but moved his hand from her breast to her hip, tapping the bone almost painfully smartly and then gripping it, reminding her that she had stopped moving. Holding her immobile, he moved his own body against her, forcing her to follow its movements and not letting go until he was satisfied with the way she matched its rhythm.

Against her mouth, he said grimly, 'Now, this time, let's try and get it all together, shall we?'

And then he bit sharply at her bottom lip so that she opened her mouth in protest.

His tongue thrust sinuously against her own, matching the movement of his body; his hand returned to her breast, cupping it and then stroking it, the intimacy catching her off guard so that for a moment she panicked and started to freeze, until her mind cancelled the warning signals from her body and told it that it had nothing to fear, and that this was simply a necessary part of what she must endure.

She tried to recapture the sense of power she had known earlier—the sense of her own infinite superiority as a woman, of being able to control and arouse this man—but the powerful movements of his body were beginning to intimidate her. She mustn't let that happen. She must remember that *she* was the one in control. His thumb touched her nipple, his nail slowly drawing a circle against its satin-covered areola. She shuddered and remembered in time her instructions, dragging her mouth from his to press it against his throat as she made a whimpering sound into his skin.

The pressure of his hand increased, something she hadn't expected. The movement of his thumb against the satin and the satin against her breast was abrasive in a way that made her skin tauten and swell. His hips lifted and thrust against her, his legs parting so that she slid between them. His hand slid down her back to the base of her spine, pressing her into his body.

Against her ear, he reminded her, 'You haven't finished yet. Tell me you want me, remember?'

For a moment her mind was blank. She couldn't think for her awareness of his arousal, and then, when she did remember what she still had to do, her control faltered.

Think of him as Charles, she told herself fiercely. Think of Charles wanting you... Think of triumph. And before that image could fade she slid her hands over the strong column of his neck and into his hair, and arched her body upwards while she pushed his head down.

'The words... remember the words...'

The words. I mustn't forget the words, she thought frantically, otherwise it will all have to be done again, and as she moved she pressed her lips against his ear and said quickly, 'T-t-touch me. I—I want to feel your mouth against my—my skin...'

She felt the heat of his breath in the V of her pyjama jacket and for a moment she thought he was actually going to prolong the lesson and take it a stage further, but to her relief he didn't. He lifted his head as he eased her away from him so that she could sink on to the floor and gather her knees up protectively against her body, wrapping her arms round them as she waited for his verdict.

'Not totally convincing,' he told her drily, 'but not a total disaster either. Now we both know just how much work we have to do, on a scale of nought to ten.

'Tomorrow we'll take a different look at what being seductive involves. A woman can be just as alluring fully dressed as she can in a situation like this evening's, but that involves knowing a lot more about the male body and its responses than you know at the moment.

'Starting from tomorrow, we'll go through what turns a man on. As an example, just now, instead of asking me to touch you, you could have opened my shirt and teased my nipples with your mouth...' He got up, stretching his body until Silver heard the bones crack, and then, as he walked towards the kitchen, added unemotionally, 'Licking, sucking, even biting would have been an extremely seductive way of showing me exactly what you wanted, and of course it would have had the added benefit from your point of view of increasing my arousal.'

He stopped by the door to the kitchen and added, 'I'm not going to offer you any supper. You've got some homework to do.'

He reached down to the wooden dresser set into the wall and removed a pile of books.

'Sex manuals,' he told her drily. 'Read them.'

'I already have,' Silver told him flatly.

'Well, now you can read them again,' he told her inexorably. 'You've got a week to read them in, and at the end of that week I'll be giving you a set of questions to answer on them.'

'What?' Silver couldn't believe it. 'I've already told you, sex manuals can't give me the expertise I need. If they could, I wouldn't be here with you,' she added bitterly.

'Maybe not, but you're still going to read them.'

Angrily Silver contemplated leaving the books where he had put them on the top of the dresser, but she owned that she was really too exhausted to get involved in a lengthy argument. She could take them upstairs; she need not actually read them...and if he thought she was going to answer his damned questions...

'Amazing,' he said quietly behind her when she turned her back on him. 'I can feel your anger from here, and yet I can hold you against my body and feel nothing. Try projecting as much energy into feeling desire as you do into feeling rage,' he instructed her. 'It would be a far more worthwhile expenditure of energy.'

'I don't *want* to feel desire,' she gritted at him. 'I don't *need* to feel it...'

'If you honestly believe that, then nothing I can teach you will be of the slightest benefit to you,' he told her coldly, 'and you're wasting my time as well as your own.

Stop behaving like a petulant child, Silver. *You're* the one who wanted this, and you're paying me two million pounds to get it. If you're not prepared to take this thing seriously, then you might as well walk out of here now and save us both a lot of aggravation.'

Biting her lip, Silver walked away from him without making any response.

Later, as she lay in bed, she acknowledged the point he had made. She must learn to adopt some of his own cool ability to distance himself emotionally. This time here with him was a chasm she had to cross, no matter how painful or frightening that crossing. There was no way she could just close her eyes and will herself over it, no matter how much she might ache to be safely on the other side.

CHAPTER FOUR

IT WASN'T easy, but then nothing in her life had been, apart from her early childhood relationship with her father. But this was different from any other obstacle Silver had ever had to overcome, and her nights became haunted by the savage bite of Jake's voice, the acid-cool neutrality of his curt instructions, the calm indifference with which he blocked her every attempt to outmanoeuvre him, when, driven beyond caution, she pushed recklessly at his astounding self-control, waiting for the storm to break and his temper to overwhelm his mastery of his emotions.

It never did; she was always the one forced to back down from the confrontation. *She* was the one forced to withdraw and regroup... And on and on it went, instructions, criticism, cool, curt, matter-of-fact reminders of what she was trying to achieve, while all the time she felt she would go insane and break down completely beneath the unrelenting pressure.

Another woman *would* have done; but then another woman would never have taken the dangerous course she had chosen in the first place. She was as hard on herself as he was, grimly reminding herself that this was her own choice—a necessary means to a specific end— and that if she could not control her dislike and resentment of the man for long enough for him to teach her what she needed to know, then she had little or no chance of fulfilling her ultimate promise to herself. And all the time she clung on to the vision that drove her: the vision of Charles, awestruck, spellbound, held in total thrall to her beauty, trapped by his desire for her as she had been by hers for him. Nothing else would

70

do... nothing less would satisfy what she felt inside...
And it was for that vision that she endured when others
would have given up.

There were times when Silver thought almost fanci-
fully that it was only that granite-hard, stubborn
mingling of English and Irish blood within her that made
her go on where others, more sensible perhaps than she,
would have backed down. She was beginning to recognise within herself a certain grim relentlessness that
she had thought belonged exclusively to her father. It
was like coming abruptly face to face with a stranger
within herself—shockingly and heart-stoppingly terrifying, until she forced herself to accept that it was
simply one facet of her own personality.

She had been with Jake almost a month and, although
she herself didn't realise it yet, she had already learned
much.

He knew it, though, and he observed with a certain
detached clinicality that already her voice had developed
a subtle sensuality, that she moved differently, more vol-
uptuously, with more awareness; and he knew these
things without seeing them; felt them, heard them; sensed
them growing within her while she herself remained oblivious to what was happening to her, too caught up in
what had become a fierce personal battle to prove to
him that she *would* succeed to notice the slow, progressive steps she was already taking along the road she
had chosen for herself.

He told her as much one cold afternoon when a
blizzard outside had turned the world grey-white, and
Silver filled the sitting-room with the tension of her impatience... with her longing to break free of the con-
strictions he placed upon her, of her role as supplicator
and pupil, which she constantly wanted to challenge, and
overset.

'You're too impatient,' he told her emotionlessly after
she had flung herself away from him and gone to stand

in front of the window. 'The Chinese have a saying: "A journey of a thousand miles begins with the first step"...'

Silver narrowed her eyes and turned round, glowering at him, and then she caught herself up. It still had the power to astonish her that she should be so intensely aware of him and antagonised by him in so many minute ways, and yet that she should almost totally forget so often that he was blind.

It was as though he possessed some power that enabled him to project himself past his blindness and render it completely unimportant.

'Come back here, Silver, and we'll go through it again. Unless, of course, you've changed your mind...'

Changed her mind... She swung back to the window. How many times had she longed to do so, but stubbornly refused to allow herself to give in? Sometimes she thought his clinical detachment was meant to be deliberately abrasive... that he wanted her to give in and back down... that he was secretly and deliberately torturing her by forcing her to go over and over every tiny caress, every inflection of the words he made her say, the things he made her do.

She had learned a lot from him since that first night, had been slowly and inexorably inculcated with the information and expertise she had wanted.

Now she knew exactly how to touch a man to arouse him in desire—and not just to touch him, but to look at him, smile at him, speak to him. And now, if she managed to get through today's lesson without telling him to go to hell, she would know how to argue with him and still challenge him to desire.

The lessons... the supply of information seemed inexhaustible, like a ceaseless stream pouring relentlessly into her, so that there were times when she wanted to scream at him, 'Stop... enough!' Times when she felt as though her spirit would break in two beneath the weight of his accumulated cynicism and knowledge... when she wasn't sure which of them despised the other the more ... when for some odd, uncomfortable reason, instead of screaming defiance at him, she wanted to break down and cry, without having an atom of understanding of why she should feel that way.

And harder to bear than everything he had taught her about his own sexuality had been the knowledge he had forced on her about her own ... not as a woman, but as an individual ... She had learned for instance that the mere pressure of his fingers against the inner flesh of her arm could make her jerk back from him in fierce tension ... that the sensation of his mouth against her throat, his hand against her breast could evoke responses that had to be frozen at birth; although he said nothing, did nothing to show that he was aware of what was happening to her, instincts as ancient as the race she herself had sprung from warned her that he *had* known ... Had known and yet hadn't used that knowledge against her ... and that confused her.

She closed her eyes, blotting out the blinding whiteness of the blizzard and thinking instead of Ireland ... of the ancient castle of stone, facing out across the Atlantic, guardian of the land beyond which had been the stronghold of a race of Irish princes until one of her ancestors had seduced and married one of the noble daughters. If she closed her eyes, she could see the castle now, rising up out of the mist that blew in off the sea ... Rugged, dauntless, austere, swept by gales and storms in winter and in no way to be compared with Rothwell, that jewel of Palladian splendour and richness set in its lush green English farmlands. And yet ... and yet it was to Kilrayne that she ached to return now ... It was Kilrayne that had been her refuge, Kilrayne that offered her surcease and comfort.

Kilrayne ... If she kept her eyes closed she could almost imagine she was there, standing in front of the huge fireplace in the great hall, warming herself on the heat of the massive logs needed to fill the enormous grate. The room would smell of oak-smoke and soot, the draughts lifting the faded banners and tapestries from the walls, and outside the Atlantic gale would hurl the rain against the narrow, leaded window-slits.

Kilrayne, a dark grey fortress, built for defence and not pleasure; Kilrayne, whose stone walls had more than once run red with the blood of its enemies. Charles hated it . . . He shivered in the draughts, complained about the smoking fires, loathed the narrow passages and huge stone-walled rooms.

Silver, on the other hand, loved it . . . loved the sharp contrast between the dull grey stone and the richness of its tapestries and embroidered bed-hangings . . . its stone-flagged floors and glowing Oriental carpets, the massive heaviness of its furniture and the pewter dullness of its silver; commissioned in France and smuggled back from that country, so the story went, by an Irish Jacobite younger son of the family banished to Ireland to keep him out of the way of Hanover George's revenge.

She and her father had spent every spring there. He had always said that there was nowhere quite like Ireland in the spring, when the sky was washed clean and soft by the wind from the Atlantic and the hedgerows and fields of the south turned a green that could not be rivalled anywhere in the world.

He would arrive there at the same time as the season's first crop of foals. He used to take her with him when he visited the stables, carefully instructing her in the good points to look for, pointing out to her which foals they would keep and which they would sell, and why.

Later in the year he would go to Argentina, where he bought his polo ponies, and here again he would instruct her, tutoring her so that she learned without ever knowing that she did so.

It was only in the winter, when he always returned to Rothwell so that he could hunt with the Belvoir, that she refused to accompany him. Much as she enjoyed the spectacle and pageant of the hunt, she had never been

able to endure being in at the kill, and her father rode
to hounds at the very forefront of the chase.

Sometimes Charles had accompanied him, both of
them looking in their different ways intensely male and
virile...very much the epitome of the traditional image
of upper-class manhood.

Her father had loved to hunt—had been a first-class
rider... Other men sustained falls, broken limbs, the
jocular teasing of their peers, but her father had never
been unseated once. He had always shrugged his skill
aside, claiming modestly that it was his mounts who deserved the credit and not him.

And yet he had died on the hunting field, thrown by
a young and untried mount, who had panicked and
bolted, dragging his unconscious rider so that by the time
they were able to stop him her father was dead.

An accident...or was it? Her father's doctor had told
her gently that there was a possibility that her father
might have committed suicide. Suicide... It had come
as a shock to her to discover that there were areas of
her father's life about which she knew nothing...shadows
darkening it which might have led to his taking his own
life...

An accident...suicide...or murder...? Her mouth
twisted bitterly. She knew which it was. Charles had
murdered her father; she was sure of it. And she knew
why. Charles, upon whom she had looked as near
perfect; believing that his outer, golden perfection mirrored an equally golden heart. How wrong she had
been...how naïve... But she was naïve no longer, and
she intended to make Charles pay—and not just for what
he had done to her, for his cruelty, his cynical callousness towards her, for the threats he had used to show
her how defenceless she was without her father to protect
her—for who would believe the hysterical claims of a
fat, plain young woman who it was known was speaking
out of jealousy and spite, against the assured sophistication of a man like Charles? No, it was more for her

father's sake that she was determined to hunt him down, to stalk him, and finally to trap him, exposing him to himself and to the world for the person that he really was. Her father... God, how she missed him even now. He was the only person who had ever really loved her, who had ever really cared...

Her throat closed on a surge of deep emotion, and then, like a knife ripping into a tender, unhealed wound, she heard Jake saying coldly, 'It's *your* time we're wasting, Silver, not mine. I promised you a month...after that...'

'You'll what...?' she demanded savagely. He couldn't see her face, couldn't see the suspicious glitter of the tears she was fighting to suppress, but even so she lashed out at him verbally, hating him for being present at her moment of betrayal. 'Double the price? I haven't paid you yet, Jake,' she reminded him, driven by her own demons to taunt softly, 'What would you do if I walked out of here and refused to pay you a penny?'

That she was punishing him for Charles's faults and for her own weakness she knew quite well, but the fierce pace he was setting her, the gruelling insistence on perfection, which was like nothing she had ever undergone before, was undermining her self-control, making her want to draw retaliatory blood, making her hate herself for the way he pierced her defences and pushed her from her sanctuary of icy remoteness into the painful world of feelings and emotions. She had turned her back on that world when she had turned her back on herself, totally destroying the woman she had once been. And she hated him for making her bitterly conscious of the fact that that woman and some of her vulnerabilities still remained; that she had not, as she had thought, completely obliterated and buried her.

Jake was silent for so long that she actually began to think with relief that he hadn't heard her, and then he said quietly, and very pleasantly, 'How you do like to flirt with fire. Why not try it and see?' And without a single threat being made Silver was overwhelmed by the pressure of a menace so strong that she physically shivered beneath it, awestruck that a voice and face that could look so benign and unemotional should at the same time be able to convey such an intensity of purpose. How different he was from Charles...as dark-visaged and formidably boned as a Roman god of war, where Charles was all golden promise, all physical perfection, with the face and body of a Greek statue. Under a similar threat, though, as she now had good cause to know, Charles would have reacted with violence and malevolence, so intense and strong that the shock of it would have terrorised his victim. Jake, while equally formidable, used so little anger, and no physical force, and yet the effect he was having on her right now was far more powerful, so much more effective than anything Charles had ever said or done.

Idly she wondered who would be the victor if the two men were ever to confront one another as enemies. Pound for pound, inch for inch they were probably evenly matched, both tall, well-muscled men, although Jake had a way of moving that was somehow far more intimidating than Charles's aggressively male stride.

Physically, there was surely no comparison. Charles had the looks of a screen idol, and the charisma... Jake, on the other hand, had the kind of face that women would find challenging and a little austere.

Charles had the natural hauteur and arrogance that came from having a privileged, wealthy background; he possessed charm, sophistication—sex appeal. He also possessed, as she had good cause to know, a deep vein of cruelty, a love of inflicting emotional and physical pain...a desire to dominate and destroy. Charles, all golden beauty on the outside, was inwardly corrupt... even evil... Silver gave a tiny shudder, remembering the extent of that evil, wondering how many lives it had touched and damaged.

Jake, on the other hand, was without such cruelty. He was hard, yes, unyielding, savagely determined, completely impervious to the kind of vanities which she knew were going to be Charles's downfall.

In any kind of contest between them, Charles should have been the victor, and yet there was something about Jake that made her acknowledge that when he thought he was in the right he would hang on as grimly as the proverbial bulldog. She respected Jake, something she realised with a sudden start of shock she had never felt for Charles, despite her youthful idolatry of him.

A tiny *frisson* of unwanted sensation touched her, an awareness...sharply poignant, shockingly intense— something dangerous and not to be thought of.

She reacted to it as strongly as if Jake had physically laid hands on her and overpowered her, saying violently, 'You can't threaten me, Jake. I could walk out of here right this moment and there's not a thing you could do about it.'

She looked at him, and something cynical and world-weary in his expression tightened the coil of panic gripping her.

'You can't even see me, never mind stop me——'

She broke off, shaking with a mixture of panic-based rage and a deep sense of shame. That she, who had born so many taunts and cruel words because of her own physical handicap, should use such a weapon against someone else sickened her. She took one look at Jake's shuttered, hard face, and the words of apology stuck in her throat.

'If you want to walk out of here, Silver, I'm not going to stop you,' Jake told her quietly.

There was no recognition of her insult, her cruelty...her immaturity... Nothing other than the weary patience of an adult for a recalcitrant, awkward child. His reaction, so mild and restrained, bit into her soul like a tempered steel whip, lacerating her pride until it was raw with pain.

'You aren't the only one wishing this were over, you know,' he told her calmly. 'It would be the easiest thing in the world right now for me to let you walk away from here—as you just said, I can't stop you.'

Her face burned with guilt and self-contempt. His very acceptance where she had expected anger, his calmness where she had expected ferocity, made her feel far worse than if he had lost his temper with her.

The trouble was . . . the trouble was, she ached for him to make some betrayal of vulnerability—of humanity. At the moment she felt like a stupid child confronted by a particularly intelligent and mature adult.

She wanted to bring him down to her own level, she admitted wearily. She wanted to weaken him for the sake of her own conceit.

She closed her eyes, feeling her stomach muscles knot. When had it happened, this dangerous desire to shift the entire axis of their relationship . . . this need to make him respond to her on a personal level, even if that response came only from anger?

As she opened her eyes, she tensed, realising that he had moved and was now standing within inches of her.

'And it's not true that just because I can't see you, I can't find you,' he told her softly. His hand touched her face and he said quietly, 'It isn't very pleasant when we make discoveries about ourselves that we don't like, is it?'

And Silver knew, immediately and shockingly, that he was as fully aware of her most private thoughts as if they had been his own.

She tried to step back from him, but he wouldn't let her.

'Acknowledging that we aren't perfect and then learning to make our vices work as well for us as our virtues is an important step on the road to maturity.'

And then, before she could speak, he added almost ruefully, 'I *do* know what it's like, you know. I have been there myself . . . which is why I cautioned you against this goal you've set for yourself. All right, so you loved the guy and you lost him... He hurt you, and now you want to hurt him back...'

'There's more to it than that,' Silver told him stiffly. 'A lot more...'

His hand left her face and she discovered that she was free to move away, but for some reason she no longer felt the need to.

It was an odd sensation to be talking with him like this...to be communicating with him as one human being to another.

'Such as?'

Later, questioning the wisdom of having confided in him, she had been forced to admit that he had applied a startlingly skilful degree of emotional pressure on her, and in such a way that she had had no idea how she was being manipulated until it was too late and she had told him far more about herself than she had ever intended he should know.

'He—my cousin—wanted to marry me—he didn't love me—he told me that, and laughed at me for thinking he might. How could he love me? I was plain, fat, ugly.'

'You mean you thought he wanted to marry you?'

Silver shook her head, angry that he wouldn't believe her.

'No, I know it. He told me... boasted about it... said he would make me do it. That I had no choice. That our engagement—he said that he had to have Roth——' She broke off, biting her lip. No one, except Annie, knew who she really was... what she had originally been. And Annie might have told Jake everything else, but she wouldn't tell him that—she had promised.

'You were engaged to him?'

She could see Jake frowning, and felt a sudden shaft of pleasure that she had at last managed to surprise him after all.

'Yes, unofficially. But not because he loved me. He made that plain enough. And to think I'd been stupid enough to believe that he actually could.' She laughed bitterly. 'God, I was such a fool!'

'And then he found someone else and dumped you...'

Silver gave a bitter laugh. 'Oh, no... There was someone else, but he still intended to marry me. He gave me a choice: marriage or destruction; there was nothing I could do about it, nothing at all...at least not as Ger——'

Again she froze, realising she had once more nearly said too much, but Jake didn't appear to be listening. He was frowning, and then he raised his hand and touched her face, lightly tracing its shape with his fingers.

'So this was not merely done out of vanity, but out of necessity, as well. Out of self-protection and self-defence.'

His astuteness shocked her. Not even Annie had guessed at that second part of her need to change her appearance so totally that no one would ever recognise what she had once been... *who* she had once been.

'Partly,' she acknowledged, and then honesty forced her to admit, 'Of course I could have chosen to have a plainer face... I can't pretend that vanity didn't come into it. You see, Charles has a weakness for beautiful women...that and his greed are perhaps the only weaknesses he does have.'

She pulled away from him and said tiredly, 'There's no point in trying to dissuade me, Jake. This is something I have to do.'

She felt him weighing her up, considering, thinking, and then he said, almost reluctantly, 'It won't be easy. And I do know what I'm talking about. I have a score to settle of my own...'

'Which is why you need my money.'

'Which is why I need your money,' he agreed.

It was on the tip of her tongue to ask him what had happened, but already she could feel him withdrawing from her, his face becoming stern and remote.

'Speaking of which, unless I want you to accuse me of wasting your time, I think perhaps we ought to get back to work.'

'Work!' The man was practically inhuman. He had cleverly trapped her into confiding in him, but when it came to his own past... How many other men in this position could continue to treat her as he did, as though he was completely unaffected by her, by the intimacy of what they were doing, as though he found her flesh as coldly uninviting as if it belonged, not to another human being, but to a robot.

He kept himself completely divorced from her emotionally, and mentally, and yet he seemed to possess a diabolical awareness of her every thought and mood, as though he had some deep inner awareness of her most complicated emotional response that not even she herself was privy to. And she hated that... Hated it... resented it... defied it, and constantly tried to transfer those feelings to him, to blame him for those aspects of her own inner vulnerabilities that she couldn't bear to face.

'Thank God there's only another week to go,' she hissed at him bitterly. What would it take to break his self-control, to reduce him to need and despair? She looked at him assessingly and tried to judge him dispassionately... to single out one small chink of vulnerability in the wall of implacable indifference which he had thrown up around himself.

She studied him directly, studying each feature of his face in turn, trying to ignore the wild thumping of her heart when her scrutiny was faultlessly returned, so faultlessly and so steadfastly that it was almost as though he could see her. Her heart jolted with unease and an almost superstitious fear that he was after all deceiving her, that he and Annie had lied to her and that he could in fact see, and she recognised what she had known all along: that in his blindness she had hidden herself from him, so that everything she had to do and say, every intimacy she had to perform was mercifully made less intimate, less dangerous by the fact that once she had gone from this place she could, if she so wished, come face to face with him across a dinner table and not be betrayed by his knowledge of her.

Not that she ever expected to encounter him across any of the dinner tables she was likely to sit down at.

Her disappearance, her faked death might mean that temporarily the doors of her old acquaintances and peers were closed to her, but they would open once more, and very soon. The pedigree she had concocted for herself was impeccable... the background, the wealth, the tiny details of the persona she was creating meticulously researched... so meticulously that no one would be able to find fault with them.

She would have an immediate entrée into Charles's world; she would be able to fascinate and then ensnare him, and ultimately she would be able to destroy him.

'Stop daydreaming,' Jake told her crisply. 'You can fantasise all you like about the future in your own time... Unless, of course,' he added silkily, 'you believe I've taught you as much as you need to know...'

He was doing it again, looking straight at her with those cool, too knowing eyes, making her squirm both mentally and physically, making her want to hide herself from him. Making her flush like a child as she remembered this morning's brutally pointed object lesson in male sexuality.

It was over two weeks now since he had first questioned her like an examiner on the facts she had gleaned from the manuals he had insisted she read; questions that had turned her face fiery red, and made her clench her teeth and bite the inside of her mouth to prevent herself from stammering the answers; questions so intimate, and yet delivered in so flat, matter-of-fact a voice, that somehow or other the awful intimacy of what was happening was heightened rather than lessened.

What had followed was still a nightmare to her: a relentless period of hours which had seemed to become days, of questions and answers...questions designed to underline her ignorance and to defeat her determination not to give in to the mastery she sensed he intended to have over her, over their situation. Questions which had laid bare the paucity of her knowledge, of her awareness, of her inner essence of herself as a woman.

And not until he was satisfied that she knew by heart every last nuance of male sexuality and male anatomy had he allowed her to touch him.

Allowed her! She shuddered at the very word chosen by her mind. Were it not for the fact that she was here by her own will, he would have had to drag her screaming and kicking to within a foot of his body, never mind make her touch it! It made no difference telling herself that it was he who should feel embarrassed, he who should feel diminished by their bargain. He did not and she did, and even now it seemed he wasn't satisfied.

Her performance, while technically fair, lacked spontaneity and enthusiasm, he had told her.

Now, with her nerves stretched to breaking-point, her whole sense of purpose undermined to such an extent that she was no longer sure if she had the stamina to endure any more, she knew suddenly and bitterly that she couldn't go on.

She moved savagely, hating herself, hating him, but most of all hating Charles for making all of this necessary.

Outside the window the snow whirled and boiled, the storm as tempestuous as her emotions. As she stared into the snow she had a momentary vision of her father the last time they had skied together, and the ache of pain inside her intensified. She mustn't let him down...she must make Charles pay.

'Face it,' said Jake grimly behind her. 'You're never going to make it. You just don't have what it takes.'

The moment the jibe was spoken he regretted it, but she had been driving him to the edge of his self-control for days, whether she knew it or not, and he suspected that she did. He felt her pain as though it were a physical link between them, felt the swift stirring of air that told him what she was feeling.

Part of him wanted to take hold of her and either physically shake her or punish her with the kind of kiss that he knew full well, once given, would change their relationship for ever. And the worst of it all was that, even knowing the folly of such an action, he was still unbearably tempted to do it—to drown out all the loneliness, the frustration...the sheer heaviness of the burdens he carried by opening up that sealed well of emotion she kept so well guarded.

He knew that within them both was the capacity to destroy the privacy each of them guarded so fiercely. Fortunately for him, Silver didn't know it...not yet. She was too obsessed with keeping control of herself to worry about what he was feeling.

'I've had enough of this,' he heard her say unevenly. 'I'm going up to my room.'

'No!'

Even as he said it he knew he ought to let her go, for both their sakes. He was feeling too raw, too vulnerable to detach himself as he knew he must, and yet still he reached for her, still he touched her face and felt the warm dampness of tears he had known would be there, even though she hadn't made a single betraying sound.

When he kissed her he told himself he was doing it for Beth...that everything was for Beth...for his guilt, for her pain, for her death, and ultimately for the destruction of whoever it was in London who had ordered the taking of her life.

Drug dealing was an ugly business, he had known that from the start...had known the dangers and ignored them. That arrogance on his part had cost Beth her life.

A life for a life...but so far three men had been made to pay. Not directly by Jake; it was the information he had given the FBI which had led to the gaoling of two members of the quartet. And José Ortuga was dead,

killed in a bomb blast by a rival Colombian drug baron
just before Jake could trap him. That explosion had also
cost him his sight. Now there was one final member of
the quartet to track down and destroy: the one in charge
of the London arm of the operation...the one who had
ordered Beth's death...the one who had realised exactly
who he was and who he was working for...the one who
had so far eluded the skills of the experts he had paid
to track him down.

Without his sight there was only so much he could do
himself...but he would use Silver's money to pay for
men to find the final member of that unholy quartet.

Beneath the hard assault of his mouth he felt Silver's
soften, felt the *frisson* of shock run through her, felt her
bewilderment and distress as though they were his own,
and still he used them ruthlessly to expiate his own anger,
his own pain. Used her in a way which he knew damned
well was neither detached nor remote, refusing to release
her mouth until she was quiescent with shock beneath
his.

The moment he relaxed his hold she wrenched away
from him, as he had known she would, and he knew
quite well that if he could see her he would find her
mouth swollen and her eyes full of tears.

The anger left him as quickly as it had come.

He ought to apologise, but if he did that he would be
inviting an intimacy into their relationship which was
dangerous to them both.

Instead he said coolly, '*Now* maybe we can make some
progress. Now that you know at first hand what desire
feels like.'

Colour scorched Silver's skin. What she had just endured was surely the most humiliating episode in her
whole life...worse in some ways than finding Charles
making love to someone else. That she had actually for
one brief second of time felt desire...that Jake had
known it... She shuddered.

It was time for a break, Jake acknowledged as she fled. Both of them needed it.

It caused him a certain amount of wry self-mockery to acknowledge that increasingly there were times when he physically desired her to the point where he had difficulty with his self-control. He, who hadn't once, in the years since Beth had died, truly, instinctively desired a woman with that gut-deep, mindless male ache that owed nothing to intelligence, compassion or indeed any other emotion other than the most basic one of intense physical hunger. And very infrequently before that.

His life had been far from celibate, but he was a man who prided himself on relating to the women who shared his life and his bed as fellow human beings, who had ranked sex well down on the list of what was essential in a man-to-woman relationship. And yet here he was, his body and his mind drawn tight with an aching need that he wanted to put down to the mere intimacy of their situation, but which he knew damn well he could not.

He linked his arms behind his head and tried to ease the tension from his neck. Only another few days. Already, even if she didn't know it herself, she had learned almost all she needed to know. That jibe he had thrown at her had been without foundation, and he ought to tell her as much.

He was a trained observer who, now that the sense of sight was lost to him, made full use of those senses left to him to absorb and catalogue information about others; he wondered if she was as aware as he was of how much she suppressed her natural sexuality, even while claiming that she wanted to use it.

He knew enough about the human race and its behavioural patterns to know that it would be quite easy for him to destroy that suppression and make her respond to him personally, as she had done this afternoon.

He had told himself that he wasn't going to do it because he didn't want the complications which would inevitably ensue... because he didn't want that kind of involvement, especially not with a woman so obviously hung up on another man... Charles, she had called him... And there had been pain as well as anger in her voice when she'd said he had never loved her.

He wondered who she really was. It wouldn't be impossible for him to find out... Quickly he shut himself off from the temptation. He had other things to do with his life, things that were far more important. He had a murder to avenge. He frowned. How well he understood what motivated Silver... none better. He didn't want to allow himself to feel sympathy for her. In so many ways she was everything he despised in her sex, but that was only on the surface. Beneath that surface was a woman every bit as vulnerable as Beth had been...

Beth... why was he linking the two of them together? He shifted uncomfortably, dropping his hands and then getting up.

Force of habit drove him over to the window. He knew it was there by some complicated alteration within his inner darkness, by the difference in the scent of the air...almost by instinct...even though, standing in front of it and looking outwards, he could see nothing of the storm raging outside. His mind was on other things.

Ultimately he was going to have to fulfil the final clause of their contract and free her from the unwanted burden of her physical virginity.

His mouth curled in a humourless smile. Originally when she had made that stipulation, although he hadn't allowed her to see it, he had wondered cynically if, when the time came, he would be physically capable of entering her, whether he had the physical strength, the stamina, the mental will-power to overcome all the mental and emotional pitfalls of making love to a woman he neither liked nor desired. Now he was more concerned with making sure she didn't goad him to the point where his physical possession of her was no longer something he could mentally distance himself from—no longer merely a set task to be accomplished with clinical detachment and as much physical finesse as he could manage.

It couldn't be put off any longer. With every day they spent together now, the tension grew between them. Hers was infiltrated with fear, even though she fought hard not to show it.

He turned away from the source of light and stretched. His blindness was in its way his punishment for thinking himself invincible. He had been careless, and that carelessness had cost other men their freedom and himself his sight. It didn't matter that he hadn't been the one in charge... he should have been. He had been guilty of an error of judgement and he would pay for that error all through his life. The doctors had been brutally frank with him. There was no hope of his ever regaining his sight.

He touched his face, his fingers instinctively finding the small ridges of scars that were all that was left of the patchwork of plastic surgery Annie had done to repair the horrendous damage the bomb had inflicted.

When the eye surgeon had first recommended plastic surgery, he had told him to go to hell. What did it matter to him what he looked like? The man had persisted, though, patiently pointing out that, while *he* didn't have to look at himself, others did...

Unable to endure the thought of more surgery, he had come instinctively here to Annie and had eventually given in to her persuasion that he should have the operations. She had performed them herself. He had wondered, in one bleak moment of self-acknowledgement before the anaesthetic had claimed him, if God would punish him for Beth's death by letting him die.

Or would that have been a punishment? Life held no savour for him now. No savour, perhaps, but it did hold a purpose... a purpose that only Silver's money could help him to achieve. His mouth twisted again, a long-ago scrap of conversation floating to the surface of his mind—Beth saying awkwardly, 'She wanted you to want her...'

They had been talking about her mother. They had been lying in bed together in the apartment in Paris he had rented for their honeymoon. She had been so insecure, so young, not quite nineteen to his twenty-eight...too young, an inner voice told him as he forced himself to confront the knowledge that had been with him for a long time, but which somehow or other Silver had brought to the surface of his consciousness, adding to his already heavy burden of guilt.

He *had* loved Beth, had cherished her, but in so many ways she had still been a child. Would there ultimately have come a time when her immaturity, her dependence, even her love might have become burdensome to him? When he might have longed for a woman capable of meeting him on his own ground; a woman such as...? He blocked off the thought.

Beth...why did he find it so difficult to conjure up a mental picture of her face...to remember what it had felt like to hold her in his arms, to love her? He could remember how she had made his heart ache with tenderness...how he had wanted to protect her...but he couldn't remember what it had felt like to desire her the way he had desired Silver. They were so very different, and yet...and yet there were moments when he sensed such an intensity of vulnerability about Silver that it set off a corresponding echo deep within himself.

She had been injured, hurt, her life destroyed by the treachery of the man she loved, and now she was going to hit back at him. To destroy him in turn. Revenge, one of the most powerful human emotions there could be. And one of the most self-destructive; he should know. Yet, though he tried to warn her against taking up those burdens, he knew quite well that she would not listen to him. This need in him to warn her, to protect her almost, irked him; she was no real concern of his, but old habits died hard, and far too long he had carried the burden of being responsible for others, Beth and, before her, Justin...

Anyway, did he really have the right to tell Silver how to run her life, he who had never allowed anyone to dictate to him how *he* lived *his* life? Already in his thoughts he was betraying the fact that he was losing his emotional distance from her, that he was aware of her in ways that threatened both of them. It had to stop. Now, before things got completely out of control.

He moved restlessly around the room, acknowledging a deep inner truth he had been fighting for days.

It was time to bring things to an end...

One final lesson and they would both be free to go their own separate ways.

Silver sensed the purposefulness in him when she came down to prepare dinner. Supplies of food were delivered regularly twice a week from the town and they took it in turns to prepare the meals.

Tonight it was her turn.

Despite her father's wealth and upbringing, she could cook, a strange, eclectic collection of dishes prepared with an expertise she had garnered from her father's households throughout the world.

Tonight it was Irish stew, made in the traditional way, and served with soda bread.

As she lifted the casserole out of the oven and prepared to serve it, she commented briskly to Jake, 'It's Irish stew; that's——'

'You don't need to tell me what it is. I know.'

The vehemence in his voice startled her. She stopped what she was doing and looked at him, stunned to see a muscle twitch fiercely in his jaw. His mouth was drawn into a tight line of pain, and for the first time she saw the brilliant eyes unfocused as they stared not at her but past her, as though he were looking at something no one else could see.

He had been sitting down, since she had told him she was about to serve dinner, but now he got up abruptly, awkwardly almost, half stumbling against the table so that she reached out automatically to catch him and then withdrew her hand as she heard him swear.

He was halfway towards the door when she realised that he wasn't going to have dinner with her. Without thinking what she was doing, she asked protestingly where he was going.

'Somewhere I can't smell *that*,' he told her savagely, gesturing towards the steaming casserole, and then he added softly, 'The last time I had Irish stew, my wife made it for me. It was her favourite dish and our last meal together before I went away on business. She was dead before I returned...murdered in cold blood.'

Silver let him go in silence, too shocked to say anything. It was the first time he had ever made any kind of reference to his own personal life, and the horror of the small picture he had drawn for her remained with her long after he had gone. She found that she couldn't eat the stew herself and, picking up the casserole, she took it outside and threw it away.

When she came back in her stomach was still heaving, but there was nothing she could do. There were a thousand questions she wanted to ask...a thousand things she wanted to know...

It was unnerving and unwanted, this glimpse into the raw pain of someone else's life; this knowledge that he was after all human and vulnerable.

She had wanted that vulnerability in him, hungering for it as a weapon she could use against him, but now she realised she didn't want it after all... She was like a child suddenly discovering that a parent was frightened of the dark, and cravenly wishing she did not have to know about that fear.

She made herself go back into the kitchen, and turned on the extractor fan. She opened the fridge, and took out some fresh chicken breasts.

Half an hour later she went up to his room, knocked briefly on the door and without opening it said quietly, 'Dinner's ready. It's Chicken Maryland,' and without waiting for a response, for all the world as though the entire incident with the stew had never happened, she went back downstairs and calmly started serving the chicken.

He arrived just as she was filling her own wine glass, sitting down at the table and saying quietly, 'I've decided that you've learned as much from me as you're going to learn. That being the case, there's just one small formality left...'

Silver's hand shook. She spilt a drop of wine on the table and watched it with fixed attention, unable to bring herself to face him. Was he doing this as a reward because she had thrown away the stew, or as a punishment because she had made it in the first place?

Without appearing to notice her tension, he added coolly, 'I made up my mind this afternoon. My decision has nothing to do with any personal motivation.'

That wasn't strictly true, but he had realised from her tension exactly what she was thinking and his own pride would not allow him to let her go on thinking it.

That had been an idiotic thing to do. There was no reason why he shouldn't have eaten the damn stew... But the smell of it had reminded him too sharply of Beth, of their lives together, of her death and his own feelings afterwards.

Revenge; he knew it all, every last nuance of what it felt like.

Desperate to conceal her tension from him, Silver said the first thing that came into her head.

'Your wife... You said she was murdered...' She shivered suddenly, thinking of her father, of Charles, who would surely destroy her as ruthlessly and as cold-bloodedly as he had threatened if he should ever penetrate her disguise. But that was impossible. To all intents and purposes she was dead, and had been reborn in a different image.

'What is it you want to know?' Jake asked her bitterly. 'How Beth was killed, or why?'

Inwardly he was shocked at his own response to her question.

Silently Silver watched him, sensing his withdrawal, his anger. She had known quite well that mentioning his wife *would* anger him, but she had been desperate to divert his attention from her own tension. She half expected him to get up and walk out as he had done earlier, but to her astonishment he said grimly, 'Well, why not? It might even serve as an object lesson to you, but somehow I doubt it. I was working as a government agent, tracking down a drug-trafficking syndicate. I was close enough to exposing the ringleaders to receive threats against my life when my cover was blown. I should have stopped then, should have insisted on sending Beth away somewhere safe, but she didn't want to leave me and, God help me, I didn't want her to go.

'In my arrogance I thought they'd target any violence against *me*. I got a lead that some of the stuff was being shipped in from South America...a deliberate ruse to get me out of the way, but I was stupid enough and vain enough to fall for it.

'While I was out of the country Beth was killed by a hit-and-run driver. An accident—that was how it looked, only it was no accident. Beth had been deliberately and cold-bloodedly murdered. You want to know how I can be so sure? Easy...her murderers took the trouble to let me know what they had done.

'I only found out later that there'd been additional threats to the ones I'd received, threats that Beth hadn't told me about...you see, she knew how important my work was to me...'

He wasn't looking at her, and Silver had the feeling that he had almost forgotten she was there. It was as though the words were drawn from him like splinters of steel from a wound, and that with every word the pain increased, so that when he said under his breath, 'But, dear God, it was never more important to me than her life,' she felt a dull, paralysing ache close her own throat.

Sympathy...compassion...for Jake Fitton? Why? He had had none to spare for her.

'Since Beth's death I've spent my time tracking down the four people responsible for planning her murder...'

He had recovered with awesome speed and was once again apparently in full control of himself and his emotions.

'Two of them are in American gaols under sentence of death; one of them died in the same bomb blast that cost me my sight... So far I've been robbed of the pleasure of making those responsible for Beth's death pay personally and with compound interest for her suffering.

'There's only one member of the quartet left. No doubt he's forgotten that Beth ever existed. Once I find him I intend to make him remember.'

The icy coldness of his voice sent shivers running down Silver's spine.

'And you dare to caution me against revenge?' she demanded bitterly.

He smiled then, a humourless, chilling smile. 'Revenge demands a high price: total dedication, total commitment.'

'And you think *I* can't meet those demands?'

He felt drained to the point of exhaustion. He never discussed Beth with anyone, and it stunned him that he should have chosen this woman out of everyone he knew to unburden himself to... And it *had* been an unburdening, even if she herself was unaware of that fact. It had been an admission to himself and to her of his guilt, his pain, his need to pay whatever price was demanded of him so that Beth's death might be avenged.

And yet there was still one small, sane part of him that urged him to turn away from the past and to face forward into the future.

Was that why he was doing this? Was that why he was trying to make Silver recognise...? But why? She meant nothing to him...

Nothing other than the fact that she was a fellow human being and vulnerable. Far more vulnerable than she herself recognised.

Tiredly he told her, 'Whatever you might say to the contrary, I remain unconvinced that you *do* actually hate this man. Has it occurred to you yet that you could all too easily fall into your own trap?'

Yes, it had occurred to her. Charles was a powerfully charismatic personality. Far more sophisticated women than she was had fallen under his spell. But she knew things about him that they did not...she had a far stronger motive for hating him than Jake Fitton knew.

It gave her an odd sense of awareness about him to recognise that both of them were linked together by their desire to avenge the death of someone they had loved; and more than that. Charles was heavily involved in the London drugs scene as a pusher. Something she hadn't told Jake for reasons of her own.

Another thought struck her.

'Is that why you're doing this?' she asked him curtly. 'Because you need the money to track down the fourth man?'

'Yes,' he told her, equally briefly. 'I know he's based in London...'

Silver found she was holding her breath. Surely the fourth man couldn't be Charles? And then she released it as Jake added, 'He also does a lot of travelling, legitimately of course, using it as a means of contacting his suppliers.'

'But if he's smuggling drugs into the country——' Silver began.

Jake stopped her with a cold smile. 'This isn't someone who smuggles the stuff. He's way, way above that part of the organisation. This is someone who plans and re-cruits...who deals direct with the drug barons and who is trusted by them. This is someone who runs a country-wide network of pushers...if you like, the drug barons' ambassador to England.'

So it couldn't be Charles. He had rarely left England. She was relieved, and recognised that part of the reason she had said nothing to Jake about Charles's in-volvement with drugs was because she had been afraid that he might somehow snatch her prey away from her.

Out of some protective instinct Jake had thought he had long ago exhausted, he heard himself saying as he put down his knife and fork, 'It's not too late, you know. You can always change your mind. Revenge isn't sweet...it's acid, corrosive, bitter, and finally de-structive. It will eat into your soul until there's nothing left of you...'

Silver smiled at him, an animal baring of her teeth, her eyes glittering with resolve. Everything he had said to her had only strengthened her determination.

'Who wants sweetness?' she said evenly. 'Unless, of course, you're trying to tell me that eating Irish stew isn't the only thing you're incapable of doing.'

He picked up his knife and fork and ate some of his chicken slowly and deliberately, while she watched him with fascinated horror, wondering, as she always did, how he managed to cope so well with his blindness. Apart from a momentary hesitation as he searched for the chicken, no one would ever have guessed that he couldn't see what was on his plate, and then, when he had fin-ished chewing...when he must have known that her nerves were stretched to breaking-point by her own mindless, reckless idiocy, he said evenly, 'In that case, you'd have an excellent opportunity to show us both how well you've learned everything I've attempted to teach you, wouldn't you? The supreme test, so to speak.'

The moment of intimacy, of allowing her into his private thoughts and feelings was gone, Silver recognised, and she shivered in a return of her earlier tension.

It might have been better if Jake had not chosen to give her advance warning of what was to happen. And then she admitted, with the percipient intelligence that had been honed to such sharpness under her father's tutelage, that whichever route he had chosen to take towards the final culmination to her studies with him she would have criticised it, and moreover that it was not for her to criticise or accuse, since it was by her own demand that it was to take place.

There could be no shielding herself from the reality of her own decisions by trying to hide behind Jake's apparent authority.

Nevertheless . . . a tiny, uncomfortably sharp corner of her mind acknowledged that she would have felt happier had she been the one to dictate the timing of their final passage of arms.

Although she hadn't said a word, Jake was alert to every single one of the emotional vibrations she was giving off. He wondered what it was that gave rise to that specific and, to him at least, very obvious mingling of fear, anger and resentment. The anger and resentment were directed at and caused by him, he knew, but the fear . . . Was she frightened of him? He had given her no cause to be. But the fear was there, no matter how much she tried to disguise it, and for some unacknowledgeable reason that irked him. All through dinner he was sharply aware of it, like a piece of uncomfortable cloth rubbing against tender flesh, and that in itself was an annoyance. Why should he give a damn how she felt? Theirs was a financial bargain . . . an act of sale and an act of purchase . . . a necessary intimacy of the flesh without any involvement of either the emotions or the mind.

And yet, as he realised as clearly as though he could see her that she was toying with her food, he pushed his own plate to one side and said quietly, 'Well, if you're sure you don't want to change your mind, we might as well get it over and done with.'

His words, gruffly delivered, almost stiltedly so—which in itself was out of character because normally he allowed no emotion to cloud the ice-clear coldness of his voice—only increased her tension. He was almost on the brink of feeling sorry for her. Just as so many others had already felt sorry for her. Their pity... his pity were the last things she wanted. She got up jerkily and started to clear the table, saying unevenly, 'Not yet, if you don't mind... I haven't had my coffee.'

He was standing up himself and she half expected him to clear the distance between them and manhandle her out of the kitchen, but instead he shrugged and said calmly, 'Just as you like. I'll load the dishwasher, then you can make the coffee.'

As he moved efficiently and quietly between the dining area and the kitchen, Silver had the feeling that his very presence threatened her in some illogical way; that as he carefully loaded the machine and then closed the door he was just as effectively sealing off all her routes of escape from a situation she herself had deliberately engineered; and yet what, after all, was there in the slightest degree dangerous about a blind man who had already made it abundantly clear that the last person he desired was her?

As she stood in a corner of the kitchen with the percolator bubbling behind her, surrounded by the sounds and scents of the most mundane sort, she wondered why she should know instinctively that for the rest of her life she would remember them as a backdrop to the most horrible and all-encompassing sense of terror she had ever experienced.

It began in her stomach like a cold chill that slowly turned to ice and then burned as the chill itself spread through her veins; it made her head feel physically tight with tension, made her throat muscles lock and a thrill of pure fear spiral through her body so that she shuddered visibly.

And yet some stubborn, implacable hereditary awareness within her made her acknowledge that even if she could simply will herself out of this place and into another...if she could simply make Jake disappear in a thin cloud of smoke as one of her ancestresses had been reputed to be able to do, she would not have done it.

This dread...this terror...this acknowledgement that she was voluntarily stepping into a situation in which she was not going to be in control, in which she was going to be acutely vulnerable to both physical and mental abuse and mockery, in which she was voluntarily giving over her most intimate flesh into the possession of another...these were part of the price she had to pay.

Despite her education and her intelligence, Silver had a deeply atavistic awareness of darker forces running beneath the surface of her life...of currents and tides...a knowledge that went far back beyond anything that could be learned from the written word and which owed itself to the Celtic blood that ran through her veins, carrying with it hereditary memories of the magical powers of her race. It was as though that inner knowledge was telling her that this was the sacrifice she must make, this the magic talisman that would buy her success, this a very necessary crossing of her own private river of fate, and that to turn back now would mean that the whole flow of her life would have to be redirected into new channels.

Behind her the coffee still bubbled, but she no longer heard it, and her eyes no longer saw the cheerfulness of the small kitchen.

'Silver.'

The crispness of Jake's curt demand brought her back to reality. She turned and focused on him, blinking a little.

For a moment she trembled between advancing or re-treating, and then, like a sleep-walker, she heard herself saying emotionlessly, 'Yes. I'm ready.'

As he listened to her, Jake smothered his own awareness of her fear. What was it that caused that fear? He could only think of the obvious reason, and the panic he had felt emanating from her before she'd brought it under control had been far stronger than that would have merited. Beth had been a virgin and he her first lover, but she had come to him with joy and trust...Beth... He pushed his own emotions aside and said coolly, 'You haven't had your coffee.'

Her coffee. Silver had forgotten all about it. She looked at it with a pinched face and haunted eyes, not wanting to think about what she was about to go through.

'We're going to be more comfortable upstairs, and since my room has the larger bed I suggest we use that. You go up. I'll bring the coffee,' Jake told her.

He had another reason for suggesting they use his room, and it had nothing to do with the size of its bed, but rather its position. His own room was familiar to him, each object as clearly known as though he could actually see it. Every sense he possessed, and some he had never known before that he had, were warning him of impending trauma. His training, his knowledge of himself, everything he had ever learned about the human race warned him that should something go wrong, should something happen for which he was not prepared, he would be better able to deal with it from the relative familiarity of his own room.

However, as he made the coffee and took it upstairs, he told himself firmly that nothing was going to go wrong. This final act between them would be effected quickly and efficiently, and hopefully with sufficient finesse to make it endurable for both of them.

CHAPTER FIVE

NOTHING had changed in Jake's room since the first time Silver had walked into it. Then she had undressed without any outward qualms... Then she had gone to lie on his bed to wait for him without any fear other than that he would reject her proposition.

Now it was different. Now she was a mass of nerves... trembling with rejection and apprehension.

She willed herself to regain her self-control. What would she do if she reacted like this when she was with Charles? She wondered frantically if Jake had been serious when he had suggested this would be a good test for her—if he genuinely expected her to seduce him into taking her—because if so, she decided grimly...

The door opened while she was still thinking about it, and for a moment as he looked at her she could almost believe that Jake could actually see her cowering in the corner of the room. It still baffled and infuriated her, this ability of his to focus so directly on her as though he actually knew where she was. And then she realised that he did, because he had put the tray of coffee down and was walking firmly towards her. When he was within arm's reach of her, he stopped and said unequivocally, 'Before you do anything else you can have a shower. You're wearing that damned perfume again, and I have no desire to wake up in the morning with my sheets reeking of it...'

Silver had worn the perfume in a mood of angry defiance, thinking she was going to eat dinner alone. She had forgotten about it, but now suddenly she could actually smell it: the sweet, cloying scent of the tuberoses suffocating her senses, making her almost feel nauseous; and although the last thing she wanted to do was to obey any instruction he gave her, she found herself actually mentally imagining the relief of soaping her skin clean of its too-sweet scent.

'Do it, Silver,' he told her grimly. 'Otherwise I'll do it for you, and I assure you that if I do it will be something that neither of us enjoys.'

His relentlessness seemed to restore her courage. She marched away from him and into the bathroom, slamming the door behind her, stripping off her clothes and standing behind the stinging spray of the shower before she could change her mind.

The vapour of the hot water seemed to intensify the scent, so that when she closed her eyes she could actually see Charles and his lover entwined in bed...as she had seen them that time, Charles's hand caressing the silky thigh of the blonde-haired woman, his mouth feeding greedily on her breast while he moaned and twisted against her in semi-tortured ecstasy... An ecstasy that made Silver feel physically sick.

She cried out without realising she had done so, causing Jake to frown and head for the bathroom door and then stop.

Tuberoses. God, how he hated that scent... And she, with that Machiavellian instinct of hers, seemed to know it instinctively. He moved uncomfortably, conscious of a certain ache in his thigh where it had been pierced by a piece of flying debris from the bomb.

He realised from the silence that the shower had stopped running, and started to undress, methodically removing his clothes, folding them neatly, so that when Silver emerged from the bathroom wrapped in a towel, her hair a damp, tangled mass on her shoulders, he was standing naked beside the bed, removing the quilt.

For some reason her heart jolted physically at the sight of him. She was no stranger to his nudity, or indeed to any part of his body, not any more, and yet she felt shaken each time she was confronted by its power.

He had taught her with admirably clinical detachment how to appreciate and stimulate every part of it, instructing her in acts of intimacy that seemed impossible to believe when later, fully dressed, he would matter-of-factly cross-question her about what she had learned.

His total indifference to her flesh and his own had helped her then to apply herself to what she wanted to learn with a detachment that almost matched his own, but suddenly she felt far from detached, and her face burned with memories she would rather not have had surface.

As she looked at him and knew that he was waiting for her to shed her towel and get on the bed, she wanted to protest that she needed to dry her hair and drink her coffee, to tell him that she wasn't ready...that she needed more time. But what would such delaying tactics achieve other than an increase in her fear? So, trying not to think about what she was doing, she removed her towel, folding it as neatly as he had folded his clothes, although her fingers trembled dreadfully over the task. Then she skirted the bed, going to the opposite side from where he was standing.

For a moment they stood facing one another across its width: two adversaries in a duel, each acknowledging the strength and power of the other in a silent exchange that encompassed more than any amount of words; and beneath the covert testing of one another's will, beneath the subtle shifting and weighing of strengths and judging of weaknesses, like a current felt but unseen, ran the secret flow of Silver's fears.

In one clear, sharp second of time before she fought them down, as she looked at Jake, challenging him with the only power she had that he did not—that of her sight—she almost felt the silence around them pulse with her fear, and, as though she had said the words out loud, her mind received from his an assurance so clear that her mouth dropped open, her brain unable to comprehend that neither of them had actually spoken. Like a child in the dark, she had cried out her dread and, like an ever-watchful parent, he had heard it and comforted her.

The shock of that mental intimacy, so unexpected and so dangerous, drove away her fear. The sheets felt cold, making her shiver, and she told herself she had imagined the intense inner reassurance...that it could not have existed. Must not have existed.

As she felt him move on to the bed beside her, without looking at him she said tautly, 'I'd like to get it over with as quickly as possible.'

For one mind-destroying, bitter moment she thought he was actually going to laugh, but then she saw that the faint twitch of his mouth was caused, not by amusement, but by tension.

'My feelings exactly,' he told her drily. 'But unfortunately it isn't going to be as easy as that. While it might be possible for your body to accept mine merely at your command, mine, I'm afraid, is not quite so accommodating.'

Silver felt her face burn, as much with indignation as with irritation, but what had she expected? she derided herself: that just because it was convenient for her, despite his having shown her beyond any shadow of a doubt that he felt no desire for her, his flesh should suddenly and miraculously pulse and swell with excitement at her proximity?

Or was this simply his way of testing her, of making her prove that she had learned her lessons well? She reminded herself that if this were Charles she was with, she would not be able to have any qualms about her course of action.

But if she had been with Charles she would *want* to arouse him, to excite him, to overwhelm him with the intensity of his desire for her, and there could be no Charles until this final hurdle was cleared. So she turned to him and asked distastefully, 'What exactly do you want me to do?'

'Don't for God's sake speak to your potential victim like that, will you?' he murmured drily. 'You'll terrify him into a state of permanent impotence. Actually I don't want you to *do* anything other than come and lie here beside me...and on this occasion I think we can dispense with these,' he added, reaching out and switching off the lights.

How had he known they were on? Silver wondered. In the past, while he was teaching her, he had refused her initial attempts to persuade him that she would prove a more apt pupil if she didn't have to see what she was doing, and he had taunted her so unmercifully with her squeamishness that she had stopped asking.

So why now, of all times, did he offer her the panacea he had withheld from her before? Not for his own sake...his darkness was permanent.

For hers? Never! More likely because he sensed her tension and wanted to ease it, for his own sake as much as hers.

As she moved closer to him, the unexpectedness of his arm curling round her and drawing her down against his side until her flesh touched his startled her. Before, there had been no physical contact between them other than that which he had deemed necessary as part of her sexual education, no casual, almost comfortable embrace of the type they were sharing now, and it bewildered her, sending out conflicting messages which her brain couldn't unravel.

There was the silky brush of skin against skin, sensually pleasing, as her own flesh already recognised, vaguely dangerous and forbidden in a way that was slightly exhilarating, and yet the casualness of his attitude towards her was the opposite of sensual; deprived of any sensuality or hint of desire, the firm pressure of his arm around her was more comradely than anything else, somehow or other defusing the situation of some of its terror. His hand rested against her waist, not caressing her or stroking her, simply touching her, so that her skin absorbed the sensation of it, noting the hardness of his fingers, their relaxed strength, their knowledge and experience.

Even though he was silent, there was no tension in his silence; rather, it was almost as though he was in some subtle way inviting her to share it, coaxing her to relax into it, although why she should have felt that she had no idea. She had the most peculiar urge to ask him what he was thinking about, something she had never done before nor ever imagined doing. She moved restlessly, and his hand slid to her hip, turning her with some slight pressure so that almost half the length of her body rested on him.

His hand still sat lightly on her, but now the pressure of his silent demand that she open her mind to him was so strong that she had to use all her own strength to resist it. His assault on her body she had expected... but this assault on her mind... She lay against him angrily, using all her concentration to fight free of the subtle lure he was throwing out to her, unaware of the slow drift of his hand against her skin as it stroked the warm flesh of her hip and the round curve of her buttock, slowly easing her into his own flesh so that each fierce beat of her angry heart and every quick, impassioned breath from her lungs reinforced for him the physical reality of her femininity.

If all else failed, Jake told himself cynically, he could always try blocking everything else out and remembering how it had been with Beth, but he didn't want to do that. Partly because it would desecrate what had been, and partly... He swore explosively under his breath, at the same moment as Silver chose to wriggle protestingly against his touch, and, by some alchemy he wasn't going to bother to even think about trying to analyse, the angry, resentful movement aroused him with unexpected intensity.

Silver gasped and then choked on her protest as he rolled her over on to her back, only just managing to stop herself from curling her body into an angry foetal ball of rejection and instead opening it to accommodate the unexpectedly heavy weight of him.

She wanted to scream at him to hurry and get it over with, and at the same time acknowledged that she could hardly behave in such an irrational way.

Intelligence told her that it would all be much easier if she could instruct her tense muscles to relax, but some instincts were too ingrained for intelligence, and when Jake withdrew slightly from her she realised he was as aware of her tension as she was herself.

'All this would be a lot easier if you let me help you to relax first,' he told her calmly.

Silver stared up into his eyes, marvelling at his ability to remain so calm. She knew exactly what he meant; he had already told her, in explicit and sometimes pithy detail that warned her that in some way he enjoyed her mental and emotional shrinking from what he was saying, that everything he was teaching her to do to him could be reversed to exactly the same effect, and that she would have a much deeper and more instinctive awareness of how to manipulate male arousal if she had experienced her own female arousal first.

But she had told him it wasn't necessary. And she still considered that it wasn't.

Because she was afraid of that experience... Even more afraid than she was of his physical possession?

The answer was there in the sharp, shrill denial that came instinctively to her lips.

'No!' she spat at him. 'I don't want you to do anything other than get this whole damned thing over with.'

For the first time, she sensed his self-control slip. One brief burn of anger beneath the cold clarity of his eyes, one hard tensing of muscles as her frailer flesh took the weight of his body, and she almost gave in and told him she'd changed her mind.

Only pride stopped her. Pride and a certain desperate awareness that if she once allowed him to arouse her to desire, she would somehow have lost a very important part of herself to him ... A part of herself that could never be recovered ... Her emotional virginity, perhaps? She scorned herself for the thought, and then heard him say grimly, 'Very well, then, if that's the way you want it.'

And then she felt his hands on her body, moving her, positioning her as he loomed over her, suddenly dark and alien. She held her breath and forgot to tense her muscles against him, so that his first thrust carried him into her and caused her only to gasp a little at the un-expected ease of it, only to discover as he moved again and then again that she had been too confident too soon, and that the pain that now shot through her was every-thing she had imagined it would be and more: sharp, tearing, inescapable, filling her so that she cried out and twisted beneath him, dragging her nails against his skin as she fought for release and wasn't granted it.

The pain went on and on as he drove further into her, ignoring her cries ... ignoring her demands, ignoring everything but the goal he had set himself.

And then, miraculously, when she had thought it would last forever, it was over and she was free to curl herself into a ball of fading scalding agony, sick and dizzy with relief, so that she was barely aware of him leaving the bed and going into the bathroom until he came back wearing his bathrobe, holding a glass of water and a small white tablet.

'I'm sorry it was so bad,' he told her coolly. 'But it's over now and it won't ever bother you again. Sit up and take this ...'

'What is it?' she asked him, eyeing the tablet warily, but for some reason she couldn't understand obeying his command to uncurl her body and crawl into a sitting position. She winced as she did so, still sore and tender inside, even though the pain had abated.

'Pain-killer,' he told her. 'I need them sometimes. It won't harm you. You're going to bleed for a while, I suspect. If you're still bleeding in the morning...' He frowned and Silver looked away from him, even though he couldn't see her flush of embarrassment.

She looked at him and for the first time said quietly, 'Thank you...'

An odd expression crossed his face. One she couldn't define at all.

He looked down at her almost broodingly, and she wondered what was going on behind the implacable hardness of his face...what thoughts were locked away in that over-alert and too perceptive mind. He had known her fear, felt it, touched it, tasted it; she had given him a unique weapon against herself and yet he had not used it.

And now, when another man might have experienced discomfort, impatience, embarrassment or just the sheer plain desire to turn his back on the whole incident and on her, he was still standing beside her, his fingers resting lightly against her inner wrist, monitoring the feverish race of her pulse.

The deep understanding which had led him not to betray either surprise or anger, the compassion which had given her the pain-killer, his calm, matter-of-fact awareness of the possible physical consequence of the tearing of that too-protective unwanted veil of flesh, betrayed a much deeper awareness of her than she had known.

'You'll want to sleep alone,' he commented now, and then, when she started to move, his fingers curled round her wrist, making her yield to their pressure.

'No...you stay here. I'll sleep in your bed tonight.' His mouth curled and then softened into an incredibly illuminating smile, one she had never seen curve his mouth before, and for a heart-stopping moment she was breathless and motionless beneath its potency, dazzled by its lure and promise. And then it vanished and his mouth was the cynical curl of contempt with which she was so familiar as he added drily, 'I trust that you don't go to bed wearing that appalling perfume.'

'It isn't appalling. It's very expensive, and I happen to like it,' she told him fiercely, hating herself for the odd sensations she had just experienced, wanting to push them out of her mind and bury them deep where she would never have to face them again. They were too disturbing, too distressing, especially now, when not just her body but her mind as well felt drained of all energy and will to combat anything.

'Liar,' he derided her softly. 'It isn't you at all. You should wear something sharp and fresh, something that smells of young fresh grass after spring rain...something subtle and tormenting——' He broke off suddenly, and Silver knew instinctively that he had spoken words he had not intended to say.

'We both need to get some sleep,' he told her curtly. 'But if you need me for...anything during the night...'

She shot up in bed, simultaneously reaching for the sheet to cover her body—a wasted gesture since he couldn't see it—and wincing sharply with the pain that splintered inside her, so that he heard her sharp indrawn breath. Then she realised that he had not been taunting her with sexual innuendo, as she had thought, but had simply meant if she was in any physical discomfort.

She had spent enough dreary hours recovering from the pain of her own operations to know why he should be so aware of how long and dark those nights could be when the physical body was tormented by its ills and the pain stretched out tentacle-like fingers, which it hooked into vulnerable flesh and raked it into an agony that never seemed to subside.

'This tablet should do the trick if it's one of Annie's wonder pills,' she told him gruffly, not knowing why now, after all that had happened, she should feel awkward and embarrassed by his detached concern...why the mere thought of having to ask him for comfort and relief of any kind should make her skin go hot and cold and her mind shudder back from the edge of some unsuspected chasm which lured her to its edge even while she cringed back from it.

She wanted him to leave so that she could go into the bathroom and clean her body, not of his touch, which at all times had been minimal and clinical, but of the evidence of her own humanity and weakness. But he stayed where he was, hovering over her like a dark eagle while she swallowed the pill and drank the water, and even after that, until the pain started to subside and her eyes started to close.

They parted the next morning, outside the bank, where Silver formally handed over to him his money and where they faced one another gravely, still two antagonists. Her body felt stiff and slightly sore, but there was no bleeding and she knew with inner conviction that she would soon heal.

As he took the money he said firmly, 'I won't wish you good luck. I know you believe you're right in what you're doing, but I can tell you that you're not. Unfortunately, by the time you come to that realisation yourself, it will be too late. It's one of life's more bitter truisms that we can't learn from the experience of others.

'I, too, have had my time of black despair, my thirst for destruction, my need to reach out and contaminate with my hatred those who contaminated me and mine with theirs; I, too, have known what it means to set myself above the law and consider myself justified in doing so.

'Revenge is a drug; once it gets hold of you it doesn't let go, it pervades your whole life.'

He couldn't have said anything more calculated to strengthen her hand.

'That might be your experience, it won't necessarily be mine. My father taught me to shoot when I was twelve years old,' Silver told him thinly, angry with him that he should choose now of all times to give her an unwanted moral lecture. 'Always shoot to kill, he told me. And always kill cleanly...'

He smiled at her then, mocking her with his soul-deep awareness of her thoughts as he said softly, 'Yes, but mutilation has such a subtle appeal, doesn't it? What point is there in inflicting a wound if the victim doesn't feel it...and it *is* mutilation you thirst for, isn't it, Silver? Mutilation and destruction...'

'What I plan to do has nothing to do with you,' she told him distantly, dismissing him with the ice that ran through her voice like the chill of northern snows. 'I did what I had to do, and now it's over.'

She turned her back on him and swung down the street, a tall, silver-haired woman whose arresting beauty drew glances from everyone she passed. But for once she was unconcerned with the effect of her looks, and for the first time, although she herself didn't know it, her face was that of a woman real and alive, full of emotion and character, and not simply a mask of beauty almost unreal in its perfection.

She had two more days before she left Switzerland and returned to London. She took a taxi back to her rented chalet, dismissing the maid, who was so well trained that she exhibited no surprise either at Silver's command or at her reappearance in the middle of the day, after an unexplained absence of several weeks.

From the chalet she rang Annie, who expressed pleasure at hearing from her.

'Where have you been?' she scolded. 'I've been worried about you.'

'Oh, I had things to do,' Silver told her vaguely, quickly changing the subject. 'Annie, I'm leaving in a couple of days... How about dinner this evening?'

'I'd have loved to, but Jake beat you to it. Unless of course you want to join us...'

Silver paused for a moment, her heartbeat quickening. Would Jake tell Annie what had happened?

Somehow she doubted it, and anyway, what would it matter if he did? There was no point in joining them for dinner simply to sit in torment all evening waiting for Jake to mock her by revealing their arrangement. Despite the fact that she felt that Jake and Annie were not lovers, she wondered if perhaps tonight they would be together...if Jake would want to wipe from his memory any record of her by superimposing another woman's essence over hers.

What did it matter who the hell he slept with? she derided herself as she refused the invitation and hung up.

She had things to do...phone-calls to make...

In London she had an agent who would be expecting to hear from her. The apartment she had purchased through that agent and handed over to a very up-market and expensive interior designer should be ready for her by now. It was time to start psyching herself up to her new image. From now on she was leaving the past behind her.

When she returned to London it would be as a completely different person. A person who was already in some ways familiar to her, and yet in very many others still a stranger.

She walked into her bedroom and removed from her case a thick file. In it were all the details she had assembled for her new life...for her new image, right down to her name. From the moment she left this chalet behind her, she would be playing that new role. Silver Montaine, that was who she was now, widow of a Swiss, but wholly an Anglophile.

One more night and then she would be on her way home. She looked around the large, impersonal bedroom, shivering despite its almost sub-tropical temperature, conscious of a sensation of loss which crept up on her, taking her unawares, making her frown and glance over her shoulder as though half expecting to see Jake walk through the door.

Jake! She tried to dismiss him from her mind and found she could not. Last night the bed had carried his scent; she had woken with it all around her. She shuddered at the memory. Tonight was going to be a very long night indeed. Then she remembered the mild sedatives Annie had prescribed for her just after she had first left hospital.

She found them at the bottom of her leather handbag and took one, grimacing as she swallowed it, trying not to remember last night and the way Jake had watched her while she took his pain-killer; the medical palliative offered to her after she had refused the physical one.

An early night, a sound sleep, the ability to switch herself off from Switzerland and Jake... These were the things she needed now... And then Paris and her new wardrobe, and then home with her new face... her new personality... her new name and past...

She had a bath, experimentally stretching her muscles and discovering that last night's pain had completely gone. That pleased her. It seemed a good omen for the future. She was reaching for the perfumed body lotion to stroke into her skin when she stopped and instead lifted the jar to her nose, sniffing it delicately and then hesitating.

She had chosen that particular perfume for a specific reason and yet now she felt reluctant to wear it. Impatient with herself, she recapped the jar and pulled on the ancient brushed cotton nightdress that was a legacy from her past, grimacing at her own reflection as she did so. How disparate the two images of herself looked. Her face was all perfect, stunning beauty, her eyes as they had always been, in colour at least, although in the past they had not been so almond-tipped and mystically slumberous... and her mouth no longer over-large for her face, but instead sensually full.

She studied the silver tangle of her hair, curling slightly in the steam from her bath, and then switched her attention to the homeliness of her nightdress, subduing the faint bubble of laughter. From the neck down she looked like an unawakened adolescent, the curves of her breasts barely discernible, her nipples unaroused and flat against the fabric, her wrists and ankles betraying the fact that the nightdress was something she had outgrown.

But from the throat up... She threw back her head, studying the arch of her throat with concentration, pouting slightly, trying to imagine how a man would visualise her...how Charles would react to the sight of her. On impulse she tugged off the nightdress and studied the lines of her body. That at least was her own, she reflected acidly, far thinner and more shapely than it had been, perhaps, but still untouched by the surgeon's knife. The fullness of her breasts, the glowing coral of her nipples, the narrow indentation of her waist, the smooth flatness of her belly, the unexpectedness of the triangle of russet hair at the apex of her thighs, and then her thighs themselves, slender, sleek, fluidly muscled, an athlete's body, softening into femininity but hinting at sensual strength...that at least was her own...

Suddenly her head had begun to ache and her mouth felt dry. The sedative was making her drowsy, and she left the nightdress where it lay and padded into the bedroom, switching off the lamps as she went and flipping back the silk sheets, grimacing a little at their almost vulgar opulence, trying not to think of the cool crispness of the cotton sheets on Jake's bed... Sheets that had reminded her of Ireland, and of her childhood and the lavender-scented sheets on her bed there. Sheets embroidered with her family's crest, and a little worn in places. Sheets which had been ordered by a bride who had married into the family while Victoria was still on the throne.

The bed was vast, and Silver moved restlessly in it, disliking the over-softness of the mattress, instinctively trying to resist the pull of the drug, but ultimately giving in to it.

On the other side of the valley Jake and Annie had finished dinner and were sitting in her small private sitting-room in her quarters at the back of the Institute.

Jake stood up. 'Thanks for dinner, Annie.'

She got up too. 'There are some letters for you. Do you want me to read them?'

When he nodded, she did so, her own expression growing grave when she had finished.

'So...confirmation that your fourth man is in London, but your tracing agents haven't been able to discover where or who he is...'

'No...I'm going to have to go over there myself.'

'Jake, isn't it time that you let it rest? That you let *Beth* rest?' Annie suggested gently. She knew that she was taking a risk, that Jake hated any mention of his wife's death, and she could sympathise with him.

She had felt much the same way when her own husband had died.

Tom and Jake had been in the same regiment and had become good friends, a friendship which had continued when they had both left the army to join the government department of special agents fighting against the growing menace of the drug traffickers.

After Tom had been killed in the bomb blast which had taken Jake's sight, Annie had insisted on removing her husband's friend from the overcrowded hospital where she had found him, and bringing him here to Switzerland.

After his recovery physically, he had spent several months at a special rehabilitation centre run for the blind.

It had been during the early days of his recuperation that he had told her what he was doing.

Initially the government had turned a blind eye to the personal vendetta he was carrying out against Beth's killers—after all, as drug dealers they *were* his legitimate quarry—but once he had lost his sight he was no longer employable as a government agent, and so he had to pursue his one remaining quarry at second hand.

Several times Annie had tried to counsel him to forget the past, even while she knew he wouldn't listen to her.

She had known and liked Beth, but she suspected that had she not been killed there would have come a time when Jake might have tired of carrying the burden of a wife who would never really have been able to match him in either intelligence or maturity. Beth had been a young man's love, and Jake was a young man no longer.

He was also intelligent enough to recognise for himself what she herself had seen, and she suspected that it was this knowledge that added to his guilt and reinforced his determination to hunt down Beth's killers.

After his return from the rehabilitation centre she had offered him the use of the chalet which had been given to her by the parents of one of her young patients. She suspected he would have liked to refuse her offer, but both of them knew he had nowhere else to go. He wasn't a rich man; government agents did not receive pensions, and he had used what money he had in trying to track down the final member of the quartet.

'I can't let it rest, Annie,' he told her quietly. 'You know that. Not yet.'

She wondered if he knew how much he betrayed in those two final words. This was the first time she had ever heard him express any desire to be free of his self-imposed task.

He moved away from her and, sensing his withdrawal, she guessed that he was thinking of Beth.

If she had only known it, she was wrong. It was an entirely different woman who was occupying his thoughts as he said his goodnights and left.

He had already made all his arrangements. His driver was waiting and took him in silence to his destination, dropping him at a pre-arranged point and then driving away, the big car crunching heavily over the snow.

The landscape was in darkness, illuminated only by the silvering of a crescent moon, which of course was no help to Jake. He had to find his way by instinct and by careful, pre-worked-out calculations, moving as silently and delicately as a mountain cat, keeping his breathing in check until he felt the first step under his feet and knew that his calculations were correct.

It was a crazy, illogical thing to do, and he wasn't even sure now why he was doing it, only that it was something he had to do—that he needed to do. Male pride, he acknowledged with cynical self-mockery. Even now, after all he had undergone, there was still that, and yet if he had learned nothing else he had learned that pride was the most wanton and wasteful of all human emotions.

He had reached the door, and he felt in his pocket for the key... A key he had made himself, having stolen the original and then replaced it. His mouth twisted into a humourless smile. The army taught a man many skills, all of them potentially anti-social.

He held his breath as he inserted the key and then turned the lock. It moved easily, making a mockery of the building's sophisticated alarm systems.

Being blind had one advantage, Jake thought wryly as he moved inside. There was no need for him to worry about the dark.

He wondered if Silver knew how much she had given away to him about this place, how after questioning her he had virtually been able to draw a plan of it in his mind.

What he didn't know was which was her room.

He tried three before he found it. He could tell she was asleep simply from the depth and rhythm of her breathing.

He paused for a moment on the threshold of the room. Now was the time to turn back. He hesitated for the space of a heartbeat and then moved forwards.

Very carefully he paced the perimeter of the bed, and even more carefully found her position on it, and then, swiftly and economically, he undressed and lowered himself down beside her without betraying his presence.

Her skin smelled of soap, clean and fresh, the scent oddly erotic although he couldn't have said why. His fingers touched the silk sheets with distaste. Silk was fine on a woman, but he didn't like sleeping in it. He pushed back the covers and moved alongside her, sinuous and silent as a cat. It didn't take his hands long to discover her nakedness. That did surprise him, causing him a tiny stab of chagrin, because he knew damned well that she had never slept naked while she was with him. He wondered what her dreams were as she lay asleep, whether they featured the man she had set out to destroy. Did she dream of him here beside her? Did she dream of his touch, of his desire, or did she dream only of revenge?

And then, deliberately, he clamped down on any thoughts other than those needed to focus his mind on his purpose in being here. His final payment of the account between them.

And then he reached out and touched her with subtle, knowing hands that disturbed her flesh and her senses while allowing her mind to sleep. That caused her to sigh and soften and turn to him with a voluptuous innocence that welcomed the smooth caress of his touch against her skin.

Silver was dreaming, a confusing, brilliant dream shot through with sensations dazzling her like a rainbow in the sun, that teased her to pursue them, and that, when she did, retreated, only to beckon and tease again and again so that she chased after them until she was out of breath and out of temper, waking abruptly to find her face damp with tears of emotion and a pulsing between her thighs that made her tense and lift her head off the pillow in confusion.

And then she froze, her mind and body locked in the same rigour of shock as she felt the lazy, knowing touch of fingers that stroked her intimately and slowly as though they found pleasure in the task. As she lay there, rigid with shock, the caress was repeated and a red-hot wire tugged through her body, making it convulse.

In the darkness she saw and recognised the familiar outline of Jake's head and shoulders and her heart stood still, until she was released from her shock by a massive, rolling surge of anger.

She reached out to push him away and demanded fiercely, 'Jake, what the hell do you think you're doing?'

'Giving you full value for your money,' he told her bluntly, easily ignoring her attempts to evade him, rolling her on to her back.

'You've given me everything I want,' she told him in a stifled voice, unable to take in what was happening.

He laughed then, a savage, mocking sound that made her body tremble.

'Not yet, I haven't,' he told her silkily. 'But I shall.'

And while she struggled against him she felt the searing heat of his mouth against her skin, burning her throat and then moving down over her body, his hands twisting and turning her until her torso was wet and slick from the caress of his mouth and tongue. All apart from her breasts. He hadn't touched her breasts. And she told herself she didn't want him to, couldn't bear him to, while all the time, against her will, she could feel their sensitive nerve-endings pulsing and throbbing. When his mouth moved over her stomach and his hand slid between her legs, the pad of his thumb rubbing slowly and deliberately over and over her, she clenched her muscles and screamed at him to stop, until her throat was raw and the silent screaming inside her body threatened to overwhelm her determination to withstand what he was doing to her.

'I don't want this,' she told him, over and over again, as though by saying the words and holding on to them she could make them true. But she knew already that they were lies, and that there was nothing she wanted more now than the heat of his mouth on her skin, the bite of his teeth against her aching, needing flesh, the penetration of him so deep inside her that she would feel him there for the rest of her life. And, while she fought frantically against what was happening to her, she tried to understand *why* it was happening. She had been so careful, so conscious of the danger of this kind of intimacy, so mindful of avoiding it, of allowing him nothing of herself, that she couldn't understand where he had got this intimate, dangerous knowledge of her. How he had *known* that she would be vulnerable to him like this. How he had *known* that her flesh would melt and burn for his mouth and his hands. And she tried desperately to cling on to her determination to reject him while all the time she felt as though she was drowning beneath tides so heavy that nothing could withstand them.

His thumb stopped tormenting her, his hand slid back to her waist and she trembled in relief, her body quivering like a finely drawn wire and bathed in sweat. She thought he had given up, but she should have known better.

His mouth touched her skin between her breasts, beneath them, above them, almost touching them, almost, but not quite, and as she felt the silky drift of its heat against her she acknowledged that her impatient twistings and turnings were not because she wanted to escape but because she wanted that heat on her breasts, between her legs... Her body shuddered and out of the darkness she heard him ask softly, with appalling awareness of her need, 'What is it you want, Silver? Is it this?' His mouth brushed the curve of her breast and she shuddered wildly. 'This?' His tongue traced its hard tip and she bit the inside of her mouth to stop herself from screaming out loud. 'You only have to ask, you know,' he tormented her, laying his head against her, his hands either side of her ribcage, his breath warm against her skin. 'Just ask me, Silver, and I'll do anything you want... please you any way you want...'

She shuddered again, like a soul in mortal torment. How easy it would be to give in, to submit; she didn't even need to say anything. She could simply turn her body, place her hands on his head and guide the tormented pinnacles of flesh into the soothing balm of his mouth. The mere thought of what it would be like to have the pain drawn from her by its slow, thorough suckling made her break out in a fresh wave of sweat.

'Is it really so hard?'

He seemed almost amused. He moved and blew gently on her hot skin and then licked languorously at the beads of sweat drenching it. She couldn't bear it. She was going to die, to fall apart, to dissolve in a massive explosion of pain and need.

'Too proud to ask?' he taunted softly, and then added shockingly, 'I could make you.'

It was no less than the truth, and something inside her broke apart at the knowledge. 'But this is payment of a debt between us, not punishment, so I'll make it easy for you, shall I?' he told her.

And his hand slid down over her hip and along the outside of her thigh, and then the inside, while he moved against her in that slow, drugging rhythm that had been one of the first things he had taught her; and as though her body recognised a command indelibly imprinted on it, it started to move with him, so that her pulses fluttered beneath her skin and her heart thudded frantically beneath the weight of his head. His head moved, his mouth touching her breast, his tongue curling round the hard, eager tip, his teeth dragging so tormentingly against it that she ground her teeth in an audible agony of need.

As he opened his mouth fully over her swollen nipple, she fought desperately to break free of the current dragging her down into darkness, drowning her in its hot, sweet tide, but it was too strong for her; *he* was too strong for her. Suddenly she stopped fighting and allowed herself to be pulled down, down, down into the hot, suffocating darkness of her own passion, abandoning herself completely to sensation.

She surfaced once, briefly dragged out of the welling pleasure by the sharp sound of her own voice, and she

realised that the salt taste in her mouth was his flesh and
the hard thud beneath her palm his heart, and that at
some stage she must have reached out and touched him,
caressed him as he had taught her. She just had time to
be shocked by the mindless sensuality of her own he-
donistic and unthinking abandonment of her defences
before she sank back into the darkness where there was
nothing but the taste and feel of him, where nothing
mattered more than the sensual glide of his hands on
her body as he touched her, turned her, stroked her with
his hands and mouth until her bones turned liquid and
the ache inside her was the focus of her whole world.

When he entered her she shuddered beneath the weight
of her need and her awareness that she would rather die
than withdraw from him now. She reached for him,
digging her nails into his flesh, arching desperately
beneath him, begging him with incoherent pleas not to
stop what he was doing to her. The heat and weight of
him surrounded her, engulfed her; the scent of him, the
feel of him around her and within her overwhelmed her.
She raked her nails against his skin, arched her throat,
and then moved her head restlessly from side to side,
taking quick, short snatches of air as he started to move
inside her.

She cried out that she couldn't bear it and moved
frantically beneath him, her movements impatient and
untutored, but explicit enough to make him surge inside
her and hold her head still on the pillow while he silenced
her husky litany of need with his mouth, so that briefly
she surfaced from her mind-destroying passion to the
knowledge that he was kissing her, really kissing her,
something he had never done before. And more: that
the hard, sure pressure of his mouth was setting off cat-
aclysmic, seismic reactions inside her...that the scent
of him, the taste of him, the reality of him was feeding
her hunger so that she kissed him back, biting at his
mouth, letting him coax and seduce her with his tongue,
letting him cause her to want him in a way she had never

dreamed was possible. Her heart gave a frantic leap and then started hammering against her ribs. Her eyes opened on his face and saw with a tiny stab of compassion that his were closed. Almost wonderingly she reached up and touched him, feeling the alienness of his stubble beneath her fingertips. And then he moved inside her, fiercely, urgently, compellingly, and she forgot reality and clung to him, driven by the ache that pulsed inside her.

When she felt the first convulsion of pleasure she stiffened and cried out sharply, trying to deny it, the doors of her mind, closed by the need he had awakened within her, bursting open to admit the shocking reality of what was happening. And now, when it was too late to stop it, when it was too late to do anything other than let the pleasure pulse through her in convulsion after convulsion, she knew who it was whose arms she lay in, whose body filled hers, whose mouth and hands had so skilfully drawn from her a response she would have given a hundred thousand lifetimes to have suppressed.

And, even worse, as he lay with her, waiting for her laboured breathing to slow down, holding her in an embrace she could not break, was the knowledge that while he had driven her into a frenzied abandonment of herself to the passion he had induced, he had not similarly lost control.

When she could finally breathe evenly enough to speak, she said roughly, 'All right, you've done what you came to do. Now would you mind leaving and letting me get some sleep?'

She expected him to withdraw from her and make some taunting comment, but instead, shockingly, he did not. Instead his hands tightened almost possessively on her body in the darkness, and against her ear he mouthed softly, 'Not yet... That was for you... Now this is for me.'

For him, he had said, and that might have been his intention, but whatever pleasure he took from her he gave her back tenfold, so that she touched him, caressed him, pleasured him with her hands and her mouth without a thought in her head other than a driving desire to wring from him the same submission he had got from her.

And when she did, when he groaned her name and shuddered, holding her, filling her, flooding her with the evidence of his arousal, her own body dissolved in heat and fierce, sharp pleasure.

When she woke in the morning he was gone. The events of the night seemed unreal and dreamlike, clinging to her consciousness like threads of mist on sun-touched hedgerows of Kilrayne. But he *had* been there; it *had* happened; and the evidence of his presence lay on her skin in small passion-given bruises; it lay within her body in the unfamiliar satiated ache of her muscles. But most of all it lay across her mind, an irrefutable knowledge she had fought against accepting, an awareness she would have destroyed mountains not to have had, a learning that she already knew could alter the whole direction of her life, if she allowed it to do so. If... but there would be no ifs in her life... no uncertainties... no doubts.

What had happened was unfortunate, unnecessary from her point of view—unwanted and undesirable. It would never happen again. Never.

PART TWO
Geraldine Frances

CHAPTER SIX

In Paris Silver shopped, with the single-minded determination of a woman who knew exactly what it was she was shopping for, rather than the bored self-indulgence of a woman with too much money, too much time, and too much loneliness.

In the couture houses the *vendeuses* raised their eyebrows and hardened their mouths, wishing they could tell her that what she wanted was impossible. They didn't like her, this tall, silver-haired woman who refused to play the game by the rules, who refused to treat the matter of buying couture clothes with the reverence and seriousness it deserved. *Vendeuse* after *vendeuse* found herself giving way and agreeing both to discounts and alteration dates that made them wonder, once removed from the compelling determination of Silver's presence, if they had gone a little mad.

A month in Paris, buying her new wardrobe, polishing her new personality, watching assiduously for flaws in the new role she had created for herself, and then she was ready to go home...

Home... Her mouth twisted cynically. Where was home? The castle in Ireland...the shooting lodge in Scotland...the apartment in New York...the Palladian mansion near Bath which had been the principal seat of the Earls of Rothwell since the end of the seventeenth century and which was now inhabited by her cousin?

At Charles de Gaulle she boarded the plane and lay back in her seat closing her eyes. Her luggage was all stamped with her initials, S.M., and her new identity was to be that of a widow of an extremely rich and reclusive Swiss businessman...the daughter illegitimately of a long-dead English peer whose name she was not allowed to mention; a woman whose past was spiced with a small amount of teasing mystery; a woman whose dress, whose manner, whose looks whispered subtly that she was an enchantress, and dangerous.

The metamorphosis was complete. Silver wondered what her father would have thought of her had he met her now, and her smile deepened, betraying a soul-deep awareness of the irony of what she had become . . . what, in choosing to abandon her real identity, she had voluntarily given up.

Geraldine Elizabeth Sophie Frances Fitzcarlton, Countess of Rothwell, each one of her Christian names marking her family's allegiance to those who had held the English throne . . . apart from Geraldine . . . Geraldine had been her mother's personal choice. Elizabeth was for the Tudors, Sophie the Hanovers, and Frances the Stuarts, and each one of them in turn had heaped fresh honours on her forebears.

Her father had once said that he—or she—who carried the mantle of their inheritance carried a heavy weight indeed, not just of prestige and power, but of guilt and responsibility.

The plane started to lift into the air, and Silver opened her eyes, wanting to let her thoughts drift, yet driven by some self-imposed discipline to accept the need within herself to go back, to examine her life, to study it as though she herself stood outside it, as indeed she now did.

She closed her eyes again, concentrating her mind. She had been born in Ireland towards the end of an exceptionally hot summer, her arrival ill timed, coming in her mother's seventh month of pregnancy.

It had been so early as a result of the shock her mother had received when one of her father's prize racehorses had broken free of its groom in the stableyard, lashing out at everyone who came near it with wicked steel hoofs and snapping teeth before clearing the main gates with a jump that Padraic O'Connor, her father's head trainer, who had been little more than a trainee stablehand at the time, was still inclined to marvel over.

Unfortunately, her mother had always been terrified of horses, a fear that sprang from a bad fall from a too highly bred filly at her father's second cousin's stud farm in Kentucky's Blue Grass country. She had panicked and, thinking that the horse intended to harm her, had run across the cobbled yard, catching the heel of her shoe between the cobbles and pitching forwards on to the ground before anyone could save her.

That night, while in the stables John Kincaid the vet laboured to save the recaptured filly, upstairs in the ancient keep of the original castle—a bleak, dark room, so the new bride always complained fretfully, despite its expensive refurbishment—the local doctor, summoned despairingly when Bridie Donovan, the housekeeper, had announced that the new Countess had begun to give birth, laboured to save the lives both of the frail, sweating woman lying in the ancient tester-bed that her husband's ancestors had commissioned in France, and of the child she carried.

He was an honest country doctor, used to dealing with births and deaths, but the young Countess was narrow across the pelvis, her hipless body as slender as a child's, too slender for her ever to have been able to give birth easily, and the child inside her was a large one, fighting to be born too soon.

It was Bridie herself who had told her the full story, not once but over and over again until she knew it off by heart.

'Well, Geraldine Frances,' she would say, because it was her father's decision that she should be known by both her first and last Christian names, 'Well, Geraldine Frances, it was like this . . . We had sent to Limerick for the ambulance and old Doyle was in a rare lather, that worried he was that it wouldn't arrive in time. Your poor father was pacing the floor, cursing himself and the filly to damnation and back, swearing that he should never have brought your mother out of England...that he should never have taken such a risk, with her so near the time and knowing how much she hated the castle. Just about given up hope, we had, when we heard the ambulance, but you were too quick for them...' Here she would always give a rich chuckle. 'You knew where your rightful place was even then. Determined to be born here, you was, in the same bed as your ancestors before you.'

Yes, she had been born in Ireland, in the grim, grey castle of those doughty warrior princes who had mingled their blood with the Norman line of her Elizabethan ancestors. She had been the first Rothwell to be born there in eight generations.

The ambulance which had come too late for her birth had taken her mother to hospital, and she had gone with her. But she hadn't stayed there long. Her mother had been too frail to withstand such an ordeal, and her life had seeped slowly away from her so that, within a week of Geraldine Frances's birth, her mother was dead.

She had little recollection of those early years, knowing only what she had been told about them by her father, and by the people who worked for him. How he had returned to London grim-faced and bleak...how he had refused to allow his American mother-in-law to take the responsibility of the child off his hands... How he had himself interviewed and appointed a nanny for her and how he had then retreated from the London social scene which he enjoyed so much to spend a year mourning the death of his wife and watching over the life of his child.

She had had an idyllic childhood, with the almost constant companionship of her father, for he had refused to send her away to school, hiring tutors for her instead, taking her with him on his annual and fixed progression around his personal world. By the time she was ten she had learned, like him, to adapt herself to her surroundings, and to accept the almost chameleon-like change in her father as they moved from the almost austere formality of the great Palladian mansion of Rothwell to the casual, almost fecklessly relaxed lifestyle of Castle Kilrayne.

And then there was formality of another kind when they visited the pampas country of Argentina, and she was obliged to speak the pure Castilian Spanish of their hosts.

Until her grandmother's death when she was seven, summer almost always contained an obligatory month of purgatory cooped up in the stiff formality with which her grandmother ran her Palm Beach household; it was no place for a young girl used to running free with the wind in her hair, a young girl to whom the music of life was made up of her father's voice and the sound of horses' hoofs, be it on the racecourse, on the polo field, or on the crisp, frosted hunting fields of the Belvoir Hunt, of which he was a member.

Theirs was an enclosed world, and she liked it that way. The obligatory Christmas visits of her father's sister and her son, who always spent that time of year with them at Rothwell, were the only events that shadowed her life. For Charles, her cousin, six years her senior, tall, golden-haired and almost impossibly good-looking, she had mixed feelings, half of her inclined to hero-worship him and the other half just a little afraid of something within him that she didn't really recognise, but which intimidated her. An older, wiser person would have discerned that towards Geraldine Frances Charles felt both resentment and jealousy, but, since he was careful to disguise those feelings whenever someone more astute might have recognised them, Geraldine Frances's father was unaware of how his nephew really felt about his daughter.

James himself had ambivalent feelings towards Charles, feelings which he freely acknowledged arose from his own guilt over the way his sister had been treated by their father after she had married, and the fact that Charles was so very much like the man who had fathered him, a man so far removed from their own social sphere that marriage to him had virtually reduced his sister to a social outcast.

Willingly he had offered to pay for Charles to attend one of the country's foremost public schools, but the school didn't have a place for Charles and his sister had announced that she preferred to send him to another equally expensive but less regimental institution.

Since the first choice had been his own public school, James had not been too pleased, none the less he had complied with her demands, and now Charles was attending a very prestigious public school which admitted both sexes.

If Geraldine Frances wasn't sure quite how she felt about her cousin, she knew exactly what her feelings were for her aunt. Between Geraldine Frances and her aunt there existed a mutual animosity that neither of them tried to conceal.

Looking into her cold, pale blue eyes, Geraldine Frances found it hard to accept that this unlikeable, grim woman was her father's sister. It seemed impossible that any blood relationship could actually exist between them, and she didn't envy Charles, having her for a mother.

Her annual visits to Rothwell always followed the same pattern. A week before Christmas she would descend on them, sending the staff into a panic of preparation and bustle. She would sweep into the elegant oval hallway, studying it with gimlet eyes, reminding Geraldine Frances of an angry cat swishing its tail, waiting to pounce on its intended victim; and more often than not *she* was that victim.

With her she would always bring Charles; a Charles whose attitude towards Geraldine Frances confused and puzzled her. There had been one year when he had wandered into the kitchen and found the place in turmoil, the reason being that one of the stable cats had brought in a live mouse and set it free.

The maids were screaming for someone to do something, and Geraldine Frances, whose heart was tender, was desperately trying to catch the poor, terrified creature before the cat reached it, so that she could set it free outside.

Panicked by fear, it ran straight for Charles as he opened the door.

Geraldine Frances saw him lift his foot and cried out sharply to him, 'No...don't!'

And he looked at her and gave her such a warm, tender smile that she forgot, as she always did when she was basking in the warmth of that smile, the other side of him, the cruel side, and rushed forward to pick up the mouse. He waited until she reached him, and then brought down his foot with deliberate and open purpose.

She heard the crunching of small bones, felt the tiny animal's fear and shock as though it had been her own, and while she stood there, transfixed by horror and anguish, she heard him saying solicitously, 'Gerry, I'm so sorry... I thought you wanted me to kill it. I thought you were frightened.' He gave her another smile. 'Girls are always frightened of mice...'

And as always within a tiny space of time he managed to confuse and upset her to such an extent that she felt the blame for what had happened lay on her shoulders; that she hadn't made her meaning plain...that she had unwittingly orchestrated the poor little beast's death.

And underlying that was another fear, deeper, stronger—a fear that was somehow beginning to shadow her whole life. Whenever he saw her, Charles always managed to make her feel that somehow or other she wasn't like other girls, those girls who attended the same prestigious school he went to himself...that she was somehow lacking, incomplete...

His new school had taught Charles a great deal, including the fact that girls were often open to male mockery and criticism. That they could be subtly bullied and tormented, made to cry and plead.

A victim of his mother's domination himself, Charles relished the opportunity to dominate others in turn.

The year she was eight, Christmas was overshadowed by the fact that her father was ill. James was one of those fortunate souls who rarely suffered ill health, but there had been an epidemic of mumps in the village, and Geraldine Frances had contracted it on an illicit visit to the gamekeeper's cottage to play with his children. Because of her father's peripatetic lifestyle she had no real friends of her own age and class, and was often lonely for the company of her peers without even realising it herself.

The gamekeeper's wife, who had been out shopping, discovered her in the sick-room when she returned, and was obliged to escort her back to Rothwell and explain to the Earl what had happened.

Inevitably, Geraldine Frances went down with the virus herself, but what no one had foreseen was that she would pass it on to her father.

For what seemed like weeks the house was shrouded in an unfamiliar silence, busy with the comings and goings of the doctor, who always seemed to wear a far more abstracted air when he attended her father than he had done when he attended her.

Everyone within the house seemed to be affected by a strange tension, and then abruptly, one afternoon, much earlier in the month than expected, her aunt arrived.

Standing outside the library door, waiting to see her father, who was now allowed out of bed, Geraldine Frances heard Aunt Margaret saying triumphantly to him, 'Well, James, you only have yourself to blame. I warned you years ago that you should remarry, and now, of course, it's too late.'

Too late for what? Geraldine Frances puzzled, bewildered by both the constrained excitement in her aunt's voice and the grim anger in her father's when he replied to her.

Despite her curiosity, some sensitive inner knowledge warned her not to mention what she had over-heard . . . not to question.

After that Christmas Charles had not only spent the Christmas holidays with them, but others as well.

Sometimes she had surprised him watching her, gloat-ingly, as though he knew some secret she did not. He confused her and continued to tease her, almost to the point of torment at times. But still he intrigued her, casting a spell over her which she was far too young to recognise.

Charles as a teenager was a perfect golden god; handsome was far too mundane a word to describe him.

In vain Geraldine Frances searched in her own mirror for some echo of Charles's perfect beauty in her own face. There was none.

'A plain little thing,' was how she had once overheard one of the staff describing her, almost disparagingly. 'Not like the other one . . . Handsome as a prince, he is.'

The summer was cold and wet, her father distant with her, indifferent to her almost, in a way that hurt. She ached to ask him if she had done something to offend him, but couldn't find the words, and so she suffered in silence, missing their old closeness, growing unhappy and afraid, sensing that somehow her life was changing but not knowing why or how.

One afternoon, to escape from her aunt's constant nagging about how far beneath the standards she herself had achieved as a child Geraldine Frances fell, she made her way to the long gallery. Here she liked to play im-aginary games with the paintings of her ancestors, creating from their portraits three-dimensional com-panions to ease her loneliness.

When Charles came into the gallery behind her, his presence surprised her. He too had changed towards her since Christmas; he no longer bothered to be kind, to charm . . . and deep down inside there was a small part of her that was almost frightened of him without knowing why.

Instinctively edging away from him, she wished she were somewhere else.

It seemed to her this summer that, whenever she saw her father, Charles was with him, the gold head close to the black, the blue eyes taunting her with the knowledge that he had formed a relationship with her father from which she was excluded... For the first time in her life she was being made aware of the fact that her father preferred another's company, and it hurt.

And, what was more, Charles knew that it hurt.

'Poor Gerry,' he mocked now. 'All on your own.'

Driven by a defensive impulse she could neither control nor explain, she said rudely, 'Go away. Rothwell is my home, not yours. You have no right to be here...'

She stopped then, suddenly afraid as she saw the look in his eyes, but even as she stepped back from him it vanished, and he said softly, 'You're wrong, Gerry. I have far more right to be here than you. The right of succession... One day, when your father is dead, Rothwell and everything else will be mine.'

Geraldine Frances stared at him. She couldn't imagine her father being dead... never thought about it nor considered it, and now, suddenly, with a few careless words, Charles had made her conscious of how very vulnerable her whole world was... But what did he mean about Rothwell?

As though she had asked him, he added dulcetly, 'Only a male can inherit Rothwell, you know, and your father can't have any sons now... And that's *your* fault... No wonder he can't bear the sight of you any more.' He was smiling at her, smiling as though he was being kind, and inside... inside she felt as though she were being ripped apart with sharp, poison-tipped knives. She wanted to deny what he was saying, to challenge him, but instinctively she felt a deep inner insecurity that made her hesitate, and then, to her relief, she saw that her father was standing behind Charles. She opened her mouth to appeal to him to defend her and then, when she saw the look of bitter fury in his eyes, she fell silent, quelled by an emotion she couldn't totally understand.

Charles, sensing that they weren't alone, swung round, his eyes widening with shock as he saw his uncle standing there. He left the gallery without a word, and she, childlike, burst into tears and ran to her father, taking comfort from the safe, protective feeling of his arms round her as he picked her up and held her, telling her that everything was all right and that of course he still loved her.

That evening her aunt and her father spent a long time in the library. But the seed of the destruction of her feeling of self-worth had already been sown. Her aunt emerged with anger in her eyes and a dark, hectic flush mantling her cheekbones. She and Charles left the next day.

It had been shortly after that that her father had suddenly started talking seriously to her about the burden she would one day have to carry, of the need she would have to marry and produce a son who would carry on the family name, the family tradition. It had been then that he had started to tutor her in all she would need to know.

It had been then that they had drawn closer together, and that year there had been no Aunt Margaret or Charles at Rothwell for Christmas. She had been glad to be relieved of their presence, sensing in both her aunt and Charles a resentment and dislike of her that fell on her like an oppressive weight, even while at the same time part of her missed Charles's presence.

It was almost a year before she saw either her aunt or Charles again, and when she did she was conscious of a change in their attitude towards her.

Generously she had accepted Charles's overtures of friendship, sensing that her father wouldn't object to the new relationship that was developing between them, and then suddenly, the year she was twelve, her feelings towards Charles changed dramatically.

She was at that age when the hormonal changes of her body were making themselves felt, and Charles, six years her senior, already so much more mature, enthralled her. She was lonely that year because, for the first time, her father had gone away without her. That had hurt her, and she had found an unexpected source of solace in Charles, who seemed eager for her company.

Her aunt and Charles spent less and less time at the tall, narrow London house which belonged to her father, but which he allowed his sister to live in rent-free. They were almost constantly at Rothwell, and Geraldine Frances found herself drawing closer and closer to her cousin as a bulwark against her aunt's dislike of her.

She began to see how burdensome her aunt's possessive love of Charles must be to him, and she began to sympathise with him because of it. Yes, the year she was twelve was a watershed in her life. Her father had become distant from her again, and sometimes she saw him looking at her almost as though in some way he resented her.

Always acutely sensitive to the moods of others, she withdrew into herself.

She was fast developing a crush on her cousin, even though she herself wasn't aware of it. Others had noted it though, older, more mature eyes, and Margaret was well satisfied with the results of her conversations with her son. The day she had discovered that her brother had no intention of allowing his daughter to be disinherited in favour of his only male heir, she had subdued the bitter rage and resentment burning inside her and determined that if Charles could not get Rothwell and the Rothwell fortune directly, then he would have them indirectly, through marriage to her, his cousin.

All this she had relayed to him, not bothering to mask her bitterness over what she considered to be the wrongful allocation of her brother's title and assets.

'Marry Geraldine Frances?' he had sneered, and Margaret had looked back at him and told him explicitly and carefully exactly what his life would be if he allowed someone else to take what she believed was rightfully his.

She herself had no money, no assets, nothing. She lived virtually on the charity of her brother. Was that what he wanted from life, she asked him, when with only the very slightest effort he could have everything?

'It should be mine without my having to marry her,' he had responded bitterly.

She had tutored him well from the moment she had discovered that her brother would never have a son of his own; she had taught Charles that everything that was his uncle's would one day be his—as long as he married Geraldine Frances.

With the onset of her teens, Geraldine Frances found herself putting on weight. Almost overnight her body seemed to change, thickening and softening from the hard athleticism of almost boyish slenderness into something she herself was repulsed by and unable to accept. She became moody and withdrawn without being able to understand why.

Her aunt announced that what she needed was to go to school, to be with girls of her own age, and for once her father seemed prepared to listen to his sister's advice. Despairingly Geraldine Frances protested that she didn't want to go to school, that she was happy here with him and her private tutors.

It made no difference. His sister had suddenly alerted him to the fact that his daughter was growing up alienated from her peers. No argument would sway him, and Geraldine Frances finally acknowledged that she had lost the battle and that she was going to school.

Looking sadly into his daughter's pale, set face, knowing how much she hated the idea of going to school, James wished he could explain to her that he was only doing what he thought was best for her. He had seen for himself how alone she was.

Selfishly he had kept her with him, wanting, since he had made the discovery that she would be his only child, to prepare her for the burdens she would one day have to carry. It was true that for a while he had toyed with the idea of making Charles his heir, following the rule of succession in favour of the male heir, but Charles was not his son and Geraldine Frances was his daughter.

He had petitioned the Queen so that she could inherit his title from him. It had been done before, after all, and only one small estate in England was entailed, thanks to the forethought of his predecessors. No, it was best for Geraldine Frances now that she went to school and had a few years at least of finding out what it meant to be a young girl, and so he withstood the numb pleading he saw in her eyes and firmly distanced himself from her, so that she felt forlornly that he had deserted her completely, and that there was only Charles who understood how she felt.

Charles, who had changed so much towards her that she found it hard to believe she had ever disliked him.

James saw the crush she was developing for her cousin and wondered how much it had been engineered by his sister's machinations. She had already pointed out to him how sensible it would be if Charles and Geraldine Frances were to marry, and she was right, of course. It would be an ideal solution. Too ideal, perhaps.

He was bringing his child up more boy than girl, his sister had accused him, and so for Geraldine Frances there were no more dawn rides through the woods and over the fields, no more midnight treks into the wood to watch the badgers, no more shooting rabbits in the cool haze of the summer dawn.

Geraldine Frances had to stay in and prepare herself for school, and when she wasn't doing that she had to be dragged round London stores being equipped with new clothes.

It was on one of these trips that Geraldine Frances was confronted with the hateful image of herself that was to remain with her all through her teens.

Her aunt, out of temper and exasperated, had dragged her into an expensive children's outfitters, insisting that the saleswoman produce the kind of clothes that Geraldine Frances loathed: smocked-bodice dresses in velvets and silks, velvet-collared coats, plaid skirts and cashmere sweaters.

Hot and furious, Geraldine Frances had glared mutinously at her aunt, steadfastly refusing to try on anything.

'Well, if you won't try them on, then we'll just have to buy them without your doing so. What size are you?' Margaret had demanded imperiously.

Geraldine Frances had had no idea. The clothes she most liked were made for her by her father's tailors: soft riding jackets, jodhpurs, handmade boots, masculine, tweedy suits of a type favoured by the feminine members of the Irish hunting society...capable, useful clothes.

The saleswoman, sensing the impending storm, had interrupted unhappily.

'I doubt if we'll have anything in *mademoiselle*'s size... She *is* rather large...' Her voice had trailed off as all three of them had confronted Geraldine Frances's image in the mirror. In silence their eyes had met and acknowledged the bulky, overweight reflection of Geraldine Frances's teenage flesh.

A malicious smile had curled her aunt's mouth. Her aunt was thin, brittly so, with sharp bones, a sharp mouth and sharp eyes.

'Yes... Really, Geraldine Frances, you do look appalling...you're enormous. It's bad enough that you're so plain, but this... We'll have to put you on a diet...' And then, in an aside to the assistant that wasn't an aside at all, she had added disparagingly, 'Heaven knows where she gets it from. But then, I suppose every family has its changeling.'

Geraldine Frances knew all about changelings...
Ireland's folklore was full of stories about them: ugly,
unwanted children, usurping the rightful place of
others...

She had looked in the mirror, hating her aunt with
burning, loathing eyes, hating the assistant, who was
trying to look everywhere but at her, and most of all
hating herself.

When they had got back to Rothwell she had gone
straight to the kitchen and eaten half a dozen freshly
made scones thick with home-farm butter. With them
she had drunk a pint of full cream milk.

It had made her feel better, for a little while...filled
that craving empty space inside her, for a little while.

Her aunt had put her on a diet, knowing that Geraldine
Frances would break it and feel worse for doing so.
Charles loathed food as much as she loved it. She ate
what he refused and her body, suffering anyway under
the onslaught of its hormonal changes, became bloated
and strained at the seams of her clothes. Her glossy russet
hair dulled. Her eyes became small and round and her
skin, overloaded with a surfeit of fats, broke out in a
rash of spots.

She missed her father, who was away in Argentina,
desperately, ached to be with him, sharing the companionship they had always known. But now it seemed
that he did not want her with him, and that hurt her,
confused her. She felt as though she was in some way
to blame for his withdrawal from her; that she had done
something wrong. And her aunt, sensing this insecurity
in her, subtly encouraged and fed it, as Geraldine Frances
fed her increasingly bloated body, trying to subdue the
ache of misery inside her with food.

She was so used to being a part of her father's life,
to travelling with him, that the sharp severing of the bond
between them was an open wound she didn't have the
experience to heal.

There were short, uncommunicative phone-calls from him that exacerbated her misery rather than easing it. Her aunt always remained in the room while she spoke to him, and was quick to put an end to their conversations long before Geraldine Frances could say anything that might have alerted her father to what she was suffering.

And, although she didn't know it, James was missing her too; he hadn't realised how much he enjoyed her company, how closely attuned their minds were...how intelligent she was.

He felt unusually restless, unable to take his normal pleasure in life. Because he was still suffering the after-effects of his illness...or because he was missing Geraldine Frances?

Argentina wasn't the same without her. James had picked up a fever that lingered rather longer than it should have done, making him fret and fume. He hated being tied down to any one place for too long. He had been born restless, his mother had always said, and it was true that he hated tedium. Already it was July... Soon it would be August, and he began to daydream longingly for Scotland's heather-purple moors and cool, misty mornings.

The flirtation with his host's daughter had grown more dangerously intimate than he wanted; sex was an appetite he indulged whenever he felt its bite, knowing without conceit that he was giving and taking pleasure in the act, choosing his partners with care and circumspection.

The discovery that he could no longer father a child had made it unnecessary for him to marry again. He had loved his wife, but he was not so sure that that love would have survived a lifetime of marriage. He grew bored easily...jaded... He liked young flesh, silken hair, soft eyes, and eager, hungry bodies, but he also liked women with intelligent minds, women skilled in the art of conversation, women who could keep him entertained over dinner with their subtlety and wit.

A young body and an old mind...the ideal combination, but he was not searching for an ideal...He had no intention of allowing himself to be inveigled into a second marriage. He had his child, his daughter...and if she was not a son...if there was never to be a son...well, there would be grandchildren, a boy to take up the reins when he eventually had to put them down. But Carmelita, so soft and passionate in his arms, was beginning to pout and sulk. The air was heavy with subtle persuasion and there was much talk of marriages among other members of Don Felipe's extensive family.

James knew when a net was being cast for him. Fever or no fever, it was time for him to go.

He shifted uncomfortably in the smothering comfort of the high Spanish bed, the call of his blood stirring him into urgent activity.

The *estancia*, with its endless prairies, its black-eyed, dulcet-mouthed women, was beginning to cloy. He wanted to go home.

He could almost smell the crisp scent of heather and gorse, hear the soft Scots burr of his gillie, see the sharp blue arc of a northern sky...

He sent a telegram to warn them that he was coming home.

It had been a long flight, and the fever still gnawed at his bones. James had forgotten how grey and miserable London could be under rainy August skies. There were delays at Heathrow, and his chauffeur was late picking him up.

Feeling irritated and enervated, he settled down in the back of the Bentley and closed his eyes.

Geraldine Frances knew all about her father's temper... 'A black temper he has, and there's a fact,' Bridie Donovan had told her more than once, half admiringly, half disapprovingly. 'Oh, your father suffers

from the curse of the Celts,' Padraic O'Connor had said,
and in Scotland the gillies and beaters said that the Earl
could be a dangerous man to cross when the mood was
on him. But Geraldine Frances had never experienced
at first hand that fierce pulse of pride and rage that could
possess her father and overwhelm all the carefully garnered, land-honed accoutrements of civilisation and
training, peeling them back to reveal the essential man:
the dangerous blending of Scots and Irish, Saxon and
Norman blood...stirred through with their combust-
ible Angevin inheritance... It had been said that, even
before Henry married Eleanor of Aquitaine, the
Plantagenets were all descended from the devil; that they
were dangerous and volatile and that none could withstand the smite of their fearsome temper.

A long hold-up on the motorway; the discovery that
he was not immortal, and that his flesh was as vulnerable to the aches and pains of ageing as the rest of
the human race, did nothing to ease his temper.

He was just pouring himself a glass of whiskey when
the library door opened and Geraldine Frances walked
in.

He didn't recognise her at first, and in the crystal light
from the chandeliers made in Bohemia to the special
design of the Georgian dandy who had commissioned
them Geraldine Frances saw the shock and distaste widen
his eyes as he stared at her.

He stood and stared at her in disbelief. He had always
known her to be plain. She lacked her mother's beauty
and the finely drawn autocratic looks of his own family,
but he had never in a thousand lifetimes imagined she
would become this...this bloated parody of everything
feminine... She looked grotesque...like a gar-
goyle...inhuman almost...and the cruel clarity of the
crystal light faithfully relayed to her every one of the
emotions crossing his face.

'My God,' he asked thoughtlessly, 'what have you
done to yourself?'

It was the beginning of the end...the first hurtful severing of a bond she had foolishly believed could never be severed. Both of them suffered for it: he because she was his child and he loved her, but could not reach out across the chasm of his instinctive revulsion of her physical appearance to find the spirit he had cherished and tutored; she because she had never quite forgotten the fear Charles had instilled in her, the fear that her father loved her because he felt he *had* to, because she was his only child...his heiress. And she wanted to be loved for herself.

Only she knew how desperately she strove these days to make up to her father for all that she was not and never could be.

Charles had intimated that, as a girl, she was unworthy of her father's love, and she was haunted by the fear that it was true.

Sometimes she managed to forget the fear, to push it to the back of her mind, but too frequently these days it resurfaced, larger, more dangerous, threatening her...and on these occasions she would creep into the kitchen and comfort herself with food.

Her father wanted her to go to school, and she could not rid herself of the belief that perhaps he wanted that because he no longer wanted her with him. And because she loved him and wanted to please him, she kept these thoughts to herself and stoically accepted what she knew was going to be a time of intense misery and loneliness for her.

School was everything she had dreaded and more. She lacked the ability to make friends, distancing herself from those who would have befriended her out of shyness and the fear that they too, like Charles, would quickly discern her feelings.

As a scholar she was intelligent...too intelligent in some ways, her teachers believed, with a knowledge far too sophisticated for a girl of her age...with the kind

of education more suited to a boy... The school was
old-fashioned and heavily into role-models, something
which the Earl, in his ignorance of girls' schools, had
not realised... But Margaret had. She was determined
to destroy the close relationship between father and
daughter.

She hated her brother almost as much as she hated
his child. Ten years older than James, she had become
used by the time he was born to considering herself the
only child her parents were going to have, with all that
that implied. And then James was born, and overnight
it seemed that everything changed. She was no longer
important, no longer wanted almost; she was relegated
to a secondary and far less important place. She had
now a brother... a brother who was far more important
than she would ever be. And gradually, as she grew older
and realised all that James's birth meant to her in terms
of inheritance and importance, her resentment of him
grew.

She should have been the one to inherit Rothwell... not
James.

It had been in a mood of bitter defiance, following
an argument with her father over her allowance and the
fact that she, as a mere girl, merited little if anything
from the estate, that she had met Irvine Leyland. She
had seen him... wanted him, and she had made a mistake
that, because it was her misfortune to have been born
into an age where girls of her class had to be seen to be
pure and virginal until they were married, was immensely catastrophic.

That she of all people had succumbed to the facile
charm of a man like Irvine Leyland was still something
Margaret hated to acknowledge. Even now, more than
eighteen years later, she still found it almost impossible
to understand how he had managed to undermine her
defences, to make her fall in love with him and allow
him to seduce her, both of them knowing that it was the
only way her parents would ever accept a marriage be-

tween them...both of them knowing that, without her father's financial support, there could be no marriage.

Irvine Leyland was one of that breed of men commonly known as fortune-hunters; he lived on the fringes of society, generally supported by a doting older woman all too eager to pay for the pleasure of having him as her lover... At thirty years old, with the way he had lived his life beginning to show on the face and body that were his only assets, he needed to find himself a wife...a rich wife... And then he had met Margaret Fitzcarlton, only daughter of the Earl of Rothwell, and he saw in her his opportunity not only to marry money, but into society as well...real society...not the kind that his past activities limited him to.

Margaret, of course, had known about his reputation. Her girlfriends had been delighted to tell her, but she hadn't cared; she wanted Irvine and she was determined to have him, as much to spite her father as anything else, although she hadn't acknowledged that then... *He* thought she was unimportant...that James was all that mattered to the family...well, she would show him just how important she was...

Of course, it hadn't been easy... She grew hot beneath the tight bodice of her dark wool dress, remembering that look on her father's face when she had challenged him to refuse to acknowledge her marriage to Irvine, telling him that it was already too late and that she was already carrying Irvine's child.

She had been old enough to marry without her parents' permission, but she had of course known exactly how her father would feel. She had had the satisfaction of making her father accept what to him was the unacceptable. And then he hated her as much as she hated him.

It was James on whom he lavished what tenderness there was in him, James who was cherished and fêted, James who was the heir, the future earl, while she was nothing...nothing at all...and it was only because she

was nothing that he was allowing himself to be manoeuvred into giving public acceptance to a marriage to
a man who, he told her coldly, was totally unacceptable
to *him*, and who *should* have been totally unacceptable
to *her*. How he had humiliated her pride that day! She
had never forgiven him for it.

'By God,' he had roared at her in a voice loud enough
for the entire staff to hear, 'if you had to behave like a
bitch on heat, I'd have rather you'd picked someone
from our own stables! At least then it would be honest
yeoman blood we'd be getting... Do you know what he
is, this man you're so desperate to call your husband?
He's a gambler and a cheat... he lives off stupid old
women whom he flatters into thinking he wants them.
He's worse than a pimp. Very well, marry him, then,
but he'll never be welcome here.'

'And you'll continue my allowance,' she had pressed
grimly, hating him with a searing, bitter hatred, because
he was telling her what she already knew.

'Yes. I'll pay it. Just as long as you keep away from
Rothwell,' he had agreed grimly.

It was Margaret's good fortune that he had died so
soon after her marriage. She had read about the freak
sailing accident while she and Irvine were in the South
of France, he living with one of his rich old women while
she and her young son were forced to endure the privations of a narrow tenement house in the poorer quarter
of town, their relationship kept secret from his patroness.

Her parents' death changed things. Without waiting
to consult Irvine she had made her arrangements, ar-
riving at Rothwell in time for the funeral, knowing with
that keen instinct of hers that James was not like their
father... that he would not find it possible to deny her.

She and Charles had lived off her brother ever since.
Charles was a family name; she had chosen it without
consulting Irvine. The mad desire that had taken her
into his bed and driven her into such a frenzy of need
for him that she had had to marry him had gone. They

separated without regrets on either side. He was killed in a car accident when Charles was five years old, and by that time, even though James had responsibilities himself, he had grown so used to the necessity of supporting his sister financially that neither of them thought to question it.

But living as a pensioner of her brother wasn't enough. She didn't want to live life on the sidelines; she wanted the full glory of centre-stage. And then came the event that could give her the ultimate opportunity to claim it.

Her sister-in-law died, leaving her brother with a very young child to care for.

Naturally she had hurried to his side, offering compassion and soft-voiced suggestions that he should hand the child over into her care.

Already she had it planned... Not yet, but in another year or so, she would gently remind her brother that she was caring for his child...that it was wrong, surely, that his heiress should be brought up in a tiny London house...that she as his sister was willing to forgo the quietude of her widowhood and her small circle of friends and establish herself as the châtelaine of Rothwell...and, once there, she intended to see that she was never removed from that position.

Rothwell...what opportunities it could give her... She envisaged herself as a great political hostess, a powerful figure moving behind the scenes, directing the actions of others.

But the child, the infant who was so vital to these plans, had taken one look at her and started screaming, and had not stopped until her embarrassed and apologetic nurse had removed her from her aunt's rigid arms.

James had softened his refusal of her offer, pointing out that he could hardly let his sister take charge of his daughter when he had already refused a similar offer from his mother-in-law.

What could she say? The golden future she had envisaged for herself faded into dust. She looked at the child and mentally wished her ill, promising herself that there would come an accounting and that she would pay...oh, yes, she would pay.

All her life, fate had seemed to be against Margaret, letting her hope and then disappointing her, but this time she was not going to be disappointed. Geraldine Frances: that hated child of her brother's was going to be the instrument by which she regained her rightful place in life.

With Geraldine Frances married to Charles, *she* would be able to return to Rothwell permanently.

Margaret spared no thought for her niece's ultimate suffering in a marriage that she knew would destroy her.

At long last it seemed that the pendulum of fate was swinging in her direction, and she intended to make the most of it.

CHAPTER SEVEN

SEVERAL years passed, and Geraldine Frances found a dull acceptance of her new life.

Miserable at school, shunned by most of her fellow pupils, too proud and too afraid to confide in her father, she had nevertheless managed to excel scholastically. She had a gift for languages, for science, for maths... She possessed a brilliant mind... an ability to reason on an intellectual level that far outstripped that of her peers.

These were gifts she had received from her father... gifts the years with him had honed and polished... Gifts Margaret resented as savagely as she resented her niece's existence.

Reflecting that life was after all turning her way for once, and that she had much to look forward to, Margaret gave in to an impulse to wander into Harrods.

Intent on the mental shopping list she had compiled and the dinner party she had planned for the evening, she hurried into the shop and then out, grimacing, irritated by the jostling crowds that filled the wide pavement. There was a long queue at the taxi-rank. Tourists in the main... all of them clutching their souvenirs and waiting patiently for the line to go down. Well she had no intention of waiting. Her eyes were caught by a taxi slowing down on the opposite side of the road and imperiously she stepped off the pavement to summon it, never seeing the motorcyclist sweep round the corner.

It made *The Times*, a small two-line acknowledgement of the accident, in addition to the entry in the Deaths column.

The funeral was thinly attended; the day blazed with late spring sunshine and promise as the small group watched while her coffin was interred in the family crypt. Charles, sombre and hauntingly handsome in a black suit that really belonged to his uncle. Geraldine Frances, her face blank and strained with the effort of not betraying what she was really feeling. Coupled with her relief that she would no longer be subject to her aunt's whims was a sense of shock that Margaret's life should be ended so mundanely and so immediately. She looked at the coffin, unable to accept that her aunt's body was inside it.

She sensed her father standing behind her and turned to look at him, wondering what he was feeling. Margaret had been his sister, but there were ten years between them...had they ever been close as children? Was that how he was remembering her now, rather than as the cold, autocratic woman she had become?

On impulse she went to him and put her hand on his arm. He looked at her, his frown dissolving into a surprisingly warm smile.

Geraldine Frances...his daughter...his child... They had grown apart recently, and that was his fault; there was nothing like death for reminding one how very fleeting life could be.

He looked at her quietly. He had missed her...missed her quick, incisive mind...her purity of spirit...her challenging intensity... He had missed her love, and he cursed the chauvinistic pride that had made him wish so desperately that she might have been a boy.

And now there would be no sons... The ache that knowledge caused never completely died, but there was nothing he could do about it. He looked across at Charles. He had never been particularly close to him. He had too much of his father in him for that...and too much of his mother.

Trust Margaret to want to promote a marriage between him and Geraldine Frances. Outwardly it would be an ideal arrangement, a neat tying-up of any potential loose ends, but he couldn't forget the triumph and intensity he had heard in Charles's voice that day when he'd caught him in the long gallery claiming to Geraldine Frances that he would inherit Rothwell.

That was Margaret's fault. *She* was the one who had taught him to believe that he was to succeed to the earldom, not knowing that from the moment James had discovered that he couldn't father any more children he had prepared plans to make a special petition to the Queen so that the title could pass direct through Geraldine Frances to her eldest son. The incident in the long gallery had confirmed that he was right to do so, and James had actually put the plans into action that week.

Margaret had quarrelled bitterly with him over that. And now Charles was subtly but surely laying claim to his cousin's affections... Was he being over-cynical in suspecting the motivation behind Charles's attitude towards Geraldine Frances?

He sighed wearily, his eyes blurring, making him frown. He had suffered from this disconcerting inability to focus both his sight and his mind on several occasions recently. There had been brief, terrifying instances when his mind had suddenly gone blank like a black hole materialising out of nowhere, a dizzying, sickening sensation of nothingness...quickly gone, but leaving behind a residue of fear and shock.

It probably meant nothing other than that he was growing older. He put his arm around Geraldine Frances, forcing Charles to step back from her slightly.

'It's over,' he said quietly. 'It's time we went home.'

And so, with Charles on one side of her, her father on the other, Geraldine Frances walked over to the waiting car.

Charles smiled inwardly as he joined his uncle and cousin. His mother was dead, but he wouldn't forget what she had taught him.

Rothwell was going to be his. He looked at Geraldine Frances, overweight and plain, and was glad she looked the way she did. That way, there was no danger of someone else stealing Rothwell from him.

He found himself wishing either that she were older, or that his uncle were less astute. If she were older he could have seduced her and persuaded her into an early marriage, but she was only just sixteen to his twenty-two, and his uncle was too astute not to see what was behind such an action. After all, it was the same one his father had used on his mother...

But somehow he must make sure of Geraldine Frances. She looked shyly at him and said quietly, 'I'm sorry... about your mother...'

He veiled his eyes so that she wouldn't see his own lack of emotion and took her hand and squeezed it, watching the hot colour flood her skin with cool detachment.

He was already more than halfway there. Left to Geraldine Frances... He knew his mother had put forward the idea of their marriage to his uncle, and he cursed mentally now that he had not worked harder to gain the latter's approval, but in the old days he had felt secure in the knowledge that, since his uncle could not have sons, *he* would inherit from him by almost divine right... the right of succession... the right that should have been his, but for his uncle's mad refusal to ignore Geraldine Frances's claims as his daughter in favour of his as his nephew... He felt the old helpless rage roll over him and gripped Geraldine Frances's hand, not re-alising what he was doing until she made a soft sound of pain.

He looked down at her, forcing back his feelings.

'I'm sorry,' he apologised softly. 'I was just thinking of Ma...'

He watched as her eyes turned liquid with emotion. God, she was such a soft touch. Getting her to the altar would be easy... getting her pregnant was a different matter. He felt revulsion for her rather than desire, but desire could be manufactured. And the marriage *would* have to be consummated... *would* have to produce a son... He toyed with the possibility of persuading her to disinherit herself in his favour... Impossible while his uncle was still alive, of course, and he was still only in his mid-forties.

All the way back to Rothwell, Charles held her hand. Geraldine Frances was suffused with so much pleasure that she couldn't speak. Instead she sat in silence, while Charles addressed her father respectfully as 'sir', and, almost without being aware of it, she recognised that Charles was setting himself out to win over her father... It bothered her sometimes, this recognition within herself that there was something facile and premeditated about Charles's charm. She didn't want to acknowledge it, and so she buried it deep within her subconscious, concentrating instead on the physical delight that being with him brought. Her stomach was quivering with a thousand butterflies... tremulous with delicate happiness... with a joy she felt guilty about feeling with her aunt so newly dead.

Poor Charles. She might not have liked her aunt, but Margaret *had* been Charles's mother. Geraldine Frances tried to think how she would feel if it had been her father who had been killed, and her fingers tightened convulsively, causing Charles to frown and glance at her.

James felt tired... Far more tired, surely, than a man of his age should feel, and slightly confused. The fear was back with him; his head buzzed with panic and a clinging, insidious apprehension as he felt his mind start to cloud over. He was only forty-four... Margaret had been ten years older... a full decade between them, just as there was a yawning gap of six years between Geraldine Frances and Charles... Charles... James frowned, not really wanting to think about his nephew, but Geraldine

Frances plainly adored him, and that worried him, nagged at him.

They *should* marry, Margaret had said. James tried to concentrate on why it was that he felt so uneasy about such a marriage, but could only summon an elusive awareness of his feelings and not the reasoning behind them. This wasn't the first time he had felt some memory slipping away from him.

Now that Charles was on his own, James supposed he would have to do something for him... He was, after all, his nephew... But what?

The answer came to him over dinner that evening, as he watched Charles's blond head turn towards Geraldine Frances's russet one, saw the open adoration in her eyes, and recognised Charles's subtle encouragement of it.

A spell apart wouldn't do either of them any harm. When dinner was over, he invited Charles to join him in the library.

'Perhaps this isn't the most propitious time to discuss your future,' he began, 'but now that you're on your own—I know that, while your mother was alive, your time was fully occupied looking after her affairs——'

It was a sop to good relations between them, since he knew quite well that Charles hadn't done a day's work in his life and that he himself had been subsidising both Margaret and her son.

'However, now she's gone...I think it might be a good idea for you to go out to Argentina. I have a half-share in an *estancia* out there, as you know, breeding polo ponies. The manager's due to retire in a couple of years. It's a good life out there.'

Charles knew quite well what his uncle was doing, and he fought down the rage boiling inside him.

'Polo ponies... It's kind of you, sir...but I'm not sure it's quite my scene. Could I have some time to think about it?'

To think of a way to get out of going without totally
alienating James, Charles reflected half an hour later as
he went upstairs.

Argentina . . . That was the last place he wanted to go.
For one thing it would mean giving up his very busy
social life in London, and for another, and more important—because after all one could find beautiful and
willing women anywhere—it would mean potentially long
separations from Geraldine Frances. And those he
couldn't afford, not now. It was too much of a risk . . .

In the library, James frowned, wondering if he should
have been blunter with his nephew . . . if he should have
warned him that he wasn't entirely happy with the relationship that was developing between him and
Geraldine Frances.

Geraldine Frances was so young . . . too young! Too
naïve, and it was his fault for keeping her to himself for
so long. Margaret had been right about that if nothing
else. He *should* have sent her to school much earlier, but
he had enjoyed her company so much . . . Now things
had changed between them and he knew it was his own
fault. How bitterly he regretted letting her see how much
her changed appearance had shocked him on his return
from Argentina that time. His reaction had driven a
wedge between them . . . caused a rift in their relationship which had meant that their old closeness had
been destroyed.

How could he tell her the reason he felt so uneasy
about this relationship which had developed between her
and Charles without hurting her? How could he destroy
the dreams he could see so clearly in her eyes by pointing
out to her how highly unlikely it was that a man of
Charles's age and looks should feel the same way about
her that she did about him?

No matter how much he himself might suspect
Charles's motives, there was nothing he could do . . .
Other than send Charles away and hope that Geraldine
Frances grew out of her crush on him.

Those were the thoughts of the father...the Earl on the other hand thought logically and coldly that a marriage between Charles and Geraldine Frances would have many advantages...but at what potential cost to his daughter?

He didn't trust Charles—he never had. There was something too smooth, too knowing, too calculating about him...something dangerous and subtle.

At the top of the stairs, Charles paused.

It was barely half-past ten. If he were in London, he would just be on his way out for the evening...an evening spent eating and drinking at one or other of the city's most expensive and fashionable venues, almost always at someone else's expense. His mother had taught him to be careful with his money. She had pleaded her widowhood and consequent poverty with a masterly skill. She had often complained bitterly to him about the size of the allowance James had given her. A man of his immense wealth could easily have afforded to make her a settlement of several million pounds, she had claimed, ignoring the fact that she had been living rent-free in a very comfortable house in one of the most exclusive parts of London...a house James had redecorated and refurnished for her at considerable expense, several times... He had paid Charles's school fees, provided her with a car, permitted her the run of all his estates and properties, but that still hadn't been enough. Nothing would ever have been enough to satisfy her craving for Rothwell itself—a craving she had passed on to her son.

And Charles continued to pursue the policy she had adopted. He moved in a circle of very wealthy young men and women. When he was at school and it was known that his uncle would never produce a male heir, he had taken to using the title applicable to a male heir presumptive; that of Lord Wesford—his uncle's second title which arose from his baronetcy—taking good care that he used it only where it would be most useful and never anywhere where it could get back to his uncle's ears. This unofficial usurpation of honours that were not strictly his had had his mother's full approval, and it had made it all the more galling that he knew privately that his uncle was in fact petitioning the Queen so that the earldom passed not to Charles, but through Geraldine Frances to her sons.

His mother had been furious. Latterly, though, she had come to realise that there was another way for Charles to get what he wanted. Marriage to Geraldine Frances might not confer the titles on him, but it would ultimately bring him Rothwell and the money, and it would be his son who eventually inherited.

Charles had listened to his mother's suggestion with cynical detachment. No wonder his father had found it so easy to seduce her. He wished he'd known his father better; he suspected the two of them would have had a lot in common... Pity he had been fool enough to marry a woman without any promise of great wealth—or had he hoped that her father would relent and that she would receive a large inheritance? Perhaps if the Earl had lived longer, he might have done so.

He had something else in common with his father, as well ... He thought about the girl who would be waiting for him in London. She was a model, only a few years older than Geraldine Frances, but oh, how very different!

That she was still naïve enough to be impressed by the people he knew, the places he went, added an extra piquancy to their affair. He teased her with promises of taking her to society events, which he had no intention of fulfilling. She had an accent that grated on his ears, and she would stick out like a sore thumb among the social set in which he moved.

Besides, when he went out in society it was normally as the discreet escort of an older woman. There were half a dozen or so to whom he paid subtle court... nothing too over-the-top...just enough to convince them that his flattery was genuine...just enough to make sure that he was always welcome at their parties...in their homes...that he was always included in their invitations and never expected to pay.

He hadn't had to take any of them to bed yet...but if that became a necessity... He shrugged cynically. He had his little hot-eyed model for pleasure, and for the rest... Well, it would stand him in good stead when the time finally came for him to bed Geraldine Frances.

He had reached her bedroom door. He stopped outside it. There was no way he was going to be sent to Argentina. Did his uncle really not know how easily he could see through that manoeuvre? Separate him from Geraldine Frances and that fierce, vulnerable teenage idolatry of him would easily die; but he wasn't going to allow that to happen.

He wished again that she were a couple of years older. As it was... He knocked briefly on the door and pushed it open.

Geraldine Frances hadn't gone straight to bed. She was too wound up...too thrilled and excited by having Charles's company and attention.

Charles... Her eyes shone with pleasure. How handsome he was...how sophisticated... How gentle and tender with her. How much she loved him.

She sat on the window-seat, looking out into the darkness, hugging her knees, letting herself melt with the pleasure of imagining herself married to Charles.

And then her face clouded and she looked miserably at her own ungainly body. If only she were prettier, slimmer... She had tried to diet, but she just couldn't do it... Going without food seemed to make her hungrier than ever, so that she simply stuffed herself until she felt almost sick. She was the fattest girl at school, and she knew that the others made fun of her behind her back. She comforted herself by thinking how jealous they would be if they saw her with Charles...

She heard the faint knock on the door and got up, expecting her father. She hadn't changed out of the unflattering black dress she had worn for the funeral.

When Charles walked in, she stared at him in surprised delight.

His fair hair was ruffled, a haggard expression tormenting his eyes.

'Forgive me, little one,' he said huskily as he came towards her. 'I shouldn't be here like this...'

A delicious tremor raced through her at the implications of his words...and the way he looked at her.

'But I wanted so much to be with you...' His voice sounded muffled, hoarse with emotion...with passion? Her heart thumped and she went instinctively towards him.

'Charles, what is it?'

'It just came to me that, now Ma's gone, I'm completely alone...' He waited, wondering if she would take the bait, hiding his triumph when she did, reacting as he had anticipated she would, her plump face creasing into a look of intense compassion, melting with the pleasure she felt in his having come to her.

'Oh, no...you're not alone...' she breathed unsteadily, thrilled beyond words that he had come to her to unburden himself, to find solace for his unhappiness at his mother's death. 'You've got us...Daddy and me...'

Dared she go up to him and put her arms round him, offering him physical comfort? She hesitated and then, when he bowed his head as though overcome with emotion, caution was forgotten and she ran towards him, flinging her arms around him and crying out passionately, 'Oh, Charles, don't! Don't be upset...'

Upset! He grinned to himself while theatrically portraying agonised emotion, putting his head on her shoulder and letting her think he was overwhelmed by the loss of his mother...letting her hold him in her inexperienced, naïve embrace, and ignoring the unpleasantness of her too-soft flesh pressing against him.

'Oh, God, I shouldn't be here with you like this...'

He started to push himself away from her, and Geraldine Frances tensed and then quivered with joy as he murmured, 'You aren't a child any more. When I hold you in my arms you don't feel like a child...'

He drew her back against him and added, 'It's going to be hell being so far away from you...'

So far away...? Warning bells jangled in her ears. This time it was Geraldine Frances who reluctantly detached herself from their embrace.

'So far away? But——'

'Your father's sending me to Argentina,' he told her, and then added, in a voice which he muffled against her hair as he pulled her back against him, 'I think he's guessed how I feel about you and he doesn't approve— and who can blame him? I'm no catch for the future Countess of Rothwell, am I?' He nuzzled her hair and Geraldine Frances was ablaze with delirious joy, incandescent with it. He loved her... He must love her... That was what he was saying, wasn't it? And her father was going to send him away! She couldn't let it happen.

'I expect he thinks you're too young to know your own mind... and perhaps he's right... Oh, God,' he added in tones of apparent self-loathing, 'I shouldn't be saying any of this to you. I shouldn't be laying this kind of burden on you... it's only that I'm so frightened of losing you...'

Well, that much was true, but Geraldine Frances, dazzled by what she was hearing, could only stand motionless within the circle of his arms, feeling as though she had just been given the greatest gift that life could offer.

And that was how James found them when he opened the door to Geraldine Frances's room and walked in. He had intended, after a long inner battle with himself, to give her a gentle warning about attaching too much importance to Charles's attentions. To walk into her bedroom and find her standing in her cousin's arms, her young face turned up to his as though she were looking on the Holy Grail, her feelings so sharply and acutely revealed, was almost too much for him to endure.

He could only stand there, stupefied, while Charles said smoothly and, to his ears, totally falsely, 'I'm sorry, sir, I shouldn't be here, I know...' He turned his head and looked down at Geraldine Frances, a totally false look of love and promise, and said softly, 'Perhaps your father's right to send me away, my darling...you're so young...'

'Daddy, no!' Geraldine Frances pleaded, her face flushed, her eyes brilliant with tears and emotion. 'Please don't send Charles to Argentina...' And then, seeing the look on her father's face, she pressed despairingly, 'I love him and I'm going to marry him...'

The words hung on the silence in the room. Above her head, uncle and nephew exchanged looks, and it was James who was forced to look away first.

He had been outmanoeuvred...and with such skill and cynicism that it took his breath away. Why had he not realised how easily Charles could use Geraldine Frances against him? How could he tell her now what he suspected? How could he look her in the face and ask her to question if a man of Charles's looks and age could really be in love with a girl like her...a plain young girl...a very, very rich girl, who would one day own the house which Charles believed *he* should own.

Frightened by the silence and by the tension she could feel stretching between the two men who formed her entire world, Geraldine Frances panicked.

'If you send Charles to Argentina, I'm going with him,' she threatened desperately, clinging to her cousin's side...and James knew that he was defeated.

Charles didn't return to London the next day, nor for two more days. There were plans to be made.

James remained resolute that there could be no formal engagement until Geraldine Frances was eighteen.

Having bought what time he could, he was forced to pay for these concessions by giving in to the subtle pressure Charles was putting on him both to increase his allowance and to permit his continued occupation of the London house.

It was agreed that Geraldine Frances would go back to school, and stay there until she had taken her A levels. Her father had hoped she would go on to university; she had a good brain, and she would need to learn how to use it to its best advantage if she was to hold together what first his father and then he himself had gathered together to support Rothwell... Already he had started to teach her all the complexities of the many trusts he had set up...of the involved and multi-national financial basis that underpinned their fortune. Such things couldn't be trusted to Charles... James had no illusions on that score.

Geraldine Frances had been too happy to object to his decree that no formal engagement should be announced until she was over eighteen.

James felt as though he was caught in a trap that was largely of his own making. He wanted Geraldine Frances to marry, and he wanted grandsons, but at the same time he wasn't sure that he wanted her to marry Charles. And yet she loved her cousin, or thought she did, and, much as it seemed to be a betrayal of her as a human being and his daughter, he was forced to admit that physically she would repel far more men than she would attract... And those who did seem to be attracted to her... He suppressed a sigh. They would undoubtedly be motivated by the same things that he felt sure motivated Charles.

In a way he was desperately hoping that time would solve the problem for him; that by some miracle time would reduce Geraldine Frances's undoubted emotional dependence on Charles, and that it would also somehow work the miracle necessary to make his daughter into the woman she truly deserved to be.

It had also occurred to him that Charles, being made to wait, might grow impatient and look for another, easier victim.

CHAPTER EIGHT

CHARLES had no intention of doing any such thing. He wanted Rothwell and he fully intended to have it.

From the moment he had first experienced awareness of another human being's emotions, Charles had known that his mother neither loved nor wanted him.

The brief flare of passion which had brought his parents together in the first place had died out long before Charles himself was born, and his mother, used to being treated with the deference and awe which being the daughter of the Earl of Rothwell accorded her, hated the privations forced on her by her new way of life.

Charles might have been born in the exclusive and fashionably private wing of one of London's foremost hospitals, but it was with that one concession on the part of his grandfather that the similarities between himself and the other children born there began and ended.

Charles had no privileged, luxurious home, but a shabby, cheap rented flat in a part of London which his mother had barely known existed until after her marriage.

Her husband, bored already with his wife and bitterly disappointed in her father's refusal to either fully support or acknowledge him, had made other arrangements to finance the lifestyle he wanted, long before Charles's arrival.

Margaret grimly refusing to admit publicly what she knew privately, followed her husband to the South of France, but, while he enjoyed the luxurious comfort of his mistress's Mediterranean villa, she and Charles lived in what was virtually a slum.

For Charles the earliest years of his life had left an indelible memory on his personality which translated into an abhorrence of poverty so deeply ingrained that it was almost a phobia. Allied to that was an awareness that to his parents, the father he scarcely remembered, and the mother whose acid bitterness against that father coloured his entire childhood, he was an unwanted encumbrance.

Furious that she had conceived in the first place, furious with the father who had rejected her, the brother who had superseded her and the husband who had deserted her, Margaret had turned the full force of that fury against the male child to whom she gave birth.

Not that she was physically cruel to him, but from the moment he was born all her resentment and bitterness at the supremacy of the male sex coalesced and overflowed, finding a focus and an outlet in Charles.

It was only later, after the death of her parents and her husband, that she began to see what a useful pawn her child really was.

And yet even there she found something for which to blame Charles. Had she not had a child, she was sure she would have been able to persuade James to allow her to make her home at Rothwell, where she could have surreptitiously taken over the reins of the great house's management so that it would always have been far more hers than his.

It was a fallacy that Rothwell belonged to the earls; in truth it had always belonged to their countesses, because Rothwell, with its vast treasure of furniture, carpets, paintings and other *objets d'art*, needed the love and control of a mistress to provide it with the care and attention that made it flourish.

Charles had always known of his mother's obsession for Rothwell, just as he always had known of her lack of love for him. Rothwell should have been hers, she would tell him frustratedly after a visit to the house to see James. These visits always left her on edge and bitter, and it was then that he would feel the verbal sting of her acid tongue.

And so, as Charles grew from infancy to childhood, somewhere within him also grew a deep-rooted belief that Rothwell was the magic that would turn the base metal of his mother's dislike and resentment of him into love.

Charles was not by nature a timid or gentle child, he had too much of both of his parents in him for that, but he had learned young that it was impossible for him to pit himself against his mother and win.

However, once he started attending the exclusive school Margaret had convinced James was the only possible place she should send her child to to begin his education, he quickly discovered a wonderful outlet for all his aggression.

School was his first real contact with other children. Margaret complained quite untruthfully to James that the allowance he permitted her was far too miserly to allow her to employ a proper nanny, and so Charles had had to make do with the impatient and irritated attentions of the various housekeepers his mother employed, and who were generally told to 'Keep him quiet and out of the way'.

It seemed to Charles, growing up, that women held an awesome and unfair power, and he had enough of his grandfather in him to feel bitterly resentful of that unfair distribution of control and authority.

The school was old-fashioned, and followed the old methods of permitting boys to be boys, while girls were expected to be demure, clean, tidy and neat, and Charles very quickly developed a sharp sense of pleasure in discovering subtle ways of punishing those unprotected female children for the power his mother held over him.

It was fortunate that the day school only took pupils from four to seven, the age when most boys of his class started at their exclusive prep schools, because by the time he was seven years old his teachers were becoming uncomfortably aware of the number of complaints they were receiving from the parents of some of their pupils about his bullying tactics.

Confrontations and unpleasantness of any kind were abhorrent to them and, safe in the knowledge that in another few months they would be thankfully relieved of such a troublemaker's presence, and that it would be up to the far harder and tougher regime of a boy's school to deal with the character faults he was fast developing, they soothed the agitated mothers and took care to make sure that Charles was isolated as much as possible from the most vulnerable sections of his class, praying that the next few months would pass without any more incident.

One of the three sisters who ran the school did tentatively suggest having a word with Charles's mother, but she had not met Margaret, and was quickly assured by her sisters that such a course of action would not be a good idea. For, though the woman had little enough love herself for her son, the stiffly ingrained sense of family pride she had inherited from her father made it necessary for her to believe, where the rest of the world was concerned, that her son was as near perfect as it was possible for any child to be.

At home, in the privacy of their solitude, she might refer to him as a nuisance and an unwanted burden on her finances and her emotions, but publicly he was her darling boy... her precious child... and to his already dangerous repertoire of adult emotions Charles added a new one: an awareness of the necessity to create a public image which did not reflect the truer, more private one.

He learned that responding in a pretty, deferential way to his mother's cooing voice and flattering comments when they were in public earned him certain small indulgences in private, although it would be several years yet before he recognised that there were women who, no matter how great the evidence to the contrary, would self-woundingly allow themselves to believe that even the most fictitious and deliberate flattery was the truth.

Towards James, his uncle, he felt almost as great a resentment as he did towards his mother, because it was James who was responsible for his mother's bitterness... James who had taken from his mother something which should have been hers. Rothwell!

She took scant interest in all other aspects of his education, but where their family history was concerned she was relentless in inculcating into Charles an awareness of her family and its greatness... its importance... an importance that focused on whoever was fortunate enough in their generation to be the eldest or only son, for, no matter how privileged in their time other members of the family might have been, in reality they were nothing, because eventually there would come a time when the doors of Rothwell would be closed to them.

Rothwell represented power, prestige and wealth. Rothwell, and her obsession for it, was the sickness that clouded his mother's soul and shadowed her whole life, and Charles, through her, had become infected with the same disease.

By the time Margaret was petitioning her brother to provide the money to pay Charles's fees at one of the exclusive prep schools, Charles was already recognised by his peers as someone to be feared.

Cruel he might be, but Charles was no fool. He quickly understood the advantages to be gained from the cooing admiration of his mother's cronies—and the reason for that admiration.

He had grown so used to the words, 'Such a handsome boy...' that it wasn't until he heard his mother commenting disparagingly on the plainness of Uncle James's baby daughter that he began to understand the benefits that went with the face he saw reflected in his mirror every morning.

After that, he began to study the faces of his peers and astutely saw that those with the more attractive features received indulgences from adults that the plainer children did not.

On the death of James's wife, Margaret had immediately rushed to her brother's side, offering to take charge of his motherless daughter.

Charles, who had not been allowed to accompany her, suffered the full brunt of her rage once she returned home at being thwarted in her plan by Geraldine Frances's refusal to take to her, but once she had calmed down Margaret began to see other advantages in the fact that her brother's marriage had only produced one female child... But, while there was the possibility that James could marry again and produce sons, it would be dangerous to hope for too much. Even so, she began to look at Charles with new eyes, to see him as a potential asset.

Margaret kept constant pressure on James until in exasperation he gave in and used his influence to get Charles a place at his own old prep school.

It hadn't been easy, and so he was less than pleased when within eighteen months he received a telephone call from the headmaster to inform him discreetly of his concern over Charles's, as he termed it, 'inability to mix well with his peer group'.

A deeper investigation revealed charges of bullying and mental if not physical cruelty which Margaret, when taxed about them, dismissed as jealous lies on the part of the other children.

Charles, summoned to his uncle's study to account for himself, lowered his head and used his most convincing expression of bewilderment.

'It's true that there have been some problems at school,' he told James earnestly, and by skilful manipulation of the truth he lied so convincingly that James was forced to accept Margaret's assertion that Charles was being picked on because she, his mother, lacked the social and financial standing of his fellow pupils' parents.

As always, Margaret managed to make James feel guilty by reminding him that he had been the one to receive their parents' love and attention, that he had been the one to inherit the earldom and everything that went with it, while she, neglected by her parents, had rushed into a foolish marriage...had been pushed into it almost, by her desperate craving to be loved. And James gave in.

Privately he shared the headmaster's views of his nephew, but Charles was Margaret's child and there was little he could do personally.

He shied away from the knowledge that he could perhaps have taken a more 'fatherly' role in Charles's life, and from the extra burden of guilt that went with it. He didn't like Charles, and if he were honest with himself he didn't particularly like his sister either.

Academically, Charles's years at prep school were not a success, but in other ways they established a pattern he was to follow throughout his life: that of the subjugation and domination of others weaker than himself.

He had quickly discovered that his good looks acted on the unwary like a spider's web trapping flies; the only problem was that sooner or later his 'friends' discovered the more unpleasant side of his nature and quickly abandoned him.

Emotionally that didn't bother him at all. The early neglect he had suffered from his mother had cut him off from any ability he might have had to react emotionally to others, and had bred in him instead a deep core of inner coldness that successfully isolated him from the pain of any peer rejection.

However, what did bother him was the fact that, in losing his admirers, he was also losing 'face', and so he learned to cloak his desire to hurt and dominate, so that each of his victims thought himself alone and, fearing the ridicule he thought exposure might bring, kept his misery to himself, outwardly still forming a part of Charles's 'court', but resentful and frightened.

From subjugating his peers emotionally, it was a short and simple step for Charles to dominate them in other ways; especially financially.

No matter how generous James was to her, Margaret never forgot the humiliating poverty of her marriage. She was careful with her money to the point of meanness. From her Charles learned that money represented power, and that power in his mother's life lay vested not in her, but in James. He also observed and learned how skilful his mother was at playing on her brother's guilt and extracting money from him, and he too began to develop the same skill. Draw someone within your power, subjugate them, and then subtly threaten them. Charles soon found it possible to increase the miserly pocket money his mother allowed him almost tenfold by this means.

But a restless, driving dissatisfaction was beginning to infiltrate his life.

Real power, true power came from Rothwell and everything it represented. Rothwell should have been his, his mother had told him as much.

Sometimes, driven by a frenzy of irritation and compulsion, his mother would say, 'She's only a girl; she can't inherit...Rothwell could be yours yet. *If* your uncle doesn't remarry and produce sons, *then* you will inherit Rothwell.' If James *did*, then he, Charles, would have *nothing*. But in either case, Geraldine Frances, that plain, pampered girl-child on whom his uncle so inexplicably appeared to dote, would lose out, because as a girl she could not inherit Rothwell. And that pleased Charles.

Sometimes it amused him to use his charm to bedazzle his much younger cousin. He liked the way she followed him with her eyes, the way she gazed at him with open adoration. At the same time he despised her for her weakness in allowing him to see how she felt, and he would then be unable to resist punishing her. No one of any sense ever revealed their real feelings; he had learned that from his mother.

It was nearing the time for Charles to leave prep school to go on to the famous public school attended by his uncle, and before that, since the school's inception, by each and every one of his male ancestors. Only Charles had other ideas. Ideas which would allow him to widen the scope of his own particularly non-academic talents.

He knew all about the type of school his mother had in mind; there he would be nothing, no one...the son of a man whom his fellow pupils' parents would remember as a social climber, and worse.

His mother had reverted to her maiden name after his father's death and had his name changed to it by deed poll, but in their world such things deceived no one, and if there was one thing Charles hated it was being made to feel inferior to his peers... At the school he had in mind things were different; money ruled there, not social status. It was a progressive, modern establishment favoured by actors and pop stars for their offspring, and it had received a good deal of media attention, since it catered for both boys and girls, and moreover did not provide any kind of strict regime but allowed its pupils to choose which subjects they wished to study and the time when they wanted to study them.

Charles had discovered one very important fact: how much easier it was to manipulate girls than boys. Young girls, like their elders, were so much more susceptible to his good looks and spurious charm...girls were so malleable...so trusting...so easy to hurt; and in hurting them he had discovered the perfect way of punishing his mother for the way she had hurt him.

He broached the subject carefully with his mother, knowing quite well by now how best to bring her round to his point of view.

At first she demurred. She wanted him to attend the school the males of her family had always attended, but when an interview with its headmaster informed her that, despite everything James had been able to do, there was no place there for Charles, she hid her chagrin and said airily to her cronies that she wanted something more for Charles than the outdated, regimented, institutionalised education offered by a traditional public school.

Charles took to life at his relaxed, easygoing co-educational boarding school better than a duck to water.

It offered him limitless opportunities to refine and hone his skills, providing as it did a wide field of victims only too ready to offer themselves up to him.

He was tall and well developed for his age, and it wasn't very long before he lost his virginity and, in doing so, took that of the shy, rather nervous girl in his class whom he had picked out from among her peers.

Not because he desired her more than the others, but because he knew she would keep her mouth shut, and because it amused him to torment her by letting her believe he cared about her when in reality he felt nothing for her at all.

The school acted like a forcing house of burgeoning teenage emotions, throwing the sexes together without any parental supervision and fostering a network of small, secret groups, each devoted to the pursuance of their own particular pleasure.

When Charles discovered he had been nominated by an older class of girls to join the select group of boys they allowed to have sex with them he went readily to a secret meeting to undergo an initiation ceremony of which he had already heard exciting whispers.

The leader of the group was a tall, heavily built girl with dark hair and curiously flat pale blue eyes that seemed to have an almost magnetic quality.

Not at all attractive in the accepted sense, she nevertheless possessed a formidable charisma, which Charles recognised and duly paid homage to.

This girl knew and recognised power. What was more, she also knew how to take control of it and to use it. Older than Charles by almost three years, outwardly, to her tutors at least, a rather dull, plain girl who worked reasonably well, she had another side to her personality which only those admitted to her secret sect knew.

The initiation ceremonies took place in an abandoned hut in the grounds of the school, and involved group sexual acts that focused mainly on the oldest girls in the group and the boy they had chosen to admit to their ranks, but which also occasionally permitted a chosen and favoured male to remove from a young and newly admitted female member of the sect the unwanted burden of her virginity.

Charles's initiation ceremony was very well attended.

Two girls, masked and robed, met him at the doorway of the room. Its windows were covered so that the room was dark, illuminated only by candles which gave off an odd sweetish scent.

He was given something to drink that quickly made him feel light-headed and euphoric. And, while he watched, more of the same stuff was passed around between the watching girls.

By the time they started to undress him he was conscious only of the distant pleasure of their hands on his flesh . . . that and the burning power of the pale blue eyes of the one girl who stood aloof from the others . . . silent, motionless, and yet so exciting him with the unblinking, unwavering intensity of her stare that merely to look into her face brought him to such a state of sexual arousal that his body was eagerly responsive to everything that his initiators demanded of it.

At no time at all did the girl who stood aloof touch him or communicate with him in any way, but it was she who filled his consciousness as the eager hands and mouths of the others explored and tested the endurance of his arousal.

When he woke up the next day he was violently sick, his head and body hurt, and for the first time in his memory he was aware of having lost control, not only of a situation but of himself as well.

A fellow pupil observing his nausea and inability to concentrate, asked mockingly, 'Been drinking Helen's magic brew, have you? Watch out you don't get hooked on it.'

And it was then that Charles realised what had happened to him. He had heard whispers about drugs, but only whispers, and they hadn't meant a great deal to him. Now, suddenly, they did, and he recognised the power they conferred, not on the person who took them, but on the one who supplied them.

That was to be his one and only experimentation with taking drugs. Anything that robbed him of his powers of self-control, and through that his power to control others, was something there was no room for in his life, but, for the supplier rather than the taker, drugs opened up a whole new world, one which he was anxious to be a part of.

His enquiries brought him into contact with a boy two years ahead of him in school, the son of a pop star who had unlimited access to supplies of drugs.

By cultivating Mike Rigby, Charles soon became one of the chosen few to whom he 'sold' drugs acquired in secret on his visits home.

Charles in turn sold his supply to his own carefully chosen and discreetly monitored group of users. He was always careful to sell only to those who he knew had the money to pay and who he knew to be well under his own control.

For Charles there were no moral qualms or compunction about what he was doing. In this world the strongest survived and the weakest went to the wall; and he intended to be among the strong.

And then came the master stroke of fate that suddenly cleared the way for him to inherit Rothwell ... And all through a childish virus that Geraldine Frances had so helpfully passed on to her father.

Margaret was ecstatic. When Charles went home for the school holidays she could barely wait to tell him.

'Poor old Geraldine Frances,' he gloated. 'She won't have a bean...'

Margaret frowned. As she had good cause to know, her brother's private fortune, the money he had inherited from their father and so miraculously expanded, was his to do with as he pleased. *If* he wished, he could leave every penny of it to Geraldine Frances... Money which by rights ought to go to Rothwell.

Charles was in a high state of exultation. That Christmas he alternately bullied and bewitched Geraldine Frances, secretly despising her... looking at her with the sexual cynicism he had developed, half of him wanting the pleasure of revealing that knowledge to her, just for the sheer thrill of savagery it would give him to smash down the barriers his uncle had placed too protectively around her, the other half of him holding back... just a little bit afraid.

And then, that summer, just when the wave of exultation was reaching its peak, everything came crashing down. And it was all his fault, or so his mother claimed, turning on him in a fury of anger as she demanded to know *why* he had been so stupid as to boast of his inheritance, and in front of James of all people.

Did he realise the damage he had done? she stormed at him. Did he realise that, because of him, James had told her that he had finally decided to petition the Queen so that the earldom and Rothwell would pass not to Charles, the next male in line, but to Geraldine Frances... his daughter... and a woman.

At first Charles hadn't believed her... it couldn't happen. He was the male, the heir! But gradually he had been forced to accept that it was true.

'There's only one thing for it now,' his mother told him acidly. 'You'll have to marry Geraldine Frances. That's the only way you're going to get Rothwell now...'

'Marry Geraldine Frances?' Charles stared at her, the words of denial spilling from his mouth. He felt trapped, infuriated... full of hatred for his mother, his uncle and

most of all against Geraldine Frances herself, because
he knew that, no matter how much he fought against it,
the only way he was going to hold the power that was
Rothwell was through that plain, hated girl who was his
cousin.

He knew blindingly in that moment that nothing,
nothing would make him give up Rothwell. He had to
have it, no matter what the cost...and if that meant
marriage to Geraldine Frances then a marriage there
would be. But, as he vowed to have the earldom and all
that went with it, he also vowed to make his cousin pay
for standing in his way, for forcing him to marry her.
Oh, yes, he would make her pay...

His mother was saying something about him having
to be nicer to Geraldine Frances... He suppressed an
acid, jeering comment. Did she really not *know* that he
knew exactly what had to be done? He looked at her
with distaste and dislike. Over the years she had changed
her attitude towards him and had somehow managed to
convince herself that she had always adored and cherished him; that he *was* the 'precious child' she had so
often referred to, and, even more unbelievably, she
seemed to have convinced herself that he felt the same
way about her. A sudden thought struck him and he said
casually, 'Ma, I'll eventually be leaving school...when
I do...'

'You'll go on to Oxford, of course. I——'

'No,' he told her curtly. 'No...I think it would be a
better idea if I did something to convince Uncle James
that, as his only male heir, I ought to be taught something about his business affairs.'

His mother looked at him.

'You're right,' she agreed. 'But we'll have to wait until
James is in a better frame of mind. And I don't know
if he——'

'You'll have to talk to him,' Charles told her smoothly.
'Persuade him to fix something up for me. Something

which will enable me to keep in close contact with Rothwell and Geraldine Frances...'

Again his mother stared.

'Yes, I should have thought of that...you're going to have to make sure someone else doesn't steal her away from you, Charles. Without her...'

He laughed bitterly. 'It's a pity she didn't die with her damned mother... Then there'd be nothing to stand in between me and Rothwell.' And Margaret, who had once felt very much the same thing about her young brother, could say nothing.

Charles had raised a very salient point, though. It was essential that he remain in close contact with Rothwell and his cousin, and if James could be persuaded to take Charles into his confidence about his financial affairs, to teach him all that he was so unnecessarily teaching Geraldine Frances...

'I think your cousin will have to go away to school in a few years,' Margaret announced thoughtfully... And Charles, who knew quite well the lines on which his mother's mind ran, agreed softly.

'An excellent idea. Divide and conquer, unite and rule... We must make sure that the only person my dear cousin unites herself with is me...so that through her I can make sure that *I'm* the one to rule Rothwell.'

By the time he left school Charles had established a strong network of drug users to whom he supplied a variety of drugs, no longer obtained merely from his original source of supply.

Once he was free of school, the network spread, and as always Charles was careful only to supply to those he knew could afford to buy.

His sexual experimentation while at school had led him to the discovery that there was a certain type of woman he enjoyed sex with best.

Physically she had to be attractive, and, equally as important, physically desired by other males. She had to be a woman who was in some way a challenge, but not so much of a challenge that she might ultimately refuse or reject him, and, most of all, she had to be the kind of woman who, once she had accepted him sexually, would let him establish over her an ascendancy which would allow him to dominate and direct their relationship.

He quickly found out that the easiest place for him to find this woman was among the ranks of young models attached to the fringes of the groups in which he mixed. Physically beautiful, they were almost always also insecure enough to be gratified by the attention he paid them, by the title he waved under their nose with just the right amount of modesty, by the names he dropped so carefully and nonchalantly. And then, when he had had enough of them, there was no problem in getting rid of them.

Tearful threats of suicide, protestations of loving him... Charles ignored them all. He was, as they soon discovered, impossible to blackmail emotionally.

With his uncle, knowing the control James ultimately had over his future, Charles was very careful to preserve an outward image of probity and seriousness, but, while James was never unpleasant to him, Charles knew that his uncle did not like him.

Another fault he laid at Geraldine Frances's door. Another crime for which she would ultimately pay.

Sometimes, lying in bed with his latest lover, sated and relaxed, he would study the body of the woman lying next to him, comparing her lissom lines with those of his grotesquely overweight cousin...comparing her sexual experience and skill with Geraldine Frances's total lack of it. It made him shudder to think of Geraldine Frances in the same state of wild abandonment reached by his lovers when he skilfully encouraged them to take just the right amount of drug to ensure that they gave him the maximum amount of pleasure.

Later, when the drug began to matter more to them than sex, he was quite happy to supply them so long as they could afford it. Once they could not afford it...well, that was their hard luck.

James's name and wealth admitted him to privileged circles which would otherwise have been completely closed to him, and he was beginning to find that there was a market for his drugs which far outstripped anything he had previously known.

Wealthy young socialites with their parents' money behind them, secure in their positions of privilege, soon learned what he was able to supply.

He began to receive invitations to the kind of parties where drugs were openly passed round...where there was no risk of anyone betraying a friend's habit...where people could afford to pay virtually whatever Charles chose to ask.

He had only one problem. Demand was beginning to outstrip what he could supply.

So far he had dealt discreetly and cautiously with other suppliers, wary of allowing himself to get dragged into water he might later find too deep. Once he was married to Geraldine Frances—once he had control of her wealth, of Rothwell—there would be no necessity for him to earn an income by drug dealing.

But now there was, and once he realised the extent of the money he could make supplying his wealthy, aristocratic peers he lost a little of his caution and decided that it was time to find a new and better source of supply.

Discreet questioning of all his existing sources gave him the same answer. The supply of drugs in London was controlled from one source. If he wanted a larger supply, they could give him a name... If he tried to bring in supplies from a source outside the city, those who controlled it would react in swift and dangerous retaliation.

For a month Charles hesitated, but in the end his greed won. He was invited to a coming out ball, held in the private home of one of the country's wealthiest peers. The ball was being held to celebrate the man's niece's eighteenth birthday. It was the most prestigious event Charles had so far attended, and he had been invited, he knew, purely because he had happened to drop James's name in the right ears.

This was no marquee-erected-on-the-lawn affair, but a glittering extravaganza held in a ballroom which almost rivalled that at Versailles.

The supper provided was as parsimonious as only the very, very wealthy could get away with, but the drink flowed generously, and Charles had the dubious privilege of being approached by the giggling and tipsy girl who was the focus of the whole affair, who had been 'dared' by her chums to invite Charles to help her celebrate achieving her majority by making love to her.

Charles cautiously refused. He had no wish to find himself the victim of a paternity suit, and certainly not for the dubious pleasure of having a rather plain and certainly dull young girl, who he knew quite well was unlikely to inherit anything more than a hundred thousand pounds.

Besides, he had other, far more important business to attend to.

He had been approached over and over again throughout the evening for drugs, and the greed that was so much part of his inheritance from his mother finally urged him to push caution aside and to make contact with the name he had been given.

The ball was well attended by representatives of the more up-market gossip Press. Charles dutifully posed for photographs with half a dozen carefully selected young men and women, all of whom in their own way were physically outstanding.

The photographer was a woman, bone-thin, dark-haired, sharp-featured, and Charles had to look at her twice before he recognised the pale blue eyes and re-alised who it was—she had slimmed down dramatically since their first unconventional meeting.

She raised her eyebrows mockingly when he approached her and said softly, 'Well, well, fancy meeting you here.'

She was not the kind of woman Charles would ever be drawn to, but he had never forgotten his initiation ceremony, the excitement she had engendered within him, the power he had sensed emanating from her.

'You still enjoy watching others play, I see,' he responded.

If she recognised the subtle threat of his words, the recognition he had that for her pleasure would always come from being in control...from being apart from rather than involved in...from being an observer rather than a participant, she didn't betray it.

'It's a job,' she told him, shrugging her shoulders. 'Speaking of which, here comes my boss...'

The man approaching them was tall and dark, very vigorous-looking despite the fact that he was well into his forties.

'Come along, Helen, my love,' he demanded. 'Stop making a play for the belle of the ball, and remember that you're here to work, not play...'

Homosexual, Charles recognised immediately, equally immediately making it subtly clear that he was anything but.

Homosexuals were outsiders...aliens...their particular pleasure had to be kept a secret if they wanted any kind of public life. The man who inherited Rothwell could never be gay.

Charles was no longer living with his mother, but rented a flat from a friend of a friend.

When he returned to it in the early hours of the morning, he discovered that his newly discarded lover had somehow or other managed to obtain a key and had destroyed everything capable of being destroyed in the place.

His mouth hardened. He would make her pay for that particular piece of folly, but in the meantime...the flat wasn't his and would have to be restored to what it had originally been... That would take money... Before he could change his mind he found the note he had made of the name he had been given and the telephone number, and punched the numbers into his phone.

The interview he had later with the anonymous man, who he was quite sure was not the one he had spoken to on the phone, was mutually beneficial. The interviewer was plainly impressed by his contacts, by the promise of the business he could bring in, by the amount of drugs he was prepared to take, and the business he could virtually guarantee already, and Charles in turn was impressed by the discretion and wariness evidenced by the fact that whomever he had spoken to was keeping his own real identity a secret and using a go-between.

Charles was particularly insistent about the precautions to be taken over the delivery of the drugs to him and his payment for them. In the end it was agreed that Charles would employ a cleaner, whose name he would be given, who would act as his contact with his supplier.

He found a new lover to replace the one he had abandoned, quickly discovered just how much money he could make from his drug dealing and for the first time in his life experienced something approaching contentment.

And then his mother died, and the realisation that he might after all find that his uncle might manage to alienate Geraldine Frances from him, and thus destroy his chances of ever possessing Rothwell, was brought sourly home to him.

Too well he understood what his uncle was trying to do, but he wasn't going to allow James to succeed... Geraldine Frances would marry him. No matter what he had to do to make sure of it, he *would* have Rothwell.

CHAPTER NINE

CHRISTMAS this year had been the happiest one she could ever remember, Geraldine Frances reflected blissfully, looking back on the short, ecstatic time she had spent with Charles, learned of his love and received her father's permission for Charles and herself to be unofficially engaged.

She frowned suddenly. Her father's enthusiasm for her future with Charles did not match hers, she knew, but he had not proffered any explanation for that lack of enthusiasm, and for some reason she was reluctant to press him for any. It was far easier and far, far more pleasurable for her to concentrate on the fact that she and Charles still had two whole precious days together before he had to return to London, rather than to worry about her father's lacklustre response to the announcement of their love for one another.

Tomorrow her father would be joining other members of the Belvoir hunt, and Charles would be going with him, while she remained here at Rothwell. While she loved the pageantry of the hunt, she hated its end result, and had long ago opted out of sharing her father's pleasure in that particular sport.

If she could change just one thing about this wonderful Christmas, it would have been its venue, she decided, staring out of the window across the frosted park of Rothwell. She would have preferred to spend Christmas in Ireland at Castle Kilrayne.

Charles had mocked her when she had told him as much. 'Gerry, *you* may love that monstrous heap of rocks, but I'm afraid I don't share your feelings. Rothwell, now...' His voice had softened betrayingly and she had recognised with almost a chill shrewdness, for the first time in her life, that it was possible for a human being to love an inanimate object or a place almost to the point of an obsession. But since it was an awareness she didn't want to have, since it showed her idol to have faults and flaws, and since she was still young enough to want Charles and her love for him to be totally without flaw or fault, she had dismissed the vague feeling of distaste that the look in his eyes had given her, turning away from him so that she didn't have to see it. She loved Rothwell herself, was proud of its history, its beauty, but it was, after all, only a house. A house filled with art treasures beyond price...a house which had belonged to her family for many generations...but still only a house, and the avid, hungry look in Charles's eyes when he spoke about it had frightened her.

The two of them had been alone in the huge book-filled room. It was over twenty feet high, with an arched ceiling covered in ornate plasterwork squares, each one depicting various hereditary arms appertaining to the family. Painted and gilded, the ceiling echoed the richness of the mahogany bookshelves, which ran the full height of the walls. A gallery encircled the room, reached by a curling wrought-iron staircase.

The original Aubusson carpet, now faded and slightly worn, still covered the polished floor. It had been woven to the special order of the eighth Earl.

Her father had been with the estate manager. Once, houses like Rothwell were supported by the income from the lands on which they stood, but no longer.

Geraldine Frances had looked at Charles... She could still not believe they were virtually engaged. He had been frowning, staring down into the fire, and a tiny *frisson* of disquiet had touched her skin, running coldly down her spine. She had wondered anxiously what his thoughts were and why he looked so distant, and she had ached for the confidence and the experience to go up to him...to touch that beautiful sculptured face...to see his mouth soften and smile, and to know that his smile, his attention, his love were for her and her alone.

Remembering those feelings now, she shivered a little. It was stupid of her to harbour these kind of insecurities, to worry that...

That what? That Charles's love for her was not as intense, as fierce, as all consuming as hers was for him? He was a man, she reminded herself, and men did not always show their feelings as easily as women. He had told her he loved her, hadn't he? Had said that he wanted her to be his wife? So why was she suffering this ridiculous mood of self-doubt...why did she wish she could keep Charles permanently at her side, when she knew that just wasn't possible?

The sound of the door to the sitting-room opening made her swing round, her worried expression changing to one of brilliant pleasure as Charles came in. He checked in the doorway, almost as though he hadn't expected her to be there. Almost as though he hadn't wanted her to be there...but even as the disquieting thought struck her, he was coming towards her, smiling his golden, caressing smile, holding out his hands to her as he exclaimed, 'Gerry...here you are! I thought you were cooped up with your father and Harding.'

John Harding was her father's estate manager, and traditionally whenever they were at Rothwell her father spent his mornings in the library going over estate matters with him.

'It's a pity your father doesn't do a bit more entertaining here at Rothwell,' Charles commented, releasing her quickly, after kissing her lightly on her forehead.

Quelling her disappointment at the brevity of his caress, guilty about her rebellious flesh's longing for something more intimate...more...intense, Geraldine Frances felt the sting of the lightly said words and looked at him miserably.

Charles led a very sociable life in London, she knew, and it was probably only natural that he should miss it when he was here. He was naturally gregarious where she was not, and as always when she suffered his displeasure she hunted round despairingly in her mind for something to placate him with.

'There's the hunt tomorrow,' she reminded him. 'You always enjoy that...'

His eyebrows rose, a look of cynicism hardening his face; someone older and more experienced than Geraldine Frances would have recognised his pleasure in tormenting and hurting her, but she was too young, too much in love to see below the dazzling, magnificent surface of his physical good looks.

'Hearty country types who live and breathe horses... Hardly my scene, Gerry...' He looked at his fingernails and said idly, 'I ought to be attending a dinner party in London tonight...'

And Geraldine Frances, frantic to keep him with her, fell immediately into his trap and cried out, 'Oh, no...no, please stay. You'll be gone so quickly, and I'm going to miss you so much...'

She blushed and stammered to a halt as she saw his amused expression, feeling that she had blundered emotionally in much the same way as her ungainly body made her blunder physically.

'My poor sweet.' Charles's voice caressed her. It gave him such pleasure to hurt her like this. He had lain in bed last night furiously assessing Rothwell and all its treasures, its titles and honours, the vast tracts of land and the huge secret investments that funded everything. He wanted it all, every smallest part of it. Like a refrain in his head he heard his mother saying that he should have had it all...that it was obscene that a girl should snatch it all away from him, and such a girl... He looked at her and shuddered inwardly, disgusted by the sight of her grossness. He compared her with his latest lover. *She* had a thick mane of glossy dark hair and a tiny, delicate face, high, firm breasts and long, long legs that twined themselves around him while she pleaded and begged for his possession.

His breathing quickened suddenly, his body going hard with triumphant arousal as he remembered the last night they had spent together before his coming down to Rothwell.

He had spent the night at her flat. She liked to use cocaine to increase her pleasure and she had tried to get him to do the same, but he was wary of using drugs and so had refused.

She had been excited, insatiable, doing things to him that had driven him out of his mind with pleasure.

Lost in his own thoughts, he wasn't aware of Geraldine Frances's approach. She touched his arm tentatively; beneath the thin cashmere of his sweater she could feel the silken rasp of body hair and the hardness of taut muscle.

She whispered his name uncertainly. His eyes glittered oddly. He seemed not to be looking at her, but past her, and as she touched him, unexpectedly and thrillingly he grabbed hold of her, gripping her flaccid flesh so hard that it hurt, dragging her against him and kissing her with fierce, demanding passion that made her body melt inside and her heart turn somersaults.

She cried out in pleasure and tried awkwardly to respond to his passion, but he was already releasing her...turning his back on her...

God, how he loathed her, and even loathing her he knew that he wasn't going to let her go...

But someone was going to have to pay for the humiliation he would have to endure in marrying Geraldine Frances...and who better than Geraldine Frances herself? He looked at her, her eyes bright with stunned pleasure, her fat fingers touching the trembling outline of her mouth as she looked at him with gratitude and adoration...with all the humble worship of a bitch for its master...and he felt a fierce, savage thrill of power. Oh, yes, he would make Geraldine Frances pay... His eyes narrowed and he remembered his mother telling him how necessary it was for him to marry Geraldine Frances. How important it was that he be nice to her...

Nice to her... My God, what he really wanted to do was to take hold of her throat and choke the life out of her... to destroy her and then to forget that she had ever existed. But he mustn't let her guess what he really felt. If she broke their engagement...if she married someone else... And there would always be someone shrewd enough and greedy enough to marry the sole heiress of the Earl of Rothwell.

His skin broke out in a cold sweat and he started to shake as the enormity of losing Rothwell hit him... No, he couldn't afford to alienate Geraldine Frances... But there were other ways...ways of subtle, delicate torment...ways in which he could keep that blind look of adoration in her eyes and yet punish her at the same time.

Geraldine Frances saw him shiver and asked uncertainly, 'What's wrong?'

Had she seen that bitter look of revulsion in his eyes? Charles looked at her and knew that he stood at the most important crossroads of his life. Alienate her now and he would lose everything. He must be careful not to betray to her how he really felt.

He said to her soothingly, 'Nothing...it's just... You're so very young, Gerry...and it's going to be a long time before we can marry...' He gave her the charming, insincere smile he had inherited from his father and shrugged disarmingly. 'I'm only human,' he told her, pausing meaningfully, while she blushed and looked openly stunned and delighted as his implication reached her. 'I want you,' he said softly. 'But your father won't approve if we become lovers before we're married.'

That cold moment of clarity when he realised how easily Rothwell could still slip through his fingers touched him again, like ice against his spine, warning him of his vulnerability.

'I wish we didn't have to wait so long.'

It had occurred to him that his safest course might be to get her pregnant, but he feared his uncle too much to take the risk.

'I'll speak to him,' Geraldine Frances told him breathlessly. 'I'll tell him we want to be married sooner than we planned.'

'I only wish we could...' A thought had occurred to him...a clever, dangerous thought. 'But I'm afraid it isn't possible, my darling. For one thing, I'm hardly in a position to support a wife...not yet...' He made a wry face. 'Of course, I'll get a small inheritance from Ma when I'm thirty-five...' It wasn't exactly a lie. There was a small inheritance...a very small inheritance, and he had no intention of spending it on anyone apart from himself. Of course, he could have afforded to marry had he wanted to; his earnings from his drug trafficking brought him in a very good income indeed.

'And I suppose your father will let us have the London house...'

He knew quite well that Geraldine Frances hated the London house because of its association with his mother...

He saw her frown and then she said uncertainly, 'But we could live on my money, couldn't we?'

Got her. She'd taken the bait. Fighting not to appear too eager, he forced a doubtful, tender look into his eyes and said softly, 'When I get married, I want to be able to support my wife myself...and besides...' a hard note entered his voice, but Geraldine Frances didn't hear it; she was too much in love...too wrapped up in her own delirious joy '...you don't *have* any money of your own yet, do you, my pet? It all belongs to Uncle James...'

Checked, Geraldine Frances frowned. What he said was quite true, though... She wouldn't come into any of the trust fund monies her father had established for her, to avoid death duties, until she was twenty-five.

'Well...yes.' She frowned, and then her face brightened. 'But I could ask Daddy to increase my al-

lowance. We could live here at Rothwell. I know how
much you like the house.'

Did she? He gave her a hard, bitter look, quickly
masked. Had she any real idea how he felt about
Rothwell... *his* Rothwell, not hers?

Another indulgent smile... a light touch on her hand,
making sure he didn't betray his physical revulsion at
the contact with her obese flesh.

'My darling, you weren't listening to what I said... I
couldn't live off my wife... No, I'm afraid we'll have
to wait until I'm going to earn enough to support you
myself...' He gave a theatrical sigh. 'Heaven knows how
long that will be...'

Geraldine Frances was normally very astute, but she was
barely seventeen years old and very much in love. No
one had ever warned her that men could and did use
women and their emotional vulnerabilities... No one
had ever urged her to use her head before her heart, and
just as soon as she could she went to her father, excitedly
begging him to find a way to boost Charles's income so
that they could be married immediately.

James looked sharply at his daughter, hiding his shock
from her. He had almost given up hope of her realising
the truth about her cousin, but he couldn't let them
marry yet. Charles was not fit to marry her, to take on
with her the burdens and responsibilities of her eventual
inheritance.

One had to be bred for such a role, he acknowledged
tiredly. *He* himself had been trained to do it from birth,
warned repeatedly by his father of how easily all that
his ancestors had garnered could slip through careless
fingers; and he, once he had realised she was to be his
only child, had in turn tutored Geraldine Frances. She
had a quick brain... she was already beginning to grasp
the complexities of the financial empire that supported
Rothwell, Castle Kilrayne and all their other properties... the necessity of generating income for their

preservation and protection. She already knew that her role was only one of guardian . . . that it was her duty to nurture and protect what they held and to pass it on to the next generation. But Charles would never have that instinctive inner knowledge . . .

He looked at Geraldine Frances and his heart ached for her. He wanted to warn her, to caution her, but how could he destroy the happiness in her eyes, the joy he could almost see burning in her? She needed time to come back down to earth . . . to accept reality . . . to understand that Charles was weak, and that it would always be on her shoulders that the responsibilities would rest.

If he allowed her to marry Charles now . . .

He was an astute man and knew well that it was Charles who was behind this sudden urgent desire for an immediate wedding. Charles was trying to force his hand. Well, Charles had a lot to learn.

Hiding his thoughts from his daughter, he took her hand and held it warmly in his own.

'So Charles wants to take you away from me already, does he?' he said lightly. 'Forgive me, Geraldine Frances, but I had hoped to have at least another summer with you, just the two of us, as it used to be before you went away to school . . . Remember, darling, you agreed, no formal engagement until you're eighteen.

'I don't want to stand in your way. It's selfish of me to want you all to myself. But once you and Charles *are* married . . .'

She was wavering, he could see it in her eyes.

'Let me speak to Charles and see if I can persuade him to allow us to have more time together,' he suggested softly, watching her.

She thought of the long, lonely years at school when she had ached to be with her father.

Please God let her agree, James prayed inwardly. There was still so much she had to learn.

'Well, if Charles doesn't mind,' she said uncertainly.

Charles minded very much, but there was nothing he could do about it. Geraldine Frances wasn't eighteen yet and couldn't marry him without her father's consent, and then there was the other problem of her inheritance. All she had until she was twenty-five was the allowance her father made her. If he forced the issue and married Gerry the moment she was eighteen, her father would retaliate by refusing to increase her allowance. Reluctantly he was forced to curb his impatience, his fear that Rothwell could still slip through his fingers. He knew he had an opponent in his uncle, but James was tied by his love for Geraldine Frances.

Two days later he left Rothwell to return to London. Geraldine Frances watched him go with sadness in her eyes, wishing they had had the privacy to exchange more than a mere kiss on the cheek as a goodbye, never dreaming that Charles had deliberately manoeuvred events so that he wouldn't have to be alone with her.

In February, after enjoying a good fortnight's hunting, and before he and Geraldine Frances left for Gstaad, James visited his doctor—a second visit.

His doctor had rooms in an elegant Georgian terrace in London. He was a tall, grey-haired, distinguished man who was adept at judging the temperaments of his patients.

With James he was shatteringly direct and honest.

'The results of the tests are back,' he confirmed. 'The news isn't good, I'm afraid. It's a progressive disease.' He named it and then interpreted briefly, 'Senile dementia.'

'Senile . . .?' James stared at him. He was in his mid-forties and outwardly looked vigorous and healthy.

'So far it's only in its very early stages,' the specialist told him. 'That's why it's been necessary to re-check the tests.' He pursed his lips and looked down at the floor.

'I have to be honest with you. There's no way the deterioration will regress once it starts, and no way of checking the progression of the illness. However, so far you are only in the very, very early stages, and progression, with luck, will be very slow. There are certain vitamin-based injections we can give you that may help, and new discoveries are being made every day...'

Slowly James shook his head, trying to clear his mind of the hideous fog engulfing it.

'Senile dementia... what is it?'

'Basically,' the doctor told him, 'it's caused by the death of certain brain cells at a faster rate than the usual ageing process. Once they *are* dead...'

'And its effects are physical?' James pressed.

'Physical and mental,' the specialist told him. And then waited while the shock of his announcement sank in.

He was more sorry for his patient than he wanted him to know. He was a man who virtually had everything a man *could* want... but twice now, three times if one included the death of his wife, he had suffered tremendous blows: once in losing his ability to produce children, and now this fresh blow.

Even he, with all his experience of life, shuddered a little as he contemplated James's future. The progression of his illness could be swift or it could be slow. There was no way of knowing... no way of knowing anything other than that, ultimately, James would be reduced to a totally dependent shell of the man he now was, suffering both mental and physical deterioration.

'No platitudes,' James said thickly. 'Just tell me the truth. How long...?'

'How long is a piece of string?' the doctor replied drily. 'There is no quantifiable period of time. It can be months, a rapid deterioration to the point where the patient is totally helpless, or it can be years before the deterioration becomes... noticeable.

'In your case, you're still only in the very early stages... Depending on what happens in the next, say,

twelve months, we should have a better idea of how
long...'

'Noticeable?' James, staring into the doctor's unblinking, pitying eyes, knew sickly what he was saying.

Rheumatism, arthritis, some kind of muscular
ageing...that was what he had assumed... Not this...not
this sentence of death while he was living.

He listened to everything the doctor had to say, then
got up and shook hands with him, noticing with grim
bitterness that this was one of the occasions on which
his muscle control did not fail him.

And then he walked out into the street. The air was
raw with the bitterness of an east wind, but he ignored
its coldness, hailing a cab and instructing the driver to
take him to the nearest public library.

Once there, he made straight for the medical section.

When he eventually emerged from the library it was
dark. He was glad. He couldn't have borne anyone to
see him... Not now, not when he was still trying to
grapple with the stark truth. He had been sentenced to
die...to gradually lose all physical and mental command
of himself...to become a parody of all that he was...had
been...

Oh, God... Why? Why? He wanted to scream the
words to the sky, but they were locked inside him like
the panic he refused to acknowledge.

One thought thundered in his head.

Geraldine Frances...Geraldine Frances... He must
prepare Geraldine Frances... Not for his death—he
couldn't lay that burden on her—but he must speed up
her preparation to take on the role that would be hers.
There were things he had to do...plans he had to make.

Her marriage to Charles... Too late now to wish that
he hadn't agreed to it. She loved him, or thought she
did...too late now to acknowledge what he had always
known: that Charles was no husband for his daughter.
No successor for him. God, if only Geraldine Frances

had been a son... That sharp brain, that keen intelligence...

If only he hadn't agreed to that unofficial engagement...if only he knew how much time he was going to have. He prayed to God it would be enough for him to make sure she would be ready to take over from him...enough for her to grow to maturity and realise Charles's lack of worth.

He toyed with the idea of telling her what he suspected her cousin was, but he knew he just couldn't do it to her... She was so young...so vulnerable. It was something within her that made his daughter vulnerable, he realised tiredly. She needed to be loved...to be cherished. In so many ways she was strong and intelligent, but she was still a woman. If he told her now that he suspected Charles only wanted to marry her because he wanted Rothwell, it would destroy her.

And besides...at the back of his mind, barely acknowledged but there, his first and most important fear was not for Geraldine Frances, not for his child, much as he loved her, but for Rothwell itself and all that it represented...the lands and titles held by his family through so many vicissitudes...lands and titles now vested in him...held by him in a form of sacred trust for future generations. Without Geraldine Frances's marriage to Charles there could well be no more generations...at least, not carrying the direct line of his blood. Another fear struck him. At all costs he must keep his illness a secret, for if Charles found out there would be nothing to stop him deserting Geraldine Frances, secure in the knowledge that ultimately, even if she should outlive him, Rothwell and all it stood for must eventually pass to his own offspring. For James was sure that if Charles destroyed his daughter's trust now, she would never ever be able to trust herself to another man, and Geraldine Frances, for all her strengths, was still too young, too immature to contemplate marrying for the sake of Rothwell alone.

He prayed as he had never prayed before that if he was granted no other boon, he was granted the ability to resist the slow destruction of his mind and body until Geraldine Frances had the wisdom and maturity to see, as he could now see, that in the end it was not the present that was important, but the future...that it was *Rothwell* that must come first, above personal feelings...above personal desires; that it was *Rothwell* that must survive, no matter what else might have to be destroyed to enable that to happen.

CHAPTER TEN

GERALDINE FRANCES found it hard to believe that two years had passed so quickly, but that was how long it had been since the Christmas Charles had declared his love for her. Now she was almost nineteen, and in all the time since she and Charles had become unofficially engaged she doubted that they had spent more than two months together.

At first she had missed him dreadfully, ached to be with him, scanned the British gossip Press when they were out of the country, hungrily gleaning what snatches of information she could.

Charles featured regularly in such articles. And why not? He was an extremely social and handsome man, always popular as a dinner party guest...as an escort...

She tried not to torment herself by wondering how many other women had tried to seduce him into their beds. *She* was the one he loved, and she must hold on to that knowledge.

There were times when it was hard, times when she saw him photographed with some lovely girl hanging on his arm and jealousy raked her with painfully sharp claws, making her reach for the phone, desperate for the sound of his voice, but always she managed to stop herself, to remind herself that their relationship must include trust...that she must learn to accept that they could not as yet spend all their time together.

When she *did* see him, he always seemed to be almost amused by the pain she tried so hard to hide, telling her carelessly that she had nothing to worry about, that *she* was to be his wife, and adding that her father had made him promise that there was to be no mention of their

203

new relationship until he himself gave permission for their engagement to be formally announced.

The last time she had broached the subject, after having seen him photographed in a society ball dancing with a girl who so plainly adored him that she had been unable to prevent herself from questioning him jealously about her, he had shrugged and said nonchalantly, 'My dear Gerry, what would you have me do? You don't know these carrion who feed off the social scene as I do. If I turned my back on women completely they'd be suggesting that I was gay... is that what you'd prefer?'

Poor Geraldine Frances hadn't known what to say. The truth was that she wanted Charles with *her*, that she suffered agonies every time she saw him photographed with someone else, or read about him escorting someone else, and was unable to stop comparing the partners he favoured with herself. *She* was so fat, so plain, and *they* were so lovely...

The sensible thing to have done would be to resist the temptation to read such articles, but they were a compulsion akin to her need to eat, and there was no way she could control it.

She ached to be with Charles, longed for his company, but there were so many things her father wanted to do... people he wanted her to meet... things he wanted her to learn.

And he, too, seemed to have changed. He had lost a lot of his old insouciance and become far more serious... far more intent. He had also started wearing glasses, complaining that he was having a small problem with his sight. Geraldine Frances had noticed when she was out with him that occasionally he seemed to hesitate or stumble, and she had teased him about it at first, until she had seen how much he disliked it.

It seemed a rather odd vanity in her father that he should resent becoming a little short-sighted, but she loved him too much to want to hurt him, so when he told her tersely that he didn't want his short-sightedness mentioned to anyone else, not even Charles, she accepted his dictate.

In the past two years they had spent very little time in England, and even less in Ireland, which she loved so much. Instead there had been months in New York, weeks in Switzerland, long hours and exhausting days spent listening to lawyers and accountants, meeting bankers and financiers, learning, always learning about the vast powerhouse of wealth that existed to feed and protect her inheritance... Wealth which had been accumulated mostly by her father, whose genius for financial affairs was something she herself had apparently inherited.

Three months ago she had learned all about the Queen granting her father a petition so that Geraldine Frances could be allowed to inherit his titles, and, through her, her children.

She had been touched and amused by her father's determination to transfer them to her. After all, Charles was the next male in line, and when she was his wife their children would in any case inherit through him, but her father had been adamant, refusing to say anything other than that he wanted *her* to carry the title.

The fortune he had made was different; it was his personally, and would not have been entailed with the title. Her grandfather had had the foresight to protect what monies did go with the earldom and Rothwell itself from the ravages of death duties, and her father had done exactly the same thing. But he wasn't just making sure of her inheritance, he was ensuring that she would be competent to deal with it. To nurture it and protect it, and most of all to nurture and protect Rothwell.

It had come as something of a surprise to her to discover how strongly her father felt about Rothwell. He had spent so much of his life travelling that she had not realised how passionately he felt about the house and land. Again and again he made her promise that she would always remember that Rothwell itself, the titles, the land were a sacred trust and that they must be passed over into no other hands...not even those of her husband... Hopefully, he told her, *she* would have the sons he had been denied.

'Teach them well,' he had said. 'Because it is on their shoulders that the future of Rothwell will fall.'

Dutifully she gave him her promise, while at the same time reminding him cheerfully that he himself would probably be able to see his grandsons growing up.

'You aren't senile yet,' she had teased him, and James, the specialist's words always there in his mind, had turned away from her so that she shouldn't see the helpless anguish he knew must be in his eyes. No, he wasn't senile yet...but the deterioration had begun. Slowly, oh, so slowly...barely perceptible on his good days...but there were other times... He shuddered and prayed that his daughter's children would have longer to grow up in than he could allow her.

Already he could see the signs of maturity touching her, signs of which she herself was unaware. He was shamed by the desire he still had that if he must only have a female child she might at least have been physically attractive. It was not Geraldine Frances's fault that she was the way she was, and, worse, he knew that inwardly she *did* have beauty and grace.

It grieved him beyond measure to acknowledge that even he, knowing of that beauty and grace, should still look upon her and wish that fate had been generous enough to bestow an outer façade to match that inner beauty, and not just for her own sake.

James Fitzcarlton was a man who, all his adult life, had enjoyed the company of beautiful women. Geraldine Frances's mother had been one of them. Small, delicate, she had possessed all the fragility and high breeding that went with being the daughter of one of America's first WASP families. Their marriage had been a dynastic one, each of them aware of what they were bringing to it, but they *had* shared mutual desire, mutual respect, and, even

though he suspected that they might not have remained
faithful to one another, James knew their marriage would
have endured.

During the years since her death, there had been many
discreet, orderly affairs, in the main with women who
moved within the same social circles as he did himself—
generally married or divorced women, especially after
he discovered that he couldn't father any more children.

How bitterly that had rankled. Margaret, coming upon
him at a weak moment, just after he had discovered that
the childish disease he had picked up from Geraldine
Frances had left him sterile, had listened to his furious
burst of temper against fate... against his wife for
dying... against Geraldine Frances for being a girl and
against himself for thinking he had all the time in the
world to provide Rothwell with an heir.

Now there would be no heir other than his daughter.

Margaret hadn't liked that. Her son was his heir, she
had objected angrily. It was ridiculous to even think of
leaving such a vast inheritance to Geraldine Frances... a
girl. And James had known illuminatingly then, without
her having to say it, how much she had resented his birth,
his taking from her Rothwell and all that it stood for.
He had always known she resented him, but until then
he had not known how much... or why.

After that he had watched Charles closely, acknowledging that the boy had the all-important Fitzcarlton
blood. But he also had his father's weaknesses... He
was right to believe that the responsibilities of Rothwell
could not be left safely in his hands—right to have begun
his petition to the Queen.

As the year drew to a close, James watched his daughter
closely. Her intelligence, her astuteness outmatched even
his own; her quick grasp of essential data, and the sheer
breadth of her ability to use that data, delighted him.

Sitting round a boardroom table, she commanded respect...sitting at a dinner table was a different matter altogether.

She had lost little weight during the year, and when she spoke of Charles her eyes glowed with love, but that only served to emphasise the paucity of her physical gifts, and it was with terrible sadness that James admitted that she would probably marry Charles and that there was nothing he could do to stop it—but not just because *his* time was running short and his love for her was such that he wanted to protect her for now and for the future. Not even because he knew how desperately she loved her cousin...loved him, adored him, ate, dreamed and talked him every day of her life.

It was the broader view he had to consider...the future which he would never see. Above and beyond his instinctive desire to protect his daughter from the pain he already knew her marriage would bring was his duty to protect Rothwell.

If he told her of his doubts about Charles...if he destroyed her trust in him, her love for him, she would be left alone. He wondered how long then it would take her to realise that if she didn't marry and have a child...children...Rothwell would eventually pass to Charles and to *his* children.

If only he could be sure that he could hold off the devastation that threatened him...

Their travels had had a secondary purpose, and one which he had kept hidden from Geraldine Frances.

She must have a husband; that was clear to him. She *had* to marry and have children, otherwise Charles's children would inherit on her death, and he knew his nephew well enough to know that Charles *would* marry and produce those children.

Throughout their travels he had been carefully assessing the sons of his business acquaintances and friends, watching their reaction to Geraldine Frances at the skilfully arranged meetings that threw them into her company. Their reaction was depressingly similar. They were invariably polite to her, well mannered and sometimes even kind, but nothing could hide the fact that physically they were unresponsive to her as a woman.

There would be no husband for Geraldine Frances among their ranks, that much was obvious to him.

In the most private recesses of his soul he acknowledged his hope that somehow a miracle might occur: that Geraldine Frances would somehow or other metamorphose into, if not a beautiful, then at least a passably attractive young woman, attractive enough to appeal to a man who wanted her for more than the fact that she was James's heiress, a man whom he could like and respect, whom he could trust...a man who was not Charles.

No, those hopes were fading. In London Charles was waiting...knowing...James would not be able to fob Geraldine Frances off with well-intentioned fibs much longer. Soon she would be asking him to make good his promise to allow her and Charles formally to announce their engagement.

He had done all he could to safeguard her future, and, more important, to safeguard Rothwell. There was no way Charles could break the trusts he had set up for Geraldine Frances and her children, no way he could overset his explicit instructions, but once he, James, was dead Geraldine Frances would have total control of everything. Could he trust her to hold to her promise to him, not to allow anyone, not even Charles, to take over that control? She was so vulnerable where her love for Charles was concerned...

Already, without her knowledge, he had made other provisions...signed powers of attorney so that, when the inevitable happened, she would be able to smoothly take over the reins he would be forced to relinquish, and without Charles being able to interfere.

His lawyers, those grey, shadowy men in Switzerland and the equally skilled firm he employed in London,

knew all there was to know, and they would not fail
him. Legally he had made everything just as secure as
he could, but there was no way he could legislate for
Geraldine Frances's emotions, or for Charles's greed.

He ached to be at Rothwell . . . longed for it with an
intensity that was unfamiliar, as though his very soul
was starved for the tranquil familiarity of it . . . He who
had always been so restless, who had always enjoyed
travel and variety, now wanted nothing more than to sit
in his library and look out over Rothwell's magnificent
park.

He told Geraldine Frances they would be going home
for Christmas, wishing her delight were not so obviously
caused by the thought of seeing Charles.

That evening she wrote to Charles telling him they
would soon be on their way home.

Charles read the letter and laughed cruelly over its shy
declarations of love. That fat, boring lump . . . Did she
really believe he could love something like her? Hadn't
she got the wit to see it was *Rothwell* he wanted, and
that *she* was simply the price he had to pay for getting
it?

After James had refused to admit him to his confidence financially, and to share his business dealings with
him, Charles had ostensibly gone into business with an
acquaintance as a financial consultant.

The business was a good screen for his drug dealing,
and gave a plausible explanation for the generous income
he seemed to receive.

When his partner left to set up in business on his own,
Charles announced that he was closing down the office
and intended to conduct his future business from the
Rothwell Square house. It was a very convenient arrangement. The clients who visited the house were invariably young, wealthy, and often socially well
connected. The pretence that Charles was advising them
on their business affairs was one that suited both parties.

In reality, the fees that Charles charged them were indirect payments for the drugs he was supplying to them.

His reputation passed by word of mouth and the number of clients he supplied increased. He was invited everywhere. Occasionally he came into contact with some of his fellow pupils from school, but very few of them were privileged enough to move in the same social milieux he inhabited.

Helen Cartwright was the one exception to that rule. She was fast gaining a reputation as a first-rate photographer, and was now a personality in her own right, no longer photographing social affairs for glossy magazines but flying all over the world to different locations, commissioned by a variety of top-quality journals.

Charles saw her occasionally, sometimes with a man in tow, more often not. When they met, neither of them mentioned their shared schooldays. Charles had sometimes wondered if she might be gay; if so, she concealed it very well.

The thought of spending Christmas with Geraldine Frances held no appeal at all.

He had a new lover—not one of his insecure models this time, but the daughter of a prominent Catholic barrister to whom he had been introduced at one of the many parties he attended.

She was the same age as Geraldine Frances, but there the similarity ended. Outwardly quiet, almost enough to be described as unfashionably chaste, beneath her demure exterior she concealed a sexual appetite like nothing he had ever known.

For the first time in his adult life he came close to experiencing something approaching the intense sexual ecstasy he had felt during that unforgettable initiation ceremony.

She had the ability to drive him outside his normal caution and discretion, and, even while he was aware of the risk he was taking in openly squiring her at so many social events, he was powerless to stop himself... He didn't love her, his emotions weren't engaged in the least, but he desired her, lusted for her, needed her with an intensity that refused to be sated.

She had an expensive taste for cocaine, which was how he had first come to know her. When they made love she liked to rub the stuff on his body and then inhale it. He shuddered suddenly, his body urgently aroused. It was always like this when he thought about her. Sometimes he could barely wait to get her inside the house before taking her, quickly, savagely tearing at her clothes and her flesh, driving into her until she screamed with pleasure.

She was the first woman he had allowed to stay overnight at the Rothwell Square house. So far he had resisted her urgings to allow her to move in. If she had one fault it was her jealousy... She had no idea about Geraldine Frances, but then no one had; he had taken good care to make sure they did not. Obeying his uncle's dictate that nothing was to be said about any potential relationship until he gave his permission for the formal announcement of their engagement suited Charles admirably.

But now he sensed time running out on him. At first, when James had announced his intention to travel and to take Geraldine Frances with him, he had worried that he might lose her...that someone else might see her value and snatch Rothwell away from him. But, if anything, her absence from him had only strengthened her feelings for him. Her letters bore witness to that.

Now she was coming home and he was summoned to Rothwell for Christmas. It would be the usual boring affair. A very dull Christmas Eve, handing out presents and bonuses to the staff. Church on Christmas Day morning, with James reading the lesson in the local village church. Lunch at Rothwell, just the three of them, and afterwards the opening of the presents, followed by a cold and dreary walk through Rothwell's parkland, before supper.

On Boxing Day there would be a small and very dull round of cocktail parties to attend, and then possibly a couple of days' hunting with the Belvoir.

One of his biggest problems was going to be getting Thérèse to accept that he couldn't spend Christmas with her, but luckily, before he could broach the subject, she told him that she had been summoned home by her father in order to spend Christmas with her family.

Wrinkling her nose at him, she said wryly, 'I suppose he wants to read me another lecture, poor darling...he's so strict and uptight, it just isn't true. He's dying for me to get married and produce lots and lots of little Catholic grandchildren...' She gave a deep, throaty laugh, her hand caressing Charles's bare thigh, sliding upwards to torment his flesh.

'It won't be for long, though, darling... I should be back well before the New Year...'

She laughed as he caught hold of her, taking her nipple between his teeth and savaging it roughly in the way he knew aroused her.

On their way home James and Geraldine Frances stopped off in Geneva, ostensibly for James to hand over to her her Christmas present, which was a case holding her mother's jewels, but in reality so that he could visit a specialist whom his own doctor had recommended to him.

It was just as he himself had known. The disease was slowly advancing...taking hold... Over the months there had been small signs. His brain was usually as alert as ever, but sometimes he suffered attacks of confusion and panic, even more terrifying in their way than the realisation that neither his eyesight nor his co-ordination were all they had once been...

'You're a very fit man,' the specialist told him, 'in many ways far more healthy than most men of your age.

Because of that, it will probably be some time before your condition starts to become noticeable. When it does...' James shuddered inwardly. There was no point in hoping for a miracle.

That night he told Geraldine Frances that if it was still what she wanted he was prepared to announce her engagement to Charles on her next birthday.

She was ecstatic. They had been travelling on her eighteenth birthday when the engagement should have been announced, and she had despaired that they would ever return home to make her and Charles's news official.

As they flew into London James acknowledged his bitter sense of failure. All he could pray for now was that Charles might have had a change of heart... or that he would do something so spectacularly damaging to the image Geraldine Frances had of him that the scales would fall from her eyes and she herself would break free of her enchantment.

If that happened, it would bring problems of its own, problems to which he had been giving a great deal of thought. As yet he had found no solution to them, or at least, not one that would be acceptable to his daughter, but the gut feeling he had that Charles would somehow or other contrive to destroy everything that Rothwell was would not go away. Better to pay some unknown man to impregnate his daughter with the son she needed to keep Charles from inheriting after her than to allow Charles to marry her, but that could only happen if she chose it of her own accord, if she was driven to it by the recognition of what Charles really was and of how impossible it would be to allow him any kind of control over Rothwell. Women were rarely as logical and far-sighted in these things as men, James mused, especially women like Geraldine Frances.

As the plane landed James acknowledged that, even in his wildest flights of fancy, such an outcome was impossible.

Charles was far too clever to make the kind of mistake that would lead to Geraldine Frances's becoming disillusioned with him and rejecting him.

Charles delayed his arrival at Rothwell until as late on Christmas Eve as possible. Geraldine Frances waited up to welcome him, and the moment he stepped into the hallway and saw her, his gorge rose.

She hadn't changed, unless it was to become even more gross than ever.

He fended her off quickly as she approached him, yawning and complaining that he was exhausted.

Geraldine Frances had been waiting for him all day, her excitement dimming to anxiety as the hours passed; and now, swiftly, that anxiety turned into aching despair and disappointment. She had longed for him so much...wanted him so much—spent endless nights imagining how it would feel to be held in his arms.

He was as handsome as ever, even more so than she had remembered, if that was possible, his hair and skin still the same warm gold. So why was it that for a moment his image seemed to dull and tarnish?

Charles saw his mistake and quickly retrieved it, taking hold of her hands, ignoring the soft unpleasantness of her almost boneless flesh.

'Forgive me, my love. Hardly a romantic reunion, I know, but I'm so damned tired... I didn't think you'd be wonderful enough to wait up for me...' He gave her his special smile, that blend of humour and coaxing that was so effective. 'Will you hate me for ever if I go straight to bed?'

Geraldine Frances thought about the special supper she had ordered, the bottle of her father's best burgundy that was open and breathing in the small sitting-room...she thought about the news she had for him, the excitement with which she had planned telling him that they could be formally engaged; and then she quelled her disappointment as childish and rather silly, responding to Charles's smile and saying with an attempt at light-heartedness, 'Only because you're going there without me...'

Thank God! Charles thought, but said instead, 'Ah, don't tempt me... Your father seems determined to keep us apart...'

He was already walking towards the stairs, but Geraldine Frances followed him eagerly.

'Not any more,' she told him excitedly, halting him. 'Oh, Charles, isn't it wonderful? Daddy says we can get engaged officially on my next birthday.'

Concealing his expression from her, Charles reminded himself that it wasn't Geraldine Frances he was marrying, it was Rothwell...Rothwell. As always, the thought of losing the house and everything it represented acted on him like a goad, and he felt a resurgence of his old fear that somehow or other his uncle would contrive to wrest it from him. That mustn't be allowed to happen.

Turning round, he took hold of Geraldine Frances's hands again and, lifting them to his mouth, said thickly, 'My darling, that's wonderful news...wonderful.'

And with that Geraldine Frances had to be satisfied, because Charles had already adroitly released himself and was heading upstairs.

Why, when he had called her his darling, and accepted her announcement with every evidence of real pleasure, did she somehow feel cheated...anxious... fearful almost?

Telling herself she was being a fool, she lumbered miserably after him, heading for her own room.

Christmas Day was very much as Charles had known it would be. His gift to Geraldine Frances was the triple strand of pearls which had once been his mother's.

She received it bleakly, trying not to think of the long hours she herself had spent looking for just the right gift... In the end she had chosen not one but several.

In Paris there had been the irresistible Fabergé egg covered in gold and ornamented with lapis lazuli in exactly the same deep, dense shade of blue as Charles's eyes.

In New York she had commissioned for him an expensive set of luggage, and in Switzerland, following a hunch of her own, she had bought him shares in a newly formed computer technology company, which she personally thought was going to go places.

James's mouth tightened as he looked at the pearls and recognised that they had not even been restrung. They had been his parents' twenty-first birthday gift to his sister. He thought bitterly of his daughter's open adoration of Charles and reflected that it would have cost little for him to buy Geraldine Frances something which genuinely was from himself, instead of simply handing her his mother's pearls.

Geraldine Frances affected to be thrilled. In reality she was deeply upset. Charles knew how she felt about his mother, and yet he had given her her pearls. She knew as she closed the leather case that she would never wear them.

Her father gave her a portfolio of shares and her eyes had gleamed with anticipation as she read through them. All of them were companies they had discussed during the year, most of them small and as yet unprofitable, but she and her father knew their real value.

He also gave her a pair of diamond earrings, solitaire studs to wear in the ears she had had pierced in New York.

She didn't put them on immediately. As always, she was acutely conscious of her physical appearance. She was wearing one of the dresses she had had made to order, a dull, thick tweed that did nothing for her colouring but which she believed, in its plainness, helped not to draw attention to her fatness.

Surreptitiously during the last year she had started dieting, but with limited success. The heavy business lunches and dinners...the hunger pangs that attacked her almost constantly...the misery she felt at being away from Charles so much...her own inner despair over the way she looked. She longed for some reassurance...for Charles to look at her and know what she was feeling, to tell her lovingly that it was she, the person whom he was marrying, whom he loved, and not the outer casing of bulging flesh.

Her initial bright, fierce pleasure in their love had become tainted and weakened by insecurity. She so rarely saw Charles, and when she did there was a distance between them, a lack of opportunity for any real intimacy, a suffocating awareness on her part of how different they were physically... She had gone from delirious awe and joy that Charles, so male, so handsome, so almost godlike, should by some miracle choose to love her, to a sick fear that one day Charles would look at her and see her not as he did now, with his eyes dazzled by their love, but as others saw her: bloated, unattractive, unappealing physically in every way.

Oddly, in some ways when she was with him her self-doubts were increased rather than reduced. She longed for Charles to banish her fears, to take her in his arms, to show her physically and passionately that he wanted her.

And at the same time she was vaguely ashamed of such feelings, of the desires that tormented her at night when she was alone, of the intense, secret excitement she felt at the thought of Charles wanting her, touching her.

Tomorrow Charles would be leaving. He had pressing business to attend to in London before joining her father for several days' hunting with the Belvoir. Because her dislike of hunting was so well known to him, the host, with the best motives no doubt, had not included her in the invitation.

She looked at Charles; he was leafing through a copy of *Tatler*. As she watched, he frowned suddenly, studying one of the pages closely.

Curiosity took her to his side. He was studying a group photograph taken at the kind of social party Geraldine Frances most disliked, but she hid this as she said lightly, 'They look as though they're having fun. Anyone you know?'

Charles heard the jealousy in her voice and hid his triumph. In point of fact he knew all of them, but cleverly he picked out from among the soft, pretty if rather vacuous faces of the girls the one who he knew would soothe Geraldine Frances's fears. Now was not the time to let her know how plain and dull he found her.

'Yes, as a matter of fact. I know this girl. Helen Cartwright. She and I were at school together. She's getting quite a name for herself as a photographer.'

There was a note in his voice that Geraldine Frances couldn't quite analyse, but one look at the face of the girl in the photograph was enough to reassure her that she was no beauty and, besides, she had more important things to worry about than one of Charles's old schoolfriends.

Tonight was her last chance to be alone with Charles. She knew which was his room, of course. The colour came and went in her face at the thought of what she was contemplating.

But why not? They were practically formally engaged now, and they would not be having a long engagement. Other couples in their situation made love . . . and, since Charles had already said that he could not spare the time to come skiing with them, it would be another two months at least before she was able to see him again.

Buoyed up by the excitement-cum-dread of what she was planning, Geraldine Frances went to bed early. Charles watched her go with well-hidden relief.

He was going to marry her—nothing could change his determination on that point; he had to marry her to get Rothwell—but that didn't alter the fact that physically he found her revolting. He would have to bed her, of

course, and not just to make the marriage legal. He
wanted sons, the sons for Rothwell that fate had denied
his uncle. As he said goodnight to her, smiling falsely
into her eyes, lifting her hand to his mouth and feeling
her tremble as he touched the hot, moist flesh of her
wrist, he hoped cynically that she would prove fertile.

Geraldine Frances, with no idea of what was really in
his mind, left the room, her heart thudding with excitement. There had been such promise, such pleasure
in his eyes as they had said goodnight. Her excitement
rose...

She had left her door open slightly so that she would
hear Charles when he walked down the corridor to his
own bedroom.

She waited for five minutes after he had closed the
door behind him, her stomach muscles clenched with
tension. She was undressed, wearing one of the plain
cotton nightdresses that had been part of her school
uniform. Over it she pulled on an ancient dressing-gown
that had been her father's, refusing to look at herself in
the Adam pier glass as she passed it, knowing too well
what she would see. She couldn't bear to see that billow-
ing, fat, plain reflection, not now when she needed all
her faith, all her frail belief in her inward femininity to
give her the courage she needed.

When she walked into his bedroom Charles was just
picking up the telephone receiver. He saw her and
dropped it, a look of acute disgust crossing his face and
transfixing her where she stood just inside the door.

She started to tremble with shock, knowing sicken-
ingly that she had done the wrong thing.

Tears filled her eyes. She turned for the door, stumbling over the hem of her dressing-gown, and Charles,
who had realised a fraction too late just what he was
betraying, resisted his body's physical command to let
her go, quelling its inner revulsion as he rushed to the
door ahead of her and slammed it shut.

She stared at him, and he forced his features not to betray what he was feeling. God, but she was ugly. The thought of touching her...those layers of fat tissue...

'Geraldine, darling... My God, what are you doing here?'

Geraldine Frances stopped and looked at him, desperately wanting to believe the soft promise of that 'darling', willing herself to forget the look she had seen on his face, trembling agitatedly as she tried to think of a logical explanation and, finding none, having to say humbly, and awkwardly, 'I wanted to be with you. I hardly ever see you. We're never alone together; I thought...'

Her face betrayed her, as she looked past him and at the bed.

Charles felt himself starting to sweat. Dear God, not now...he couldn't face that now... But neither could he think of alienating her.

Controlling his loathing, he gave a small soft groan, but didn't touch her, swinging round so that he wouldn't have to look at her, bowing his head in a gesture of mock defeat.

'Darling, I know, I know...I want you, too...I want to be with you, to hold you...but you must see that it isn't possible...' He heard her move behind him and knew that he must convince her, that he couldn't let her leave the room until he had. Stifling all his inner revulsion, he turned round and took her in his arms. She was almost his height now, and when she leaned her head on his shoulder he felt smothered by the weight of her.

'You must see how it is. If I made love to you now, I could easily make you pregnant...' He felt the shudder run through her and ached to push her away. Unlike James, he couldn't see her inner beauty and gentleness, nor did he want to. He saw only the outer image...an image that revolted him.

'My darling, much as I want you to stay, you must see that that isn't possible.'

She ached inside for him; being so close to him was making her feel dizzy with the pain of it. She moved against him, instinctively seeking relief from the tormenting sensation in her breasts.

Charles tensed. Oh, God...he wasn't going to be able to persuade her... He couldn't touch her now, not now...he needed time...

'Gerry, please...don't make this hard for me...' His voice grated and for a moment it was almost like listening to his mother.

She frowned and looked up at him, knowing that what he was saying made sense, but longing to stay with him.

'We can't take that kind of risk,' he told her softly. 'You must realise that...'

She looked at him...a dogged look of determination...an aching look of need.

And then, ducking her head, she said huskily, 'But we needn't do that, need we? I mean...there are other ways...other things... We don't actually have to...' The frustration driving her welled up inside her, and she clung to him desperately, 'Charles, please let me stay. I want you so much. I love you so much.'

Of course she did, he thought mirthlessly. *He* had made sure of that fact, but why on earth couldn't the fat fool see that the very last thing he wanted was her gross physical presence? And yet one part of him was reminding him that it would do no harm to make absolutely sure of her, to make sure of James, who he knew quite well would have moved heaven and earth to stop the marriage if it weren't for the need for Geraldine Frances to produce sons. It was one thing for him to feel sure that no man would even think of trying to take her from him; the world was full of unscrupulous, hungry people, and it only needed one of them to realise what marriage to Geraldine Frances would give him.

He ground his teeth, his eyes narrowing on Geraldine Frances's flushed, unhappy face. If he got her pregnant now, he wouldn't have to touch her again for nine months, and James would be down on his knees begging him to marry her... He liked the idea of that... he liked it very much... He began to smile... He could even torment them both a little by pretending to have second thoughts... by...

Geraldine Frances saw the look he was giving her and couldn't interpret it. Her heart started to pound. He was going to let her stay after all. And then someone rapped on the heavy door, and she heard her father say calmly, 'Charles, is Geraldine Frances here? I wanted to have a word with her. I'm leaving for the City early in the morning...'

And as Charles stepped back from her she knew that the moment was lost. Her heart and body ached tormentingly for what might have been as she lumbered unhappily away from Charles and towards the door.

CHAPTER ELEVEN

GERALDINE FRANCES stared resignedly out of her bedroom window. Rothwell felt so vast and empty with both Charles and her father gone.

They had left within an hour of one another, immediately after an early breakfast.

Charles had business to attend to, and, while she could applaud his industry, Geraldine Frances couldn't help wishing that he could have put his clients off so that they could have spent this last day together, especially since her father was absent.

He, too, had business in the City, a lunch appointment with an old friend who was seeking his advice on some investment matters. Their lunch would extend until well into the afternoon, he had told Geraldine, and so instead of returning to Rothwell he would stay overnight at his London club before leaving for Belvoir in the morning.

Now, when it was too late, she was beginning to regret that she had not been included in the invitation. She need not have hunted, and at least she would have seen Charles in the evenings.

When she had suggested that instead of accompanying her father he might return to Rothwell, Charles had reminded her that he was not a wealthy man, that he had a living to earn, and that mingling with the other guests might, if he was lucky, bring him in some new clients.

Once again Geraldine Frances had not been able to find any fault with the business logic of his statement, but her heart felt sore all the same.

She went downstairs, and wandered aimlessly through the house. Most of the staff were on holiday, spending time with their families. The huge portraits of past earls and their countesses stared down at her as she walked down the stairs. She searched their aristocratic features, looking in vain for some resemblance to her own plainness, but there was none.

Had the artists flattered their sitters, or was it just some malevolent act of fate that had decreed that she, and she alone, should be marked out so excruciatingly?

Downstairs she walked into the library and picked up a handful of trade journals. She might as well catch up with her reading; there was nothing else for her to do.

She looked outside. It was a cold, crisp day, with frost whitening the grass. Ideal hunting weather, and just treacherous enough underfoot to add that extra exhilaration of danger that her father loved so much.

Once she would have enjoyed the cold freshness of such a day herself, either riding or walking, but oddly, since she had grown so obese, she felt the cold in a way she had never done before.

Now she shivered, despite the central heating and the vast fire burning in the library grate.

The coldness was inside, she recognised...and not just a coldness, but an emptiness as well. Despite the fact that it was less than an hour since she had finished her breakfast, she put down the journals and headed resolutely for the kitchen.

The atmosphere of breathless silence that greeted her as she walked in made her ears burn. She had hoped that the kitchen would be empty, but the staff were having their coffee-break, and so she was forced to retreat in stumbling disorder. Both the girls sitting at the table were about her own age, small, dark-haired and enviably slender. Tears welled in her eyes as she hurried back to the library. Upstairs in her wardrobe, hidden behind her clothes, were tins of biscuits and sweets, huge bars of chocolate...cheese and biscuits... She needed

their comfort now to warm the cold place deep inside
her... She needed it so badly...

Later she knew would come the inevitable self-disgust
and loathing...the silent vows never to touch another
morsel of food until she was thin...never again to indulge in anything so disgusting, so—primitive—but while
she was gorging herself on her hoarded food nothing
mattered but the need to cram it into her mouth as
quickly as she could.

The day stretched emptily in front of her. She had no
friends she could telephone or visit, and even if she had,
it was *Charles's* company she wanted, not another
woman's.

In London, James's lunch went on even longer than
he had anticipated. It was dark before he eventually left
the Connaught. Inhaling the cold crispness of the winter
air, he decided against using a taxi. He would walk instead. Do him good to have a bit of exercise... All that
food and port was sitting far too heavily on his stomach,
and he had a hard few days ahead of him... The walk
would clear his head.

Halfway to his club, he suddenly remembered that he
had intended to telephone Charles to ask if he wanted
a lift down to Belvoir in the morning.

Much as he might privately dislike his nephew, James
had a highly developed sense of family pride; an old-
fashioned trait which demanded that, no matter what
went on privately, in public the family put up a united
front. It was something he had developed through his
father's training.

And so he changed direction and headed for Rothwell
Square.

Realising the value of the London property he had
inherited from his father, investing in it by improving
the tall Georgian houses and having them restored and
renovated, had been one of his earliest financial coups.
Now the leases on these properties brought into the estate
a very good income indeed.

The difference between the worth of selling the property outright and holding on to it, letting it out on lease, had been one of the first things he had taught Geraldine Frances.

In every lease was the stipulation that no alterations whatsoever could be made to the plain, almost austere Georgian façades of the houses, nor could the rows of iron railings that separated their basements from the pavement be painted anything other than very dark green tipped with gold that made Rothwell Square stand out so distinctively from its fellows.

The small enclosed private garden to which only inhabitants of the square had access had rails of the same colour, tall, elegant plane trees underplanted with bulbs that flowered in the spring, smooth green lawns, and an ornamental fountain flowing into a circular stone pond inhabited by some large, fat goldfish, said to have been put there by his great-grandfather.

By a stroke of luck, thanks to the family habit of never discarding anything, the original gas-lamps, installed in the mid-eighteen-hundreds, had been found stored away in the old carriage house at Rothwell.

James had had them re-installed, and the effect as one turned the corner and entered the square was almost of stepping back into the nineteenth century.

Another of James's decrees was that no inhabitant of the square was allowed to park his car, no matter how grand, in front of the houses. To their rear all of them retained their original coach-houses, and it was here that present-day leaseholders were able to garage their Rollses and Mercedeses.

No one who was anything short of a millionaire had the wherewithal to lease a property in Rothwell Square, but, despite that fact, there was always a waiting-list of eager applicants when a lease became available.

Rothwell Square was undoubtedly one of London's most prestigious addresses. When he remembered the run-down and shabby state in which it had been when he had inherited it, James reflected that it was perhaps not surprising that he should stand at its entrance himself, momentarily admiring its elegance.

Perhaps it was a fanciful notion, but he rather thought that even Robert Adam himself would have found little to cavil at in its present-day appearance.

Such modern vulgarities as festoon blinds, bay trees in tubs and sundry other fashionable items had no place in Rothwell Square.

The house he had deeded to his sister, in a rash moment of impulsive guilt, was the largest in the square. When Margaret had been wont to describe herself to her closest cronies as 'virtually penniless', she had conveniently overlooked the fact that she was living rent-free in one of London's most elegant 'small' houses, if a four-storey town house possessing six bedrooms, three bathrooms, a drawing-room, a library, a dining-room plus, on the ground floor, a kitchen, sitting-room, and another sitting-room for the staff, could ever be described as small.

In an equally rash moment James had allowed her to plunder Rothwell's attics in order to furnish it, and then, because she had insisted that what furniture she had been able to find was all in need of restoration and re-covering, he had also allowed her to call in Colefax and Fowler and others of their like to transform what she had described as a positive hovel into something suitable in which she could live.

All too conscious of the fact that to his sister, having grown up at Rothwell, nothing else would ever be truly acceptable, James had said nothing about the size of the bills with which he had been ultimately presented.

Now, however, as he looked at the first and most imposing house in the square, he started to frown.

A car had drawn up outside the flight of stone steps leading up to the front door, and a young man was pacing the pavement impatiently.

He looked up as James approached, and James hid a swift stab of distaste as he observed his haggard face and wild expression. He had come across far too many drug addicts through his travels not to recognise immediately what the young man was.

Every nervous, unco-ordinated gesture betrayed him, every wild, uncontrollable movement of his body. By the looks of him he was a heavy user, quite probably overdue for the fix that would, for a time at least, quiet his spasms.

When he saw James approaching the house he came towards him.

'It's no use,' he told James, intercepting him. 'He's not here. He told me to come round now...he promised me he would be here...' His voice dropped to a fretful whine, his eyes suddenly dull where they had been overbright, and as James watched him frowningly he muttered thickly, 'Bloody pushers... They're all the same.' And then he added despairingly, 'Where is he? He *knows* I need the stuff.'

And before James could stop him he rushed up the stone steps and began to pound maniacally on the door, frantically calling out Charles's name.

James stared at him. At first he had thought his presence in the square was pure mischance, but now, listening to him, watching him, hearing him refer to Charles by name...

He followed him up the steps and said quietly, 'This man who lives here—does he just supply you, or...'

The man looked at him, his expression truculent and suspicious. 'What's it to you?' And then the awareness faded from his eyes and he said ramblingly, 'He doesn't like us coming here unannounced, we're supposed to ring and arrange a meet, but I'm desperate, don't you see?'

He had started to whine again, plucking at James's coat, his body trembling convulsively.

Charles, supplying drugs...pushing drugs... James had asked for a miracle, never expecting to receive one, and now it seemed he had. No matter what her feelings for her cousin, he could not allow Geraldine Frances to marry Charles now...he could not take the risk of Rothwell's becoming tainted with all that Charles so obviously was.

He paused on the steps, torn between waiting for Charles to return so that he could confront him with his knowledge, and pity for Charles's victim, now a crumpled heap of flesh, crouching on the top step, howling mournfully.

Compassion won. Summoning a taxi, he briskly manhandled the other down the steps and into the cab. James told the cabbie to take them to the nearest hospital, and left the man there in the outpatients department. It was the best he could do for him, even if the fellow didn't seem to think so... He had alternately raved and cursed at James throughout the entire drive.

When James returned to his taxi, the driver grunted.

''e won't stay there, you know, guv. Be out again as soon as their back's turned...seen it all before. Don't matter who they are, once that stuff's got a hold of them they're all the same. Course, it's them as sells it who I blame—pity the government can't do more about it, but you've got to prove what they're up to first, haven't you? And they're as full of tricks as a bagful of monkeys.'

Deep in thought, James gave him the address of his club. Once there, he went up to his room and picked up the telephone.

There was a man in London, an agent, for want of a better description, whom he had used on numerous occasions in the past whenever he had wanted something doing discreetly and quietly. He was a past master at extracting information from all manner of unlikely sources.

To James's relief he was in, and agreed to see him straight away.

Peter Vincent lived in a small, plain house of no apparent distinction. Quiet and subdued, it was very like the man himself, but, as James already knew, Peter Vincent was a very astute and intelligent man indeed.

He was also a man whom James trusted absolutely. He, and certain other chosen men in Switzerland, in New York and in certain other countries, provided James with the network of information which enabled him to keep control of his vast financial empire. Geraldine Frances had already been meticulously introduced to all these men, and all of them had recognised within her much of her father's financial astuteness.

Peter Vincent let James in, and frowned a little as he saw him. He had rarely seen his client in such an impatient mood.

Quickly James explained to him what he wanted him to do.

'It won't be easy,' Peter confirmed, frowning a little. 'You're convinced that your nephew *is* dealing in drugs...it isn't possible that the man had mistaken the address...?'

'And the name?' James asked wryly. 'It's possible, I suppose, but unlikely.'

What was in his mind was that Geraldine Frances, vulnerable as she was to Charles, might refuse to believe him unless he was able to produce incontrovertible proof of what Charles was doing, and it was to this end that he was seeking Peter Vincent's aid.

'If your nephew is supplying, it will probably be to close circles of acquaintances...people known to him. That's generally the way it works. It's a pity you didn't hang on to that young man; we might have been able to find out a little more. Leave it with me,' he suggested. 'I'll be in touch as soon as I've discovered something concrete...'

James returned to his club, his mind preoccupied. There was no going back now. Geraldine Frances could not marry Charles...not now...

She would *have* to marry, of course, but he would deal with that problem later. First he must convince her about what Charles was doing.

He remembered that he would be seeing Charles in the morning, and he also remembered that he had intended to ask him if he wanted a lift.

He was tempted to let him make his own way to Belvoir. If there was one thing that James detested, it was someone who caused the kind of physical and mental suffering to his fellow human beings which Charles was so wantonly and deliberately causing. He doubted he had the stomach to face Charles without betraying what he was feeling, and of course it was essential that he did not do so...

It was also essential that he did not arouse Charles's suspicions in any way, and, although his nephew should have no reason to suppose that James had the slightest idea what he was doing, James well knew the value of paying attention to the smallest detail. Charles was well aware of his feelings about maintaining an outward appearance of family harmony. For James to neglect to suggest they travelled to Belvoir together would be out of character. He might not like Charles, but he could not ignore the fact that his nephew was a dangerous and shrewd man. It was unlikely that he would connect his refusal to offer him a lift with the possibility of his discovery that Charles was supplying drugs...highly unlikely...none the less...

This time James drove round to Rothwell Square. The car which had been parked so haphazardly there had gone. He frowned over this, wondering if it had been removed by the police or...

He parked his own car outside Charles's house. There were exceptions to every rule...*he* might not permit others to park in the square, but he who made the rules might also break them.

He went up the steps and rapped on the door.

Charles answered it himself. He didn't employ any live-in staff, just a daily woman, claiming that permanent staff were a luxury he could not afford.

He looked a little less urbane than was normal, James recognised, as Charles moved back to allow him to step into the hallway but did not invite him further into the house.

'I was just passing and it occurred to me you might care to travel down to Belvoir with me in the morning,' James told him.

Charles nodded. He had been expecting James to either call or telephone with such a suggestion; that was one of the reasons he had got in such a panic when he'd realised that something had gone wrong with his communications system, and that the drugs he had arranged to collect from a pre-arranged source had somehow been delayed.

He refused to keep any supplies in the house; there had been an increased demand before Christmas, and one of the reasons he had had to return to London was because he had known quite well that many of his 'customers' would be waiting for fresh supplies.

In the end he had got the supplies he wanted; the delay had been caused by some confusion in the address of the pick-up spot, and he had had to drive what seemed like halfway across London before being able to find a telephone box he could use to find out what had happened and arrange a fresh pick-up.

It had taken him two hours longer than he had expected, and he had been starting to sweat with anxiety when he finally got the stuff. Charles hated it when things did not run according to plan; he had 'customers' waiting.

All of his users knew far better than to come to the house these days, a precaution which he had adopted on the advice of his supplier. He normally called on them, or arranged to meet them, and that was why...

He tensed and said tersely to James, 'Thanks. I take it you'll want a fairly early start?'

'I thought we'd leave at six,' James told him.

Charles still hadn't invited him to sit down or offered him a drink, and now, as he confirmed that he would be ready, he was edging the older man back towards the front door.

'Sorry I can't be more hospitable,' he apologised insincerely, as he opened it. 'Afraid I've got a dinner engagement, and I'm already running late.'

A dinner engagement, or a meeting with one of his victims? James wondered cynically as he allowed himself to be ushered out and down the steps towards his car.

Charles waited until he had seen James drive off, and then he walked quickly over to the door that opened into the library.

The man standing inside it was staring out of the window.

'That's him...' he told Charles excitedly. 'That's the guy who was here earlier... the one I was telling you about.'

Charles stared at him.

'Who is he?' the man asked.

'No one who need concern you,' Charles told him grimly. 'Here's your stuff...'

He removed a small package from his pocket and handed it to him, gripping hold of his wrist so hard that the other winced as he said fiercely, 'Oh, no, you don't, not in here. Wait until you're well clear of this place before you touch it, damn you, or that will be the last lot you get from me... and remember, the next time you want something, wait for me to bring it to you. Don't come round here!'

The rage in his voice penetrated the other's ecstatic relief. He stopped greedily fingering the small package and stared at Charles.

'But I had to come,' he whined. 'I needed something——'

'If you come here again, I promise you you will be more sorry than you ever dreamed possible,' Charles told him softly. 'Now get out...and use the back way.'

Once he had gone, Charles stood staring unseeingly into the fire, and then, with great deliberation and intensity, he picked up a fragile Sèvres ornament from the mantelpiece and flung it the width of the room so that it hit the wall and splintered into a mass of tiny fragments.

That the ornament was probably worth more than he made in a whole month of dealing didn't matter. What mattered was that he had been found out...that James knew what he was doing...he *must* know. James was no fool, and it was obvious to anyone with any intelligence just what Tony Byres was. Tony had told him himself that James had questioned him.

At first when he had come home and found Tony waiting for him, Charles's greatest fear had been that one of his neighbours might have alerted the police to the fact that a drug addict was apparently camped out outside one of their houses, but fortunately it seemed that most of the inhabitants of the square were away in the country for Christmas, and so, after cursing him and making him remove his disreputable car from outside the house to the service area at the rear, Charles had been forced to let him in.

Once there, Tony had given him some garbled tale about a meeting with another 'user' who had taken him off to hospital and left him there.

Tony had grown very aggrieved and loquacious at this point, and Charles might not have got any more information at all out of him if Tony hadn't remembered that this other man had questioned him about whether or not Charles supplied him.

Hoping against hope that his unknown visitor must have been another of his customers, Charles had bundled Tony into the library and warned him to keep quiet when he'd seen James's car outside.

He didn't doubt for one moment Tony's recognition of James; it was all too plausible. So why had James said nothing to him? What was he waiting for? Had he told Geraldine Frances yet? He must intend to.

Charles's greatest hope lay in the fact that so far James had said nothing to him. That must surely be because James himself was not entirely sure of his ground. Somehow or other he would have to persuade James that his suspicions were unfounded.

He had not lied to James about having a dinner engagement. He was supposed to be meeting Thérèse. Sex was the last thing on his mind right now, but she was the most temperamental of all his lovers, and if he cancelled their date... Time enough to worry about James and what he intended to do tomorrow. As he went upstairs to get ready for the evening, it came to Charles that he was back where he best liked being: right on the edge of a crevasse, walking the tightrope between safety and danger.

As he always had done, as he always intended to do, he would survive.

When James picked him up in the morning there was no evidence in Charles's face or manner that he was suffering from any kind of stress or tension. Beneath his clothes his flesh was marred with small bruises and bites inflicted by his lover. She liked inflicting pain as well as receiving it, and it had been well into the early hours of the morning before Charles had finally persuaded her to go home.

There was nothing in James's attitude towards him to give him any indication of what his uncle might be thinking. He was sitting in the back of the Bentley reading the *Financial Times* when the chauffeur picked Charles up, and only raised his head from his paper to murmur a brief good morning.

Now was not the time to try to find out just how much James knew, Charles recognised. He wanted to make

sure they were completely alone when he did that, with
no one to overhear him.

His opportunity came earlier than he had expected. Both
he and James were riding borrowed hunters; James's was
nervous and edgy, and obviously not very experienced,
balking at the hounds, and causing James to fall behind
the rest of the field.

Charles fell back with him, and drew alongside him.

'I wanted to ask you something,' he told James.

The older man wasn't in a good mood. His mount
was proving hard to handle. This morning he had suffered an attack of palsied unsteadiness which had left
him weak and edgy. He hated these reminders of what
lay ahead of him, and tried his best to ignore them.

'When you called round last night, why didn't you say
you had also called earlier?'

James couldn't control his start of surprise. How had
Charles known about that? His mouth set firmly, and
Charles knew that Tony had been right. James made no
attempt to evade the confrontation.

'You realise that this means the end of your hopes of
marrying Geraldine Frances,' James told him flatly.
'Once she knows...'

Once she knows... Charles's heart leapt. Perhaps he
hadn't told her... but he had to be sure; too much was
at stake for any mistake now.

'She'll what?' he taunted. 'Break our engagement? Oh,
I don't think so... She loves me, you see...' He laughed
softly when he saw James's bitter expression. 'You don't
believe me? Why not try telling her and see?'

'I fully intend to tell her,' James told him acidly. 'Just
as soon as——'

He cursed as Charles's mount came too close to his
own and the animal sawed at its bit, dancing nervously.

He was an excellent rider, but this horse was too highly
strung to be used as a hunter, he acknowledged
disgustedly.

So he was right, Charles gloated. James hadn't told her...not yet... And he mustn't be allowed to do so. It was one thing for Charles to boast to his uncle that Geraldine Frances would refuse to break their engagement, but what if James chose to expose him publicly, to hand him over to the police? He started to sweat nervously.

James's horse had pulled a little in front of his own. A rabbit shooting out from the undergrowth startled it, and it reared up sharply, almost unseating James. Watching, Charles was suddenly struck by a thought. A thought so dangerous...but so right...

His crop was already in his hand; it was the easiest thing in the world to lift it and bring it down hard on the other animal's exposed flank.

It screamed in pain, reared up as it had done before, almost unseating James, and then bolted out of control, while Charles watched, narrow-eyed and unmoving.

James was an expert rider, but the horse was unpredictable and the ground treacherous. A hedge loomed in front of them, one which it should have been easy for the horse to jump, but instead the animal swung violently sideways and James, unable to save himself, was flung off, his foot still tangled in the stirrup. He was dragged across the hard ground, unable to prevent the horse from continuing its panicked course.

Normally James's quick reactions would have saved him, but those increasingly frequent muscle-seizures, those panicky moments of confusion betrayed the fact that his co-ordination was not what it had once been.

James had one moment's stark disbelief that it was after all happening like this, that he was going to die, and another of tremendous fear for Geraldine Frances, and then it was all over.

Charles reached him first, seconds ahead of two other riders.

'Is he all right?' one of them demanded anxiously.

Charles, already on the ground, shook his head, his expression appropriately shocked.

'He's dead... His neck...'

'Oh, my God! What happened?'

He was asked that question over and over again during the next few confused hours.

The master of the hunt, too far ahead of them to know what had happened, had to be informed, a doctor summoned who confirmed Charles's own statement.

'Get one every year,' he said unemotionally. 'Someone will have to tell his family.'

'I'll do it,' Charles told him. 'He is... was my uncle. There's only me and a daughter...'

Significantly he put himself first, before Geraldine Frances, because that was where he now intended to come.

All through the questions and concern that followed he acted superbly; he was the shocked, disbelieving, grief-stricken nephew of a very great man, who had seen his uncle thrown in front of his eyes...

'But he was such a good rider,' the master muttered in disbelief when he was given the news. 'Could have ridden anything... did...'

'His mount was very nervous,' Charles commented, and then improvised, 'Uncle James was in London yesterday meeting an old friend... they were dining at the Connaught...' He frowned, and looked self-conscious, but everyone there knew what he wasn't saying. Drink could play havoc with a man's concentration, and no one there thought the worse of James for having imbibed it, only sorry that his indulgence should have had such tragic results.

There was of course a whole host of necessary formalities to be gone through, and it was several hours before Charles was free to instruct James's chauffeur to drive him to Rothwell.

Gloatingly, he was saving for himself the pleasure of telling Geraldine Frances about her father's death.

She would be devastated, of course, all too ready to allow him to assume full responsibility for everything, including Rothwell. And once he had done so...

It struck him, as he automatically assumed the seat in the rear of the Bentley which had always been his uncle's, that the sooner he and Geraldine Frances were married, the better. Once they were married... well, there was no James to protect her now. He would be able to do as he wished. Geraldine Frances had always liked Ireland and Castle Kilrayne... well, he might suggest to her that she took up permanent residence there. He would visit her as infrequently as possible, and would take the reins of Rothwell and its fortune firmly in his hands... because of course, once they *were* married, he would have no difficulty whatsoever in persuading Geraldine Frances to hand over control of her inheritance to him.

Safe from prying eyes in the back of the Bentley, he permitted himself the luxury of a small smile.

It had all been so easy. Just the merest flick of his crop, and fate had done the rest. His smile broadened. Really, it couldn't have been better. For as long as he'd lived James would have stood between him and Rothwell. Charles mused on how long it would be before he could assume the title, because of course Geraldine Frances must be brought to see how impossible it was for her to refuse to allow him to overset James's petition for her to hold it... What difference could it make to her, anyway? As his wife she would still have the title of Countess, and their sons...

For the first time it occurred to him how pleasurable his life might be if only he could dispose of Geraldine Frances as easily as he had disposed of James, but he dismissed the temptation. Once, yes, but twice—that was too much of a risk; it would raise too many questions, too much suspicion. He couldn't *kill* Geraldine Frances, but there were other, equally effective means of banishing her from his life and yet at the same time holding on to everything that marriage to her would bring him.

CHAPTER TWELVE

GERALDINE FRANCES observed the Bentley's stately process down the lime-lined avenue with frowning eyes, knowing immediately that something was wrong.

Her father wasn't scheduled to return for another two days at least, and she was downstairs and waiting in the hall when the door opened and Charles walked in.

Automatically she looked past him for her father, pleasure radiating from her as her concern died beneath the delight of seeing Charles so unexpectedly.

'Where's Daddy?' she asked him incuriously as he came towards her.

Charles took hold of her—one never knew, after all, who might be watching—and held on to her forearms firmly, keeping her grotesque body out of contact with his own.

'Geraldine Frances, my dearest girl...I'm sorry... there's been an accident...'

An accident... Geraldine Frances stared at him, and then suddenly she knew. Cold shock seized her.

'No...not Daddy...tell me he's all right...' she begged pitifully, but Charles, enjoying his role far too much to relinquish it, said gravely,,

'If only I could... You must be brave, dearest. Your father is dead...'

Geraldine Frances gave a low moan of shock, and as the chauffeur, who was standing behind Charles discreetly awaiting his instructions, told the rest of the staff later, 'You'd have thought he'd have told her somewhere private, like. The poor thing looked fit to collapse.'

'And well she might...she was that close to her father...' someone else commented.

'What happened?' Geraldine Frances whispered. Her whole body felt icy cold... She ached for Charles to take hold of her and warm her...to comfort her, to wrap her in his arms and tell her that everything was all right and that it was a mistake. But he did no such thing.

Instead he said, almost pleasantly, 'He was thrown from and dragged along by his horse... When I got to him it was all over, he had broken his neck.'

He heard her whimper, but refused to reduce his own pleasure. 'I thought for a moment when I reached him that he might still be alive...' He saw her face and the look on it gave him great pleasure. 'I've arranged for his body to be brought back here to Rothwell, of course,' he added almost casually. 'Kingscombe is coming down tomorrow, so I'll be staying overnight... Will you tell Soames to have a bed made up for me, Gerry? Not your father's on this occasion, of course, but in future...until we're married at least... I suppose I ought to have his old room...as head of the family...'

Geraldine Frances was too shocked to feel pain at what he was saying. Her father, dead. She couldn't take it in...couldn't believe it.

Only yesterday she had seen him, said goodbye to him...he had been so alive and vital. To accept that he was now dead, that she would never see him again...

Her composure shattered abruptly, her self-control disintegrating as she gave a terrible cry of anguish and sobbed, 'No...no...please, it isn't true...'

She was still sobbing hysterically when the local doctor arrived, hastily summoned on Charles's orders.

'Shock,' he pronounced kindly, wondering why on earth this very good-looking but obviously incredibly stupid young man had chosen to give her such shocking news here, in this lofty, cold marble hall, when surely the privacy of a smaller, more comfortable room would have been a far wiser choice. He was only small himself, and he viewed the vast bulk of Geraldine Frances's obese body with despair, wondering how on earth they were going to get her upstairs to her room. She was virtually on the point of collapse already.

Charles solved the problem for him, saying coldly, 'Gerry, for goodness' sake remember who you are and pull yourself together... She *is* rather prone to hysteria,' he told the doctor untruthfully. 'I'm afraid she tends to be highly strung...'

'She's had a terrible shock,' the doctor sympathised. 'Perhaps if we could get her upstairs...'

It was Soames, her father's butler, who had known her since she was a child, who managed to coax Geraldine Frances upstairs to her own room, while Charles stood by and watched with cynical enjoyment... And this was just the start... she was going to pay, and pay over and over again, for every small slight of his childhood, every tiny humiliation... and when he was tired of punishing her, of making her pay, then he would banish her to Ireland where she could stay for the rest of her life— just as long as she produced his sons.

In the morning Geraldine Frances was calmer and insisted on getting up. Her father's solicitor arrived, and to Charles's fury insisted on seeing her on her own.

'Tell him that you want me with you... that we're going to be married,' he demanded, but she shook her head, too exhausted with grief to do anything other than listen to the contents of her father's will in numb acceptance.

There was nothing she didn't already know. Various bequests to members of the staff, various requests as to the disposal of some of his private possessions, but, as she had already known, the bulk of his assets, Rothwell itself and the titles, all came direct to her, and would pass into her control and hers alone.

The solicitor coughed and said uncertainly, 'You *do* know, I am sure, that your father was most insistent that only *you* control his estate... that not even your husband should be allowed to have any say...'

'Yes . . . yes . . .' Geraldine Frances assured him tiredly. 'I'm sorry, I'm not feeling very well,' she told him. 'I wonder if you would excuse me.'

She escaped to her room to cry the tears she felt would never stop flowing. They poured from her like blood, liquid anguish that could never be dammed.

And worse was to come. Charles had attended to all the arrangements for the funeral, organising a far grander affair than she suspected her father would have wanted . . . A quiet ceremony here at Rothwell was what he would have preferred.

The service itself was bad enough, but afterwards, ignoring her pleas, Charles had arranged for the most important of the mourners to return to Rothwell, and having to circulate among them, accepting their condolences, behaving as though she were at some kind of society cocktail party, was the last thing she wanted to endure.

Her father's doctor stopped her as she was trying to escape. He at least had been genuinely fond of her father, Geraldine Frances knew. 'I am sorry,' he told her quietly. 'Not so much for your father, of course, but I know how much you will miss him . . .'

Geraldine Frances stared at him.

'What do you mean, not so much for my father?'

The doctor looked uncomfortable and then said quietly, 'I was thinking of his illness . . . I know how much he was dreading the inevitable physical and mental deterioration it would have caused . . .' He paused and then looked directly at her. 'He was such a good rider; I did wonder . . .'

Geraldine Frances couldn't believe what she was hearing. She saw Charles approaching her with relief . . . he would be able to explain what was happening, make the doctor understand that her father's death had been an accident, and not, as he was implying, suicide. Her father had been perfectly well . . . perfectly healthy . . .

'Charles . . .'

Both men ignored her. The doctor looked at Charles and said curtly, 'I thought you told me that Geraldine Frances *knew* about her father's condition.'

'I thought she did,' Charles managed to lie smoothly, giving her a faked look of concern. He hadn't known, of course, but he had managed to conceal his own shock when the doctor had revealed the facts about James's illness earlier that day. 'Surely James told you about his dementia, Gerry?'

His *dementia*... The floor rocked beneath her. She went white, and she heard the doctor curse Charles under his breath and then say to her, 'Geraldine Frances, it's all right...your father wasn't mad...he was suffering from a progressive deterioration—an acceleration of the natural ageing process, known as Altzheimer's disease. His condition was diagnosed some time ago...'

'He never said a word,' she managed through stiff lips.

Charles continued to look both puzzled and contrite, while hiding his cruel pleasure in her anguish.

'Didn't he? That's odd. He was discussing it with me only minutes before...before his accident. That was why, when your father's doctor here asked me if I'd realised how ill he was, I did wonder if... well, none of us would have blamed him if he had chosen to take the easy way out, would we?'

The discovery that James had been ill had in fact been almost as great a shock to Charles as it had obviously been to his cousin, but for different reasons. What a pity he hadn't known earlier about James's illness. What a weapon it would have been against him, against them both...it might not ever have been necessary for him to arrange James's 'accidental' death. The mere threat of exposure might have been sufficient to make his uncle keep his mouth shut about his own private affairs. But it was too late for that now. However, her father's medical history, physical and mental, was something he could and would use against Geraldine Frances—and who knew? With that threat it might even be possible to drive her into mental instability herself, to take from her her inheritance, and to have her locked away in an institution.

Geraldine Frances felt numb...numb...everywhere except for one tiny place inside her which seemed to throb with agony.

Her father, ill...frightened...confiding in Charles and not her...taking his own life...

'I think he did it for you,' Charles was murmuring to her. 'Better a clean end now than to become a dribbling, gaga——'

It was the doctor's curt command that silenced him, while Geraldine Frances stood there trembling, white and sick, unable to believe what she was hearing. She looked at the doctor and asked painfully, 'Is it true...would my father...?'

Much as he wanted to lie, to soften the cruelty of Charles's unkind description, there was nothing he could do, other than to say, 'Ultimately, yes, but I believe your father had a good many years of excellent health still in front of him. I don't think...'

I don't think he would have killed himself, he had been about to say, but checked the words, knowing they would do no good now, and patted her hand silently instead.

In his opinion Charles Fitzcarlton was one of the most tactless young fools it had ever been his misfortune to meet. Why on earth a man as mature and wise as James had chosen to confide in him rather than his own daughter, he had no idea, unless it was because of the innate deep-rooted chauvinism that still seemed to infest certain members of the upper class.

Charles smiled as he drew Geraldine Frances away. Of course he had had no idea of James's illness, until the doctor had asked him if he had been aware that his uncle was ill. It had been all too easy to get the man to confide in him by pretending he had known the truth. And *what*

a truth... How he had enjoyed taunting Geraldine
Frances with it... what a weapon it would be in the
future. The threat of madness...even if not exactly true,
it would still be a very powerful part of his future
ammunition.

Almost immediately after the funeral Charles left for
London, his absence carefully calculated to intensify
Geraldine Frances's dependence on him. He wanted to
make sure she was fully aware of how much she needed
him when he told her that his principles would not allow
him to marry her while she was so wealthy and he so
poor. She would, of course, immediately offer to transfer
all her assets to him, he knew... After that it would be
a simple exercise to get her to transfer the titles as well.

He had another reason for returning to London. His
affair with Thérèse would have to be brought to an end.
She was not the kind of woman to remain discreetly in
the background while he married someone else.

It was a pity... In bed she was the best he had ever
known, but sex, while enjoyable, wasn't everything... it
certainly fell a long, long way short of being as important to him as Rothwell.

Telling himself that he deserved the reward of enjoying her for a few more nights before he told her it
was over, he smiled his false, betraying smile into
Geraldine Frances's eyes and promised her that he would
return just as soon as he possibly could.

'I have my own business affairs to attend to,' he told
her, not untruthfully.

There would be no more drug dealing. *That* part of
his life was over. Yes, there was plenty to occupy his
attention in London, before he could return to Rothwell
to assume his rightful place as its master.

In London, Peter Vincent, who had read of James's
death in the papers, pondered and considered. He was

not a man who ever acted rashly, and it took him some time to make his decision.

Geraldine Frances listened, uncaring, while Soames told her that she had a visitor. There had been so many, all of them wanting to convey their condolences, coming to see her out of curiosity or pity, but her father's training refused to allow her to hide behind the convenient excuse of her own grief.

'Who is he, Soames?' she asked tiredly.

'A Mr Peter Vincent.'

Peter Vincent. She knew him, of course. One of her father's very special agents...

She saw him in the library, offering him a glass of the twenty-year-old malt she knew he favoured, surprised when he shook his head in refusal.

'I—er—take it you are here alone,' Peter asked her awkwardly. 'That is, your cousin, Charles——'

'Charles is in London,' Geraldine Frances interrupted, and was surprised by the look of relief that crossed his face.

'What I have to tell you isn't very pleasant. I've searched my conscience, wondered...but your father's instructions to me were clear... Had he been alive, I know it was his intention...and perhaps it's even more important that you should know now...'

Geraldine Frances stared at him. 'Know what, Mr Vincent?'

'That your cousin Charles has been dealing in drugs...acting as a supplier...a pusher...' He said the word distastefully and, seeing her expression, added quietly, 'I'm sorry...I know how difficult this must be for you. Were it not for the fact that your father came to me himself and asked me to check...'

'My father asked you...? But when?' Geraldine Frances asked him, frowning.

'The day before he died,' Peter Vincent told her simply. 'He telephoned me at my home and asked if he could see me... He told me that he'd had reason to visit your cousin, and that when he'd arrived at the Rothwell Square house Charles wasn't there, but that a young man very obviously a drug addict was, and that, moreover, he made it plain to your father that he was waiting for his supplier and that the supplier was your cousin, Charles.

'Naturally your father was extremely concerned... He asked me to find out as much as I could about Charles's activities... discreetly, of course...'

'And?' Geraldine Frances asked him tensely.

He gave an apologetic shrug. 'I'm afraid it's true...'

Charles, a drug dealer... she couldn't believe it... *wouldn't* believe it.

'I wasn't sure what to do,' Peter Vincent was saying. 'Whether or not your father would have wanted me to pass on to you the information he had requested...'

'I'm sure he would,' Geraldine Frances told him absently. Of course he would... but she couldn't believe it was true. There must be some mistake... there had to be... Not until she had heard it from Charles's own lips would she believe it. She *had* to see him... to talk to him...

She got up clumsily, thanking Peter Vincent for taking the trouble to visit her, aching for him to leave so that she could think, but, once he had gone, calm, rational thinking was the last thing she could do.

Instead she paced her bedroom, alternately trembling with shock and half distraught with pain. It couldn't be true... she wouldn't *let* it be true...

Her whole world had turned upside-down, and the only person who could make it right again was Charles himself. She had to see him... she had to...

For the first time in many, many years she forgot that she hadn't eaten, that Cook would be preparing her dinner, and instead pulled on a coat over the shapeless plaid dress whose dark colours were supposed to disguise her ungainly bulk.

Her car was in the garage alongside the Bentley. She got in and started the engine, ignoring the fact that she was really in no state to drive.

She had to see Charles. She *had* to hear from his own lips that Peter Vincent was mistaken...that her *father* had been mistaken... There had to be a rational explanation...there must be.

Charles was going to be her husband...they were going to be *married*... He was all she had in the world, and she loved him so much.

Too much, an inner voice taunted her, but she refused to listen to it. She dared not listen to it, just as she dared not listen to the other cold, clinical little voice that told her that her father would scarcely have gone to the lengths of asking Peter Vincent to investigate Charles's activities if he had not been firmly convinced that Charles was involved in drug dealing. Her father had never been a vindictive man. He *knew* how much she loved Charles. He must have known how much pain it would cause her to discover...

Her mind sheered off, unable to cope with the enormity of the pain waiting for her. Frantically she concentrated on believing that there *was* an explanation, that she only had to see Charles, to talk to him for everything to be explained.

Mercifully, London was relatively free of traffic, and as her father had done before her Geraldine Frances ignored the ban on parking in front of Charles's house.

She knew he must be in. Lights blazed from the downstairs windows, and to her surprise as she mounted the steps she saw that the front door was actually open.

She stepped into the hall, frowning as she saw a woman's coat lying on the floor. Sable... She gave a small shudder; she loathed the very idea of wearing animal pelts herself... Beside the coat was a shoe, impossibly small and equally impossibly high. She called Charles's name, but there was no response... Her fear and panic mounting with every second, she climbed the stairs heading for the library, which was the room Charles used most.

She opened the door and then stood staring into the room, her body seized in a sudden spasm of shock as she whispered Charles's name.

Charles hadn't heard her... Charles hadn't seen her... Charles was oblivious to everything but the fierce, thrusting ecstasy that pulsed through him as he pushed fiercely into the woman lying beneath him.

Clothes were scattered everywhere... The woman was laughing a low, mocking sound, her arms and legs wrapped around Charles as she taunted, 'Tired already? Surely not?' and then, as Charles responded violently to her taunt, she screamed loudly in pleasure, a wild, mindless sound, punctuating the things Charles was saying to her, things that made Geraldine Frances's skin burn with heat and then freeze with ice both at the same time.

She couldn't move. Couldn't do anything but stare with some sort of horrible, compulsive fascination at the intimate entwining of their bodies and their savagely triumphant movements.

It was almost as though someone was holding her, forcing her to watch... refusing to allow her to turn away... as though someone outside herself was directing her movements.

She felt the sickness stir in her stomach, the disbelief, the pain... the shocked anguish of a knowledge she asked not to have... heard the woman whispering mindlessly... heard Charles's guttural, primitive cry of pleasure... saw, as though it was happening at a distance from her, and in slow motion, like a film instead of real life, his flesh withdraw from the woman's, his head turn, his eyes widen and then dilate with shock and then fury as he saw her...

As he saw her...

Abruptly, something inside her snapped, and with it the pressure that was keeping her where she stood.

She heard Charles swear, ugly, savage words that hit like pieces of molten, flying metal embedding themselves into her, wounding her, as she turned to flee... She heard the woman's voice, soft and frightened, asking something...

She tried to escape... to run... but her weight was against her.

Long before she reached the front door, Charles caught up with her. He had even had time to fasten his trousers, she noticed savagely.

'Gerry, what the hell are you doing here?'

His arm barred her way out. His eyes... how had she ever thought them warm and tender? They were cold... deeply, dangerously cold. Even now, after what she had seen, after what she knew was not to be ignored, she still couldn't lie.

'I wanted to see you,' she told him unsteadily, while tears filled her eyes and flooded down her cheeks.

She sensed rather than saw him relax slightly.

'Look, it isn't what you think,' he told her easily.

'You mean you weren't making love to her?' she demanded huskily, hating him for what she had seen and hating herself for standing here, howling like a child... for listening to him, when everything else inside her screamed in outraged pain and pride against what she had witnessed.

'Come on, Gerry, you're not a child. I'm a man...' He was trying to shrug it off... to make it seem unimportant. She could almost feel him willing her to be convinced, but behind the coaxing was a coldness that chilled her.

'Look, let's be sensible about this,' she heard him saying. 'It doesn't make any difference to us. It isn't important...'

Not important? How could he expect her to believe that, when she had seen in his face, in those unguarded seconds of agonised ecstasy, the truth?

'It's important to *me*,' she told him fiercely, despising herself for wanting to be convinced...persuaded. Wanting to wipe out all that she had seen and heard.

'Oh, for God's sake!' Charles swore savagely, no longer bothering to hide what he was feeling. 'What the hell did you expect? That I would wait, virgin-like, pure and unsullied until we got married? Grow up and stop being so ridiculous.

'Look at yourself,' he derided her. 'And then tell me honestly that you believed my refusal to make love to you was for any reason other than one of revulsion. Let's be honest with one another, Gerry. You need me because that's the only way you're going to get a husband and children...and I need you because that's the only way I'm going to get Rothwell.'

She felt as though her whole world was falling apart.

'You said you loved me,' she stammered pitifully.

Charles laughed sadistically, and derided, 'And *you* believed me? *No* man could ever love you, Geraldine Frances...no man could ever desire you. You're grotesque...obscene. Do you think anyone will blame me for taking my pleasures with someone else? Once we're married——'

Something inside her snapped. She had borne enough...

'We aren't going to be married,' she told him huskily. 'That's what I came here to tell you.'

Now, when it was almost too late, her pride had come to her rescue. Geraldine Frances lifted her head and looked at him, saw the mockery and contempt in his eyes.

'Liar,' he told her cruelly. 'You came here because you wanted a fuck and I'm the only man who's ever likely to give you one.'

His obscenity appalled her... She had never dreamed he would treat her like this...had never dreamed there was another Charles behind the golden mask she had thought was the real man. It stung her into flinging the truth recklessly at him.

'No,' she contradicted him flatly. 'I came here to tell you that I know the truth.'

She was savagely pleased by the sudden look of fear in his eyes; it gave her the courage to press on and say, 'I know all about your drug trafficking, Charles...you see, my father found out what you were up to before he died, and he instructed one of his agents to investigate you. I couldn't marry you now, even if I wanted to,' she told him disdainfully.

Inside she was falling apart. She wanted to scream and rage, to tear the very flesh from her bones, to throw back her head and howl to the heavens that she had been betrayed, that she was in mortal pain.

Charles's hand on her wrist shackled her, but behind them his lover emerged from the library and demanded mockingly, 'Who on earth is this ridiculous creature, Charles? And what is she doing here?' And while Charles's attention was distracted, Geraldine Frances slipped free of his hold and made for the front door.

She might have seemed strong and resolute outwardly, but she knew quite well that inwardly she was not. Logic, reason might dictate that she abandon any thought of marrying Charles, might tell her that she had now seen him revealed as he really was, but her feelings... her emotions...her deepest feminine needs were not so easily disposed of. She loved him...even now...even knowing...

She discovered that she was sitting in her car with tears streaming down her face. She started the engine and headed for Rothwell, knowing full well that it wasn't over, that sooner or later Charles would follow her, would try to persuade and browbeat her into marrying him. The only truth he had told her tonight had been that he wanted Rothwell...And wanted it badly—badly enough to marry her without loving her, without wanting her—and without even liking her!

At Rothwell she abandoned her car outside the front door, and after Soames had let her in she went straight upstairs to her room. Uncapping the small jar the doctor had left for her, she took two of the sleeping tablets inside it, her hand shaking. Somehow or other she had to blot out those awful pictures of Charles with that woman...those awful words he had thrown at her, those appalling home truths she had had to face.

Tomorrow would be soon enough to deal with her problems; for tonight she needed to escape. She needed sleep, she needed oblivion, and as she undressed and prepared for bed she wondered agonisingly if this was how her father had felt, knowing what lay ahead of him, and if after all he had, as the doctor and Charles had implied, taken his own life... But no... Everything she knew about him said otherwise. His death had been an accident...an accident...

She woke up early, her head aching, her mouth dry from the effects of the sleeping tablets.

The thought of food nauseated her. All she wanted was coffee. Hot, strong coffee, the way her father had always enjoyed it. She gulped at it downstairs in the library, scalding her mouth, but not caring.

Charles hadn't slept. He had been awake all night, alternately cursing both Thérèse and Geraldine Frances. Why had she come here in the first place, the fool...and why the hell had he been so stupid as to give in to Thérèse's pleading that they have one last evening together?

And over and above his rage and feeling of being trapped lay a darker, more insidious anger. James had done the one thing Charles had not allowed for...he had told someone else his suspicions.

Normally Charles knew he would have had no problem persuading her that her father was wrong, coaxing and bemusing her into ignoring whatever she had been told, but last night's discovery of him with someone else had destroyed that blind, worshipful adoration she had had for him, even if only temporarily.

He cursed again, reaching for the phone. He couldn't trust himself to see her right now...if he did, he'd probably be tempted to put his hands around that fat neck of hers and squeeze it until she had no breath left to defy him.

If he had had any sense he would have thrown Thérèse out last night and then taken Geraldine Frances to bed...telling her that she had come to him because she wanted laying had possibly been his worst mistake, even if it was the truth. How much easier everything would have been now if he had given her what she had so plainly been asking for. Even more so if he had made her pregnant...

He cursed again before dialling Rothwell's private number.

Geraldine Frances answered the phone herself...he said her name caressingly, but she made no response.

'Darling, we have to talk...'

'What about?' she asked tonelessly. 'My father——'

Rage seized hold of him. 'Your damned father is dead,' he told her viciously, and suddenly, as she stood there in the library at Rothwell, Geraldine Frances knew quite definitely that somehow or other Charles had been responsible for her father's death.

It was like standing under a freezing fall of water, the shock numbing her.

'Gerry, are you still there...?'

She stared out of the window, and then said quietly, 'And my love for you is dead, too, Charles.' She knew that it was a lie. She still loved him; she must, otherwise she would not be feeling this excruciating pain, but that love would have to be destroyed...before Charles used it to destroy her.

'You killed him,' she accused him shakily. 'I know you did. I won't marry you, Charles.'

His very silence betrayed him, and then he said venomously, 'Oh, yes, you will. I intend to make sure of that. You *are* going to be my wife, Gerry.'

And suddenly they were the most frightening words she had ever heard. She had his measure now... He might not risk killing her as he had killed her father, but there were other ways, other things... Right now he needed her so that he could get Rothwell, but once he had her... She started to shake. Oh, God, what could she do? She had no one to turn to... nowhere to go... but no—that was wrong. There *was* somewhere, somewhere where, she hoped, Charles would not follow her. Somewhere where she would be safe, for a little while at least.

CHAPTER THIRTEEN

GERALDINE FRANCES didn't waste time once she had made up her mind. She fled to the only place she could think of where he wouldn't follow her. Ireland and Castle Kilrayne. For the second time in her life, she knew what it was to experience fear of the power of another human being. Like mother, like son, she thought wretchedly as she boarded the plane, a tall, plain woman, whose clothes were already beginning to hang a little loosely on her bulky frame.

The shock of discovering the truth about Charles, coupled with her father's death, had achieved what no amount of stringent self-lecturing could... Geraldine Frances did not want to eat. She herself was totally unaware of the fact that already she was losing weight. Her width was the very last thing on her mind... totally unimportant when set against other and more urgent troubles.

On the plane she had a window-seat; another woman took the seat adjacent to her, but Geraldine Frances didn't even glance at her.

When the stewardess came round with food and drink, she dismissed her with a small shake of her head, and the uniformed girl wondered sympathetically if the poor woman was afraid of flying. She looked so tense and white-faced, and the girl remembered how nervous she herself had been when she'd first started to train.

Perhaps it was that that made her keep an extra special eye on Geraldine Frances, so that when the passengers disembarked she found the glossy magazine in the seat next to Geraldine Frances, and carefully tucked it into Geraldine Frances's large shoulder-bag as she solicitously guided her off the plane. The poor thing looked as though she was in a state of shock, her movements disjointed, her eyes unfocused. She almost fell on the metal steps leading off the plane, and, once down on the ground, stared bleakly and dazedly around as though confused by her surroundings.

Bridie clucked over her like an anxious hen once she'd arrived at Kilrayne, offering her the comfort of her freshly baked soda bread, and talking about these things being 'God's will and not for the likes of us to question'.

Geraldine Frances ignored her. Bridie obviously hadn't noticed that she wasn't wearing her engagement ring, because she made no comment on its absence, and, if nothing else, the older woman was outspoken in her views, in the way of the Irish. But then, Bridie had never taken to Charles, never been impressed by his charm and his good looks.

Bridie had more sense than she had herself, Geraldine Frances acknowledged bitterly as she ignored the older woman's anxious cluckings and made her way slowly, almost zombie-like, to her tower rooms.

Once there, she barred the door, a symbolic gesture only, because, despite the thickness of the door and the stoutness of the heavy iron bar that closed her sitting-room and the bedroom above it off from the staircase, barring it couldn't prevent Charles from breaking it down if he wished, just as he could break down her determination not to marry him.

She sat down in a chair without removing the jacket she had travelled in, dropping the shoulder-bag that contained everything she had brought with her on to the floor with a dull thud.

She was exhausted, spiritually and emotionally. She hadn't slept properly since her father's death; she mourned him deeply, had lost her closest and only friend, her confidant. She had no one she could now turn to...no one at all. There was no one who could help to ease the pain of Charles's treachery...no one to ease the shock of the discovery of his emotional and sexual betrayal. And now to discover that he was not, as his outward appearance suggested, a golden, shining example of the perfection that humanity could attain, but just the very opposite—cruel, destructive, violent, greedy, completely without ethics or morals—was tearing her apart. He had killed her father. She would never forgive him for that. Never!

Her eyes burned as though they had been washed with grit, but, much as she ached to close them, she could not. Every time she did so she saw Charles and his lover, their bodies entwined, interlocked...she heard the elemental sound of their passion, felt the heat it generated...felt her insides turn to liquid with the agony of jealousy and pain.

To know that a man you loved was unfaithful was one thing. To witness the act of that infidelity was another, far more painful cross to bear.

The sun was starting to drop over the sea when she heard footsteps on the stairs. Bridie called out to her, but she ignored her and eventually she heard the older woman muttering complainingly as she announced that she was leaving her a tray.

Long after Bridie had gone away, Geraldine Frances roused herself enough to open the door and retrieve it. Instinct told her that she ought to eat, but when she was confronted by the food her stomach rose nauseously and she shuddered in sick distaste.

Bridie, whether from habit or on purpose, had placed a full bottle of Geraldine Frances's father's favourite claret on the tray, and on some savage impulse she barely understood Geraldine Frances poured herself a glass and drank it, not as the claret deserved to be drunk, savoured, but quickly and savagely, for no other reason than her instinctive knowledge that it would provide some kind of panacea for her pain.

By the time the bottle was empty, the wine had already hit her stomach…a stomach deprived of food for several days.

She went under the influence of the alcohol so quickly that she barely realised what was happening.

She surfaced from it briefly, shuddering at the almost animalistic, howling cries of pain filling the room, trying to blot out the sound of some tormented, hunted fox in its dying agony, and then abruptly realised that *she* was the one who had cried her pain into the silence of the room, letting it be absorbed by the ancient stones that had absorbed so much pain before hers.

Her glance fell on the fragile, delicate furniture that had been her mother's; pretty, feminine furniture that reminded her vividly and unbearably of the slim, small-boned woman whose body had been wrapped so sensuously around Charles's, and without knowing why or what she was doing she picked up one of the valuable chairs and smashed it against the wall.

Bridie, partly deaf, insulated from the sound of destruction in the tower room by the thickness of its walls and the distance that separated it from her private quarters near the kitchen, heard nothing…

Geraldine Frances, sobbing for breath, crying frenziedly, moved blindly round the room, goaded and driven by the pain inside her, unaware of the destruction she was wreaking, unaware of anything other than her own agony, her own helplessness…knowing she had no way of escape…that she would marry Charles, and that he would destroy her, just as she was destroying her mother's pretty French furniture. And if she didn't? As her father had known would happen, with the knowledge that she could no longer marry Charles had come the grim realisation of all that her own lack of a husband and children, especially sons, would set in train. She had no illusions left now. Charles had seen to that. No man could possibly want her…desire her…give her a child. She loathed and derided herself for ever thinking that they might. No, she would have no sons for Rothwell. So Charles would ultimately win...for his sons, if not for himself. Unless...unless *what*? What could she do?

She collapsed eventually, lying on the floor, shuddering and nauseous, somehow managing to find her way up the flight of stairs to her private bathroom, where she was violently and painfully sick.

Afterwards, her stomach and brain cleansed of alcohol, she staggered under the shower, turning the cold jet on full, letting the icy water burn her skin until she was covered in goose-bumps.

Weak and empty, she hid the bulk of her ungainly body in a voluminous towelling robe and padded through into her bedroom, wanting to sleep so that she could find the strength to face the morning and ultimately her next confrontation with Charles, but unable to do so.

Restlessly she moved round the room, and then, admitting she was not going to be able to sleep, she went back down to her private sitting-room.

As she opened the door, she couldn't believe what she was seeing. Broken furniture littered the room... Someone had written on the delicate French wallpaper with lipstick the words: 'I hate her...I hate her...' Someone had torn the curtains from the window and smashed the valuable antique lamps... Someone, in a frenzy of destruction, had attacked the room and virtually destroyed everything in it... And that someone was herself, she recognised dazedly as she surveyed the destruction and shuddered in self-revulsion. How could she have done such a thing?

No need to ask why she had done it. She had tried to destroy the room's beauty because she wanted to destroy the beauty of the woman who had taken Charles from her... Taken him? He had never been hers to lose.

She touched the wild lipstick message slashed across the wall, her fingers trembling. Who was it she hated? The other woman...or herself? As she removed her fingers, she knew the truth. She hated herself...hated and loathed herself with a soul-deep, terrible hatred that whispered to her that she deserved to be punished, to be humiliated, to be destroyed the way marriage to Charles was going to punish, humiliate and destroy her.

Bravely she pushed back the final barrier, admitting the knowledge she ached to suppress. Charles had been responsible for the death of her father. Oh, he had not perhaps killed him physically with his own hands, but she knew instinctively and irreversibly that he was responsible. Knew it as though Charles himself had told her so, even if her knowledge could probably never be proved. He had killed her father and now he intended to marry her. Because he wanted Rothwell.

She lifted her hands to her face in a helpless gesture of defeat, and as she did so her attention was caught by the magazine sticking out of her leather bag.

She stared at it, focusing on its unfamiliarity... frowning as she wondered how it got there. She never bought glossy magazines. Curiously she pulled it from her bag... There was a beautiful girl on the cover, and a large caption reading, 'Would you like to have this face? Read inside about the miracles of modern plastic surgery,' and before she knew what she was doing she was opening the magazine, flicking faster and faster through its pages as though driven by a mind beyond the control of her own.

By the time she found the article, her hands were trembling so much she could hardly hold the magazine straight enough to read. She devoured it quickly, dizzily, and had to go back and read it again, more slowly this time, as the fierce surge of adrenalin pumped through her and she ignored the destruction all around her, an idea so fantastic, so unthinkable forming in her mind that she hardly dared to contemplate it.

She stayed up all night, reading and rereading the article. She memorised it, and with it the name and address of the surgeon the magazine claimed was the most skilled and potentially the most expensive in the world.

There were interviews with women who had committed themselves, their faces and bodies to the woman's scalpel... Beautiful women... but none of them had undergone anything as radical as the kind of changes Geraldine Frances contemplated. And then she came to the final part of the article... the surgeon's description of work she had carried out on the victims of Beirut's internecine war... faces that had been completely rebuilt...

Completely rebuilt. Geraldine Frances felt her heart leap and pound. Impossible... crazy. She would have to be mad to contemplate such a thing. Mad. Or desperate...

She had a fleeting, momentary vision of the way Charles had looked at her when she'd told him that she wasn't going to marry him, and she shivered, recognising now what she had not recognised then, knowing illuminatingly all that her life would be if she ever allowed Charles to have control over any part of it.

A kind of fierce, desperate and instinctive need to survive pulsed through her. She thought of her father, of all that he had been, and then she thought of Charles and all that he was not and never would be, and she knew that, no matter what the cost to her in terms of physical pain, she had to take whatever route she could to escape from Charles, to punish him for what he had done, to make him suffer as she was suffering. Not just to suffer for the emotional pain and degradation he had caused her, but, far more importantly, to be brought down, destroyed for what he had done to her father.

Yes, she wanted to destroy him. But how? And then, as she looked at the magazine again, she knew.

Only by destroying Geraldine Frances as though she had never been and re-creating in her place a woman whom Charles would never recognise, only by allowing him to think that Rothwell was his, that he was secure, and then taking everything from him as he had wanted to take everything from her, would she be able to avenge her father's death.

Yes, she would destroy Charles... and, when she had done so, she would tell him why...

She picked up the magazine again, this time with determination and purpose.

Charles arrived at Castle Kilrayne five days later, alerted too late by Geraldine Frances's failure either to return to Rothwell or to get in touch with him, as he had confidently anticipated she would. After all, what other options were open to her? Either she married him and he gave her the son who would one day inherit from her, or he married someone else and gave another woman that child.

He knew his cousin well. After the blows he had dealt her, the home truths he had told her, she would never recover enough to let another man within a mile of her.

However, when he got there all he found waiting for him was a room that looked as though it had been torn apart by a force of nature and a note from Geraldine Frances saying that her life was something she could no longer endure.

The police made enquiries, of course, but her apparent suicide so soon after the death of the father she had adored was accepted as the action of a woman whose mind was disturbed and disorientated by shock and grief. Finding one of her shoes washed up on the beach, and surmising that she had thrown herself from the cliffs into the sea, they had instituted a search for her body, and when none was found Charles was told that legally it would be seven years before Geraldine Frances could be pronounced dead and he could inherit her estate and titles.

A minor inconvenience. To all intents and purposes he was now the Earl of Rothwell. Rothwell itself was his, and without the necessity of marrying Geraldine Frances.

Gleefully he reflected that she had done him the best favour she could have done him in taking her own life.

It was a pity, though, that she had not also seen fit to do so in a way that would have provided the authorities with her body, he reflected callously.

All through the highly secret negotiations Geraldine Frances carried out with her father's Swiss bankers and lawyers, she held on to the magazine as though it was some sort of talisman.

This was not the first time those astute Swiss bankers had been approached by someone who wanted to 'disappear' while still having access to their wealth. There were ways and means, if one was adept and skilled, and they were, but their skills came at a high price. Geraldine Frances paid it.

The desire for revenge now burned within her with the strong, unquenchable flame of a funeral pyre, overtaking the anguish and fear that had obsessed her in Ireland. They had been emotions far too turbulent and intense to endure. The feelings she had now, the need that burned ice-cold inside her, was different.

It was almost as though the person who had been Geraldine Frances no longer existed, almost as though that person had indeed died. Had in fact been killed by Charles's callousness.

The new Geraldine Frances was different. Stronger... surer...colder...*thinner*, she acknowledged with a bitter, acid smile as she caught sight of her reflection as she left the discreet and private entrance to the equally discreet and private venue the bankers had chosen for their meeting.

Her appetite, the appetite that had remorselessly driven her for so many years, had gone. The mere thought of food now nauseated her...now there was a different hunger within her...a new greed that would not allow any other need to exist in competition with it.

She was going to destroy Charles. She was going to destroy him just as surely and as uncaringly as he had destroyed her father; as he had wanted to destroy *her*.

Thoughts, plans, ideas whirled through her head, each one a venom-tipped arrow seeking its target. Outwardly

she was cold, controlled; admirable traits, if rather unusual in a woman, thought those bankers who were un-
knowingly her allies, listening to her and watching her.

From Zurich it was only a two-hour drive to the small
clinic owned and run by Annie Rogers. The clinic had
originally been a sanatorium for people suffering from
TB and was set high up in the Alps, approachable only
by a winding zigzag road.

The clinic was almost as difficult to find as Annie
Rogers herself, the celebrated plastic surgeon who had
made her name by creating beautiful faces, but who now,
it seemed, had eschewed that world, instead concentrating on mending the broken bodies of children from
all over the world, children who through no fault of their
own were paying the full penalty of the wars engaged in
by their elders.

The discovery that the clinic was funded in the main
by charitable donations had given Geraldine Frances the
lever she needed to ensure that Annie would see her.

There was no price she was not prepared to pay for
what she wanted…what she *needed* if she was to succeed
in her determination to destroy Charles.

Annie Rogers wasn't easy to persuade. The magazine
article was out of date, she told Geraldine Frances dispassionately but briskly, hardly even glancing at it. She
no longer performed plastic surgery purely for cosmetic
reasons, except in very rare and special cases.

It took Geraldine Frances almost two weeks to persuade Annie Rogers to accept her as a patient… What
she was suggesting wasn't impossible to achieve, but there
would be dangerous psychological barriers for her to
overcome…there would be pain such as she had never
known before; there would be weeks, months of physical
and mental agony, Annie warned Geraldine Frances, and
then was surprised when her patient said grimly, 'Good.
The more I suffer, the more I shall enjoy exacting every
last measure of atonement…'

Very much against her will, Geraldine Frances had been forced to tell Annie Rogers the purpose behind her request. Without knowing the reason, Annie had firmly refused to even consider taking her on as a patient.

She had made it plain that she did not consider what Geraldine Frances was contemplating was wise, but she had read in the other woman's eyes her unwavering determination to go through with her plans, and she had known that if she did not help her she would find someone else who would.

Intensely compassionate and intensely aware of the feelings of others, Annie had not been able to dismiss Geraldine Frances, knowing that she could all too easily end up in the hands of some unscrupulous and unskilled surgeon who could maim and even kill her.

She soothed her conscience by reminding herself that the fabulous fee Geraldine Frances was prepared to pay was desperately needed for the clinic.

Human emotions...they caused such problems, such havoc. She was beyond that now. She had loved only one man in her whole life. He was now dead, his death a result of his chosen way of life. She had loved him and she mourned him, but for her the clinic had become a retreat from the physical world in much the same way as women widowed had once retired into convents. All she now asked from life was to be allowed to perform the work which had become for her a personal crusade.

'It won't be easy,' she warned Geraldine Frances, once she had agreed to her request. 'There will be countless operations and almost unendurable pain. It will take at least a year, maybe longer, perhaps even closer to two, as it would be better if you slimmed down before we start on the surgery. We shall have to see how quickly your flesh heals.'

Two years. Geraldine Frances smiled grimly to herself. Time enough for Charles to grow secure...to feel safe...time enough for her suicide to have become an accepted fact...for people to have forgotten that anyone called Geraldine Frances had ever lived.

Seeing that she was not going to be put off, Annie said calmly, 'I shall assign you a room here. You can move in tomorrow.'

Geraldine Frances hadn't given her her real name; among the other things the men in Zurich had given her had been a new identity. From now on she was Silver Montaine. This name was a joke against herself as she had noticed a shock of white hair which had dramatically appeared at her left temple. All her recent trauma was gradually changing her life in every way.

Annie rang through to her assistant, and when the girl came said briskly to her, 'Jeannette, could you please take Miss Montaine over to the private wing and admit her?'

Geraldine Frances's eyebrows rose mockingly.

'A private wing...for orphans from Third World countries?'

'I do occasionally take private patients,' Annie reminded her drily. She frowned as something occurred to her, a small complication which she had not so far thought of.

'As a matter of fact,' she added casually, looking down at the papers on her desk, just in case this extraordinary young woman, who for all the obese plainness of her face and body had already demonstrated that she had a razor-sharp brain and the kind of perceptiveness that most people would find very daunting, should prove curious, 'I have another private patient here at the moment.'

It wasn't strictly true. Jake was not staying at the clinic as a patient in the strictest sense of the word. No amount of surgical skill could give him back his sight; and as for his scars...well, he had a few more painful operations to go before she could be content that she had done everything she could for him. His outward scars she could handle, but it was the ones he carried inside which worried her...

She sighed to herself. Only one thing, it seemed, would heal those.

Strange to think that both occupants of her private wing, in their very different ways, sought the same goal.

It was rare, in Annie's experience, for human beings to feel a need for retribution that was so strong that it superseded every other emotion and need. Revenge was normally a fierce but short-lived desire, quickly burning itself out, a form of desperate madness that sooner or later had to give way to sanity.

And yet there was nothing impulsive or short-lived about the feelings of either of these two. They were united, although they themselves did not know it, by the very logical determination, the resoluteness, the relentlessness, the sheer, cold, hard intentness of their separate purposes.

Even so, she reflected with wry humour, she doubted that either of them would welcome such knowledge, and she suspected that it might be a sensible idea to keep them apart.

She had only been able to persuade Jake to come here because he had needed her surgeon's skills... and because he needed a base... somewhere from which he could work towards his goal.

An impossible goal, some might think. Annie sighed softly. She was very fond of Jake... He and her husband had been in the army together, Jake a junior officer under Tom's command.

Tom had liked and respected him, and their friendship had developed as they continued working together in the drugs field.

Now Tom was dead and, while Jake had tried to reject her offer of help, in the end he had had nowhere else to go.

She looked down at her desk. On it was a small parcel containing, she suspected, tapes from Jake's contacts...the men he was using to try and track down his wife's murderers. Tapes...but then a blind man could hardly read letters...

PART THREE
Jake

CHAPTER FOURTEEN

JAKE heard Annie's familiar footsteps as she walked down the corridor outside his room and he discovered he was holding his breath, not really knowing whether or not he wanted her to come in.

There was someone else with her. They walked past his door and into the next room. He heard Annie's voice, and that of her companion. Another woman, her voice cool and controlled, the vowels effortlessly clear and sharp. His mouth twisted as he recognised the tell-tale accent of a member of the British upper classes.

He tried to fit a face and body to the voice, a supposedly therapeutic task, but one which left him feeling angry and frustrated with the limitations of his blindness.

When they had first told him in the small, bare military hospital that he had lost his sight, he had been in too much pain to care. It had been later, in London, that the full realisation of what that was going to mean, how it was going to affect the purpose which had driven him for the last four years, had really sunk in.

At headquarters they had commiserated with him, offering him awkward, uncomfortable pity, treating him with an unfamiliar blending of caution and unease, no one wanting to say what was now obvious.

That there was no place there for him now. What good was an agent who could no longer see? He would be a liability, not just to himself, but to others as well. There had been some talk of a desk job, but he had refused it angrily, and had sensed that they had been relieved by his refusal. The life that had been his for so long was now over.

They had sent him to a military hospital where he had received the very best treatment, both physical and psychological. They had taught him as best they could how to come to terms with the reality of his blindness, and then, later, when he received his final discharge, there had been an interview in London, with an anonymous man in an anonymous office, who had told him quietly and without emotion that his days of usefulness to the agency were now at an end.

The agency... He smiled grimly to himself, trying not to let his mind slip back across the years... trying to focus on the voice of the woman in the next room... a cool, sharp voice that reminded him of the voice of another woman from another time...

'Of course, it will have to be the army for Jake... I can't say that I approve, but you know how my father thinks. It's difficult enough financially as it is, and once Daddy dies, what with death duties and everything, I suppose the Park will have to go, probably to some ghastly *nouveau riche* pop star.'

The sharp, querulous voice was that of his aunt. Jake was standing outside the drawing-room door listening to her.

It was the sight of the gleaming Aston Martin car drawn up outside on the drive that had drawn him in, its immaculate refinement sharply in contrast to the house's neglected shabbiness.

The once pristine gravel drive was now infested with weeds, the elegance of Fitton Park's frontage marred by peeling paintwork. During heavy storms the roof leaked into the attic rooms and the stone façade was stained with rust where the gutter had rotted away.

Inside, the results of neglect through lack of money were even more visible. The once elegant plastered ceiling in the upper-floor ballroom now sagged ominously. Damp stained the walls, mould stretched grey-green tentacles across expensive silk wallpapers.

The whole house wore an air of shabby hopelessness, as though it had sunk into a state of apathy. Its rooms smelled of decay and damp; its furniture bloomed with fungus and rot.

His aunt tried to, as she described it, 'keep up appearances', which meant having a fire in the drawing-room to banish the damp, even though the rest of the house was freezing cold. It also meant that, whenever anyone visited, Finks, Grandfather's batman, had to walk along the maze of corridors from the ancient cavernous kitchen to the drawing-room, carrying a heavy silver tea-tray and its precious burden of delicate china Sèvres cups, despite the fact that he only had one leg. The other had been lost at Ypres. Jake's grandfather had lost an arm in the same action.

Jake had lost count of the number of times he and Justin had listened to their grandfather describing the incident.

Justin always flinched and looked sick, and Jake had learned long ago to manoeuvre himself so that he was standing or sitting in front of his elder brother, shielding him from their grandfather's fierce gaze.

Fittons did not look sick at the thought of losing a limb in action; rather, they gloried in the knowledge that they were doing what their ancestors had done since William the Conqueror had landed his force of men on English soil...fighting for Crown and Country. Portraits of generations of Fittons in military dress from various periods adorned the walls of the gallery that overlooked the enclosed Tudor gardens. The men of their family had a long and proud record as fighting men, a tradition which had cost their grandfather his arm and their father his life.

Their mother, whom their grandfather had dismissed as a wishy-washy creature, had died when Jake was four. A car accident dismissed by their grandfather as not being worthy of note.

The brothers, orphaned by the death of first their father and then their mother, were dispatched to live with their grandfather and his unmarried daughter.

Mary Fitton had been born seven years before their father. She was what had once been described as a spinster, both in inclination and by circumstance. She did not particularly like small children, especially dirty, noisy little boys.

Justin she could tolerate... just. He was quiet and biddable, and this she approved of, not seeing that behind the seven-year-old's meek, obedient behaviour lay the trauma of losing first his father and then the mother he adored, and then finding himself removed from the comfortable environment of a small London house to the rambling originally Tudor mansion that was Fitton Park, and to the care of a man who frankly terrified him.

Boys did not cry, Richard Fitton told his grandson disgustedly, the first time he discovered the seven-year-old weeping for his mother, and Jake, despite the fact that he was three years his brother's junior, had realised then, with the clear-sighted astuteness he had inherited from his father, that *he* must be the one to protect Justin now that their mother was no longer there to do it.

Justin had always been their mother's favourite. Jake had recognised that fact and accepted it with a stoicism that was part of his heritage from his grandfather. Justin was delicate, fine-boned, blond-haired like their mother, while he, Jake, took after their father, being far more robust, dark-haired and blue-eyed. People looking at the boys were often astonished to discover the age difference between them, because Jake was such a large, sturdy child and Justin so obviously delicate.

Delicate was a word that Richard Fitton associated purely with the female sex, and it was not one with which anyone was ever going to be allowed to describe his grandsons, especially his elder grandson. Already in his mind, Richard Fitton had decided that both boys would follow him into the army. It was their tradition...their heritage...their duty. He scowled ominously when, after Justin had been away at boarding school for six months, the headmaster approached him and tactfully suggested that Justin was a child who might benefit more scholastically from being educated at a good day school where he could return to the comfort and security of his home each night.

What was the man trying to suggest? Richard had roared at the headmaster. That his grandson was a weakling?

The man, who had been trying tactfully to explain that for a boy as sensitive and delicate as Justin a robust boarding-school atmosphere, especially one run on the semi-military lines of his establishment—which was favoured by those families who, like Richard Fitton, considered their sons from the day they were born to be destined for the élite regiments of the army, such as the Household Cavalry, the Guards, the Blues and Royals— was not perhaps the best place for him to spend his growing years.

There were other and quite frankly more dubious aspects of his grandson's personality that the headmaster had wanted to take up with Richard Fitton, but it had only taken a very few minutes in that gentleman's company for him to realise that to bring up the concern that was at the forefront of his mind would be a sheer waste of time.

The headmaster was not one of the old school, who believed that in allowing his pupils to brutalise one another he was doing them a favour and preparing them for what life would force them to endure sooner or later, but in a school full of boys, crammed together in the particular hothouse atmosphere such an establishment was bound to engender, it was impossible to prevent a certain degree of bullying, and worse...and Justin Fitton was just the kind of delicate, almost effeminate child who would quickly become the victim of both types of vice, which he privately considered the very worst aspects of single-sex private education.

A radical man in many ways, he was campaigning among the board of directors to permit the school to open its doors to girls as well as boys, but so far his campaigning had produced only a hardening of the die-hard attitude of its guardians.

Dismissed by Richard Fitton with a curt injunction to 'toughen the boy up a bit, it will do him good', the head-master reflected bitterly as he drove home that the only effect such a regime was likely to have on such a sensitive child was to destroy him completely.

Richard Fitton had two grandsons. The younger was due to join his brother at the beginning of the new autumn term. He could only hope that the younger child was made of hardier stuff than the elder.

During the Easter holidays, when Justin cried out in the night, it was Jake who crawled out of his own bed and crossed the freezing cold, cracked linoleum floor of their shared room on the nursery floor of the old house to comfort him and to whisper to him stoutly, 'Don't worry, Justin. I'll be there soon, and I'll look after you...'

Now, with only a matter of weeks to go before Justin returned home for the summer holidays, Jake paused outside the drawing-room door.

The car belonged to his aunt's godson, Noel Davenport-Legh; a young man of whom his grandfather disapproved and treated with the same cursory contempt he dished out to anyone who did not meet his favour.

'Where is the old boy?' he heard Noel asking in amusement.

'He's gone to Chester...on estate business...'

'Selling off more land?' Noel asked knowingly, and outside the door Jake winced... Although there were times when he resented his grandfather, hated him almost

for the way he treated Justin, they were linked by a
common bond that neither of them wanted to acknowledge...and that bond was their deep atavistic love of
their home and land.

Right from the start, Jake and his grandfather had
been at loggerheads, too alike to fit in easily with one
another. When Jake had constituted himself his brother's
champion, he had set himself on the opposing side to
his grandfather...

And it was almost always on Jake that the full brunt
of the old man's irascible temper fell. The loss of his
arm during the First World War had left him with a
wound that ached and tormented him, especially when
the weather was damp, and when autumn came and the
mist lay over the Cheshire plain like a thick veil the agony
of his aching flesh drove him into furious outbursts of
temper which often resulted in Jake's incurring the older
man's wrath to the point where he would be summoned
to the stables to receive the ritual beating which Richard
Fitton believed was a necessary part of a boy's upbringing.

He had received many a beating himself from his
father's hand, and was firmly convinced that it was the
only real way to discipline an unruly boy—and Jake was
most certainly unruly.

All the more so when Justin was at home, and, since
Richard Fitton did not have the insight to realise that
the younger boy was simply running interference for the
older with his determined, defiant stance against his
grandfather's edicts, it was on Jake's head, or rather on
Jake's buttocks, that the full weight of their grandfather's disapproval fell.

Afterwards, when he had stoically endured the humiliating agony of his grandfather's heavy leather belt
and his grandfather's equally heavy arm, wielding the
regulation 'six of the best' against his naked flesh, he
would be allowed to pull on his clothes and walk, stiff
and straight-backed, up to the nursery, where Mrs Finks

would be waiting for him, clucking with anxiety and concern as she bathed the afflicted flesh with a stinging concoction of her own design which healed the raw flesh even if it inflicted even more pain in doing so.

Noel Davenport-Legh was descended, like the Fittons, from an ancient Cheshire family, but, unlike Richard Fitton, *his* grandfather had seen the writing on the wall, and had cheerfully and unapologetically married the daughter of a wealthy Liverpool merchant, thus ensuring that his family would not suffer the financial hardships presently afflicting Fitton Park.

Noel was a cheerful if spoilt young man, genuinely fond of his godmother, who, as he saw it, did not have much of a life, cooped up in a crumbling, decaying house with her irascible and unreasonable father, and two dependent children who were not her own.

Once, long ago, Mary Fitton had been a pretty young woman; he had seen photographs of her with his mother to prove it. But now, while his mother had softened into middle age, cosseted by wealth and the love of her husband and children, Mary Fitton had hardened into it, so that it had cast her into an embittered and resentful mould.

Noel and his mother were possibly the only two people who genuinely cared for her, and she clung to their visits like lifelines in an otherwise viciously unkind sea. She hated her father for the life he made her lead, deprived of the comfort of a husband and family of her own, because he had insisted after his wife's death that she must take charge of her younger brother's children.

She didn't like small children. She never had and she never would, and to add to that she had resented the brothers both inwardly and outwardly because of their dependence upon her... just as she resented the lack of financial independence of her own which made it impossible to break free of her domineering father and his old-fashioned way of life.

From his position outside the door, Jake worryingly heard Noel saying, 'Well, as far as young Jake is concerned, the army will suit him fine. He's a real chip off the old block, as tough and hard-headed as the old man himself. But Justin...'

He paused, and there was something about the way he said Justin's name, something softer and subtly different about the sound of it that made Jake's stomach roll protestingly and his muscles clench as they always did whenever he sensed that Justin was in danger.

'The poor kid's finding school difficult enough. He'll never make the army——'

'He has no choice,' Mary Fitton interrupted him abruptly. 'When father goes, the death duties will eat up what's left of the estate...' Her voice shook with the bitterness and resentment which had begun to colour so much of her life. 'There'll be nothing left...nothing...'

There was silence inside the room, and Jake scuffed the toe of his shoe against the worn floorboards outside it. He didn't like Noel. There was something about him that made him withdraw from him without knowing what engendered his instinctive withdrawal.

'Pity you can't persuade the old man to let young Justin come home. The poor kid hates that damned school...'

'How do you know?'

Again the sharpness of his aunt's voice fell unpleasantly against Jake's ears.

'Oh, didn't I tell you? I called at the school on the off chance of being allowed to take him out for lunch a few weeks ago. I was in the area, staying with friends...and I remembered how miserable the poor little blighter had been the last time he was home...'

'You're too soft with him, Noel,' Mary Fitton chastised him. 'Father is right about one thing. Justin is far too sensitive for his own good. He needs toughening up, not spoiling...'

Outside the door, Jake felt his body tighten in anger and frustration. He hated his aunt for what she was saying about his brother. And yet at the same time he felt equally resentful of Noel Davenport-Legh. This perplexed him when he knew that he should feel grateful to him for taking the trouble to spend time with his brother. Something about Noel made him feel uneasy, like the stable cats when he brushed their fur the wrong way. It was an uncomfortable sensation...an uncomfortable awareness, and one that made him cross and worried inside.

Inside the room his aunt was saying brittly, 'I'd invite you to stay for lunch, but...'

'No, thanks,' Noel declined. 'Ma's having a dinner party next Saturday. She sent me to tell you that you're invited.'

His aunt laughed... A strained, high-pitched sound that jarred against Jake's ear.

'That's kind of her, Noel, but please tell her that I won't be able to accept.'

She had her pride, Mary acknowledged bitterly later as she watched him drive away. Even if she could persuade her father to allow her to accept the invitation, how on earth could she attend a dinner party wearing the one and only evening dress in her wardrobe, a garment which dated back more years than she cared to remember?

Upstairs, from the barred window of the old nursery, Jake watched Noel drive away. He envied him his car, but he knew that that wasn't why he disliked the man so much. No...his dislike was rooted in the funny, twisting, painful sensation inside him when Noel talked about his brother, and, although he didn't realise he was doing it, his small fists clenched hard against his side as he watched the Aston Martin drive away.

The world of an all-male boarding school had its own rules and hierarchies, and ordinarily Jake would soon have settled down quite quickly and happily within it. Added to the hardiness he had inherited from his grandfather was a sturdy independence which the deaths of both his parents had fostered, making him one of those rare individuals who genuinely did not feel the need to court the goodwill and approval of his peers, and yet at the same time was not one of nature's natural outsiders, the race apart who were somehow born knowing that they must march to a different drum.

He was a popular boy who wore his popularity lightly, a boy with a very advanced sense of responsibility twinned with a totally unexpected and deep-running vein of compassion which made Frederick Hesketh feel that he had discovered gold in a totally unexpected source.

At first sight, the headmaster had put Jake in the same mould as his grandfather. Unlike his brother, Jake would settle easily into the life his grandfather had chosen for him, but it was not very long before Frederick Hesketh was obliged to change his mind.

Not only did Jake display outstanding qualities of leadership, he also displayed an amazing sensitivity for the feelings of others . . . most especially for his older brother.

'It almost breaks my heart,' his wife told him sadly one afternoon. 'Do you think he knows yet . . . about his brother?'

Frederick Hesketh frowned. Homosexuality among the pupils was one of the more unpleasant aspects of all-male boarding schools, and one he personally was trying to stamp out, not from moral principles, but because he knew that the sexual relationships that sprang up between the boys were often based on cruelty and bullying on the part of the older boy and fear on the part of the younger, who was often, but not necessarily always, terrified into playing his part in the relationship.

It was a very invidious situation, underground and unacknowledged; something that, if acknowledged at all, was described as 'just a phase', 'something he will grow out of', or as a necessary outlet for the boys' growing sexual awareness.

But sometimes it would happen that one of the boys would discover that for him homosexuality was not just a passing phase, but that this involvement with his own sex was ultimately to be his way of life, and Frederick Hesketh was almost sure that this was the case with Justin Fitton.

The boy was almost femininely attractive physically, and thus designed by nature to be the focus of his peers' curiosity and attention...and not just his peers, Frederick acknowledged, frowning as he remembered the man who had visited the school the previous term, claiming that he was in some distant way related to Justin, and insisting on taking him out for the day.

Justin Fitton and his brother were both destined for the army, their grandfather had made that abundantly clear, but Frederick Hesketh knew already that Justin was simply not equipped physically or mentally for the rigours of army life. He was intelligent...they both were...intelligent enough to win a scholarship to Oxford, if he could persuade his grandfather to allow him to accept it. The old man was suspicious of education, and considered that the army taught a man all he needed to know.

If Frederick Hesketh could somehow or other persuade Richard Fitton to allow his older grandson to take an Oxford scholarship, he might be able to buy the boy a little more time in which to learn enough about himself to find a way of convincing his grandfather that he was simply not designed to take on the role the former had planned for him.

It would probably mean sacrificing the younger boy, which was a pity; he was equally intelligent, and equally capable of winning an Oxford scholarship, but he was far more suited to an army career than his elder brother. He wondered how Jake would react when the inevitable happened and he discovered the truth about his brother.

*   *   *

The inevitable happened within six months of Jake's joining the school. He was, as the headmaster had already observed, keenly intelligent.

The discovery came through the crude taunts of a couple of older boys and, once their meaning had sunk through, it didn't take Jake long to realise that inwardly he had always known about his brother. It didn't alter the way he felt about him; if anything he was more protective of him, his instinctive need to protect Justin growing rather than abating.

At home, during the school holidays, he deliberately brought himself to the forefront of his grandfather's attention, flouting his rules so that the old man was kept too busy chastising him to concern himself overmuch with Justin.

But then, one holiday, for the first time in their lives, the two boys quarrelled. The cause of the quarrel was Noel Davenport-Legh's frequent visits to the house, visits which inevitably concluded with his making an excuse to be alone with Justin.

The boys were now nine and twelve respectively, and bitterly Jake was forced to acknowledge that his brother was growing away from him.

The years passed; Justin sat and won his Oxford scholarship and reluctantly their grandfather was persuaded to allow him to accept it.

Justin shuddered with relief. He was now a finely drawn, effete young man so different from his younger brother that a stranger would never have known they were related.

Privately Jake acknowledged that he too would have enjoyed the challenge of Oxford. He had a good brain and enjoyed using it; the modern army was not the army his grandfather remembered, and he felt no resentment at Richard Fitton's insistence that it was to be his career. He already knew that he had a gift for managing men...plus a talent for organisation which would find a natural outlet as an army officer.

After school he would be going on to Sandhurst before joining an élite Guards regiment...his grandfather's and his grandfather's before him...and then, the Christmas when Justin was in his third year at Oxford, the blow fell.

Justin came home for Christmas, but not alone. He brought a friend with him, a tall, languid fellow undergraduate whose relationship with his brother was so obvious that Jake was stunned at Justin's folly in bringing him home.

The pair were infatuated with one another...and in the ancient rambling house, with its empty rooms and dusty corridors, it was easy for them to find somewhere to be alone. Until the day they went too far...

It was the day of the Boxing Day hunt. Although now well into his eighties, their grandfather had insisted on riding out with the hounds on a borrowed hunter, since he himself could no longer afford the luxury of his own stable. Justin hated hunting and refused point-blank to go with him, and Jake, running his customary interference, drew the old man's fire by telling him that, while he was totally against the wanton hunting down and killing of an animal for no better reason than that it gave the hunters some kind of barbaric pleasure, he would ride out with him if only to make sure that no accident befell him.

With the young man at just over six feet tall, and with the breadth of chest to match his height, it was no longer possible for the old man to take his belt to his grandson, but his remarks had the desired effect, and Richard Fitton turned his temper away from Justin and on to Jake.

What no one could have foreseen was that the hunt would be cut short by the appearance of a group of hunt saboteurs, who, while trying to protect the hunters' quarry, managed to lame Richard Fitton's borrowed hunter to such an extent that Richard had to dismount, and both he and Jake had to leave the others and make their way home.

Naturally the older man was furious at this abrupt end to one of the few pleasures his life still held. The lamed horse had been driven back to the house in a borrowed horsebox, and while Jake, who was driving, stopped the Land Rover, his grandfather got out and went to lead the horse into the stables.

It was the curse his grandfather bellowed that alerted Jake to the fact that something was wrong. He sprinted across the yard and burst into the dilapidated stable to find his grandfather standing over the prone and naked figures of Justin and his lover, his face purple with rage, his hand clenched round the whip he had snatched up in his fury.

It whistled through the air, biting into Justin's pale soft flesh, drawing an almost inhuman scream of pain from the young man's throat as he tried desperately to protect both himself and his lover.

The shock of what was happening held Jake motionless until he heard Justin's scream. Fury galvanised him into action, and he leapt forward, snatching the whip from their grandfather, his strength far superior to that of the older man as he wrenched it out of his hand and then threw it the length of the stable.

'You knew about this, didn't you?' Richard Fitton accused him bitterly, ignoring Justin and turning on Jake, his face congested with blood as he almost stammered in the intensity of his fury. 'My grandson, a damned sodomite, and you knew... Get out!' he demanded thickly. 'Now... both of you. I never want to set eyes on the pair of you again.'

In the corner of the stable Justin was whimpering with pain and shock, while his lover cowered beside him. Without giving them another look, Richard Fitton walked out into the stableyard.

'We can't leave...' Justin whimpered, appealing to Jake. 'There's nowhere we can go...'

Jake focused blindly on him. It hurt him that he should feel this welling of resentment and anger against his brother... How *could* he have been so stupid? He must have known the risks he was taking.

There was blood oozing from the welt across his buttocks and he was crying brokenly, and Jake, who had withstood many a worse beating without a murmur, felt tears stinging his own eyes... He felt Justin's pain and yet at the same time he felt a strong sense of revulsion. He knew what Justin was, but the sight of him naked in the arms of his lover angered him... And not just angered him, but sickened him as well, he acknowledged as he felt the nausea burn his stomach and knew he had to escape from the stable before he betrayed himself completely.

Because of that need to escape, he didn't focus properly on what Justin was saying, and, desperate for fresh air... for solitude... he said curtly, 'Don't worry about it... By tomorrow the old man will have forgotten he told you to go...'

He saw from the relief in Justin's eyes that he had said the right thing. Privately he doubted that their grandfather would ever forgive or forget, but now wasn't the time to tell Justin so. Despite his scholarship, Justin was heavily dependent on their grandfather for the allowance he gave him... an allowance which, though grudging, the old man considered to be Justin's right as his eldest grandson and heir.

Wanting only to be alone, unable to face the thought of either drawing his grandfather's fire or of giving Justin the comfort he knew his brother craved and needed, Jake headed for the horsebox and said curtly that he ought to deliver it back to its rightful owner.

As he got in the driver's seat, Justin's lover scrambled into his clothes and said jerkily to him, 'Hang on a few minutes, will you?' Then, 'I think I'd better leave,' he said awkwardly to Justin, who had followed him to the door of the stable. 'I'll just go and get my things...'

Jake knew he shouldn't blame him, and that probably, had the circumstances been reversed, Justin would have behaved in exactly the same way as Leo, but he couldn't help the fierce surge of resentment on his brother's behalf that burned through him as he watched, cold-eyed and unhelpful, as Leo Saunders loaded his hastily packed case into the horsebox and got in beside him.

Jake drove him to the station in silence, refusing to respond to any of his attempts to make conversation. He knew that the other man was not his brother's seducer, nor indeed his first lover, and that it had probably not even been his idea that they should make love in the stable, but because Justin *was* his brother, because he loved him and had all his life protected him, he couldn't deal with the situation logically, and found that by the time he had dropped his unwanted passenger off outside the station he was feeling as violent towards him as their grandfather had been towards Justin.

Reversing the horsebox, he drove far too dangerously and far too fast down the narrow country lanes, heading for the home of the man who had loaned it to them.

He was a relative newcomer to the area, a businessman who had bought up a small local estate, which he ran as more of a hobby than anything else.

The small Queen Anne house had received the attentions of one of London's most prestigious interior designers...the gardens had been meticulously planned and redesigned to provide the perfect backdrop for the house, and Jake's mouth twisted bitterly as he drove down the immaculate drive, so very different from the drive at Fitton Park.

Here everything breathed order and wealth...when Jake drove the horsebox to the rear of the house, the courtyard was empty apart from a brilliant red Porsche car and a girl standing beside it.

She was a stranger to Jake, a smart, pert-looking girl with a narrow waist and generous breasts. She looked him over with frank curiosity as he got out of the Land Rover, surveying him slowly without the slightest degree of embarrassment.

He hadn't seen her at the hunt; she was wearing not riding clothes but a longish suede skirt that made the most of her narrow waist and a silk shirt that showed quite plainly that she wasn't wearing a bra.

'If you've come to collect someone from the hunt, I'm afraid you've come to the wrong house,' she told him assessingly. 'They're all over at Colonel Walters's.'

Her accent was pure Sloane Ranger, her teeth sharp and white.

'I'm not here to collect anyone,' he told her curtly. 'Just to return the box...'

Interest quickened in her eyes. 'My father isn't back yet. Why don't you come inside and wait for him...? I could run you back later, if you like...'

He hadn't given the fact that he had no means of getting home a thought in his urgent need to escape from the stable and its almost tangible emotions.

He didn't want to go back, he acknowledged. He needed time before he could cope with what was waiting for him there.

She saw the hesitation in his eyes and smiled coaxingly.

'Come on...it will be ages before Daddy gets back. I'm all on my own here and in need of a bit of company.' She wrinkled her nose. 'God, I hate the country, don't you?'

Without giving him a chance to reply, she swung round so that the soft suede flared round her hips and lovingly outlined the curves of her buttocks, and, without even realising what he was doing, Jake found that he was following her.

They went into the house via the rear entrance, into a kitchen almost as cavernous as the one at Fitton Park, but far, far better equipped.

A small, plump woman eyed them both disapprovingly as they walked in.

'I thought you said you were going out, Miss Saffron,' she complained. 'It's my night off, you know, and if you want something to eat——'

'Stop fussing, Belle,' the girl drawled arrogantly, and then, ignoring her, turned to Jake and took hold of his arm, pushing open the door with her free hand so that as they passed through it the softness of her breast was pressed against the hard muscle of his forearm.

The sensation disturbed him; he wanted to pull away, but pride wouldn't allow him to do so.

'Are you hungry?' she asked him softly and suggestively once she had let the door swing closed behind them. 'Because if so...'

She gave a small giggle, and Jake realised that the dizzying, provocative scent he was breathing in came from her, and that the way she was rubbing her body against his arm was not accidental at all, but perfectly deliberate.

He was not totally inexperienced, although his contact with the opposite sex had been limited to half a dozen or so fumbled exchanges at various Christmas parties.

He had, up until now, been warily cautious about his own sexuality. Initially there had been a need to prove that he was not like his brother, but once he had realised that he felt no desire at all for any kind of sexual relationship with his own sex, he had realised that what mattered to him most was his own ability to feel at ease with himself rather than any need to prove to others that he was rampantly heterosexual.

After the various school holidays he had listened closely to the inevitable sexual boastings of his contemporaries, but as yet the awkward and hasty fumblings with girls' clothing, while they giggled and protested, came nowhere near affording him the satisfaction he got from masturbation.

Up until now the arousal of his body had been caused by his own actions, and he stopped dead in the corridor

as she rubbed against him and for the first time his body
responded violently and uncontrollably to the stimu-
lation of someone else.

There was enough light for her to see what had happened to him, and she obviously felt none of his embarrassment, because she looked openly at him and then,
lifting limpid eyes to his face, stretched out her hand
and pressed it caressingly against him, saying huskily,
'My goodness. I think we'd better do something about
that, don't you?'

The shock in his eyes made her laugh.

'What's wrong?' she taunted. 'Not frightened that
Daddy might come home and find us, are you?' She
gave a tiny, dismissive shrug. 'He won't. He'll be far too
busy bonking the Colonel's wife to care what we're
doing...'

There was an acid bitterness in her voice that Jake was
still too young to wholly define. What he did know was
that this girl was both bitter and unhappy, and that on
closer inspection she was older than he had first supposed... probably at least twenty-one to his seventeen.

In fact Saffron Howard was twenty-five, although she
knew she looked younger. She was also on the point of
getting engaged to a very dull but rich young man whose
father was something in the City, and for the sake of
propriety and the future of her marriage she had been
forced to limit her sexual activities exclusively to the
partner who was going to be her husband.

Sexually Christopher bored her out of her mind. Once
they were married she had no intention of being faithful.
Christopher would make her an ideal husband—rich,
indulgent, very much in love with her... She would be
able to wind him round her little finger, but right now
the ache between her thighs was far more important than
her impending marriage, and every feminine instinct she
possessed—and she possessed more than her fair share—
told her that this silent boy-man would be able to more
than adequately assuage it.

She took him upstairs to her own suite of rooms. Jake wasn't stupid. He knew very well now what she wanted from him.

Normally he would have withdrawn from the situation, but for once his customary caution was overruled by his need to find something to stop him thinking about that scene in the stable.

There was a raw, burning anger inside him . . . a pain that wouldn't let him go . . . and mingled with that pain a guilt that he had somehow let down both his brother and his grandfather . . . And oddly, despite the old man's behaviour towards him, he was unwillingly fond of him, finding it far easier to understand Richard Fitton's attitude and beliefs than Richard Fitton could understand his grandson's.

Saffron's suite of rooms consisted of an over-prettily furnished sitting-room, crammed with chintz-covered furniture in pastel pinks and blues, and matching curtains caught up with an over-abundance of bows and tassels; a bedroom decorated in the same style and, if anything even more chintzily feminine, her bathroom and dressing-room.

It was the sitting-room to which she led Jake, offering him a dainty little armchair in front of the open fire.

'Good, Bert's left plenty of logs,' was her only remark as she invited him to sit down. 'He and Belle think they can get away with murder with my father . . . He spoils them rotten . . . Just as well it's their night off, though,' she added suggestively.

A fierce thrill of sensation went through Jake as she trailed her fingers down over his thigh, and his body leapt in obvious response to her touch. She laughed softly, and made a sound in her throat not unlike a cat purring before digging her nails almost painfully into the hardness of his arousal.

She was leaning towards him, her breasts virtually on a level with his mouth.

He could see the hardness of her nipples pressing against her silk shirt. He could even see, through the fabric, the darkness of the areola surrounding them. He took a deep breath, the air rattling in his lungs. When she moved back from him, he felt dizzy and light-headed with arousal. His whole body pulsed with the intensity of it. He could feel himself, swollen and hard, pressing against the fabric of his jeans so that the pressure was almost painful.

As she stood back from him, her hands went to the buttons on her blouse. She unfastened them slowly, a catlike smile curling her mouth as she deliberately let the silky fabric slide down her arms so that only the top half of her breasts was exposed, the dark hardness of her nipples almost but not quite buried in the soft folds of silk.

Jake couldn't take his eyes off her. He swallowed visibly, aching with excitement and apprehension.

Half of him didn't really believe what was happening. It was as though this were a dream he had invented to stop himself thinking about the trauma of that scene in the stable.

'What's the matter?' Saffron's voice taunted him. 'Never seen a woman's breasts before?'

She laughed as he lied in denial.

'What's wrong, then?' she whispered tormentingly against his ear, as her tongue shiveringly investigated the hard whorls of flesh, her breath making him shudder in a fresh paroxysm of pleasure. 'If it isn't that you don't know what to do...perhaps it's because you don't like women...'

The taunt came too close to home, acting on him like acid applied to an open wound. He forgot his inexperience and awkwardness, reaching clumsily for her, spanning her ribcage with his hands while he buried his face in the provocative softness of her breasts... She made a tiny explosive sound which could have been laughter or could have been pain, taking his hands and

moving them upwards from her ribcage to her breasts
and then holding them there while she moved her body
so that her nipples rubbed erotically against the palms
of his hands. The sensation of her hard nipples moving
sensuously against his flesh made pleasure burst through
him, his body straining upwards to reach her, but she
laughed and evaded him mockingly, whispering...

'Ah, no, not yet. First you've got to show me that
you know how to please a woman.'

And yet, while she denied him, her hand was deliberately caressing him through the taut fabric of his jeans,
arousing the hard pulse within him to the point where
he felt he was going to burst with the agony of what she
was doing to him.

'Not so impatient,' she chided him. 'There's no
hurry... Daddy won't be back until morning.'

She was moving her body against him, rubbing herself
sinuously against him. She made a soft purring sound
in her throat and then bit sharply into his earlobe and
complained throatily, 'Come on...or do I have to do
all the work myself?' She felt him tense and moved away
from him, watching him with mocking eyes as his skin
darkened with excitement at the thought of what she
was implying. 'Ah, so that's what turns you on, is it...?'

She had begun to realise that he was probably younger
than she had first thought. His height and breadth of
shoulder had initially deceived her, and now the sense
of humour that was one of her major assets briefly
lightened the fierce need burning inside her, and made
her deride herself mentally, Trust you to find yourself
the only man in a fifty-mile radius who's probably still
a virgin...

A virgin... There was something vaguely piquant
about that thought...something that titillated and intrigued... She wondered what it would be like to teach
him...to show him how... There was certainly nothing
wrong with the equipment that nature had seen fit to
bestow on him. She wondered wryly how old he *was*,

and if there was a chance that what she was contemplating was illegal, and then banished the thought as the ache inside her intensified. She was pretty sure now that he was totally inexperienced, but because her own sexual drive was such that it often caused her to walk the very fine line that sometimes divided physical pleasure from physical pain, she didn't let him know she had realised it.

'I think we'd be more comfortable in my bedroom,' she told him in that purring voice that raised goose-bumps all over his skin. 'I perform so much better on a stage,' she added obliquely, hiding her amusement when she saw that he had no idea what she meant.

Well, tonight was going to change all that. A virgin he might be, but that did not absolve him from paying for his initiation by learning how he could satisfy her...*and* learning that *that* was far more important than satisfying himself.

Numbly Jake followed her as she turned her back on him and walked through to the bedroom.

Here too a fire burned in the open grate... The bed was a four-poster, hung with chintz curtains, and beneath the cover, which she swished back, the bed was surprisingly covered in cool white linen.

She saw the way he looked at it and smiled wickedly at him.

'What did you expect, black satin?' She shook her head. 'Linen is so much nicer... Come and feel.'

Idiotically, he did as she commanded, almost as though he were a puppet programmed to obey her commands, but he was barely aware of the cold crispness of the linen beneath his fingertips, because, as she stood next to him, she slowly and deliberately finished removing her blouse.

Her breasts were large and firm, the pigmentation of the areola around her nipples very dark in contrast to her creamy skin... Her flesh had a sheen which made him ache to reach out and touch it, and her nipples...

He found he had forgotten to breathe, and his chest constricted. He wondered what it would feel like to have her lying on top of him while he sucked hard on those hard nipples. The thought made him go hot and dizzy. She looked a little like a gypsy standing there with her bare breasts and her dark curls, her eyes sparkling with wanton amusement, the suede skirt clinging to her narrow waist.

Her legs were bare beneath it, and the pupils of his eyes dilated as he realised it.

She was tiny, barely five feet, he recognised absently as they stood together, the heat and scent coming off her body making him tremble.

He wondered what she was wearing beneath the skirt, and as though he had said the words out loud she smiled provocatively at him and, taking his free hand, placed it on her suede-covered thigh and said softly, 'Now you know how nice linen feels to touch, why not see if you can't touch something even nicer?'

She didn't laugh as she felt the violent tremor that ran through him, but as his hand inched awkwardly up her thigh, and then got caught in the folds of her skirt, so that he had to release it and her before he could slide his hot, dry palm beneath the fabric to discover the cool bareness of her skin, she moved towards him, so that her naked breasts were pressed flat against his chest. Her mouth stroked his throat, drawing a convulsive shudder from him, and as her small, sharp teeth bit delicately into his skin he forgot his nervousness in the tide of sharp need that overwhelmed him. By the time his brain had assimilated what his hand was doing, he had already discovered the fact that beneath the skirt she was completely naked and that his cupped hand could easily hold the soft mound covered with a mat of curls that prickled against his palm. She made a sound against his throat and her sharp teeth bit almost painfully into his flesh. His hand tightened involuntarily and she moved against him.

The blood roared in his ears; his body pulsed frantically as the heat devoured him; he felt her tugging at his shirt, releasing him from both it and his jeans, and then removing her own skirt, casually dismissive of both his nakedness and her own as she moved on to the bed and patted the empty space beside her.

He was trembling so much he could hardly move, his awkwardness and lack of experience forgotten in the burning need that drove him.

He kissed her fiercely and eagerly, grinding his mouth down against hers, his hands kneading the fullness of her breasts as her legs opened to receive him and her nails raked sharply along his spine.

He thrust into her blindly and inexpertly, grinding his teeth with impatience and resentment when her hands caught his hips and held him off for a few seconds that seemed like an eternity as she positioned herself to receive him.

The sensation of being inside her both awed and shocked him, stilling him momentarily as he savoured the silken wrapping of her heated flesh, and then the fierce, pounding desire swept over him, and he moved inexpertly once, twice...and then the hot, flooding torrent of sexual release burst through him, leaving him slumped on top of her, exhausted and drained, and suddenly uncomfortably aware of what he was doing.

He withdrew from her with a stammered apology that made her raise her eyes to heaven and say crisply, 'Well, you've certainly got something to apologise for. Haven't you ever heard that gentlemen come last?' she derided him, watching the hot colour sting his face without sympathy.

'I suppose I'll have to let you off, seeing as that was your first time,' she added acidly, and then laughed as she saw the shock dawn in his eyes.

'What's wrong? Did you think I wouldn't know?' she demanded mockingly. 'My God, if it *wasn't* your first time, then all I can say is that you're a pretty poor specimen... You didn't even try to give me any satisfaction...'

She rolled over and said briskly, 'OK, little boy, you've had your fun... now it's *my* turn to have mine.' She looked at him, and he was cringingly conscious of the exhausted limpness of his body. As though something of his confusion and misery reached out to her, she said half scornfully, 'Oh, the equipment's fine... you just don't know how to use it, that's all.'

She gave him a smile which was at the same time both bewitching and mocking.

'This is your lucky night, little boy, because I'm feeling generous enough to teach you...'

She grimaced herself, knowing full well that it wasn't generosity that was motivating her, but frustration. She could send him away and then give herself the physical release she needed, but it wouldn't be the same as feeling this superbly male creature moving inside her, filling her with the hard pulse of his flesh... pleasuring her as she was sure he would pleasure her once *she* had shown him how.

'The first thing you need to know is that you must forget about that...' she told him, indicating his limp penis, 'and concentrate instead on this.'

Her hand briefly covered her own sex and was then removed. Her total lack of embarrassment was something new to him, and it both puzzled and intrigued him. According to the experiences of his schoolmates, women were something that had to be pursued and coaxed into allowing them the freedom of their bodies, but this one wasn't like that...

Half of him wanted to run from her, sensing that he was way, way out of his league, but the other half noted the way her fingers rested lightly against her sex for the merest heartbeat, pressing firmly against the mound of flesh, and that same part of him also noted the thrust of her nipples and how they too were slightly swollen, and some of the things he had heard about and read about came back to him illuminatingly, so that when she said coolly, 'It takes far longer for a woman to become aroused than a man, so the first thing you need to know is how to initiate that arousal,' he was able to move towards her with a creditable assumption of sophistication and say casually as he cupped her breasts with his hands,

'Like this, you mean?'

He trembled a little as he ran the pads of his thumbs over and around her nipples, not sure if she was going to laugh at him, and then he felt her body jerk as though an electric current had run through it, and he ran the pads of his thumbs over and over her nipples again, this time pressing them against the swollen flesh and rubbing it experimentally.

When she arched her back and her head fell back, he stopped abruptly, confused by her action.

She swore briefly under her breath, and when she raised her head he could see that her eyes had narrowed to slumberous cats' slits and that her face had suffused with colour.

'I didn't want you to stop, you idiot,' she derided him, adding tauntingly, 'You don't know *anything*, do you? Women don't just like to be touched ... They like to be stroked, kissed, sucked, bitten.'

Fire burned through his guts as she caught hold of his head and lowered it to her breasts.

She moaned as he sucked on her, arching her back and dragging his hands down her body, holding one of them between her thighs while she rubbed herself rhythmically against it and then lifted her head to whisper commands in his ear that he followed blindly and implicitly.

This time, when he entered her, he was sure he was going to pleasure her, and when after no more than a few fiercely blissful thrusts it was over and she was moving angrily away from him he felt sick with mortification that he had failed her.

The exhaustion that made his body tremble uncontrollably made it impossible for him to do anything other than lie on the bed, fighting for breath and self-control, his eyes closed as he tried to shut out her angry, sullen face.

When he felt the rhythmic movement of the bed he opened his eyes in bewilderment, his muscles locking in shocked amazement as he saw what she was doing.

She was lying with her legs wide open, her back against the mound of pillows, her fingers moving quickly and knowledgeably against her own sex.

She saw that he was watching her and her fingers stilled.

'What's wrong?' she taunted him. 'If you can't satisfy me, I'll have to do it myself, won't I?'

And, quite calmly, as though he weren't there, she closed her eyes and went back to her subtle and skilled manipulation of her own flesh.

Appalled and fascinated, Jake found that he couldn't look away...couldn't do anything other than simply stare and feel his breath lock in his throat as his body registered the rhythmic movements of hers.

He was young enough and fit enough to recover very quickly from his own climax and Saffron, furiously angry both with him for disappointing her and with herself for being stupid enough to have thought that he might be able to satisfy her, resolutely continued to shut him out, keeping her eyes tightly closed while her body slowly hummed with pleasure and the quick, delicate movements of her fingers aroused the familiar onset of pre-climax sensation.

She didn't see Jake move, and indeed had almost forgotten he was even there as she concentrated wholly on reaching her own inner goal, so that the totally unexpected sensation of his teeth raking her sensitive breasts, and his hands pushing away her own so that he could enter her stimulated, eager body with a fierce, hard thrust and then another, made her jerk convulsively as an electric sensation raced from her breast to her groin and then convulsed her again as his body enforced its rhythm on her, and his teeth savaged the tender bud of her nipple so that she felt the delicious onset of sharp desire.

This time it was different... This time he was slow to climax, driving into her and into her so that her flesh convulsed around him and held him while she cried out and raked him with her nails.

Even then it wasn't enough, and he stayed with her, driving both her and himself to an ecstasy that made her scream her pleasure until her throat was raw and so was his back.

Afterwards, satisfied, and almost purring with the release of it, she was disposed to be indulgent.

Before he left her in the cool shadows of the winter dawn, borrowing her car to drive back to Fitton Park and then crawl into his familiar narrow bed in a state of mental and physical exhaustion, she had shown him what it felt like to have her hands and mouth caressing his flesh, and she had shown him also what it felt like to take her into his mouth and to pleasure her until her stifled whimpers of pleasure became guttural sounds of need, only silenced by the hot thrust of his flesh deep within the silken net of hers.

CHAPTER FIFTEEN

IT WAS Jake's aunt who woke him, gabbling something unintelligible in his ear about Justin and his grandfather as she shook him frantically, her voice high-pitched and hysterical with shocked fear.

He opened his eyes reluctantly, coming out of his deep sleep like a swimmer coming up through too-deep water. He was naked under the bedclothes, but his aunt, who was normally frigidly obsessive about what she termed 'keeping to decent standards', made no move to turn away from the bed as the sheet slipped down over his bare torso.

He shook his head, trying to clear his brain; images of last night still lingered hauntingly there, and his body, young and strong, was still in a state of semi-arousal.

'What is it? What's wrong?' he demanded thickly, suddenly remembering the scene in the stable and his grandfather's bitter rejection of Justin.

'It's Justin and Father... Come quickly... Oh, my God, what are we going to do?'

He was alert now, reaching to the other side of the bed for his discarded jeans, pulling them on as quickly and discreetly as he could under the cover of the bed-clothes, while at the other side of the bed his aunt continued to wring her hands and gabble hysterically.

What was happening downstairs? He knew his grandfather's temper, and knew that the old man would not hesitate to unleash it on Justin. He flinched as he thought of his over-sensitive brother being subjected to the same kind of beating he himself had endured so often.

Justin could not stand physical pain. He would weep and beg, and that would drive his grandfather to even further paroxysms of fury...

'Where are they?' he demanded tersely, getting out of bed, pulling on a pair of tennis shoes,

'In the gun-room... Oh, God, what's going to happen...what will people say...?'

He was already halfway down the narrow stairs that led up to this third storey of humble rooms and corridors, but he hesitated, a cold finger of horror touching his spine. His stomach moved queasily as the fear spread. Without a word to his aunt, he started to run, not stopping until he had burst into the small, narrow room behind his grandfather's study, where his grandfather's shotguns were kept chained and padlocked to their stands.

He had known with one part of his mind what he would find, but the shock of it numbed him so that for what seemed to be a lifetime he could only stand and stare at the two bodies.

The effect of a powerful service revolver fired at such short range had made both their faces indistinguishable...pulped masses of flesh, blood and bone that he wanted to turn away from but could not.

He had started to tremble, a fierce, thrilling sensation of nausea and shock that gripped his body in fine convulsions. Sweat broke out on his forehead. Justin was holding the pistol, his fingers curled round it in the rigor of death.

'Oh, God...' He felt the tears sting his throat and eyes and backed hurriedly towards the door, bumping into his aunt.

'I heard them quarrelling last night,' she told him, calmer now that he was standing between her and the shocking sight of her father and her nephew. 'Father was shouting at Justin...' She gave a tiny shiver. 'That was after dinner when I was on my way to bed... I took one of my sleeping tablets... I never heard you come in.'

A fresh complication... How was he going to explain why he had not been here without implicating Saffron?

He was seventeen years old, but suddenly he felt as though he were seventy. He looked at his aunt and recognised that she could neither help nor support him. She was not a young woman, nor a strong one emotionally, and now she looked as though she was on the point of collapsing.

'What are we going to do?' She was wringing her hands again.

There was only one thing they could do.

'I'd better go and ring the police,' Jake said heavily.

She tried to stop him, screaming at him that he couldn't, that if he did the news would be all over Cheshire within a day, but Jake remained firm. Sickened and shocked though he was by the sight of the two bodies, and by the knowledge of all that had happened, he had enough maturity to recognise that this was something that couldn't be hidden.

After he had rung the police, he hesitated and then telephoned their local vicar, not really knowing who else to turn to. His aunt was a regular churchgoer, and it was more for her sake than anything else that he had taken this step, but later he was to reflect with gratitude that he could hardly have had anyone better to stand by him during the rigorous hours of cross-examination by the police authorities.

There was no point in concealing the truth. While his aunt had hysterics in the drawing-room, and was comforted by a WPC who looked about the same age as Saffron and reminded Jake bitterly and guiltily of the way he had spent the evening while his brother and grandfather had been dying, Jake was standing in his grandfather's study, explaining as briefly and lucidly as he could the events of the previous day.

He winced when the police inspector said tersely, 'So what you're saying, in effect, was that your brother had brought a male lover home with him and that your grandfather discovered them together...'

He inclined his head briefly, his mouth hard and terse, and, as the inspector commented later to his wife, he had felt heartily sorry for the lad, because it was obvious that he had been close to the older boy, and to wake up and find what he had found...

The police were pretty sure they knew what had happened... His aunt had confirmed that they had been quarrelling... One of them, maybe Richard Fitton, or maybe his grandson, had reached for one of the guns.

What was pretty clear was that Justin Fitton had somehow or other, whether deliberately or by accident while they were struggling, fired the gun and killed his grandfather, and had then turned the same gun on himself.

The inspector looked at the heavy service revolver and sighed faintly.

'It belonged to my father,' Jake told him quietly, and saw a faint flicker of sympathy in the older man's eyes. 'My grandfather always kept it cleaned and loaded...'

'A dangerous practice,' the inspector said heavily.

The vicar, who had arrived in time to hear his summing up of what he suspected had happened, said calmly, 'Something like this tends to get a lot of unwanted media attention, and in the circumstances I think it might be best if Miss Fitton and Jake came to stay at the vicarage for the time being, if you've no objection.'

'None at all... A lot of idiotic journalists milling around looking for enough dirt to sell their grimy rags doesn't do anything to help us,' the inspector said disgustedly. 'Scavengers, the lot of them...' He glanced at Jake's white, averted face, and said awkwardly, 'We'll do our best to keep things as quiet as we can, lad.'

Jake had already told him, without mentioning Saffron by name, why he had not been in the house the previous evening, and once again the inspector had felt a flash of sympathy for him... He looked a sensible enough lad, and if it was true that the old man had virtually been living on a small pension while the house crumbled around him, then there were going to be hard times for this boy now... He had a son of his own, just sixteen, and he wondered savagely how he would have coped with a similar situation.

While he talked to the vicar, Jake looked numbly at the now shrouded bodies of his uncle and brother. Guilt rolled through him like a sickness. If he had been there... He felt angry tears prick his eyeballs and, as though he knew what he was going through, the vicar moved away from the inspector and came to stand beside him.

He made no attempt to touch him and just said quietly, 'I know it isn't easy, but try to look on it as God's will, Jake... And remember, it would be arrogant of you, and a usurpation of a power that does not belong to you, to believe that any of this...' he gestured to the two bodies '...could have either been caused or prevented by any action of yours.'

Jake balled his fists at his sides, aching to cry out that the vicar was a fool if he hoped to placate him with such banal comfort, and yet a part of him was soothed by his words, clinging on to them with gratitude and praying that he might be right. At the same time he prayed to his brother for forgiveness...for not being there...aching inside for the tragedy and loss.

It wasn't possible to keep the story out of the papers, but by the time it broke Jake had had time to become accustomed to the reality of what had happened.

His aunt had completely collapsed, and at her own suggestion was now staying with the Davenport-Leghs.

Jake was supposed to be back at school. Term had started, but even without the interview with his grandfather's solicitor he had known that, with the crippling

burden of death duties, there could be no question of
another year at public school.

As the solicitor had explained gravely to him, the
money that would be left would be pitifully small. If
only the estate could be sold—but there was no demand
at the moment, and the house needed a fortune spent on
it.

Realising that he was waiting for him to make some
comment, Jake struggled to make his brain work. What
money there was must go to his aunt... Somewhere must
be found for her to live, since she had hysterically refused to so much as set foot back in Fitton Park.

When he explained this to the solicitor, the man pursed
his lips and then suggested, 'Your grandfather had some
investments...enough possibly to raise the money to buy
your aunt a small house of her own and to provide her
with a small income.'

He wasn't yet eighteen, and in the space of the last
few weeks he had lost his brother, his grandfather and
his youth. He stood up, and in the expression on his face
the solicitor thought he saw a trace of the man he would
be one day.

'Do it,' he instructed him emotionally.

'And Fitton Park?'

Jake had reached the door. He paused there and turned
to say violently, 'Fitton Park can burn down to ashes
for all I care.'

It wasn't true... One of the reasons he had never been
able to turn totally away from his grandfather was because he had both understood and shared the old man's
love for their home. Unlike Justin, to whom it was always
simply a draughty, ancient house that would one day
hang round his neck like a millstone.

Now it was his, for what that was worth...more of
a liability than an asset. Unsaleable, according to the
experts, with not enough land left to support it and too
much to appeal to the kind of new rich like Saffron's
father, who preferred the more controllable prettiness of

the Georgian era to the rambling decay of somewhere like Fitton Park.

Saffron. He hadn't seen or heard from her since the night she had made love to him, nor had he really expected to... or even wanted to, he acknowledged.

It was impossible for him to communicate properly with his aunt. She seemed to have retreated into a world of her own, refusing even to see him until her friend had prevailed upon her to do so... He explained as simply as he could the arrangements the solicitor was going to make, and Louise Davenport-Legh listened to him sympathetically, wondering with pity if he realised yet how much his life was going to change. He was seventeen years old, with no qualifications, no family, no money... no way of supporting himself other than the one for which he had always been destined.

It was the vicar who had gently suggested that it might be worthwhile writing to the Commander-in-Chief of his grandfather's and father's old regiment, even when Jake had protested that that was now out of the question and that the best he could hope for was to be accepted on to one of the army's training schemes for raw recruits.

He was both right and wrong. The colonel wrote back saying that, while there was nothing he could do now, should Jake be able to prove to the army that he possessed the right kind of officer material, there was a possibility that the regiment might sponsor him through Sandhurst and from there might admit him to its ranks.

Jake did not allow himself to hope for anything. Right now the only thing that mattered was finding himself somewhere where he could survive... somewhere where he could forget the horror of that scene in the gun-room. And then it struck him with dry irony, as he filled in his army application form, that, if he was accepted, the kind of scene he witnessed in the gun-room was going to be something he would have to accustom himself to.

He wasn't joining the army by way of some élite regiment. He was not going to be destined for parades outside Buckingham Palace. He was destined for the likes of Northern Ireland, where every day men, *boys* like him died ingloriously and unheralded.

The army was much as he had expected it to be. At first he was chivvied and taunted by the others because of his accent, but once they realised that whatever they said to him apparently meant nothing, and that, if anything, he was actually tougher and harder than they were themselves—although the only evidence they had of this was during their training, since Jake had never and would never, he had already decided, use violence unnecessarily—they grudgingly accepted him.

During those early months a slow numbness seemed to have enveloped his emotions, an inability to feel anything other than the most cursory of emotions.

On his first leave he went home. His aunt was now established in a small cottage in the village, where it was obvious that he was not welcome. She had a new life, and made it clear that she had no desire to have anything to do with someone who was part of the old. They had never been close, but she was his only living relative, and as he walked away Jake knew that he would probably never see her again.

After that something hardened in him, something that had been broken but not destroyed by Justin's death, and, when he returned, his tutoring officers noticed that he had developed a grim resoluteness, a dedication almost, that, properly directed, could turn him into a first-rate officer.

Even that news barely touched him.

Sandhurst was familiar territory, as were its accent and shibboleths, and yet he felt distant from it, separated from those who would once have been his natural companions. And although he didn't recognise it in himself, he had now become a loner…someone who lived outside the rest of the pack.

In his final term at Sandhurst, he had an interview with the colonel of his grandfather's old regiment. The colonel had, as he had promised, kept an eye on his progress; the regiment believed in supporting its own, and he had been both pleased and a little surprised by the reports he had received. The boy had very definite potential—was not just physically equipped to become an officer, but also mentally… Additionally, he had the gift of establishing a rapport with other ranks and of getting their respect, both immeasurably valuable assets.

When he left, Jake knew that he was assured of a place in the regiment.

His mouth twisted wryly. A place he doubted that he could afford… There would be his living expenses, dress uniform and God alone knew how many more things he couldn't afford, and besides, he was no longer sure if the regiment was really what he wanted… It was *too* regimented, too stifling. But he kept his thoughts to himself because it was what he had long ago learned to do… Justin had leaned on him, not the other way around, and he was not used to seeking the counsel of others.

As it turned out, the colonel used his influence to get Jake a junior officer's post and for a number of years Jake's life was neatly mapped out for him. He responded well to army life and an added bonus was the friendship he formed with his commanding officer, Tom Rogers. Both men felt the need to move on at the same time and got to hear of an anti-drugs agency which was recruiting new men to the team. Drugs and their abuse was an issue both men felt very strongly about and the job had a certain appeal. What they would in effect be were undercover agents working for a government agency trying to fight against the illegal importation and sale of drugs. A challenge which Jake, in particular, looked forward to.

* * *

The year Jake was twenty-seven unexpected things happened. His aunt died, leaving her small estate in its entirety to her godson, Noel, something which brought a bitter smile to Jake's lips when her solicitor informed him of it, and caused the old man to grimace a little with embarrassment. He had reminded his client that the money for her house and pension had originally come from her nephew's estate and had suggested as tactfully as he could that it ought to return to this source, but she had become a very difficult woman to deal with, eccentric and prone to hysterical outbursts which both exhausted and embarrassed him.

Now she was dead, and her nephew seemed less surprised by the contents of her will than he had expected.

Three months' leave coinciding with his aunt's death had made Jake decide to go home. He had driven past the entrance to Fitton Park and had deliberately not looked towards it. It hurt him inside even now to know that the house was slowly decaying and that there was nothing he could do about it. Cheshire seemed smaller than he remembered.

He was tanned from a recent undercover trip to South America, and he had a small scar over one eye where a stray bullet had grazed him. He was tougher, leaner, harder than the men the solicitor was used to dealing with... He looked somehow dangerous and alien, the older man thought, shifting a little uncomfortably in his seat, faintly intimidated by the vague threat of this man whom he remembered as little more than a gangling boy.

As Jake waited politely for the solicitor to dismiss him, the second unexpected thing happened. The man shuffled some papers on his desk nervously and then cleared his throat before saying, 'Er...a client of mine may be interested in purchasing Fitton Park.'

Jake stared at him. This was the last piece of news he had expected.

'Someone wants to *buy* it?' he asked incredulously, and then his eyes narrowed. 'What for, to tear it down and replace it with a housing estate?'

His solicitor shook his head.

'No, she wants to restore it and live in it...'

'She?' Jake's eyebrows rose. 'She must be one hell of a wealthy woman,' he said drily.

'She is... She was married to Harold Pilling,' the solicitor informed him.

Jake frowned. He had heard vaguely of the multi-millionaire industrialist.

'He died last year. She has one child...a daughter from a previous marriage. If you're interested I can arrange for you to meet her. She's in Chester at the moment, staying at the Grosvenor...'

'Has she seen the house?' Jake asked him derisively, unable to understand why on earth the woman should want to buy and suspecting that she had perhaps only seen it from the outside and not realised the dilapidation that waited for her inside.

The solicitor cleared his throat, obviously mistaking the cause of the question, and said apologetically, 'When I couldn't get in touch with you, I—er—took the liberty of showing her round...'

Jake's frown eased. The man had no doubt written to him at his London address. He hadn't been near the flat for almost three months; he had been on the trail of a large and well-organised gang who were somehow or other managing to get huge amounts of narcotics into London. Jake had managed to infiltrate the group deeply enough to get some information, but not the names of the people bringing the stuff into the country.

'If I've done the wrong thing...'

'What...?' Jake switched his attention back to the solicitor. 'Oh, no...I'm just surprised that, having seen inside it, she still wants to buy it,' he said wryly, and wondered to himself what kind of woman she was...apart from being an extremely wealthy one.

Jake's solicitor had arranged for him to meet Gloria
Pilling at the Grosvenor Hotel in Chester. He offered to
accompany Jake to the meeting, and pointed out when
Jake refused, 'She is a very astute businesswoman, Jake;
she wants Fitton Park, I'm sure of that, but she'll fight
to make sure that financially she gets the best deal she
can.'

Something in his voice sharpened Jake's attention. His
solicitor didn't like the woman. Why?

He asked him, bluntly, watching him in a way that
the older man commented later to his wife reminded him
very strongly of his late grandfather. It also reminded
him that, while he was still addressing Jake by his
Christian name, in reality he was Sir Jake, and had been
since the sudden deaths of his grandfather and brother.

His training made it impossible for him to answer
Jake's question equally frankly. Instead he hedged and
hesitated before finally admitting faintly apologetically,
'Perhaps I'm being old-fashioned, but... Her late
husband was a good deal older than her and extremely
wealthy. When she approached me, she made it plain
that if she bought Fitton Park she would be using it as
an entrée into Cheshire society...'

'A gold digger *and* a social climber!' Jake's eyebrows
rose. He wasn't shocked or surprised by the solicitor's
revelations, and as for the woman, well, good luck to
her, he reflected cynically. She wouldn't be the first
person to use her wealth to buy her way into society. It
was his personal opinion that she was wasting her time
and her money, but if that was what she wanted and if
she was prepared to buy Fitton Park from him to facilitate her plans, then who was he to object?

As he watched Jake shrug powerful shoulders, the
solicitor reflected guiltily on what he had not said, more
than on what he had. Gloria Pilling had also made it
plain to him that she would expect the present owner of
the property to introduce her to his wealthy and aristocratic neighbours.

She had pressed him very hard for information about Jake and he had been as non-committal as he'd dared without offending her.

'Well, if you're sure,' he said uncertainly now, when Jake announced that he would not need his support, relief warring with the duty he felt towards this sole surviving member of a once prolific and great family.

'I am,' Jake told him firmly.

His time in the army had polished and tempered his ability to command the respect and obedience of others. Working as part of a team with his anti-drug colleagues, he had developed his own ability to judge situations for himself and to act on that judgement. He now had an air of maturity that made him seem much older than he was.

Louise Davenport-Legh noticed it when he paid her a brief duty call, and calmly and efficiently fielded all her curious questions. She had always felt vaguely sorry for both boys, but the tall, broad-shouldered, controlled man who sat in her drawing-room, effortlessly parrying her skilled questions, was a stranger to her, a stranger whom she found almost intimidating.

She touched briefly on the subject of Fitton Park and its possible sale.

Jake shrugged, knowing the efficiency of the local grapevine.

'I've got a meeting in Chester with a potential buyer. My solicitor fixed it up.'

Louise Davenport-Legh, who had heard all about the wealthy widow who was expressing an interest in moving into Cheshire and its society, raised her eyebrows, longing to question him further, but realised she was wasting her time.

Jake went back to Fitton Park and walked restlessly through its empty rooms. Everywhere he looked he could see signs of growing decay. The house had never been a real home for either Justin or himself, and yet the thought of losing it, of selling it, tightened emotions within him that were unexpectedly painful.

It was impossible for him to keep the place. There was no longer enough land left to fund the cost of maintaining the house; his unsettled career meant that even if he could afford to keep it he would need to employ someone else to run the estate, and that his visits home would always be infrequent.

Better to sell than let it fall into complete disrepair. And yet... And yet in his own way he was as much a victim of their joint heritage as his grandfather had been.

Ridiculous, in this rightly egalitarian age, to feel such a stirring of mingled pride and pain at the past deeds and misdeeds of his ancestors; to feel that he was betraying his heritage.

Unlike Gloria Pilling, he had no illusions about the supposed advantages of being Sir Jake. If he was going to make any mark in the world it would be as plain Jake Fitton.

As he closed and locked the massive front door behind him, Jake wondered grimly just what sort of a picture of him the solicitor had painted to Gloria Pilling. Jake was an astute man, and had quickly picked up on the older man's disquiet and guilt.

He was staying at a small hotel just outside Chester. No suite at the Grosvenor for him... The necessity to keep a low profile was too deeply ingrained and, besides, he could not afford it.

From a personal point of view, lack of wealth did not bother him. He enjoyed the life he was leading and, if it weren't for Fitton Park, would have been more than content.

The trouble was that, having spent virtually all his growing years knowing that one day Fitton Park would pass to Justin, Jake had never been prepared for inheriting it himself. And now, with his aunt having died, he had to face up to his brother's earlier death and make the necessary decisions about the family home.

He felt the pressure of his grandfather's pride and teachings pursuing him...demanding that somehow he find a way of keeping it.

But that was impossible, and the practical side of his nature told him it was foolish to let the house simply rot away and collapse because he was too proud to allow anyone else to live in it.

That was where he differed from his grandfather, who he knew would have stubbornly taken down every brick himself rather than let it pass into someone else's hands.

Boarding school had taught him how to live easily and peacefully with his peers, and the army had honed that facility. His agency training had also taught him how to make himself inconspicuous, and the other occupants of the small, rather austere hotel were barely aware of his presence.

He got up early, drove over to Fitton Park and ran alongside the perimeter wall of the park before driving to the hotel, showering and changing for his interview with Gloria Pilling.

The Grosvenor was vaguely familiar to him from visits there with his aunt.

The receptionist gave him a polite, friendly smile, concealing the sudden spark of interest his arrival gave her. It was rare for them to have single male visitors as physically attractive and compelling as this one was, and her smile hardened a little with cynicism when he asked for Mrs Pilling's suite.

Gloria Pilling was occupying the most expensive suite in the hotel, and in the short time she had been there she had managed to make herself unpopular with virtually every member of staff who had come into contact with her.

The receptionist gave Jake directions, and rang through to the suite to inform Gloria Pilling that she was sending him up.

Jake noted but didn't betray his awareness of the sudden chill in her attitude towards him. He wondered idly what she thought his business with Gloria Pilling was. He was far too sophisticated and aware now not to realise that it was quite possible for a woman of Gloria Pilling's wealth to buy the sexual attentions of a younger man.

Was that what the girl thought he was: an available piece of meat? He shrugged the thought away as being unimportant.

He rapped firmly on the outer door of the suite and had to wait several minutes before he was admitted by a tall, elegantly dressed redhead, whose looks made him revise his earlier assumption. If this woman was Gloria Pilling, he doubted that she would need to pay for her sex.

It was true that beneath the surface gloss of a near perfect bone-structure, and facial features that no man would be able to resist looking at at least twice, she was as hard-edged as polished steel; but Jake had never seen any necessity for women to conceal the fact that they had intelligence and brains as keenly sharp as any man's. Stupid women like his aunt, who didn't know how to use their intelligence, irritated him, and the few brief liaisons he had indulged in had always been with women whom he had admired initially for their conversation and wit.

He doubted that this woman would be witty. She wouldn't be able to spare the time... No, this woman would concentrate solely and exclusively on her chosen goals. Even the smile she gave him, while polite, was sharp and pointed, as though underlining the fact that he was the supplicator.

'Do come in,' she invited coolly, glancing at the heavy Cartier watch encircling her slim, tanned wrist.

She had the svelte body of a woman used to indulging and pampering her own flesh, and yet she moved with the lithe fitness of someone who used her body physi-

cally. Her hair gleamed silkily with health, and although
Jake suspected that the tautness of the delicate skin
stretched across her facial bones probably owed a little
more to the surgeon's scalpel than to nature, no one
looking at her could doubt that this was a woman in her
sexual prime. And yet Jake felt repelled by her, chilled
by her.

'You're on time...good. I've rather a lot to get through
today, so shall we get right down to business?'

He permitted himself a brief smile, recognising her
swift grasping of control of their meeting, concealing
his body's physical dislike of her.

'By all means. My solicitor informs me that you wish
to purchase Fitton Park.'

His coolness caught her off guard. He saw her hesitate momentarily.

She was a good many years his senior, and he suspected it had been a long time since she had last failed
to intimidate anyone. He was not a boy any more,
though, and he suppressed his own satisfaction at her
small betrayal and asked calmly, 'May I sit down?'

'Er—yes, please do... Would you care for some
coffee?'

'Later, perhaps... I, too, have other appointments this
morning.'

It was a lie, and he watched her body tense as though
it was under attack, wondering what had made her so
brittle and aggressive. And she was aggressive; he could
sense it beneath the deceptive cloak of sexual availability that she wore so skilfully and easily. The original
wolf in sheep's clothing, he reflected, watching her,
waiting for her to take the initiative, knowing that he
had already managed to disconcert her, and curious to
see how she would react.

She rallied quickly, coolly telling him that Fitton Park
was merely one of several properties in which she was
interested, and then promptly producing surveyors' reports on the house which Jake recognised immediately

were designed to make the property appear of such little value that an innocent, ignorant of the tactics being employed against him, might almost have given the property away just to rid himself of its potential burden.

'So, in effect, what you're saying is that in purchasing Fitton Park you would be indulging in a mere charitable impulse,' he drawled when she had finished, his voice purposely in direct contrast to her own sharp, incisive speech.

She stared at him, the sapphire brilliance of her eyes hardening.

He wondered absently if she was wearing coloured contact lenses. He had certainly never seen eyes of that spectacular shade of blue anywhere before.

He had discovered as he matured that he was surprisingly invulnerable to physical beauty... that it was the inner and not the outer person who appealed to his emotions. This woman with her perfect figure and face chilled rather than aroused him.

She gave him a thin smile. 'I'm not given to charitable impulses.'

'No,' he agreed dulcetly, smiling back at her. 'I rather thought you weren't.' He stood up easily and crossed the room, looking out of the window into the street below, a piece of skilled social manoeuvring which he was well aware had taken her completely off guard.

He turned round in time to catch her affronted, querulous expression and smiled again; this time as he might have done at a spoilt, quarrelsome child.

'Shall we dispense with the foreplay?' he suggested evenly. 'I believe my solicitor has informed you that Fitton Park is on the market and at what price... A fair price, I think, even given the dilapidation of the property. It would be insulting of me, having met you, to ask if you are aware of how much money will need to be spent on it to restore it.'

He paused, allowing the compliment to sink in, watching her battle with acceptance as she glared at him.

'You obviously want the property, but you want something else as well. What is it?'

She turned her back on him and stalked across the expensively carpeted floor. Gloria Pilling was not used to being outflanked; married first at seventeen to the son of the wealthiest residents of the small farming community in which she had grown up, once she had realised that her husband was not prepared to indulge her financially in the way she wished she had divorced him and escaped to London, where there was far more scope for her talent.

It was there that she had met Harold Pilling, the millionaire industrialist, whose friends had thought him far too intelligent and aware to be caught in the trap so obviously being laid for him by a young woman less than half his age; a young woman who, moreover, carried all the hallmarks of being unashamedly in the market for a rich husband.

Harold Pilling hadn't cared—he had wanted her and he had been prepared to pay for her—but neither had he been a complete fool. In return for her absolute faithfulness and obedience to their marriage vows he was prepared to give his new wife as much money as she could spend, but if he found out that Gloria was betraying him...if he discovered that she was indulging herself sexually with other men...

Gloria had accepted his terms, wondering cynically at the folly of the male sex. The sexual act to her was something to be despised and used; any pleasure to be gained from it was the pleasure of knowing one had the ascendancy over one's partner...of knowing that he would be made to pay and pay again for the use of her flesh.

She had learned very young the value of her stunning face and figure and had relentlessly used them to further her own ambitions. Those ambitions were to be financially and socially secure...ambitions that only someone growing up in the kind of deprived household that had been hers as a child could really appreciate.

Her father had been a farm labourer, half crippled by rheumatism by the time she, his last child, was born. He had a savage temper when he was drunk, which was five days out of seven, and every one of his six children had felt the sting of his belt against their buttocks on more than one occasion.

But Gloria was cleverer than the rest; she had soon discovered that she had the means of making her father do as she wished.

The first time her mother had realised what was happening she had screamed at Gloria and threatened to banish her from the house, but Gloria's father was the sole breadwinner, and Gloria's mother was too deeply cowed by the privations of bearing and bringing up six children in a small, damp, insanitary cottage on wages that were little more than a pittance to hold out against the combined pressure of her husband and daughter for very long.

The cottage had four bedrooms; the four girls in the family slept in two, the two boys in another, and their parents in the fourth. By the time she was fourteen Gloria had a room to herself, her three sisters being squashed in together... a privilege for which she paid by allowing her grunting, sweating father the freedom of her body into which to vent the frustrated bitterness of what he had made of his life.

No love existed between them; Gloria despised her father and felt almost equal contempt for her mother and siblings. Their life was not going to be hers.

She had watched her older sisters marry at seventeen and then eighteen and within months turn into drudges similar to their mother, slaves to the same urges that drove her father... that seemed to drive everyone but her.

She had a special gift. She was free of those urges... above them and yet able to generate them in others... able o make use of them to beguile and trap.

Before she was sixteen she had a small regular coterie of lovers, all of them chosen for what they could give her in exchange for the use of her body.

Her greatest triumph was the seduction of her form teacher, a desiccated, hungry-looking academic soured by a life of missed opportunities and by the dismal reality of his tarnished, once golden dreams.

He had dreamed of a glorious academic career at Oxford, of being fêted and honoured by his peers; of a lifetime of pleasurable academic austerity.

Instead he had had the misfortune to get the daughter of his landlady pregnant while he was still taking his degree. He had been forced to marry her—a marriage which neither of them had wanted—and with a wife and child to support he had also been forced to take the first job he could find.

Too intimidated by his fear of public outrage, he had been unable to vent his fury and hatred of his wife in any way that could bring him satisfaction, and so instead he had turned his venom on his pupils.

Parents complained, headmasters instituted discreet enquiries, and slowly he had gradually moved to poorer and poorer schools.

The large secondary school Gloria attended was notorious for its poor results, for its lack of impetus . . . its teachers worn down by the ignorance of both its pupils and their parents.

Gloria, with that inbuilt instinct she possessed, had quickly realised the potential of Andrew Johnson. He hated her so much that it had amused her to seduce him, to reduce him to a trembling, gibbering wreck of pulsing need.

She made him pay for the humiliation and torment she gave him, the same way she made others pay: in hard cash.

Cash which she was gradually saving towards the day when she would eventually be able to escape.

Only, when she was sixteen, a catastrophe occurred. Her father dropped dead while he was working, killed by a sudden heart attack, and even before her husband was buried her mother announced that she was throwing Gloria out.

'But where will I go?' Gloria had protested, wide-eyed and innocent. Her mother had laughed bitterly.

'Oh, you'll find some bed to crawl into, I make no doubt, you little trollop.'

Quickly Gloria had assessed her options. She was sixteen years old and the only way she had of supporting herself was by the prostitution of her body; but if she did that, how long would it be before she was reduced to the same state as the women she had seen hanging around the back-street pubs of their local market town, women old before their time...? Gloria had no illusions about herself or the world. She was quite prepared to sell her flesh, but not for the price of a couple of drinks or a night's fix. She wasn't ready to leave home yet... She hadn't saved enough. Panic seized her. She had four lovers at the moment, none of whom knew of the existence of the others.

Three months later she was pregnant by the only son of the farmer for whom her father had worked, and, despite all the hysterical accusations of his mother that she was nothing but a little tramp who had deliberately allowed herself to get pregnant, her twenty-one-year-old lover insisted on marrying her. It wasn't long before they divorced.

Harold Pilling had imposed another condition on her when they'd married. He had no children of his own and, since he was now virtually impotent, had no hopes of fathering one. She, though, had a child...a daughter. He would only marry her on the condition that he was able to adopt the child as his own.

Gloria had been furious. When she had divorced her husband she had left her child with him. A child was the last encumbrance she wanted or needed; she didn't want her now, but it seemed she had no choice.

It was purely by luck that she emerged victorious from the bloody custody battle that ensued. She had taken one look at the thin, plain eleven-year-old who was now legally in her care and let all her contempt for that plainness and misery show, but she had wanted marriage to Harold Pilling and she had been prepared to pay the price for that marriage, just as she was now prepared to pay the price for Fitton Park because she wanted what it and its owner could give her.

It was no longer enough for her simply to be wealthy... Now she wanted the cachet of being not just socially acceptable, but socially prominent as well.

She wanted to be on the charity committees whose notepaper carried the names of public figures like the Princess of Wales.

She wanted to be in the line-up of powerful and influential hostesses whose names were invariably associated with society's most prestigious events.

The PR firm she had contacted to advise her on how best this goal might be achieved had suggested that acceptance by the élite of one of the country's rural counties would weigh heavily in her favour and allow society to forget the publicity of her marriage to Harold Pilling.

She had taken their advice, disdaining the obviousness of Gloucestershire and the Cotswolds in favour of the quiet backwater of Cheshire.

She looked across at Jake, who was still waiting to learn what she wanted from him, and gave him the hard-edged, cold smile of a vulture.

There was no point in trying either seduction or deception on this one. It would have to be the truth.

'What I want is an introduction into local society. Your solicitor tells me that you can provide one.'

It was more or less what he had expected. He let her wait for his reply, weighing practicality against pride and heritage. He was no snob; he took people as they were, appreciating them for what they were, and he already knew that the best among those families whose names belonged to the chronicles of Cheshire's history would never admit her to the closed ranks of their friendship, not because of her birth, but because of her personality.

There were others, though, like Louise Davenport-Legh, who would use her for her wealth and allow her to use them for their social connections.

'If I do buy Fitton Park, I shall wish to hold a New Year's Eve ball there. I shall want you to supply me with a list of people I can invite, and I shall also want you to be there.'

He looked steadily at her.

'Very well,' he told her coolly. 'But that will cost you an extra fifty thousand pounds.'

He saw the triumph in her eyes and added flatly, 'That cheque is to be made out to a charity run to benefit the homeless.'

'Most noble,' she jeered, angry colour staining her immaculate skin. 'But it doesn't prove anything.'

'It does to me,' Jake told her silkily, and without saying so informed her that it was his own opinion of himself that mattered and not hers.

He left ten minutes later, knowing that he could probably have pushed her to pay another ten or twenty thousand pounds, but the game had already lost its savour.

Halfway down the corridor, he turned a corner and immediately collided with the girl running, head down, towards him.

He caught hold of her shoulders, bird-thin under the heavy cotton jumpsuit she was wearing, to steady her.

She had been running, and he could smell the fresh sweat scent of her skin. Her face, when she lifted it towards him, was flushed and hot.

She had brown hair and matching brown eyes set under thick, untidy eyebrows. The look she gave him was both embarrassed and defensive.

She looked about sixteen, and he guessed that she must be Gloria Pilling's daughter.

She was nothing like her beautiful mother...not plain, exactly—there was a hint of soft femininity in the curves of her face and body—but the way she ducked her head, the way she hunched her shoulders and backed off from him were defensive and prickly.

'I'm sorry...I wasn't looking where I was going.'

She had a soft, husky voice, and Jake wondered what she would look like if she smiled. She had a lovely mouth, her lips were soft and full, and he was shocked to discover that he was actually wondering what it would be like to kiss her.

It must be reaction to the overpowering sexuality of her mother, he decided grimly as he set her free. She was just a child.

Behind him he heard the suite door open, and Gloria Pilling say sharply, 'Beth—come here at once. Where on earth have you been? You look dreadful...'

And as he released her the girl slunk past him, head down, face flushed, her body taut with resentment and humiliation.

He half turned back towards her and then stopped, irritated by his own helpless compassion for her. She wasn't his concern, but he paused for a moment, caught on the brink of emotionalism, and yet knowing that if Fitton Park was to survive it needed an owner who could afford to cherish it.

Cherish it... For all he knew, Gloria Pilling might very well have plans to turn it into the sort of pseudo-period abomination that featured heavily in the pages of glossy magazines. Wryly acknowledging that there was perhaps at times more of his grandfather in him than he knew, he turned on his heel and headed for the lift.

'You know what this agreement entails?' his solicitor asked heavily.

The document in question lay on the desk between them and, with it, the contract for the sale of Fitton Park to Gloria Pilling.

'I have read it,' Jake answered drily.

He could see in the older man's eyes the belief that he was selling himself along with the house, but made no attempt to defend himself.

'Will you be able to fulfil that kind of commitment?' the man asked him doubtfully.

'I've got some leave due over Christmas and the New Year. A month.' And then he was going back to South America, but didn't tell him that.

'Mrs Pilling wants all the legal formalities tied up as quickly as possible,' the solicitor informed him. 'She's anxious to start work on the house as soon as she can.'

'Yes, I know,' Jake told him equably, watching the older man fumble with his papers as he wondered just how intimate a relationship had built up between his client and Gloria Pilling.

The answer was none at all. Gloria Pilling had recognised in Jake that quality that made him impervious to her particular brand of allure. She hated him for that imperviousness, and she also resented the fact that her only means left of proving to herself her superiority was to flaunt her wealth at him on every possible occasion.

Jake had learned to control his feelings too long ago to allow her to see when her sharp, raking goads met their target. He knew quite well how she felt about him.

Soon Fitton Park would be hers and he would have discharged his responsibility to his heritage to the best of his ability.

He wondered how the local gentry would react to Gloria. She was determined to have her pound of flesh from him, and he had dutifully introduced her to Louise Davenport-Legh, watching with detached amusement as Gloria subtly played up to the other woman's vanity.

Two days before the final completion of the sale took place, he gave in to a quixotic impulse and moved into Fitton Park.

His working life had inured him to discomfort and, although the damp, musty smell of the bedroom he had once shared with Justin made him grimace a little, by the time he had unearthed some clean dry bedding from one of the ancient linen chests his nose had become accustomed to the vague smell and he found himself slipping back into the familiarity of the house's odd creaks and sighs.

It had been a wet summer, with the sun only shining from the end of August, so that now, in September, the grass in the park was virtually knee-high.

As he ran through it, pacing himself, he exercised his imagination trying to imagine what Gloria Pilling would make of it. As though to make up for the wet summer, the September sun shone hot, covering his body with the slickness of sweat. The electricity had been reconnected to the house after its long period unoccupied, but Jake had forgotten to switch on the immersion heater and the prospect of a cold shower reminded him of school and his childhood. He ran to the boundary wall and then along it. The specimen trees planted by his ancestors were just beginning to show signs of the approaching autumn in the faint discoloration of their leaves.

Birds called out warning cries to one another as he ran past them, and he heard the familiar small sounds of wildlife rustling through the undergrowth.

When he had completed his run, instead of going inside, he headed for the stableyard.

The enclosed space had trapped the heat of the sun, the cobbles striking warm through the soles of his trainers. There was an old-fashioned pump in the middle of the yard. He stripped off his shorts and shoes and stepped into the stone trough, his mind full of memories of how his grandfather used to insist on both his and Justin's undergoing the pump's freezing spout of water.

Then he had often felt as though they were being encased in ice, but today the cool, silky feel of the water against his hot sticky skin was almost a sensual pleasure. He stepped out of the trough, shaking himself dry, welcoming the heat of the sun.

A door banged and he turned his head, frowning at the familiar sound. There was no one here other than himself, and yet the kitchen door only banged like that when it was opened from inside.

His frowning glare swept the emptiness of the courtyard, and then fastened abruptly on the shadowy figure standing inside the kitchen door.

He reacted immediately and instinctively, dropping the shorts he had just picked up and springing across the yard, far too fast for the intruder to do more than turn around and race across the kitchen.

He caught her easily before she was halfway across the room, spinning her round, his mouth hard and grim until he realised who it was.

'I'm sorry,' she apologised wildly, as she had done before. 'I didn't realise you were here...' She shivered suddenly. He released her, still frowning, and stepped back from her, and instantly her face burned with hot, shocked colour as her glance fell to his body and was immediately averted.

He swore under his breath, realising that he had embarrassed her... had forgotten, in the sudden instinctive reaction to the knowledge that there was an intruder, that he was completely nude.

Her embarrassment touched him with compassion and amusement. She couldn't be more than sixteen, if that, and, remembering his own vulnerability at that age, he said easily, 'I'm sorry, too. I suppose you came to see the house, did you?'

The downbent brown head nodded; one sandalled foot scuffed at a broken tile on the kitchen floor.

'I didn't think anyone would be here...' Her head lifted, her eyes suddenly wild and nervous. 'You won't tell my mother, will you...about my being here?'

'Not if you don't want me to.'

She smiled at him. A tentative, curling mouth at once so feminine and innocently provocative that he drew in his breath on a sudden sharp surge of arousal which fortunately he managed to control...just.

Her head was down again so that all he could see were two dark wings of hair. God, how in hell had *that* happened? She was a child!

'I suppose you're playing truant from school,' he said sharply.

'School!' The dark head came up again, the brown eyes wide and stunned. 'I'm eighteen years old,' she told him curtly. 'Mother likes to pretend I'm much younger, of course.' Her mouth twisted in bitterness, and then she challenged, 'Are you sleeping with her?'

'No.'

He knew that his answer was harsh, and he softened its antagonism saying quietly, 'No, I'm not.' And as he said it he wondered why he wasn't telling her, as he should, that it wasn't really any concern of hers anyway.

Instead he heard himself saying, 'Have you seen the house?'

She shook her head.

'Want me to show you round it?' he suggested.

She made an inarticulate sound in her throat and then lifted her head and said breathlessly, her face furiously flushed, 'Yes, please...but hadn't you better get dressed first?'

He had forgotten about that, and almost laughed, until he realised that if he did he would probably hurt her. She looked such a child.

But she wasn't.

Eighteen. It gave him an unpleasant jolt. He had felt safer when he had thought she was just a child. Safer...he groaned over his own thoughts and heard her say timidly,

'If you've changed your mind...about showing me the house...'

He shook his head, trying to dispel the odd sensation of awareness that was threatening him.

'Not at all,' he heard himself saying in an over-hearty, avuncular fashion. 'Just give me five minutes to go upstairs and make myself respectable.'

As he turned towards the door he had the odd feeling that if he left her there she would somehow disappear, and, dangerously, that was something he didn't want, even though common sense warned him that it might be best if she did leave.

'My bedroom's at the top of the house. Come up with me and wait for me, then we'll start at the top and work our way down.'

To spare her any further embarrassment he retrieved his shorts and pulled them on before telling her to follow him upstairs.

He used the familiar route of the servants' back stairs, taking them two at a time and then pausing to wait for her, realising that she was probably trailing miles behind him. Only she wasn't. She was standing right behind him and not even breathing fast. He frowned. Beneath that sloppy sweatshirt she was wearing, those jeans that looked as though she still had to grow into them, she must be supple and fit. He wondered briefly what her body was like, trying to visualise what lay beneath her bulky clothes and failing.

Instinct warned him that he was flirting with danger, but for some reason he didn't heed it, directing her up the next flight of stairs.

'This was once the nursery floor,' he told her when they reached the landing. 'The attics above were used for the servants.'

'The nursery floor. I suppose that's why the windows are barred.' She walked over to one and gazed out. The sun struck brilliant prisms of rich red light in the darkness of her hair. She turned round to look at him and he found himself gazing at the warm lushness of her mouth.

It was an effort to wrench away his gaze. This girl...this child had an effect on him that her mother, with all her skill and experience, could never match.

Only she wasn't a child... Not at eighteen.

'Which is your bedroom?' she asked him.

'This one,' he replied absently, pushing open the door.

She walked through it ahead of him, studying the two narrow beds and the room's starkness.

'It looks a bit like a school dormitory.'

'My grandfather believed in an austere upbringing,' he told her drily.

He hadn't bothered unpacking, and his clean clothes were still in his unopened case.

He opened it now, extracting clean briefs, a pair of jeans and a sweatshirt not dissimilar to her own.

When he turned round she was sitting on one of the beds. *His* bed, he recognised with a small stir of sensation he didn't want to feel.

'I know you've already seen all of me that there is to see,' he commented drily, 'but I think it might be as well if you waited outside while I get dressed.'

He opened the door and waited, but she stayed where she was, sitting on the bed, her body tensed with a sudden open, urgent determination.

'Are you really not my mother's lover?' she asked him fiercely.

CHAPTER SIXTEEN

JAKE looked across at Beth, already aware of what underlay the question, and why her whole body was tensed with urgency and dread.

There were a dozen or more retorts he could have made, from the light-hearted to the dismissive, all of them safe and innocuous.

He knew why he didn't choose to make any of them, just as he knew why he hadn't chosen to make her wait for him downstairs.

She was a heart-catching mixture of maturity and ingenuousness; of fierce independence and vulnerability. His own throat ached for her as she asked the question, and at the same time he knew that if he reached out to touch her it wouldn't be only compassion that motivated him.

It astounded him, how much she had the power to move him; this small, dark-haired girl-woman, who was nothing like the conventional ideal of feminine allure.

And yet, dressed in bulky jeans and an equally bulky sweatshirt, her face free of make-up and her hair tangled, she still had more sensuality, more power to arouse him simply by the way she smiled than her mother had with all her wiles and experience.

He knew he had hesitated too long to use a conventional, safe response. He knew also from the expression darkening her eyes that she thought he had lied to her the first time she'd asked the question.

'I'm not your mother's lover,' he told her quietly. 'And neither do I intend to be.' He wondered how much he could say... how far he could go. He had already witnessed the alienation between mother and daughter, but

336

how truthful could he be about the revulsion and dislike
he felt towards Gloria Pilling?

'You don't find her... attractive... or desirable?'

'No,' he told her shortly.

Her mouth quivered as though she was about to cry
and, totally unable to stop himself, he said thickly,
'Don't...'

She got off the bed and said tightly, 'I'd better go...
I'm in your way... I shouldn't be here.'

It was all there in her voice, in the way she looked at
him; her sense of rejection, of pain, of humiliation.

'No.' His fingers curled round her wrists, holding her.
'I'd like you to stay. Just turn round for a moment while
I get dressed.'

Without realising it, his thumb was stroking the
pressure-point of her wrist, trying to soothe its frantic
beat. He ought to make her wait outside, but he was
frightened that if he did she would leave, and he could
hardly show her round the house dressed in damp shorts
and trainers.

For one thing... for one thing, the physical effect she
was having on his body was not something he was going
to be able to conceal for much longer, especially not
dressed the way he was.

He released her wrists and put his hands on her
shoulders, turning her round. She was tiny, her bones
as frail as a bird's.

'Are you sure you're eighteen?' he asked her gravely.

She grimaced. 'Yes... I don't look it, I know. Of
course, Mother prefers it that way. She'd like me out of
her life altogether, but that isn't possible...'

'Not possible? Why?'

'Harold—my stepfather—made it a condition of his
will that my mother was to be responsible for me until
I marry. He was very kind to me...' She turned round,
ducking her head to avoid looking at him. 'I think he
felt guilty about taking me away from my father. My
father committed suicide after the court case and Harold

soon came to realise that my mother resented having me around. He made it a condition of his will that if I didn't make my home with her until I marry, she would forfeit half his estate.'

'He did that knowing the two of you don't get on?'

She heard the criticism in his voice and smiled wryly. 'He meant it for the best... He was very old-fashioned... very protective. When I marry, I'm to get a lump sum from his estate.

'I'd prefer to live on my own... to find a job and support myself, but I haven't had any training. A year at a fashionable French finishing school doesn't really equip one for earning one's own living.'

'So you're forced to live with Gloria...'

'Until I get married... I think that's half the reason she wants to live here,' she joked weakly. 'She probably thinks it will be easier to marry me off here than it was in London.'

Jake frowned at the bitterness in her voice.

'Of course, it might have been easier if she'd managed to resist the temptation to try out my potential husbands for their skills in bed.'

Her face flamed as she saw the way he was looking at her.

'I suppose you think I'm a bitch for saying that.'

'I would have thought that Gloria was the one who was being the bitch,' Jake corrected her.

She was so vulnerable... so desperately in need of protection. She touched some inner core of him that Justin's weakness had once touched, and it was all he could do to stop himself taking hold of her.

He shivered suddenly, a small presentiment of some unwanted emotion freezing his spine, and instantly she was concerned.

'You're cold, and that's my fault. I'll wait outside while you get changed.'

'No, you won't, you'll stay here. That way I'll know you're not going to disappear,' Jake told her wryly.

A pale flush of pleasure stained her skin and made
her eyes shine. It was so obvious that she wasn't used
to receiving compliments or praise. And yet when she
smiled she was lovely.

As he firmly took hold of her and gently turned her
round again before turning his own back and stripping
off his wet shorts, he couldn't help wondering what she
was really like beneath her clumsy, over-large clothes.

He was glad when her breathless, hesitant voice asked
softly, 'Can I turn round yet?'

'You can now,' he told her, zipping up his jeans and
pulling on his sweatshirt.

'Did you really sleep in here?' she asked him.

Her face was still flushed, and he noticed with protective amusement that she was wary of looking at him.

He wondered how much experience of his sex she had
had, and then caught himself up, sternly repressing his
self-inflammatory thoughts. She was like a burr sticking
to his skin; a pleasurable itch he ached to scratch; and
yet why? He barely knew her . . . had seen her only twice.
It wasn't like him to be overcome by this instant, overwhelming mingling of compassion and desire.

'Yes. Yes, we really did,' he told her absently.

'We?' she queried, turning from her contemplation of
the peeling whitewashed walls and barred windows.

'I shared this room with my brother. He's dead now,'
he told her briefly, and wondered how much she knew
about the history of his family.

What she didn't know now she probably soon would,
and for some reason he found he wanted to tell her
himself.

He did so as he led her from the bedroom to the room
he and Justin had once used as their playroom and then
their study.

'He killed himself?' she responded, shocked.

'Yes,' Jake confirmed briefly. 'He was a homosexual . . . My grandfather found him with his lover and
there was a quarrel . . . Justin shot my grandfather and

then turned the gun on himself...' He gave her a wry
smile. 'Do you think it would put your mother off the
house if she knew?'

She shook her head decisively.

'Nothing could put her off. She's determined to live
here and play the grand lady... At least that's one field
in which I can make use of my finishing-school training.
They sent us on a four-month antiques appreciation
course. Mother hates decorating and furnishing. She says
I can earn my keep by taking charge of the renovations
here.'

Jake was startled, but he soon discovered as they
toured the house that Beth possessed both the knowledge
and the instinctive feel for old property to give her a
loving insight into how the house could and should be.

His private dread that Gloria Pilling would turn Fitton
Park into a parody of all that it should be vanished as
he listened to Beth talking about replacing the worn silk
brocade with an identical fabric woven in France.

'It will cost the earth,' she said mischievously, her smile
warming her small face, and then she reached out and
touched him, saying seriously, 'You needn't be afraid.
I shan't spoil it...'

Spoil it... He looked up at the cracked plaster ceiling
of the long gallery and suppressed his bitterness. But he
knew what she meant, and was touched by her sensitivity.

It must be hell for her, living with a woman like Gloria,
but now that he knew the terms of Harold Pilling's will
he suspected that, no matter how much she might resent
her presence, Gloria would not allow her her freedom.

'You must hate seeing it like this,' she said gently when
they had finished the tour.

Jake shrugged.

'Yes and no... It was decaying all the time we were
growing up... I never expected to inherit it. Justin was
the elder... I was always destined for the army...'

She gave him a round-eyed, disconcerted look.

'You're in the army?'

'Not any more,' he told her quite truthfully, and then added, less truthfully, 'I'm a civil servant...'

So he was...if one could describe an undercover agent as such. Certainly his salary was paid by the government.

He thought briefly of the work he and his colleagues had undertaken in South America, working alongside the CIA in trying to suppress the spread of drug trafficking.

He doubted that they would hold back the tide for very long. With poverty so endemic in so many South American countries, anyone who provided them with a more comfortable way of living was almost guaranteed to be supported by the peasant populations of those countries.

There were South American countries with governments that strove to rise above corruption, but they didn't survive for very long. The drug barons saw to that, spreading their net of human misery until it engulfed everyone who came in contact with them.

There were rumours that certain illegal arms deals were being financed by drug trafficking. He frowned.

'It's getting late... I ought to get back... Mother's having dinner with her solicitors tonight and she wants me to be there,' she told him awkwardly.

His hand on her arm stayed her.

'Couldn't you telephone her and say you were having dinner with me?'

Her body stiffened, her eyes huge with panic as she stared at him.

'No...no...I couldn't tell her that. She'd be angry if she thought I was with you.'

For a moment he didn't understand and thought she was trying to tell him that her mother would fear for her in his company, and then he realised what she was actually saying.

'Not many men turn her down, you see,' she was almost whispering the words. 'And I expect...well, I know...'

'That she propositioned me,' he said gently for her, torn between raw pity and anger against himself for his unwanted reactions to her as he looked down at her downbent head and flushed face.

'She didn't. Your mother's astute enough to know when she's wasting her time,' he added drily. 'But I think I can see your point. You think she'll resent the fact that I find you...attractive, because I wasn't attracted to her.'

'You think *I'm* attractive?' She flushed deeply. Astonished pleasure blazed out of her eyes. Her mouth trembled over the words, making him ache to reach out and touch it, with his fingertips, with his own mouth.

He wondered how far he dared go, how much he dared say, and acknowledged that he was terrified of frightening her away. She was like a small, delicate bird that had to be reassured into giving her trust.

'I think you're *very* attractive,' he assured her gravely, and then picked up her left hand and held it against his mouth.

He had only meant to kiss it lightly, as compensation for denying himself the pleasure of kissing her mouth, but the palm of her hand was unbearably soft and vulnerable, and he could feel the quivers of reaction she was too inexperienced to hide and couldn't stop himself from nipping softly against her skin, from teasing his tongue between her fingers in a deliberately rhythmic movement.

Beneath his thumb he could feel the frantic race of her pulse, and when he released her hand he saw the twin points of her nipples pushing against the thick fabric of her sweatshirt.

She knew he was looking at her, and her face flamed scarlet, but she made no move to turn away or conceal herself. Her mouth was trembling again. The sight of it made him dizzy with aching frustration.

'Stay with me,' he asked her.

She shook her head and then bit her lip. 'I can't, but if you're still here tomorrow...'

'You'll what—escape from Mama's watchful eye and spend half an hour with me?' he scoffed. 'You're a woman, an adult, and I want——' He broke off, cursing himself for pushing her, forcing himself to relax. It took longer than he expected, and all the time she stood there, poised for flight, looking so hurt and confused that it made him sigh. What the hell was he trying to do?

'I'm sorry,' he apologised, and then added bluntly, 'I want to make love to you, and I'm having a hard time trying to behave rationally.'

Her flush deepened. She looked disbelieving...and pleased. 'You want to make love to *me*?'

She sounded dazed, as though she couldn't believe it.

'I most certainly do,' he agreed, watching her. 'But I appreciate that we both need time. I'm leaving the day after tomorrow, but I'd like to keep in touch...'

What on earth was he saying...doing? There wasn't room in his life for that kind of commitment.

'You do?' She was staring at him as though unable to believe what she was hearing.

'Yes. I've got to go away on business for a while, but I'll be here in the New Year...less than four months away. We could write...'

'But if you write to me, Mother will see the letters...'

She was whispering again, gazing at him with huge, round eyes that openly adored him.

'I could send them to my solicitor...'

God, what on earth was he doing? This was madness...lunacy. She was the last kind of complication he needed in his life.

'You'd better go now,' he told her gently. 'Will you come and see me tomorrow? There are some drawings in the library, sketches of the original house and gardens when it was remodelled by Inigo Jones. And we could have lunch...'

'Yes...yes, I'd like that.'

His gaze fastened on her mouth, and he watched her tremble in response to him. If he touched her now he'd never let her go. She hesitated, and he could almost see the thought running through her mind.

'Come on. Time to go,' he told her, adding sardonically, 'Mustn't keep Mother waiting.'

Instantly she withdrew from him, confused and hurt. He ought to have felt exasperation, irritation even, but what he did feel was an awesome mingling of protective love. She aroused feelings in him similar to those he had once felt for Justin, but these were deeper, more intense. These were sexual and not fraternal.

As he walked with her to her car, she said breathlessly, 'I could be here about ten...or is that too early?'

'I get up at six,' he told her. 'I'll be waiting for you.'

Her car was an expensive Mercedes sports, which she explained belonged to her mother. She paused as though waiting for him to kiss her and then got hurriedly into the car. He wanted to tell her that he dared not touch her, but the feelings were still too new to him himself.

She drove away with surprising skill and speed. He went back to the house, telling himself he was behaving like a complete fool.

When Jake woke up in the morning he half expected to find that his feelings had changed completely, and that he had simply been suffering from some sort of emotional daydream, but the mere thought of the girl called Beth brought an instant hardening of his body, an instant tug of need.

It took every ounce of self-discipline he possessed to follow his normal routine: a run, a brisk shower, breakfast. All the time he was thinking about her.

At nine o'clock he got in his car and drove to the local market town. He had promised her lunch in lieu of the dinner they had not had last night, and it was only when he found himself lingering over impossibly expensive bottles of champagne and handmade chocolates that he realised that he had fallen in love.

He waited for the surge of rejection and dismay he half expected to feel as he allowed himself to admit the truth, but they weren't there. In their place he felt a warmth, a breathtaking, dizzying sense of well-being and completeness combined with the feeling that if he wasn't careful he would find himself floating over the heads of the other shoppers.

He was in love, and it was like no other sensation he had ever experienced.

On the way home he found himself wondering if Justin had felt like this about his lover, the one who had run away after grandfather had found them. If so, he could well understand why his brother had shot the old man. He felt he could kill anyone who tried to take Beth away from him.

It was a ridiculous sensation. He was twenty-seven years old; the idea of making a commitment to another human being was something he had thought himself years away from.

His commitment was to his work...there was no room in his life for a girl like Beth. A girl who needed gentle handling, cherishing...protecting. And yet at the same time he knew that he was going to *make* room; that he would sacrifice anything and everything without compunction to make that room.

She liked him; he had seen it in her eyes, felt it in her shy response to him. His heartbeat quickened, his body tense with expectation.

He was back at Fitton Park for nine forty-five. At a quarter past ten, when she still hadn't arrived, he wondered if she had changed her mind. Fitton Park had no telephone installed now. The nearest one was in the village, but if he left and she arrived and found him absent...

It was just gone eleven when the pale blue Mercedes convertible pulled up in front of the house.

Jake watched her getting out of it, half expecting even now that she might disappear. She looked flushed and worried.

He went out to meet her.

'I'm sorry I'm so late. Mother wanted me to type some letters for her.'

'She makes you type her correspondence?'

Beth shrugged. 'She thinks it's a way of making me pay for my keep. Anyway, I'm not very good and she gets impatient. She's all wound up about buying Fitton Park. I think she's worried that you might pull out at the last minute.'

'I can't,' he told her drily. 'Money is owed to all quarters on Fitton Park. It's become too much of a burden to keep on.'

She was wearing the same jeans she had worn yesterday, with a different but equally bulky sweatshirt. It was a warm September day, and he was wearing a thin T-shirt. When he took her arm to lead her into the house, he noticed the contrast in their skin-tones, hers as pale as milk, his tanned, darker; his flesh clinging firmly to his muscles while hers covered the fragility of her bones with softness.

He pushed up the sleeve of her sweatshirt and ran his fingertips along her skin. The tiny blonde hairs on her arm stood up on end, a rash of goose-bumps breaking out under his touch. He was tempted to ask her if she was cold, but he couldn't bring himself to tease her.

'I thought we'd have a picnic lunch in the park,' he told her. 'We can take the original garden plans with us, if you like.'

She nodded, a silky wing of dark hair obscuring her face. He reached out and tucked it behind her ear, and the fresh, mingled scent of clean skin and perfumed hair reached him. 'You've just washed your hair.'

She moved back from him as though his touch burned. 'I wash it every day,' she told him defensively. 'It wasn't...' She stopped, and the familiar hot colour burned her skin.

'It wasn't what?' he prompted gently. 'Because you were seeing me?'

She looked away from him, scuffing her toes as she had done the previous day, and a wave of mingled pain and pleasure swept over him. She was so young...so naïve...so desperately precious to him already; and despite the fact that there were only nine years between them he felt as though he were a couple of decades her senior.

'I wasn't suggesting that it was,' he told her gently. 'I just wanted to tell you that it smells and feels good.'

'Mother thinks I should have it cut and permed.'

It was thick and silky-straight, the simple style almost schoolgirlish, but the thought of her having it tortured into the fashionable styles he saw other girls wearing made him grimace.

'It suits you as it is.'

'It needs trimming,' she told him, side-stepping his compliment. 'I used to go to a place near the house in Knightsbridge, but Mother says it's idiotic to pay all that money for a hairstyle like mine.'

Gloria Pilling was clearly a mother who delighted in undermining her daughter's self-confidence, in making her both feel and look plain and dull. Jake had met mothers like that before, but never one capable of such relentless cruelty. With most women it was unconscious, a bid to hold on to their youth by denying their growing daughters their burgeoning femininity. He doubted if Gloria Pilling had ever made an unconscious move in her life; she knew exactly what she was doing.

'Wait here,' he told her. 'I'll get the food and the plans.'

He had everything ready. When he returned, she was standing in the courtyard where he had left her, looking forlorn and hot in her thick sweatshirt.

'Couldn't I carry those for you?' she offered, indicating the plans.

He handed them over to her, watching pleasure glow in her face as though he had bestowed some wonderful gift on her.

He was used to being outdoors, to walking, and had been even before he'd joined the army, but he was careful to match his pace to hers. He knew exactly where they were going. There was a small lake set in one of the most heavily wooded parts of the park. It was surrounded by rhododendrons planted by his great-grandfather, straggly and unkempt now, but still a blazing glory of rich colour in the spring.

It was slightly cooler under the shadows of the trees. Some were already beginning to shed their leaves; the earth path was dry and packed firm, the odd tree-root the only hazard.

Their progress put up a pair of partridges. Jake pointed them out to Beth, watching the pleasure lighten her eyes.

'I grew up in the country,' she told him. 'I loved it. I'm not a city person at all...'

'You'll be happy at Fitton, then.'

'Yes,' she told him simply. 'I'll be able to think about your growing up here.'

The look he gave her made her face burn, and she stumbled a little as she stepped out of the shadowy darkness into the brilliance of the sunlit pool.

Jake reached out a hand to steady her. She was trembling slightly. He knew she was just as aware of the sexual tension stretching between them as he was himself.

Part of him wanted to say, 'Look, let's get it over with. Let's make love and then we can both relax,' but another part of him knew it was too soon, his approach too blunt.

There was a stone seat at the end of the pond, but Jake ignored it, instead spreading out the blanket he had brought with him.

He watched as Beth sat gingerly on the edge of it, and then removed the champagne from the hamper he had found in one of the old-fashioned stone pantries.

He put it in the pond, weighing it down to keep it under the water and then, calmly seating himself in the middle of the blanket, started to unroll the plans.

'This is how the garden looked before Inigo Jones's remodelling of the house,' he told her. 'Come and have a look.'

He was holding the plans so that she had to sit next to him to see them. The soft fabric of her sweatshirt brushed his bare arm.

'Aren't you hot in that?' he asked her, frowning as he looked at it. It didn't flatter her. The colour was wrong for her pale skin, robbing her of what little colour she had, turning her brown eyes as flat as pebbles when he knew they could sparkle with the same deep warmth as a good sherry.

'It's... I didn't bring many clothes to Chester with me.'

She turned her head away from him, but not before he saw the chagrin in her eyes.

While she studied the plans, he drew her out skilfully, coaxing her to relax and eventually laugh. She touched his emotions in a thousand ways he couldn't begin to name. The physical desire he felt for her was only one aspect of how he felt about her.

They ate the lunch he had provided and drank the champagne, she sparingly because she would be driving back to Chester.

As he lay on the blanket, watching her, he wondered what she would do if he reached out for her now, rolled her underneath him, kissed her soft red mouth the way he was aching to kiss it.

As though she picked up on his thoughts, she was suddenly nervous.

'Isn't it time we were getting back?'

'If that's what you want.'

He was pushing her, pressuring her, even though he despised himself for doing so. He saw her eyes cloud and cursed himself under his breath, but he had so little time. Tomorrow he would be gone, and she hadn't even promised to write to him.

'Have dinner with me tonight,' he said abruptly. 'Not here... I'll come to Chester... Take you out...'

'I... Mother's having dinner with some people she met recently. I suppose I could...' Her face flamed and she bit her lip. 'But not in Chester... we might... she might...'

'See us? Would that really be so dreadful?'

He saw from her face that it would.

'Not good enough for you, is that it?'

'No!' she said with surprising ferocity. 'No, it isn't that at all. She wants me to be married... she wants to get rid of me, but she wouldn't like me going out with you. Before she met you, I think she was hoping...'

'What?' he derided softly. 'That I'd want to take her to bed?'

'She's very beautiful,' she defended. 'Lots of men——'

'She isn't beautiful,' he contradicted harshly. 'She's ugly... inside and out. You're beautiful...'

And before he could stop himself he had taken her in his arms and was tasting the soft tremulousness of her mouth with the famished fierce hunger that had been building up inside him.

When he released her, her mouth was still trembling. He brushed it with his fingers and then couldn't resist touching it again, stroking it first with his fingertips and then with his tongue, and finally, when she made no protest, with his mouth, this time tempering his need, coaxing her into opening her mouth so that he could taste her with his tongue.

His hands found the hem of her sweatshirt and slid up inside it, stroking the narrow curve of her waist, smoothing over the soft skin of her back.

He felt her shiver when his fingertips traced her spine. He knew he ought to stop, but he couldn't. His fingers found the fastening of her bra and unclipped it. He felt the small, shocked sound she made against his mouth and stopped kissing her long enough to whisper, 'It's all right, Beth, I won't hurt you... I just want to touch you... to hold you,' and then, before he could check the words, he added rawly, 'You know I'm in love with you, don't you?'

Her eyes mirrored her shock and disbelief.

'You're lying to me... You can't be in love with me...'

'Why not? Because your damned mother wouldn't approve?'

His hands left her body and he moved away from her, but the small stifled sound she made made him turn back. She was crying, and it tore at his heart.

'Don't,' he protested thickly. 'I'm sorry... I shouldn't have said anything...'

'I know you're only trying to be kind, but you don't have to lie to me... That's what men always say, isn't it, when they want——?' She broke off and looked embarrassed, and he suddenly realised what she was thinking.

He laughed with relief and instantly felt her withdrawal. She thought he was laughing at her.

'So that's what you think of me, is it?' he teased her. 'That I'm lying to you so that I can have my wicked way with you. Well, I've got news for you.' He reached out and touched her face, sliding his fingers along her jaw, his thumb probing the soft outline of her mouth. 'I wasn't lying. I *am* in love with you. I also want to make love with you, but that can wait. This can't...'

He bent his head and kissed her slowly, whispering against her mouth, 'I love you, Beth, I love you,' until she smothered the sound with her own untutored response to him.

They spent the rest of the afternoon by the pool, talking, kissing occasionally when he felt he had enough control of himself not to frighten her with all that he wanted to show her... teach her. Because by now he had learned that he would be her first lover. Her only lover, he had mentally decided.

She had admitted to him that she was as attracted to him as he was to her, but her fear of her mother, her dread that somehow Gloria would find a way of coming between them, made her beg him to promise her that they could keep their relationship a secret.

'Just until Christmas,' he warned her. 'When I come to Fitton Park in the New Year——'

She had kissed him into silence, moaning his name softly when he slid his hands under her sweatshirt and stroked the smooth firmness of her bare breasts. He had wanted to take her sweatshirt off, so that he could see and taste the hard little nipples he could feel pressing into his palms, but he was frightened of rushing her.

She left just after three o'clock, promising to return at eight.

And it was only after she had gone that he wondered what on earth he was going to give her for dinner.

CHAPTER SEVENTEEN

'I REALLY must go.'

It was just gone midnight. Jake and Beth were sitting in front of the fire he had lit, both of them sharing the one chair.

She had come out dressed in the same clothes she had worn during the day, and this time when he questioned her she had told him simply that her mother did not believe in wasting money on clothes for her.

'She prefers to keep me looking like a schoolgirl,' she told him quietly. 'She hates people knowing that I'm eighteen. I have *got* clothes ... the things chosen for me when I was at finishing school; it's part of the deal. A suitable wardrobe for a young woman of *bon ton*...very *comme il faut* and totally ridiculous. Mother told me she'd bought me some new clothes, and until I put them on I didn't realise she'd chosen everything at least a couple of sizes too big.'

And in colours totally unflattering to her daughter's pale, delicate complexion, Jake reflected.

'Never mind,' he said softly. 'Personally I prefer you wearing nothing but your skin anyway.'

He laughed at the way she coloured, because in the firelight he could see the soft run of colour spread from her forehead downwards over her entire body, as she lay in his arms, wearing only the plain white briefs she had firmly refused to remove.

He didn't mind; or at least he was trying not to. He wanted to let her set the pace of their intimacy. The firelight played over her skin, warming its paleness to gold, darkening the flushed and swollen areolas of her nipples.

353

He touched one gently, remembering the heady pleasure of taking it into his mouth and sucking gently on it until she moaned and arched under his hands, whimpering deep in her throat as sensation quivered visibly through her body.

He gazed possessively at her love-flushed body, now swollen from his lovemaking and sensitive to his touch.

She made a sound in her throat, feral and female, and he had to quell a sudden savage impulse to take hold of her and bite urgently at her with his teeth until her whole body vibrated with the same fierce pulse he could feel dominating his own.

'Stay with me.' He whispered the words against her throat, moving her underneath him so that he could ease the ache a little against the softness of her flesh.

He knew, of course, that it was impossible, that she was far too terrified of her mother to contemplate what he was suggesting, and when he saw the way her face clouded he instantly regretted the words.

'It's all right,' he reassured her. 'I know you can't...'

'What time will you have to leave...tomorrow...?'

She was close to tears, and he felt his heart wrench with the welling, protective love she aroused in him.

'I'd planned to go just as soon as completion takes place. You are going to write to me, aren't you?'

'Yes. The New Year seems such a long time away...'

'It will soon pass.'

'I wish you lived closer... That you didn't have to go away.'

'I have to earn my living,' he told her, 'the only way I have of building a future for us.'

He frowned, wondering what she would say when he told her how he actually did earn his living. She was not the kind of woman who would find the admission sexually exciting, unlike her mother, he thought grimly.

He had seen too many of his fellow agents form relationships with women who were turned on by the thrill of danger, even when that danger was only at second hand. Ultimately such relationships were destructive and painful.

Relationships . . . He had prided himself on being far too sensible to get himself permanently involved . . . after all, what did he really have to offer a woman? Ostensibly he might be Sir Jake Fitton of Fitton Park, but in reality he was a man who risked death every day of his life, whose income was adequate rather than generous, and who could not even offer a woman any kind of emotional security, for herself or for their children.

By rights he ought to be distancing himself from Beth as quickly and painlessly as he could, for her sake as well as his own, and it amazed him that he couldn't do so. He, who had always been so in control of his emotions, who after witnessing the destruction they had brought to his brother had vowed that he himself would never admit them to his life.

What also amazed him was his instinctive, immediate knowledge that he loved Beth . . . that he did not simply want her, physically and briefly.

He wished he had more time, time to talk to her about his life, about the way he lived.

He thought briefly of leaving the agency. There were other careers, safe, profitable careers using his expertise and knowledge in other ways; but they were already so hard-pressed, so very short of manpower. . . He only had to look into the vacant, possessed eyes of the ever-growing number of young addicts to know that his job was worthwhile. Worthwhile but dangerous. And there would be periods of weeks, even months at a time when he would have to leave Beth on her own, when she wouldn't be able to contact him no matter what might go wrong. Did he have the right to subject her to that kind of life?

Did he have a right to keep the truth from her?

He took a deep breath and said huskily, 'I want to marry you, Beth.' He cupped her face in his hands, unable to resist the temptation of her half-parted lips. This time she responded with a frantic eagerness that threatened to destroy his self-control.

'I want to marry you,' he repeated softly as he released her, 'but there's something I have to tell you first.'

He couldn't allow her to become any more deeply involved with him without telling her the truth. If he lost her for doing so...

As clinically and succinctly as he could, he told her, watching her face intently.

She was shocked by his disclosures...shocked but unafraid. His heart lifted a little.

'I'm not going to make any false promises to you, Beth,' he told her gently. 'My work is very important to me. Not more important to me than you, just important in a different way. I love you and I always shall, but our marriage won't be easy. There'll be times when I shall be away for long periods...times when we can't communicate...you'll have to make all kinds of sacrifices I have no right to ask you to make,' he added bitterly, but she stopped him, placing trembling fingers against his lips.

'It's no sacrifice,' she told him fiercely. 'I love you the way you are... I don't want to change you... I'm *not* a child, Jake. I'll miss you when you're gone, but the times we're apart will make those we can spend together all the more precious.'

'I'm not a child,' she'd said, and yet in so many ways, despite her age, she was.

Despairingly Jake wished he wasn't committed to going to South America, but there was no one to take his place. Already this year they had lost two good agents.

The drug barons were ruthless...all-powerful within their own operations. The huge sums of money the business generated ensured that there was nothing they could not do...no one they could not buy.

'I want to take you with me now,' Jake told her huskily, 'but I know I can't do that... Will you wait for me, Beth? Until New Year? If you haven't changed your mind, then we can discuss the future more rationally. Tell your mother——'

'I don't *need* my mother's permission to love you,' she told him fiercely. 'Nor to be your wife...'

'No,' he agreed soberly. 'But you are afraid of her...'

'Not afraid,' she countered, flushing a little, 'At least, not afraid of *her*. Just afraid that somehow or other she'll spoil things...damage our love the way she damages everything she touches. I don't want her to know about us, Jake... Not yet...'

'Not yet,' he agreed. 'But when I come back we'll have to tell her. I realise I'm not likely to be someone she wants for her son-in-law. Materially speaking I've nothing to offer you, Beth. The money I'm getting from the sale of Fitton Park will be swallowed up by outstanding bills.'

'I don't want money,' she told him swiftly. 'I just want you.'

When she left he walked with her to her car. He hated letting her go, but couldn't pressure her to stay. There were only nine years between them, but to him she seemed so young, so vulnerable and in need of careful cherishing.

She had been gone just over twenty minutes when he heard the sound of a car coming back up the drive.

He went to the front door, frowning as he saw the now familiar outline of her Mercedes.

'What's wrong?' he asked her tersely as she stopped the engine and got out.

Her mouth was set with determination, her head held high.

'Nothing,' she told him, and then added huskily, 'I've changed my mind... I want to stay with you tonight, Jake. That's if you still want me to...'

'Want you to...?' He didn't know how he stopped himself from picking her up and carrying her straight upstairs to his room. Some final flicker of sanity and responsibility, he supposed.

'You know I do,' he told her, tempering the emotion burning inside him. He could guess how much it had cost her to turn back and make this offer. 'But it wouldn't be fair to let you do it,' he told her softly. 'And not just because you know damn well you'll be terrified of facing your mother in the morning...of explaining where you've been, and with whom...'

He saw her face and said grimly, 'And don't tell me you were going to lie... Neither of us is going to lie about our relationship...about our love.

'I want you to stay with me tonight more than I've ever wanted anything in my life, my darling, but I can't let you do it... and not just because of your mother.'

He saw her hurt and bewilderment...her hesitation and loss of self-confidence, the lovely, glowing happiness dying out of her face.

'No, *not* because I don't want you,' he groaned, taking hold of her and pulling her against his body so that she could feel the hard evidence of just how much he did want her. 'I'm not prepared...' he said against her hair. 'I can't protect you... I can't take the risk of leaving you pregnant...'

He felt her tension and released her so that he could look down into her face.

'I never thought,' she whispered dazedly. 'I never thought of that.'

'No, and half of me wishes *I* hadn't either,' he told her wryly. 'Don't tempt me into begging you to stay, Beth. I don't want to be like your mother...pressuring you...frightening you into believing you have to please me by doing what I want rather than what you want yourself. We love one another, and we're equal partners in that love.'

He kissed her again, briefly, with hard passion, aching to take what she was offering him, but knowing that for her sake he dared not.

It would kill her if he left her pregnant and she had to face her mother with that knowledge. He couldn't do that to her.

'I love you.' She whispered the words brokenly against his mouth over and over again, until he had to put her from him and still himself against the bright shimmer of her tears.

He was awake virtually all night, aching with need for her, and stubbornly refusing to give in to that need and afford his body release. It was as though by suffering himself he was protecting her... offering up an ancient sacrifice against her pain... her hurt.

'I'd like to ask you a favour.'

The solicitor frowned. Other clients frequently asked for favours, but not this one... not this stubborn young man whom he had come to respect so much even while he didn't totally understand him.

'It's a personal matter... I... I wish to correspond with someone... It's not possible for her to receive my letters personally... I was wondering if I directed them here to your office...'

'Who is she?' the man asked, too stunned to be discreet.

'Gloria Pilling's daughter.'

Jake inclined his head while the solicitor's frown deepened.

'She's frightened that her mother won't approve of our relationship. I have to go away on business; when I come back I intend to talk to Gloria Pilling and tell her that I want to marry Beth.'

'You want to marry the girl?' The solicitor's astonishment grew. It was already being rumoured around Chester that Gloria Pilling was on the look-out for a husband for her daughter. He had seen the girl once when he'd called at Gloria Pilling's suite, a plain, dull-looking young woman, who had struck him as very ordinary and uninteresting... Certainly not the type to attract someone like Jake Fitton.

Despite his lack of wealth, he was well born, and well connected... Physically he was the type of man that women found very attractive; he knew that from his own wife's observations. Privately he had half suspected that Gloria Pilling herself might have had an ulterior motive in buying Fitton Park. He wasn't so behind the times that he was unaware of the current trend for older wealthy women to take as a lover men younger than themselves.

'But——'

The intercom on his desk buzzed and he broke off to listen to his secretary announcing that his next client was waiting.

'Will you do it?' Jake asked him.

There was no reason why he shouldn't, although normally he deplored anything underhand. It wasn't as though the young woman was being wantonly seduced or dishonoured in any way. Jake had spoken of marriage, and he knew him well enough to know that he was in earnest.

'Yes,' he agreed unwillingly, and Jake, knowing that time was running out, pressed urgently,

'And if anything should happen... If she should ever come to you, you have my full authority to use the spare monies from the sale of Fitton Park for whatever she might need...'

That sounded ominous; he wanted to question Jake further, but it was too late.

Jake's last act before he drove south was to visit the small churchyard that housed the Fitton family crypt. He stood there for so long that the woman arranging the flowers inside the church began to worry about him. She was just wondering if she ought to go and call the vicar when he suddenly lifted his head and gave her his brilliant, tender smile.

'Ever so touching, it was,' she told her married daughter later as they shared a pot of tea and her grandchildren played at her feet. 'Just like he was saying goodbye to them. Awful sad it must be for him, them having lived there for so long . . .'

CHAPTER EIGHTEEN

THE months Jake spent in South America were the most difficult he had ever experienced. His work required one hundred and twenty per cent concentration. He was working alone in the field on this occasion, posing as a slightly shady businessman, and using the various contacts he had established, hoping to infiltrate a ring of drug producers and suppliers so sophisticatedly organised that, despite the fact that the CIA and the British government knew of their existence, they were unable to find out just how they were managing to get their large supplies of drugs into both countries.

One slip...one mistake could easily cost him his life, as Jake well knew. The identity he had been provided with had to fit him so comfortably and so easily that no one could penetrate its deception.

Not even when he was alone at night in his hotel bedroom dared he allow himself to think of Beth. If he thought of her he might dream of her, and he had a shrewd suspicion that his room was bugged. He didn't think he talked in his sleep, but one never knew.

The work he was doing was mentally exhausting and draining, and as his opposite number in Miami had said frustratedly the last time they had met, no matter how many of the small fry they managed to pull in and convict, the really big ones were virtually untouchable, safe behind the guarded walls of their Colombian estates, living lifestyles of unimaginable luxury, running the country from behind the scenes.

All Jake could hope for at this stage was to be tested out; that was to be allowed to either carry a small amount

of drugs through British Customs or be used as a decoy
to enable someone else to smuggle something through.

The really big shipments, the ones they were interested
in, were not carried into the country in the false base of
someone's briefcase. It would be a long time, if ever,
before the organisation trusted him enough to allow him
access to the kind of information he wanted.

They knew from the amount of drugs reaching London
how skilled the organisation was; they knew the names
of some of the smaller pushers; they knew the names of
the big suppliers. But the all-important network of people
linking them together still had to be revealed.

In Colombia there must be someone with direct responsibility for the British 'market'; in London there
must be someone the organisation trusted sufficiently to
put in overall charge of their operation; and it was these
two vitally important key figures, and perhaps one or
two others, whose identities Jake wanted to uncover.

He was under no illusions. What he was doing was
very, very dangerous indeed. In the past that hadn't
mattered, he had had no one other than himself to consider, but now it was different. Now there was Beth.

He remembered a fellow agent once remarking bitterly that the worst thing one of their numbers could do
was to fall in love. Now he was beginning to understand
why.

Over and over again he asked himself if he had the
right to expect Beth to share the dangers of his life. She
was so very young in so many ways...still half child
and half woman and so very vulnerable. But she had
told him that the last thing she wanted him to do was
to abandon his work because of her.

'It's so important...so necessary...' she had told him
with shining eyes. 'Without people like you...'

And he had realised ruefully that she was looking at
him as though he were some sort of knight in shining
armour... Very tarnished armour, he reflected tiredly,

and likely to be more so before this present mission was over.

Because it was too dangerous for him to risk reporting second hand to London, he would be flying back there just before Christmas to report directly to his superiors... After that it would be up to the organisation to contact him. Whether they did or not depended on how he convinced them that he could be of use to them.

A great deal of painstaking preparation had gone into his new identity. In London he had an ailing business, desperately in need of cash, and the kind of lifestyle to support that made him eager for money. That lifestyle came complete with an ex-wife—a fellow agent. His disappearance from London over Christmas would be covered by the need to 'disappear' for a few weeks to escape from his creditors and his ex-wife.

The operation was a long-term one, and Beth would ultimately have to be part of the deception... As his wife...

He sighed a little, remembering the forcefully blunt reactions of his superiors to the information that he intended to marry. That had angered him. Beth was too important to him for him to be able to ask her to wait, possibly many months, until the operation was over.

He wanted her with him now... wanted to establish clearly to Gloria Pilling the nature of their relationship. It wasn't going to be easy, he knew that, but somehow they would find a way.

The telephone beside his bed rang and he tensed; this was the signal he had been waiting for... the first step on the road that would take him eventually into the heart of the organisation.

He picked it up and listened.

Three weeks later, when he flew into Heathrow, he was carrying the briefcase that his contact had given him. Customs had been given instructions to treat him with kid gloves.

From the airport he drove to the apartment he rented following the break-up of his 'marriage' and, once there, waited for the contact he knew would come.

The woman who came to see him was brisk and impersonal, elegantly dressed and slightly disdainful as she took the case from him, and calmly unlocked the small hidden cavity inside it.

She smiled grimly at the expression on his face when she opened the small bags concealed inside and then poured their contents on to the coffee table.

'It's salt,' she told him, and then added mockingly, 'Surely you didn't think we'd really trust you with anything more valuable?'

'But I was told I'd be paid ten thousand pounds for bringing this stuff in,' Jake told her blusteringly, playing up to his role.

'So you will be,' she agreed, opening her shoulder-bag and removing a neatly folded roll of bank notes. She dropped them on the table beside the salt. 'It's all there...count it if you wish.'

Jake gave her a suspicious, surly look and did just that. She hadn't lied, and the notes weren't counterfeit either.

'What the hell's going on?' he demanded angrily. 'You pay me ten thousand quid just to bring in some salt?'

'We were testing you,' she told him coolly. 'After all, if this had been coke, it would have been worth far more than ten thousand pounds...' She turned round and walked towards the door, pausing there to say casually, 'We'll be in touch with you if we need you...'

'Not for the next few weeks, you won't,' Jake told her truculently, picking up the money. 'I'm going somewhere where I can enjoy this before anyone else tries to get their hands on it.'

He left London three days later, ostensibly to join a house party of like-minded 'friends' who were spending Christmas and the New Year cruising the Bahamas.

Two days after that, after a draining debriefing followed by discussions on future tactical plans, he drove down to Fitton Park.

The changes were apparent the moment he drove in through the gates. Fresh gravel covered the drive, the lawns were immaculate...and in the distance the late afternoon sunlight glinted on the cleaned and repaired mullioned windows.

He had stopped in Chester on his way to Fitton Park, to call on his solicitor. His call there had had two purposes; the first had been to collect Beth's letters.

What he had read in them angered him. It was plain that Gloria was making her daughter very unhappy, and that knowledge helped to ease Jake's own feelings of guilt that marriage to him might be placing an unfair burden on Beth's frail shoulders.

His second purpose was to collect the old-fashioned emerald and diamond ring that had been given to Fitton brides since Regency times. On his instructions his solicitor had removed it from the bank's safety deposit box and arranged for it to be cleaned.

It was heavy and ornate, and something smaller and more delicate would probably have suited Beth's tiny hand far better. But it was traditional that all Fitton brides were given this ring, and Jake had surprised within himself an odd need to continue that tradition.

He slowed his car down to a crawl as he headed down the drive, his mind registering all the subtle and infinitesimal changes wrought by skill and an inexhaustible supply of money.

Whoever had been responsible for ordering the restoration of the gardens had done so with sympathy and care, and he fancied that he detected Beth's gentle touch in their renewal.

He knew from Beth's letters that he was not going to be Gloria's only house guest.

When she had first demanded from him that he attend her New Year's Eve party he had been angered and loath to accept her invitation to stay at Fitton as her guest.

But once he had met Beth...he was smiling as he parked his car with the others and removed his bags from its boot.

Even as he approached the front door it was opening, but it wasn't Finks' familiar lop-sided figure that stood there.

The man opening the door to him bore all the hall-marks of a traditional British butler: grey-haired, stern-faced, straight-backed. When Jake gave him his name, saying casually, 'Jake Fitton,' he corrected him loftily, greeting him with,

'Good afternoon, Sir Jake. I'll inform Mrs Pilling that you've arrived. Lucy will show you up to your room; the other guests are in the conservatory. Mrs Pilling asked for tea to be served there at four o'clock, but if you would prefer something in your room...'

Tea in the conservatory. Jake suppressed a grin. The conservatory as he remembered it had been a cold, dank place, its framework rusting and many panes of glass missing. He wondered what it looked like now. Probably full of green, shiny plants and uncomfortable wrought-iron furniture.

The thought of mingling with Gloria and her guests wasn't a particularly inviting one. There was only one person he wanted to see, but he guessed that Beth would be far too apprehensive of being discovered by her mother to risk trying to see him alone.

'I'll join the others, thank you,' he told the butler, turning to follow the trimly turned-out maid who was waiting to escort him upstairs.

Following her up the cleaned and restored carved staircase, noting the delicate perfection of the plain cream-washed walls and the heavy richness of the pol-ished oak, Jake felt a small pang of regret, and he paused, one hand on the balustrade, feeling the familiar warmth of the oak beneath his skin, studying the oils grouped on the cream walls, and noting how well their sombre colours toned in with the patina of the wood.

Someone had gone to immense trouble over Fitton's reawakening, and if the other rooms were as carefully and sympathetically restored as the hallway and stairs he knew that Gloria Pilling must be receiving many compliments on all that she had achieved... Or all that her money and Beth's taste had achieved, he reflected, recalling the carefully detailed letters Beth had sent him, each one full not only of her love for him and of how she missed him, but also of the work she was doing at Fitton.

From the top of the stairs he paused to look back down into the hallway.

The huge stone fireplace had been restored and opened up again, and if the fire that burned there was fuelled by gas and not by coals, then at least this modern addition did not smoke and belch as the old one had.

Beneath the soft gleam of dulled pewter light-fittings the parquet floor glowed liquid gold, the sombre darkness of the wood highlighting the richness of the antique rugs.

The carpet on the stairs had been specially woven, Beth had told him, adding apologetically that she had not been able to dissuade her mother from having the devices of their own family's arms woven into the design.

The effect was surprisingly pleasing, even if he rather suspected that his grandfather would have had apoplexy at the thought.

At the top of the stairs where they branched left and right into the galleried landing were more oils, and beneath one of them a polished chest holding a bowl of richly scented pot-pourri.

In the darkness beyond the lights a floorboard creaked, and softly a familiar voice said quietly, 'Thank you, Lucy. I'll show Sir Jake to his room.'

'Beth.'

His heart leaped tumultuously. He barely saw the maid slip discreetly away. So she had come to him after all...too late now to regret saying he would join the others. As she came towards him out of the darkness, he couldn't help reflecting how well her surroundings became her quiet beauty.

She could have been a Puritan Fitton, all demure graces and quiet, glowing innocence. Her soft hair was pulled sleekly back off her face, her skin glowed with happiness, and as he watched her Jake ached to snatch her up into his arms and carry her away somewhere where they could be completely alone.

He heard her laugh shyly and saw the colour flood her face.

'I've missed you,' he said thickly as she put her finger to her lips and whispered,

'Wait...not yet...it's this way...'

He followed her along the gallery, frowning a little when she led the way to the flight of stairs that led to the upper storey.

When he hesitated she turned round to look at him.

'I thought you'd prefer to be up here, away from the others,' she told him softly.

The room she took him to was the old one he had shared with Justin, but so miraculously altered that for a moment he could only stand and stare.

It was her hesitant, 'Don't you like it?' that broke his concentration.

He turned to her, smiling. '*You* did all this...?'

She laughed self-consciously. 'Well, I chose everything... Mother thought I was mad...' She moved over to the window. 'I couldn't help thinking how it must have been for you and Justin when you were boys, and I wanted to make it different...to make it warm and cosy...and besides, when I was up here I felt closer to you somehow...'

She had completely transformed the cold, monastic room, turning it into the sort of bedroom-cum-study that invited the user to feel cherished and so completely at home that they would never want to leave.

'There's a bathroom...here,' she told him shyly, indicating a new door, 'and...my room's up here as well...'

His head swung round and she flushed again, her eyes uncertain and a little afraid.

'Oh, God, Beth, I've missed you so much!' He took her in his arms and kissed her, fighting to temper his need and hunger. 'Do you still love me?' he demanded unsteadily, framing her face in his hands.

Her expression gave him his answer. He kissed her again, loving the frantic pounding of her heart against his own, aching to pick her up and carry her over to the bed, so soft and inviting with its coverings of rich silk and damask... He wanted to love her here, on that bed of dark silks, with the firelight playing over their bodies, with the rest of the world shut away... He wanted to show her all the rare treasures their loving would bring. He wanted to cosset and indulge her.

'Mother's told everyone that you're spending Christmas and New Year here,' Beth told him huskily, adding, 'Gregson will have told her you've arrived. She'll be wondering where you are...'

The words, 'I don't give a damn what she's wondering,' trembled on his lips and were forced back as he saw the anxiety showing in her eyes.

He had few illusions about himself, and he doubted that Gloria Pilling would welcome him as a son-in-law, but he loved Beth, and, even if life with him would deprive her of the material luxuries that her mother could provide, he would at least see to it that that look of hesitant anxiety was banished from her eyes for ever.

'I'm going to show you the house,' she whispered palliatively to him, and suddenly his throat hurt for her that she should be so insecure, so afraid of incurring his displeasure that she felt the need to offer something in exchange for his unspoken acceptance of her fear for her mother.

'Not before I have managed to show *you* how much I love you,' he told her softly, and then took her hands in his and added firmly, 'Beth, if for any reason you've changed your mind about us, please don't be afraid of saying so. You must never be afraid of me, because I promise that, no matter what you might say or do, I'll respect that as your wish.'

'I do love you,' she responded fervently. 'I'm sorry to be like this...so afraid of Mother...' She pulled a face. 'It's ridiculous, isn't it?'

'And you're still happy with the idea of our announcing our engagement before I leave.'

Her fingers tightened convulsively in his. 'Yes,' she croaked. 'If you still want me...'

'Want you...? Come on, we'd better go downstairs before I'm tempted to show you how much. You can't imagine how tempting it is to carry you over to that bed and make love to you. You've transformed this room completely. The fabrics, the colours—they're so sensual...'

She didn't tell him that she had chosen them deliberately, or that she had spent hour after hour up here dreaming of being with him.

Instead she said quietly, 'We'd better go down separately...'

And before he could stop her she pulled away from him, hurrying quietly out of his room.

Lucy, the maid, was waiting for him when he went back downstairs. There was nothing in her expression to betray the fact that she knew he had been with Beth.

The conservatory was down a long passage which he remembered as dim and damp, lined with discarded riding paraphernalia, and smelling of wet dog and even less pleasant things.

Now, with the panelling cleaned, and hung with framed hunting cartoons, the floor polished and the vaulted ceiling restored to its original strap and plasterwork, the corridor was a different place.

As was the conservatory. There were plenty of green shiny plants there, but no uncomfortable wrought-iron furniture.

Instead the other guests were sitting very comfortably in Lloyd loom chairs, reclining against vibrant chintz cushions.

Gloria Pilling, presiding over a huge silver tea samovar when he walked in, was dressed in an outfit designed to make the most of her stunning figure. She stood up when she saw Jake and came over to him, raising herself on tiptoe, so that she could brush her over-glossed lips against his cheek. She smelled of expensive perfume and money. The light in her eyes was cold and calculating. She drew him forward, linking her arm through his.

'Jake, I think you know everyone, don't you?' she asked.

He did, only vaguely, but he saw from the expressions of curiosity and anticipation on their faces that the others all knew about him.

One of the women, more stupid than the others, gushed nervously, 'Sir Jake... Goodness, it must feel funny for you coming here... after all, it is your old home.'

Someone giggled nervously, and one of the men coughed in embarrassment. Jake smiled benignly at her, concealing his irritation.

'It's a very long time since I lived at Fitton Park,' he said easily, and then, turning to Gloria Pilling, added, 'I must congratulate you on what I've seen of the house. You've worked wonders achieving so much in such a short time.'

Gloria smiled coolly.

'Actually my daughter is responsible for most of it.' She gave a brittle laugh as though the admission didn't please her, and added disparagingly, 'I had to recoup something on the exorbitant fees of the finishing school she attended. Fortunately they included a fine arts appreciation course in the curriculum, otherwise the whole time there would have been a complete waste. Beth is so unsociable as to be positively gauche.'

Jake had to suppress a strong desire to tell her exactly what he thought of her cruelty to her daughter. The sooner he could get Beth away from her mother, the better, he decided grimly, accepting a cup of tea, and sitting down beside his hostess.

Gloria was celebrating Christmas with a magnificence that the Cheshire County set had long since abandoned... All she needed to complete the picture was a group of deserving poor to patronise, Jake reflected, watching her on Christmas morning as the Fitton Park party gathered outside the village church.

It was a cold, crisp day and Gloria was swathed from head to foot in Russian sables. The vicar and his family had been invited to join the other guests for Christmas dinner, and Jake watched the interplay between Gloria and her attendants with grim cynicism.

She was a very wealthy woman, there was no doubt about it, and he wondered how long it would take her to realise that, no matter what she did, she would never truly be accepted here. He also wondered how long it would take her to grow bored with Fitton Park, and what would happen to it when she did. He shrugged the thought aside. What did it matter? Fitton Park was no longer his concern.

The frustration of not being able to see Beth alone for more than half a dozen minutes at a time was beginning to get to him.

Gloria kept her daughter busy, treating her abominably, forever making her fetch and carry while loudly disparaging her to her friends, and more than once Jake's eyes had kindled at her behaviour.

However, much as he longed to intercede on Beth's behalf, he knew that to do so would upset her.

On Christmas Day he managed to find enough time alone with her to present her with his ring.

She cried a little as he slipped it on to her finger, and made him promise to say nothing to her mother until the night of the New Year's Eve ball.

'What is it you're so afraid of?' Jake asked her gently. 'She can't physically keep us apart, you know.'

'No...but I'm afraid that somehow she'll destroy what we feel for one another.'

'I've got a month's leave,' Jake told her quietly. 'Plenty of time to get a special licence.'

He had already decided that when he returned to London it would be with Beth as his wife, but he wanted to give her time to get used to the idea. He suspected that Gloria would oppose their marriage simply because it was what her daughter wanted.

Beth gave him a pair of gold cuff-links embellished with the Fitton arms. He kissed her in thanks, not wanting to let her out of his arms.

Her perfume seemed to cling to his skin at night, making him ache unbearably to have her with him.

Gloria's New Year's Eve ball was to be like no other party that anyone in Cheshire had ever thrown, and that included the Duke and Duchess of Westminster. She had played shamelessly on Jake's name, using it as a net to catch the kind of guests she wanted.

The ball was to be masked, and Beth told Jake that her mother had spent a fortune on her outfit, having it specially designed in London.

Oddly, Beth's costume was that of a demure Puritan girl, and Jake wondered if it was more than mere fancy that had led to him picturing her so dressed.

She came to his room after she was dressed, standing uncertainly in the doorway while he surveyed her.

She looked so ethereal...so fragile...so inno-cent...the lace collar revealing the perfection of her skin, the dark velvet of her dress and its simple style en-hancing her quiet beauty... He wondered if she knew how much the demureness of her gown incited him to remove

it from her body and to lavish her silken skin with the
attentions of his hands and mouth.

'Being very brave, aren't you?' he teased her, drawing
her into the room so that he could close the door, but
she stopped him, shaking her head.

'It's Mother...she sent me to ask you to go to her
room. She said there was something she wanted to discuss
with you.' She chewed worriedly at her bottom lip. 'You
don't think she's guessed...about us...do you?'

'Does it matter if she has?' Jake asked evenly, suddenly tired and angry. 'Oh, God, Beth...this is ridiculous. I want you as my *wife*, and I'm not leaving Fitton
without you,' he told her roughly. 'Forget your mother.
I want to marry *you*, Beth... I want to spend time with
you before I go back to South America.' And then, even
though he despised himself while he was doing it, he
added grimly, 'Who knows? It may be all the time we
can have.'

She went white, and he hated himself for what he was
doing to her and almost called back the words. He was
as bad as her mother...worse...but he recognised that
Beth would always need someone else to make her decisions for her...to coax and chivvy her. If he hadn't
been so sure that she loved him, if he hadn't known that
her life with him would be so much better than the life
she had here at Fitton Park, he doubted that he could
have done it. As it was...

'Tonight I'm going to tell your mother that we're engaged,' he told her. 'If she objects, then when I leave
here tomorrow you're coming with me.'

Her mouth trembled as she looked at him.

'If you're sure that's what you want.' And then she
said huskily, 'Oh, Jake, I don't want to be a burden to
you. I wish I could be stronger...more mature. I do
love you... I do want to be your wife...'

She was crying, and he kissed her tears away, fighting
not to give way to the fierce desire pulsing through his
blood.

'Mother's waiting…' she reminded him guiltily, easing away from him. 'She'll be wondering where you are.'

He had no idea what Gloria wanted him for. Probably to remind him what she had bought when she'd paid him that extra fifty thousand pounds, he reflected grimly as he made his way to her suite of rooms.

She was occupying the bedroom which had always been the master bedroom; and as he knocked and was admitted by Lucy, Jake grimaced at the unsuitable lavishness of the room's décor.

Every piece of furniture in her sitting-room seemed to be coated with gilt; every chair over-stuffed and over-burdened with chintz. The floor was covered in pastel carpet inches deep, and the whole effect of so many rococo gilt mirrors, so many over-trimmed French chairs, so much chintz, all ribboned and ruched, was overpowering.

But not as overpowering as the woman who stood framed in the doorway to the bedroom behind the sitting-room.

'You can go, Lucy,' she dismissed the maid.

When the door closed behind her she studied Jake. He was wearing a dinner suit and not costume; there had been a costume provided for him, that of a Regency Rake, but he had rejected it, preferring the comfort of his own familiar clothes.

Now he saw with the beginnings of speculative unease that Gloria was wearing a high-waisted, sheer fabric gown of the Regency period, her hair caught up in a vaguely Regency style.

Diamonds glittered at her ears and throat, and as she moved into the sitting-room he saw that beneath the dress her breasts were clearly discernible.

She saw him looking at her and smiled acidly.

'It was the fashion. Ladies dampened down their muslins to show off what they weren't wearing underneath.' She looked sharply at him. 'I see you aren't wearing your own costume…'

As she spoke she came towards him, saying casually, 'I've been thinking, Jake: a house like Fitton needs a son to inherit it, and as yet I only have a daughter. I'd like another child, a son, and I can't help thinking how appropriate it would be were that son to be yours.' She was looking straight at him, and he must have managed to conceal his shock. This was the last thing he had been expecting.

'I'd like you to stay on at Fitton for another week... I think that should be sufficient time, don't you?' She saw his face and smiled cruelly. 'It's what you wanted, isn't it? The reason you've been paying so much attention to my daughter...?'

She laughed at him again. 'Oh, come on, Jake, surely you didn't believe I hadn't noticed? You've hardly been very subtle. I suppose I should have expected it... after all, it's an ideal opportunity for you to regain Fitton Park, isn't it?

'Only I'm not that much of a fool... when Beth marries it will be to a man *I* choose for her...' She smiled mirthlessly. 'Poor Beth... I hope she isn't too desperately in love with you, but I suppose she must be... How amusing it will be if you make us *both* pregnant. Of course, it will be *my* child who inherits Fitton Park, not Beth's, and of course, if you're thinking of refusing me, then I must warn you that I shall simply find someone else to take your place... but there's no need for pretence between us, is there? You can't *really* have wanted Beth. She's such a dull, plain little thing... probably still a virgin, too...'

She came so close to him that her body was touching his.

'Think about it, Jake. Your son could inherit Fitton Park, and my wealth as well.'

He was already pushing her away, his face mirroring his disgust.

'I love Beth,' he told her bitingly. 'I fully intend to marry her and I don't give a damn what you do with Fitton Park!'

He saw that he had shocked her.

'You *can't* love her...' She was almost stammering. 'No man could love Beth...she's so ordinary...'

'Not to me,' Jake assured her. For the first time in his life he had come close to wanting to physically hurt a woman. Her scent filled the room, cloying and dizzying...the hot, rich scent of roses. It nauseated him, and he longed to breathe the fresh, clean perfume that was Beth's warm skin.

Gloria was furious...temper spots burned on her cheeks, hatred glittering in her eyes...and Jake recognised instantly how much she hated her daughter.

This proposition of hers had nothing to do with the desire for a second child, not even with any desire for him as a man. What she wanted was to hurt and destroy Beth. No wonder Beth feared her.

He turned for the door, but suddenly she moved, whirling round in front of him, taking hold of his jacket, clinging to him, her avaricious, hot kiss burning his mouth.

As he wrenched himself away, disgusted by the scent and taste of her, he heard her saying feverishly, 'Jake...Jake...at last...my darling...it's been so long...'

And as he stared at her he heard a small, stifled sound behind him. He turned round.

Beth was standing there in the open doorway, all the colour gone from her skin.

'Beth, darling...when will you learn to knock?' Gloria was purring...her hand touched Jake's face possessively, but he dashed it away, totally ignoring her as he turned to Beth.

'We're leaving,' he told her quietly. 'I'll come with you if you want to get changed, but I'd prefer it if you didn't bring anything with you from here...'

And then he turned to Gloria and said fiercely, 'I love Beth, and I don't give a damn about this place or your money. You want a son for Fitton... well, go ahead and have one. The children Beth and I have will know riches that no child of yours will ever experience.' And then, taking hold of Beth's hand, he almost dragged her down the corridor, not stopping until they had reached his own room.

Once there, he held her firmly and demanded, 'Don't let her hurt you, my darling, because that's just what she wants.'

Beth's hand touched his face, her fingers coming away stained with her mother's lipstick. Jake rubbed violently at the spot with his handkerchief.

'God, she's loathsome. That scent...'

Beth's calm broke... her body shook with sobs.

'Take me away from here, Jake,' she whispered brokenly. 'Just take me away. All this time I thought that underneath she *did* love me... but I was wrong...'

'She's incapable of loving anyone,' Jake told her roughly, but Beth shook her head in sadness.

'No... it must be me... something in me...'

'No,' Jake denied grimly, 'don't blame yourself for her inability to feel normal human emotions, my darling...' His hands shaped her face, smoothing the hair back against her skull.

'Do you really love me?' Beth begged uncertainly.

His heart ached. How long would it be before the uncertainty fostered by her mother could be erased? How long would it be before she recovered her self-confidence... her belief in herself and in him?

'You know I do,' he whispered against her mouth.

Gloria Pilling's New Year's Eve ball was the talk of Cheshire, all right, but not for the reasons she had intended.

It was the sight of their hostess appearing at the top of the stairs, screaming like a fishwife as Jake Fitton and Beth walked away from her, that was the memory everyone there would carry away with them, and spread, suitably embellished, until the Cheshire plain rang with amused speculation about the affair.

Jake and Beth were married by special licence five days later.

Until they were married, Jake left Beth in the care of his good friends Tom and Annie Rogers.

Beth took to Annie right away, and Annie told her husband wryly that she hoped Jake knew what he was doing.

'She's like a child, in so many ways,' she said sadly. 'Jake's turned twenty-eight now, and she's not quite nineteen. I wonder if he realises all that's going to mean. He loves her, I know, and she loves him, but she will never be able to meet him on equal ground...she will always be in need of his care...his protection...'

'Some men want that kind of relationship,' Tom pointed out to her, but Annie shook her head.

'Not Jake...he's too mature...too well rounded as a human being.'

Tom grimaced at her.

'I thought you liked Beth.'

'I do, and I feel desperately sorry for her... Maybe things will change... Now that she's free of her mother, maybe she'll start to mature...'

They had three blissful weeks together which they spent in Scotland at a small crofter's cottage that belonged to a friend of Tom's.

It snowed the first night they arrived and went on snowing almost all week... They weren't quite snowed in, but the delicious pleasure of imagining that they were, of pretending that they were cut off entirely from the rest of the world, safe and secure in this small house with its open peat fires, its low-eaved bedroom and old-fashioned high bed covered in linen sheets that smelled faintly of heather, added an extra intensity to their happiness.

They went to bed early, although it was some days before Jake was able to persuade Beth to make love with him as he had wanted to at Fitton, in front of the fire, with its light playing over their bodies, her skin so pale and delicate, his so much darker.

Watching him as he made love to her, Beth could only wonder that he should want her. She touched his skin tentatively, unable to accept still that he was hers. When he loved her he was so passionate, so male and yet so tender, never rushing her, never taking his own pleasure greedily. And as her face registered her awe and pleasure in his possession of her, Jake acknowledged a little sadly that with Beth he could not, as he might have done with another, more robust woman, admit how he had gained the skill that was giving her so much pleasure.

Beth's self-confidence was so frail, her dependence on him so great, that to know that another woman had given him the knowledge to pleasure her so that her body twisted against his in silent ecstasy would torment her, and she would never be, as another woman might have been, amused and entertained by his description of his so much younger and more naïve self.

It took him almost all the second week to convince her that there was nothing all that shocking about making love in the daylight, and most of the third to persuade her to caress him as intimately as he caressed her.

When the time came for them to return to London he was conscious of how vulnerable she was going to be without him... Too vulnerable, perhaps.

She had readily accepted the necessary change in their identity and had assured him that she was quite happy to play that role, but as he left her in the doorway of his London apartment he ached to have more time to spend with her.

For the first few months of their marriage he spent more time in South America than he did in London...

Slowly he was being permitted to know more about the organisation, but, frustratingly, he acknowledged that he was still far from discovering the identity of the small nucleus of people responsible for shipping the drugs from Colombia into London.

And then he had an unexpected piece of luck... His contact had grown confident and careless, and had permitted Jake to meet him in his office... After all, what did a member of such a successful organisation as this have to fear from the Colombian police force? In Colombia men such as himself were respected and feared, as he boasted to Jake, when Jake purposely marvelled at his careless disregard for the authorities. The man was very unimportant, vain and arrogant, but he was Jake's most important contact, and when the phone rang in his office and his voice changed from the arrogant confidence with which he spoke to Jake to a cringing, fawning subservience, Jake moved away from the phone but continued to listen.

No names were mentioned, but he heard his contact repeat an address. He himself memorised it, and when the call was finished the man turned to him and said hurriedly, 'I have to go out... on business. I will see you tomorrow.'

It was the opportunity Jake had been looking for. He followed him discreetly, photographing the man he eventually met with while staying well out of sight.

No one in London recognised the man in the photograph, but someone in Miami did.

'José Ortuga. We've had our suspicions about him for a long time, but he's been too clever for us. We think he's the brains behind the organisation of getting the drugs to their various destinations, and that he controls the small group of trusted main distributors at the other end of the chain... He travels frequently, but he's always clean... he meets a lot of people. Officially he's got a post with the Colombian government... We haven't been able to pin a thing on him. What we can't understand,' they told Jake, 'is what he's doing meeting with a small-time creep like Rodriguez.'

Jake had no idea, either... not then.

He was due to return to Colombia at the end of the week. When he did he wasn't phoned by his usual contact, but by another man, a stranger to him, who told him that a meeting had been arranged for him with someone important. He wouldn't give a name nor specify who, but Jake felt the first stirrings of excitement and tension. This must be the result of all his months of painstaking work coming to fruition at last...

In London Beth missed Jake desperately. She always did when he was away. She hadn't made any friends other than Annie... She was mortally afraid of betraying Jake in some way, so she kept her conversation with her neighbours to an absolute minimum.

She ought to have been lonely, but she wasn't. Jake was her whole world. When she was with him she knew a happiness she had never thought she could experience. When he was away she comforted herself by dreaming of the times when they were together. And now there was something else to add to her joy. She was expecting Jake's child... her doctor had only just confirmed it, and she was aching for Jake to return so that she could tell him.

Their apartment was in a large Victorian house in a quiet tree-lined street in a part of London not yet fashionable, and rather run down in a way that she found comforting and homely. Jake had given her a free hand to redecorate the apartment, and she had enjoyed herself doing so. She had a good eye for colour and fabrics, and the effect of the warm terracotta and peach walls and the rich fabrics she had chosen to go with them was very homely.

Now, in late spring, the lime-trees were in full leaf, and it was almost a pleasure to walk down the road from the apartment to the local shops.

The first phone-call came late one evening, just after she had gone to sleep. She was drowsy, unguarded, relaxed, and initially the soft soothing tones of the man's voice rang no alarm bells.

Muzzy with sleep, she thought he must be one of Jake's friends, especially as he seemed to know that Jake was in South America and why, and then, confusingly, his voice changed and became charged with menace as he warned her of the danger Jake was in. Jake must return from South America immediately, he told her. If he did not...who knew what might happen to him?

She hardly slept after that. Jake, in danger...she had known his work was dangerous, of course, he had told her that himself...but this specific and direct warning to her of that danger caused her heart to pound with fear and her stomach to tense in knots of anxiety.

Her first thought was to find someone to confide in, to help her...and the only person who came to mind was Annie, but when after a sleepless night she dialled their telephone number, no one answered.

The post arrived while she was replacing the receiver. She went to collect it, frowning as she saw that there was an additional letter with no stamp.

For some reason she knew even before she opened it what it was... The words were printed crudely as though written by a child, but there was nothing childish about the menace the letter contained...the threats against Jake's life...against their future.

Right down on the bottom line was a warning not to tell anyone else about either the phone-call or the letter itself, but just to make sure that Jake came home.

She could do it, she could write to him at the collection address she had been given, begging him to come home, but Beth wasn't a fool. She was Jake's wife; he loved her, trusted her. He was engaged in a very dangerous and important mission. She was not sure why, if these people were his enemies and, moreover, they knew what he was doing in South America, they were threatening him through her. She was intelligent enough to recognise that they must not be in as much control of the situation as they pretended if they were having to force Jake's hand via her, which meant that, despite the fact that they had apparently broken his cover, he must still remain a threat to them in some way. And then, with a thrill of pure terror, she wondered if perhaps they were trying to *use* her to lure Jake into some kind of trap. They wanted her to make him come home, for his own safety, they had said, but what if they were lying? What if they wanted him to come home for some other reason?

The effort of constantly thinking...puzzling... analysing was making her head ache. She hadn't been feeling well for days. Her hand touched her stomach lightly. Could she put it down to her pregnancy?

Was it really only yesterday that she had felt so happy that she was almost walking on air? Now she felt so much older...so much more adult...so very, very frightened for Jake. She must not allow herself to be manipulated into doing something that might place him in danger.

If only there was someone she could talk to, someone who could advise her, but they had warned her not to do so...had made it plain that she was being watched, her movements monitored...

Panic clawed through her, making her dizzy and sick, but she told herself that for Jake's sake she must remain strong. She desperately wanted him not just to love her but to be proud of her as well. To treat her not as someone vulnerable who must be cherished, but as an equal.

Three days after she had received the first telephone-call, just as she was beginning to think the whole thing had been a nightmare, just as she had managed to convince herself that the letter she had pushed to the back of the drawer beneath her underwear did not really exist, she had another phone-call.

This one was even more menacing than the first, the male voice grittily emphatic as it detailed Jake's danger and his ultimate fate if she did not persuade him to come home.

Despite her fear, she felt almost driven to convince her unseen tormentor that she was neither as weak, nor as stupid, as he seemed to think.

Breathlessly she told him that nothing he could do or say would make her do what he wanted.

She could almost hear the surprise in the silence that greeted her outburst. She felt surprised herself, elated almost that she had managed to find the courage to ignore his threats. Proudly she told herself that she had done what Jake would have done, that Jake would never have given in to threats or pressure and that neither must she.

While the elation still surged through her veins she replaced the receiver. She was trembling wildly, and had to rush to the bathroom to be sick.

As the adrenalin surge retreated, terror followed in its wake. She started shivering, her teeth chattering. She wanted Jake with her more than anything else in the world... She wanted him here beside her to hold her and comfort her, to tell her that everything was all right... and yet, horribly, her imagination kept playing and replaying to her a mental film of Jake stepping off the plane... Jake coming towards her smiling, his arms open wide...and then suddenly crumpling, blood on his face, his body still...lifeless...

She clung to that vision all day, fighting to hold on to it when the second letter arrived. She tried not to give in to the awful temptation to read it, but was unable to resist. The threats were explicit and detailed, making her run to the bathroom a second time.

She wasn't in the least bit brave, really, she acknowledged...

While Beth went to bed and pretended to herself that she was going to sleep, the man who had telephoned her made his report.

It was received in cold silence and he felt the sweat breaking out on his skin.

'I did what you told me to do,' he blustered, cursing the efficiency of the central heating, unwilling to admit that it was fear that was making him sweat so much.

'No,' the cold voice denied. '*I* told you to make sure that Jake Fitton left South America and returned to London.'

He hid his fear behind a surly expression of uninterest.

'Why bother? It would be easy enough to get rid of him over there...'

'Yes,' the cold voice agreed. 'And then his place would be filled by someone else, whose identity we would have to discover. We already know Fitton's identity. What we need now is a means of rendering him harmless... of getting him to act for us instead of against us. *That* was why I wanted him here in London. There are some men who can be bribed into changing sides; there are others, like Jake Fitton, on whom more subtle methods of persuasion are necessary. Fitton loves his wife. Any threat against her would be a very powerful means of persuading him to be, shall we say, less assiduous in his efforts to pry any further into our affairs?

'But for that kind of persuasion I need to see Fitton myself. Once his wife had given in to pressure by making him come home, he would have been that much more receptive to what I have to say. And now you, you stupid fool, have managed to ruin everything.'

It took several minutes for what he was being told to sink in. When it had done, he said angrily, 'But you never told me any of this... you said I was to threaten his wife...'

'And make her get Fitton home... not turn her into a damned martyr. I know her type. She'll be terrified, but she won't budge. You've been very stupid,

Fernandez, and there's no room in this organisation for stupidity.'

He was sweating in earnest now.

'It's not too late,' he blustered. 'We can get someone to warn Fitton that his wife's life is in danger unless he comes back...'

'No.' The scorn in the acid voice silenced him. 'You fool... He'd come back all right, but not before he'd informed his superiors... not before he'd resigned from the mission. No, I want him here, where I can deal with him myself. I didn't want him to know anything other than that that stupid little wife of his is in a panic... Now, thanks to you...'

Fernandez ignored the soft threat in the words and said as confidently as he could, 'So what do you want me to do now?'

'There is only one thing we can do. Fitton has already discovered too much. On our side, he could have been of use to us. We could allow him to live, perhaps, and feed him false information, but he's too intelligent to be deceived by that for long. If we can't disarm him, then I'm afraid we must destroy him.'

'Kill him, you mean?'

There was a small pause.

'Not, I think, at this stage. Mr Fitton has caused us rather a lot of trouble. I think he needs to be taught how foolish he's been...and it will serve as a warning to others who might be tempted to continue what he's started.

'Jake Fitton is one of that wearying breed: a man with principles. But principles must be paid for, and I think I know exactly the coin in which to make Fitton feel the weight of that payment.'

Fernandez looked confused. Intelligence was not one of his stronger points.

'What do you want me to do about the woman... his wife?' he asked cautiously, not wanting to provoke any acid gibe about his inefficiency.

'Leave her to me.'

He was not an over-imaginative man, but even he shivered as he saw the cruel smile hardening the thin mouth.

'If she's so eager to become a martyr, perhaps we ought to help her.'

Beth shopped daily, preferring fresh food, and preferring to walk rather than take the car.

The road wasn't particularly busy; there was a pedestrian crossing quite close to the shops. She checked the road before stepping out on to it, and it was empty, apart from a solitary car pulling away from the pavement some distance away.

She stepped off the pavement... and into oblivion.

A woman standing not far away saw everything. As she told the police later, she had never seen a car driven so fast... It was as if he actually wanted to hit her, she told them over and over again, and the police, aware of her shock, comforted her as best they could while they waited for the ambulance to come and remove the lifeless body of the young woman who had been killed.

Hit-and-run drivers... There were too many of them about, and they were on the increase... Of course, no one got the car number, or even its make, and they would never find it or its driver...

In Colombia Jake's meeting was mysteriously cancelled. There was no follow-up phone-call, and once his supposed business was completed he had no choice but to fly home.

At Heathrow they were calling his name over the annoy. A messenger was waiting for him... He handed Jake a large rectangular box and then disappeared. Jake opened the box.

Inside was a coffin-shaped floral decoration with a cross on top of it. His skin started to crawl, his stomach twisting in knots. There was a card as well... He picked it up and read the message on it.

'Our condolences on the loss of your wife'...and then, beneath the unsigned message, was another: 'Stay out of our business, Fitton.'

It was all the message read, but it was enough... He raced towards the airport exit and suddenly heard Annie calling his name.

One look at her face was enough.

'If it's any comfort, she wouldn't have felt a thing,' Annie told him quietly when they were back at her house.

It was only later that Jake learned *all* that he had lost...not just his wife, but his child as well. There was a small private funeral which he refused to let Gloria Pilling attend. Now that Beth was dead, Gloria was claiming that he had robbed her of her only and dearly beloved child... Listening to her made Jake want to be violently ill.

Nothing—nothing could ever wipe out of his mind the knowledge that *he* was responsible for Beth's death, and he swore that he would avenge her...that those responsible for killing her would be punished.

At first his superiors refused to allow him back in the field. He was too emotionally unstable, they told him, but when he announced that he intended to go back and root out his wife's killers, with or without their permission, they had to give way.

This time when he flew into Colombia there was no need for subterfuge or pretence...his adversaries knew exactly who he was, but that didn't stop him.

He tracked down his old contact and terrified him into giving him a list of names.

José Ortuga, that was the man he wanted, but he proved difficult to find. Ortuga was well protected... In the end it took Jake and some dedicated men, including Tom, four years to track him down, and then, just as they were closing in on him, and had uncovered information incriminating two more of Ortuga's group, their quarry had been snatched from them by a car bomb, a trap set by one of Ortuga's many enemies in the drugs business. That Ortuga had received his punishment, at other hands than his own, infuriated Jake, whose quarry had been snatched from his grasp while his own sight had been destroyed. From his hospital bed, Jake had been forced to tell the FBI what he knew of the other two men, acknowledging that he himself was too weak to track them down now, bitter though that knowledge was. They were quickly apprehended and were now awaiting trial. Four years to find three men, and there was still the all-important London controller to find; the shadowy, hidden figure who ran the London end of the organisation... the one who had ordered and organised Beth's death...

He wouldn't rest until he had found him and brought him to justice, Jake vowed. He owed it to Beth... and yet as he lay in his hospital bed he admitted that he was tired of death, of killing, of destruction...and that what he wanted more than anything else was the cool, familiar peacefulness of Fitton Park.

Instead Annie descended on him and swept him off to Switzerland. Annie who, like him, had known the agony of losing someone she loved. Tom had been killed outright in the same bomb blast that had blinded Jake. Morally, if not technically, he felt that he was to blame for Tom's death, in much the same way that he was to blame for Beth's, but Annie apparently did not share that view.

Somehow, somewhere she had found a serenity, learned an acceptance he himself had yet to know. He told himself that there was only one way he would ever again know peace of mind, and that that was by tracking down those who were responsible for Beth's murder. His own blindness he could accept as the price to be paid for the risks he took, but Beth's death—that was something different.

Tom's death hadn't really changed Annie; it had only reinforced those strengths she had already had. Knowing how much she had loved Tom, Jake wondered where she found such strength.

She had her work, of course; since, quite by chance, she had been the one to perform a life-saving operation on the son of an immensely rich American, that work had taken on an extra dimension.

The boy had been badly burned in a fire started in the family's hotel suite by accident. He had been rushed to the nearest hospital, where Annie had been on call and where she had performed a long series of operations which had ultimately restored the boy's terribly burned face and hands to normality.

It was out of gratitude for this that his father had given Annie the money which had initially allowed her to set up her private clinic, and now she was receiving patients from all over the world, children, in the main—victims of war, whose faces and bodies she rebuilt.

They had only discussed Tom once, when in a savage moment of self-loathing Jake had asked her how she could endure his presence when he was indirectly responsible for Tom's death.

'I don't look at it that way,' she told him quietly. 'Tom's work, and the risks that went with it, were something I accepted as part of him a long time ago. Tom's dead; nothing I can do will ever bring him back. I know he'd have hated to think of me spending the rest of my life living in the past.' She had looked down at her hands.

'I trained as a surgeon because I wanted to help other people. Tom's gone, but that's still there...'

And Jake had known that she was subtly trying to tell him that it was time he turned his back on the past and went on with his own life.

But *he* wasn't Annie; *he* didn't have her skills, nor her ability to accept. For him life could not go on until he had come to terms with his need to avenge Beth's death.

And so he allowed Annie to bully him and mother him, not really caring one way or the other where he was or what he did, only that somehow he had to find a way to reach out past his disabilities to search out and destroy those who had hurt Beth.

Annie, he recognised, was a crusader, a woman fiercely loyal to those she cared for, fiercely determined on his behalf that he must find a way to free himself from the past.

He was too drained to resent her interference as he might have done at another time, and so he gave in and let her think that the serenity of her Swiss mountains was an opiate, making him forget his determination to avenge Beth and to complete his original mission. Outwardly calm, inwardly he was already thinking... planning...

He was grateful to Annie, he knew she was doing her best to help, but her way... her acceptance... they were not for him. He needed more, and he intended to have it.

PART FOUR
Silver

CHAPTER NINETEEN

SILVER paused at the entrance to the dining-room of Blake's Hotel, smiling grimly to herself.

The letters of introduction she had provided herself with had proved extremely useful. She had been in London for just under a week, making Anouska Hempel's luxurious London hotel her headquarters, until such time as she was ready to move into her own apartment.

Her letters of introduction, half a dozen discreet re-commendations from members of the very rich and very wealthy aristocrats worldwide who had known her father, and about whom she knew more than enough to convince the most dedicated of sceptics, had had the desired effect.

London society was more than willing to open its door to her; their enquiries had revealed only as much about her as Silver wanted them to know: that she was rich; that she was widowed and that she was well born. Already she was beginning to receive invitations to certain prestigious society events.

She had chosen to stay at Blake's Hotel for a specific reason, that reason being the fact that Charles lunched his latest mistress there two or three times a week.

Throughout her time in Switzerland, Silver had received meticulously detailed reports of every aspect of Charles's life. She knew these reports almost off by heart; they contained every fine detail of Charles's life from the moment of her disappearance.

As she turned away from the door, and headed back to her room to change for lunch, she reflected briefly on the contents of those reports.

Once he had surfaced from his initial euphoria over her death and the fact that he would inherit from her, Charles must have found it quite a shock to discover that, not only could he not assume the title until she had been missing for a full seven years, but also that he couldn't have access in any kind of way to any of the huge fortune her father had built up.

Even if he had been able to draw on the bank accounts he would have found them empty, and he would also have found that the late Earl's bankers in Switzerland would have been remarkably unhelpful about providing him with any kind of explanation for the disappearance of such vast sums of money.

Silver knew that Charles had been advised to close up Rothwell, at least until such time as she was officially declared dead. The cost of running Rothwell and the estate had always been vast. The land did not produce sufficient income to pay the staff's wages, nor to maintain Rothwell to the high standards of perfection her father had always demanded. The fresh flowers alone that filled Rothwell's rooms created a bill that ran into many thousands of pounds per year. The insurance on Rothwell's vast amount of rare paintings, furniture, carpets and *objets d'art* cost tens of thousands more, and the salaries for the staff—for her father had always believed in paying well—had run into the hundreds of thousands.

Had Charles had access to the income generated from the leases and rents of the London properties, he might have been able to manage, just ... but he did not.

Against all advice, he had insisted not only on moving into Rothwell, but on living there in a far more lavish style than her father had ever adopted.

Before Geraldine Frances had been missing for a year, Charles had been having financial problems. She had read in her reports of his intention to sell Castle Kilrayne, and had smiled grimly to herself, knowing that it was impossible for Charles to dispose of one single asset that belonged to the earldom, until such time as *she* could legally be pronounced dead.

Four months later Charles had married the nineteen-year-old daughter of one of Britain's wealthiest industrialists, a man whose fortune ran into tens of millions of pounds.

George Lewis had been totally against the marriage, but Catherine, his adored only child, had been pregnant. Charles loved her and she loved him, she had pleaded with her father, and so, very much against his better judgement, George Lewis had had to accept the marriage, knowing it would break his daughter's heart if Charles deserted her.

He waited until after the ceremony to announce to Charles that he might have got his daughter, but he wasn't getting his money.

Charles was furious. His one purpose in seducing and marrying Catherine Lewis had been to gain access to her father's wealth. He had no love for her whatsoever; she was young, and pretty, but she was also timid and shy, and adored him so totally that he felt nothing but contempt for her.

She had been acceptable as his wife when he'd thought that in marrying her he would be financially supported by his father-in-law, but once George Lewis made it plain that he wasn't going to provide Charles with a penny, Catherine ceased to become an asset and instead became a burden.

Charles told her cruelly that her father's money was the only thing that had made him want to marry her, and that had he not been so desperately in need of that money there was no way he would have married a woman so far beneath him socially.

Although legally he could not adopt the title of earl, Charles did so whenever he could. Rothwell and its earldom, which he had so intensely longed for all his life, now that it was his was also more of a burden than an asset, but he refused to acknowledge as much.

Always jealous of James, he spent money he did not have, lavishly and desperately, but those people who had admired and venerated his uncle turned their backs on Charles, and that goaded him beyond all bearing.

He started blaming Catherine for the fact that there were certain social events, certain functions to which he was never invited.

The doors which had opened so warmly and willingly to James remained firmly closed against him. Desperate for money, Charles began surreptitiously increasing the price of the drugs he was supplying, jealously noting how small his own percentage was when compared with the vast profit made by others. It wouldn't do any harm to hold back some of the money he was supposed to hand over to his supplier, and he would repay it once his father-in-law was persuaded to part with some of his wealth.

Only George Lewis proved to be obstinate, and Charles found that he was 'borrowing' more and more from his 'employers'.

The day of reckoning would have to come, but he pushed it to the back of his mind... He needed that money and he needed it now.

It was all Geraldine Frances's fault... Why the hell couldn't she have overdosed or cut her throat and left him with a body? Then he wouldn't be having these problems.

Catherine was five months into her pregnancy when she discovered that Charles was having an affair.

Charles, in fact, had never stopped having affairs; he had just been far more careful about making sure Catherine didn't get to hear about them.

Now he didn't care. When she faced him in her bedroom at Rothwell, her face white and strained, her small, slender body swollen with their child, he laughed at her.

If she wanted his fidelity then her father could damn
well pay for it, he told her ruthlessly; until that time he
would live his life how he pleased.

As he made to walk past her Catherine clung to him,
begging him to tell her that he loved her.

Charles didn't love her; in fact, he was coming close
to hating her almost as much as he had once hated
Geraldine Frances. He pushed her away so savagely that
she fell to the floor.

At the sight of her lying there weeping, something
inside Charles snapped, her helplessness, her dependence on him, his own feeling of being trapped in a marriage that had not brought him what he wanted welled
up inside him so that he reacted immediately to her vulnerability, punching her with his fist, not once but over
and over again as she cried and screamed, finding a
savage sexual pleasure in the sound and sight of her in
pain, and a physical relief from his own tension.

When he left her she was unconscious, but he didn't
care. He drove straight to London where he spent the
night with his mistress.

When he returned to Rothwell Catherine was gone,
but George Lewis was waiting for him.

His daughter, he told Charles, was in hospital re-
covering not just from the beating he'd given her, but
from the miscarriage of her child.

The moment she was well enough his daughter would
be suing him for divorce, George Lewis told him.

When accused by George of beating his wife and
causing a miscarriage, Charles denied it. He had wanted
a child...a son... He needed that son for Rothwell. He
refused to admit that he had attacked Catherine and said
instead that *she* was to blame for what had happened...that *she* was responsible for the death of their
child. George Lewis was furious.

He left vowing that Charles would not get away with
what he had done to his daughter, but in his heart of
hearts he knew there was little he could do. Catherine,

shocked and distraught though she was, was refusing to divorce Charles on the grounds of physical cruelty, or to bring charges against him, and George had no wish to drag his only child through the trauma of such a potentially high-profile divorce case. Bitter though it made him, there was nothing he could do.

Affably Charles informed his father-in-law that the only way he would agree to a discreet divorce would be if George Lewis paid him substantially to do so.

George Lewis was outraged, but as his solicitor pointed out to him there was little he could do about that either. Catherine, still traumatised by Charles's brutality, had made it plain that she had no intention of going back to him; she was, her doctors warned George, on the verge of a complete nervous breakdown. The only way he could free her from her marriage was by giving way to Charles's outrageous demands. It wasn't the money so much as the fact that Charles was getting away scot-free but George knew he couldn't make the truth public without hurting his daughter.

A sum of money was agreed upon, half to be paid when the discreet divorce proceedings commenced and the other half when they were finalised.

George Lewis wondered how long it would be before Charles was looking for another victim...another potentially rich wife...

Yes, Silver knew all this from her reports on Charles, but there was something she did not know...something that the careful gleaning of her information had not revealed.

Charles's 'employers', the suppliers of the drugs that brought him in his only real source of income, were also concerned with Charles's affairs.

They were not, as he imagined, unaware of his misuse of their funds, and in an anonymous building in a run-down, unfashionable part of London two people were sitting either side of a table debating on what course of action they should take.

'I say we should treat him just as we would any other pusher who cheats on us. It keeps the rest in order, after all. If they thought someone else had got away with it...'

'I'm not talking about letting him get away with it,' the other corrected. 'Of course we must punish him...but there are other ways...he's very valuable to us...'

'Someone else could take over his business...'

'Not as successfully. Think about it...when he inherits the earldom...'

'When...'

'To all intents and purposes it's his now, but I'm not talking purely about the fact that he's one of our most productive suppliers. He owns a castle...it's in Ireland...on the coast. It's lonely and remote and the locals there have a long history of doing the odd bit of smuggling...who's going to be suspicious if the Earl of Rothwell buys himself a high-powered fishing-boat for the use of his friends and guests?'

'You think he'll agree?'

There was a small silence and then a grin. 'He isn't going to have much choice... Not if we make sure he has enough rope to hang himself on now. That's why I'm suggesting we turn a blind eye to what's going on at the moment...of course, if it gets out of hand...'

'I'll have to put it to *el presidente*. He may not wish...'

'He does, I've already checked. Come on, you know we've been looking for a way to bring in large supplies safely and economically... We've got the market for it here. My pushers are among the best there are. I choose them very carefully. There isn't a school within a fifty-mile radius of London I'm not supplying; there isn't a college or a university where my people aren't on hand.'

Another silence and then a grudging, 'Yes, you've built up a good organisation here, but I think you overreach yourself. I have already told *el presidente* what I think, and that is that there should be another appointed to this country to share the burden with you... With *two* of you here...one to take care of the suppliers and the other in charge of the importation...'

'There is no need... *I* can handle both ends. Haven't I proved that already...? Who was it who tipped you off about that agent, Fitton? Your people were completely deceived...'

'He is not important now. When *el presidente* took over the organisation from his cousin, Ortuga, Fitton was injured...blinded. He is no danger to us now...'

'No, but he could have been if I had not seen the danger and alerted you. Leave Charles to me. He will be more valuable to us yet, I assure you...'

'Take care you do not bite off more than you can chew, my friend...'

He stood up, glancing at his watch. 'My flight leaves in two hours and I must not delay. Remember, just as you care for your people as though they were your children, so *el presidente* cares for you. He values you highly...'

'I am grateful to him...'

They left the building separately and went their different ways.

Upstairs in her room Silver checked her appearance. Until she had made contact with Charles she intended to stay here at Blake's, despite the fact that she had an elegant and very expensive apartment waiting for her in Knightsbridge; the interior designer had presented her with a bill that ran into six figures and she had paid it without even inspecting the work. She had chosen Caroline Coleman to carry out the refurbishing of the apartment's interior, having discovered, again from her agents' disc ' enquiries, that she had been chosen to work on the w home of one of the Royal couples, and that being able to claim her as the designer of her apartment would add an extra lustre to her new persona.

Her brief to the designers had been to create an environment for a woman with a very sensual appetite; a rich woman who was female rather than feminine, subtle rather than clever, indulgent rather than intelligent; and she had purposefully chosen a designer who was well known for completing her commissions right down to supplying fresh-cut flowers, food in the fridge and magazines on all the tables, small touches that made a place looked lived-in and permanent.

All the clothes she had bought in Paris had been picked to reinforce the image she had chosen for herself; and she had been clever, buying not just new season's stock, but scouring the second-hand shops for clothes from one and even two seasons back; things that she could produce as 'old favourite' clothes for the woman who had led the kind of life she was purported to have led.

She would have had a governess as a boarding school would be too risky. It would have had to be one of the better-known ones, in order to establish her, and she didn't want to run the risk of meeting someone whom she might have been supposed to have known. Besides, a governess hinted at a sheltered, almost mysterious upbringing, with overtones of Continental royalty.

Heads turned discreetly as she walked into the dining-room.

She was wearing a Chanel outfit, stark black warmed with pink, the skirt of her suit very straight and short, ending just above the knee.

Beneath the jacket she was wearing a black silk camisole, but beneath the skirt only sheer black seamless tights.

The *maître d'* had long ago perfected the art of establishing the importance or otherwise of his diners, and she subdued a bitter smile as she was immediately shown to a small but very high-profile table, where she was seated with the maximum of attention and bravura.

The hat, which she had chosen deliberately, almost totally concealed her hair. She was lucky in being tall enough to carry off its wide brim, and she was well aware of the sharp looks of envy she was receiving from the other women diners, especially the woman seated with Charles.

She had seen them the moment she walked into the room, although no one watching her would have known that either of them meant anything to her. Her dismissive glance had swept over them with the same careless indifference with which she had surveyed the other diners.

Outwardly indifferent, inwardly she was shocked by the changes in Charles's appearance; when had the lean tautness of his jaw become puffy...when had the smooth golden flesh of his face become discoloured by the unpleasant purple flush of the heavy drinker? When had the body she remembered as hard and lean started to betray the beginnings of disintegration?

Helplessly she compared the unhealthy slackness of Charles's muscles with the taut fitness of Jake's body, and then shivered imperceptibly, infuriated that Jake's memory should dare to intrude now, when it surely had no place in her life...no excuse for being there. Jake was the past...a moment out of time which had come perilously close to getting out of hand; but that was all behind her now. She was facing the future...her future, and she intended to mould it to the form she wanted it to take.

Charles was looking at her. She was aware of his scrutiny without looking at him, just as she was aware of the pouting resentment of his companion.

Their relationship was already in its final stages; Charles was growing bored and impatient. He had almost cancelled today's lunch; now, as he looked speculatively across at the single table where Silver sat, he was glad he hadn't.

It was unusual to see such an outstandingly beautiful woman dining alone. She intrigued him.

Silver, well aware of Charles's interest, summoned a waiter and asked for a telephone to be brought to her table. She was not going to make it difficult for Charles to make contact with her. Why should she, when that was exactly what she wanted? But the lessons Jake had taught her had gone home. Subtlety was the key word here...the all-important word.

A waiter brought the telephone. She quickly dialled the number of her own apartment, and spoke to the answering machine as though holding a conversation, giving both her name and room number and allowing it to be made plain through her one-sided conversation that she was a woman of considerable wealth. Nothing obvious...just a small, delicate hint.

She knew Charles was listening. When the waiter removed the telephone she thanked him, her manner shaded to remain on the right side of slipping into flirtatiousness. One did not flirt with waiters, but one could, and did, massage their egos just sufficiently for one to obtain first-class service. No male was ever above responding to flattery.

Well, almost none. Against her will she remembered Jake. She doubted that *he* had ever responded to flattery in his life. She frowned, annoyed that she should have so suddenly and unnecessarily thought of him, and that her breasts should have inexplicably hardened, pulsing against the soft silk of her camisole as though seeking a more rough, male embrace.

Deliberately she turned her mind away from him, and with a practised motion, that she knew quite well looked artlessly natural and impulsive, she raised her hands and removed her hat so that her hair cascaded down on to her shoulders.

There were several audible gasps, more than one of them outraged. She hid her amusement. It was a shocking piece of play-acting, the sort of thing no well-brought-up English girl would ever do; and the women sitting at the other tables *were*, in the main, well-brought-up English girls.

She placed the hat on an adjacent chair and flicked back her hair in a gesture which she knew was deliberately preening. A man sitting several tables away caught her eye admiringly. She lowered her lashes and gave him a soft half-smile.

She wasn't Geraldine Frances any more. She was Silver, all soft smiles and teasing promises. A woman married young to an old, old man...a woman who was in a hurry to catch up on all that she had missed; a woman wealthy enough to be indiscreet and forgiven for it if she so chose; a woman freed from the conventions of the society she was about to enter by her 'foreignness'. She had it all well thought out and planned.

The worst was now behind her, and the game could really begin.

Some late lunchers arrived, and she tensed instinctively, recognising a couple who had been close friends of her father. The man trained racehorses and ran a large stud out at Newmarket.

When he turned to look at her, she stiffened, her heartbeat suddenly accelerating until she realised that the look he was giving her held no recognition at all, and was simply the look of a man for a beautiful woman.

With a relief came a heavy sense of euphoria. She almost wanted to laugh out loud. She could even almost imagine Jake's acerbic response to her tension and then its relief.

She frowned. What was the matter with her? *Why* was she thinking about Jake? He no longer existed for her...had never really existed other than as a means to an end. Those odd moments when she had felt so in tune with him that she had half believed he could actually read her thoughts were something she ought to have forgotten by now.

But she couldn't forget, just as she couldn't forget how it had felt to...

Stop it...stop it! She dragged at her runaway thoughts in fierce panic, not wanting to go where they were wanting to lead.

Her euphoria had vanished and in its place was a feeling of melancholy tinged with an emotion which she reluctantly recognised as loneliness.

She banished them both.

She had far more important things to think about, like Charles, for instance.

All through lunch she was conscious of the way he was watching her, almost blatantly willing her to return his regard.

But she didn't...she was too skilled for that. Instead she ate her lunch as coolly and unselfconsciously as if she were the only diner in the room.

Only as she left the table did she allow herself to be obvious in leaving behind her on the spare chair the small, exclusive carrier bag imprinted with the name of one of London's premier jewellers.

Inside it was a box containing the earrings she had specifically bought herself for this exact purpose... Expensive little trinkets of fashionable nothingness.

Charles's eyes gleamed when he saw the small parcel. Intercepting the waiter, he picked it up, assuring the other that he knew Silver and that he would return it to her.

His companion was furious.

'Can't you see she left it deliberately?' she demanded scornfully, and Charles, vulnerable always through his vanity, smirked tauntingly and retorted,

'Can't *you* see, my dear, that you are being extremely boring?'

During the ensuing altercation he was callously amused to hear her claiming that she loved him... Love had never had any role in their relationship, and she was deceiving herself if she thought she meant anything more to him than a good lay.

Once she had gone he didn't immediately go up to Silver's room. Instead he went to the foyer to use the

phone to book a table for two for dinner at a small,
intimate restaurant he favoured.

Upstairs in her room Silver wondered if Charles had
taken the bait. If he hadn't, there would be other opportunities . . . He was interested in her; curious about
her. She frowned as she caught sight of a small gift-
wrapped box on the table. The wrapping paper was silver
foil and the ribbon that wrapped it the same glittering
metallic colour.

A *frisson* of sensation raced down her spine. She stared
at the box, unwilling to touch it without knowing what
had caused her fear.

Where had it come from? How had it appeared in her
room? No one knew she was here . . . apart from Annie,
who had insisted on having details of her London addresses because, as she had said firmly to her, if anything should happen to her, however unlikely such an
accident might be, she was still very much *her* patient
and her records would be essential. The only other people
who had her London addresses were her lawyers.

Shrugging aside the prickly sensation that made her
feel almost as though there was someone in the room
beside her, she reached out for the box.

The metallic wrapping glittered in the late afternoon
sun. The package, although small, felt surprisingly heavy,
the wrapping paper warm to her touch, almost like
touching someone's skin.

She shuddered finely, tiny waves of sensation pulsing
through her, the temptation to simply throw the thing
away almost overpowering. She refused to give in to it,
unwrapping it quickly.

There was a box inside; a small, perfectly anonymous
box, which opened to reveal a small phial of perfume.

She stared at it for a moment, on the verge of relieved
hysteria. It was obviously nothing more than some kind
of publicity hype. Probably every bedroom in the hotel
had received one of these packages. It was only her own

emotions and tensions that made her believe that the silver wrapping paper had been chosen with deliberate intent . . . that it held a message that was meant solely for her.

She was just about to drop the phial into the waste-paper bin when she saw the small card inside the box.

She stared at it, transfixed. The writing was sharp and clear, and the message read, quite simply, 'This, I think, will become you better.'

She couldn't look away from the harsh initial, the sharp lines of the boldly drawn 'J', her hands trembling so wildly that she had to grip them together.

Jake had sent her this . . . Jake had known she was here . . . Jake had reached out into this new part of her life which should have contained nothing of him in it, and was in some subtle way threatening her.

Why was he doing this? What was he trying to tell her? That he knew where she was and who she was . . . oh, yes . . . undoubtedly that, she thought bitterly. But why? Blackmail? It seemed the most logical solution, yet instinctively she dismissed it, knowing that it didn't fit in with what she knew of the man.

Then why? To remind her . . . to torment her . . . or simply to warn her? She shivered a little and, without knowing what she did, broke the seal on the small bottle.

The perfume was rich and subtle, sharp and yet delicately erotic. She suspected that it had been specially blended. Why had he gone to such trouble? She replaced the stopper with hands that still trembled. If she had any sense at all, she would pour the damn stuff away. She got up to do so, then stopped.

She had worn Charles's tuberose for Jake. Perhaps she would wear Jake's perfume for Charles. The thought pleased her, freeing her in some way from the subtle domination Jake seemed to have established over her, making her stronger than either of them.

She wondered if there was any point in trying to discover how the perfume had arrived in her room, and then dismissed the notion.

The harm was done; trying to discover how it had been done would probably only multiply its aggravation.

Jake could not betray her without revealing his own part in her metamorphosis, and Jake had reasons of his own for wanting to keep a low profile.

She frowned as she studied the perfume. Had he put it here in her room himself? Her spine tingled with an odd, unfamiliar sensation...she looked round the room, trying not to imagine him in it, moving with that sure, catlike tread she had come to know so well... A blind man...he couldn't have done...he must have sent it via someone else. But the packaging, that had been chosen by him...which meant, surely, that he must be in London.

Why? Had he decided that the money she had paid him had not been enough? Had he discovered who she was...did he think he could get more money out of her...or was he simply playing some complex nerve-racking game of his own? And if so, for what purpose?

He had warned her against pursuing her vendetta against Charles, but if this perfume was meant to frighten her into dropping her plans...into making her think...

Think what? she demanded mentally, exasperated with herself. Think that Jake knew her far better than she had guessed? His choice of perfume had shown that... And she suspected he must have known how much its unheralded appearance in her room would disturb her.

What if he had followed her to London deliberately? Silver's heart started thumping with an emotion that wasn't entirely anger. She suppressed it immediately, wheeling round, impatient with herself.

Whatever game Jake was playing, she wanted no part in it. If he tried to get in touch with her she would make it plain to him that she had paid him every penny he was going to get out of her. If he threatened to betray her to Charles... But how could he? He had no idea who she really was... *No one* knew, other than a very, very small number of people, and each one of those would keep her secret. But what if he *did* know...? He couldn't know, she reassured herself. It was impossible.

She picked up the perfume, ready to throw it in the waste-paper bin, and then hesitated.

Whatever his motive in sending it to her, there was no doubt about it: the perfume might have been made exclusively for her, a gift from a man who knew her so intimately that he could unerringly choose a scent for her that immediately flowered on her skin as though she herself had produced it.

Downstairs in the foyer, his arrangements completed, Charles straightened his tie and headed for the lift.

Unlike Silver, he could not see the evidence of deterioration in his face and body. Always vain, always self-confident, always supremely conscious of his good looks, he had never thought that there might come a time when, through abuse, those good looks might desert him.

He never touched the drugs he supplied so generously to others, but there were other addictions; he drank heavily, seldom exercised other than in bed, and over the years there had been one or two minor inconveniences healthwise caused by his predilection for enjoying a wide variety of sexual partners.

Silver opened the door to his knock. She had changed out of her Chanel suit and into a sleek, body-shaping, contoured jersey outfit in soft cream.

She saw the way Charles's eyes went first to her breasts and then to the rest of her body. She didn't invite him in, but the smile she gave him was not the coldly discouraging one she had previously favoured.

He proffered the small parcel and introduced himself, giving her the smile he already knew worked to excellent effect.

'You left this in the dining-room...'

She managed an effective start of surprise, thanking him and apologising to him for putting him to the trouble of returning it personally.

His smile matched her own, both smiles saying that they were expert in a very enjoyable game.

'I was thinking of your husband's bank balance,' Charles told her suavely, looking at her rings.

Silver picked up the cue.

'Thoughtful of you, but unnecessary; my husband is dead,' she told him openly. 'That's why I came to London. I love this country so much and I thought being here would help me overcome my sorrow at becoming a widow... No matter how much money one has, there is always loneliness when one is left alone...'

'A woman as beautiful as you should never be *allowed* to be lonely. Have dinner with me tonight...'

He was so supremely confident...so sure of himself...so sure of her...

'It's very kind of you,' she told him softly. 'But I'm afraid I have an engagement for tonight. The reception given by the American Ambassador...some friends have been kind enough to include me in their invitation.'

Now she was testing him, wondering how interested he was...interested enough to find a way of attending a reception she knew full well he had not been invited to...? She would see...if he did not put in an appearance—well, there were other ways of picking up the acquaintanceship now that it was begun. She was over the first hurdle.

Charles was angry; he wasn't used to having his invitations refused. Women, at least the women he chose, were normally only too flattered and delighted to go out with him.

As he walked out of Blake's he was telling himself that he wasn't really that interested in her, but before the end of the day he was calling in favours, trying to find a way to ensure that he would be present at the Ambassador's reception.

He had discovered certain interesting facts about Silver.

He already knew that she was an extremely beautiful woman; now he knew she was a very wealthy one as well.

Wealthy...beautiful...and with no father controlling the purse-strings. Never far away from Charles's mind was the knowledge that he needed an heir...a son...a guarantee for the future, that he would not see Rothwell slip away from him as it had slipped away from James.

Only after she was sure that Charles had gone did Silver allow herself to relax. She was physically trembling as she sat down.

For the first time since her faked death she had been face to face with her cousin, with the man she had loved so desperately and so intensely, and only now could she acknowledge the fear that had stalked her all through the months she had been planning and waiting.

She had dreaded confronting Charles and discovering that she still loved him, and even while she *had* dreaded it half of her had been psyched up, almost high on the anticipation of seeing him again, remembering the powerful mingling of longing and excitement each meeting with him had once brought.

That feeling had almost been like a drug, and she had half feared she might experience it again, that she might, against all logic and common sense, discover that, while she hated Charles with her mind and that part of her heart that loved her father, she still desired him, still ached for him with that part of her that was still Geraldine Frances.

Only she hadn't... She had looked at him in the dining-room and seen only a petulant, immature man whose good looks were becoming tarnished by self-indulgence and conceit. She had felt no familiar upsurge of panicky excitement and desire, no melting aching, yearning to reach out and touch...no compulsion to beg and plead...

All that had remained of the feelings she had once known were the deep-rooted anger and bitterness she still felt at knowing that Charles was responsible for her father's death... That he had killed her father and was still walking free.

Even the hatred and agony of pain she had experienced on discovering how much he had betrayed *her* was gone. She had looked at him and seen, not a man she had once ached for, had once loved beyond everything else, but a man whose weaknesses and vices were stamped so clearly on his face that she could only marvel that she had never seen them before.

What a fool she had been... idolising him... And in doing so, she had unwittingly been partially responsible for her father's death.

She stood up, trying to control the physical reaction of her own flesh to what she was thinking and feeling.

All these months she had been haunted by the fear that once she saw Charles, once she looked at him, all that she had learned, all that she had become would be forgotten in a familiar surge of love and pain... that she would be unable to stop herself reaching out to him, begging him...

Instead, all she had felt had been contempt and a mild physical revulsion. Looking at him, listening to his heavy-handed gallantry, observing the way his glance slid eagerly over her body, she had found it easy to hold herself aloof... but not easy to stop her mind from drawing sharp and dangerous contrasts between the man she had once wanted above all others as her lover, and the man who had finally, clinically and factually, taken on that role.

Her eyes snapped open, her breathing suddenly stilted. What was she doing? Jake Fitton was gone. He had no place in her life... in her thoughts. It was *Charles* who was important now... *Charles* who was the focus of all her plans... *Charles* whom she must allow to pursue and seduce her, so that she in turn could taunt and humiliate him as he had once taunted and humiliated her...so that she could destroy him as he had once destroyed her father.

It was the goal to which she had directed her whole life, so why was she experiencing this almost physical shrinking back from it? Why was she suffering this almost overwhelming revulsion at the thought of allowing Charles to be her lover...?

Reaction, she told herself grimly. It was only reaction...reaction to the realisation of all that Charles really was...reaction to having the scales well and truly ripped from her eyes. It had nothing to do with Jake Fitton, nothing at all. And even if it had had, it wouldn't have made any difference to what she intended to do. It couldn't make any difference, she told herself hardily.

CHAPTER TWENTY

JAKE was in London. He had sold the apartment he had shared with Beth after her death, but had bought another, clinical, empty... it was simply a place to sleep and work, rather than a home. After Beth's death, a home had been the last thing he'd wanted. He picked up a tape off the desk in front of him and inserted it into the machine, frowning as he listened to it. He had played it so many times already... first in Switzerland... now here in London.

It was coded and contained information from the men he was paying to track down those responsible for Beth's death.

This one contained a list of names... names of pushers prominent on the London drug scene.

One of those names had struck Jake immediately... Charles Fitzcarlton.

His informer had been interested enough in Charles to supply Jake with a potted history of his background, and had added the fact that it was obvious that Charles was desperately short of money and more than likely milking his 'employers' of their drugs profits.

He was in a vulnerable position, so vulnerable that he might yield easily to pressure. And on the tape Jake's informant had listed the names of several other pushers who might be 'persuaded' to give more information about their sources. Charles's name had headed that list, however.

Important though that information had been, it was not that which caused Jake to play the tape over and over again. He stopped it abruptly just as his informant began to document Charles's life story.

Placing the tips of his fingers together, Jake stared into his own inner darkness.

Charles Fitzcarlton. Well connected...good-looking...ultimately a peer of the realm...*ultimately*? Once his cousin was pronounced legally dead...

Geraldine Frances Fitzcarlton...a countess in her own right. Heiress to a vast fortune...a shadowy, insubstantial figure about whom little was known, other than the fact that her father's death had caused her to commit suicide by throwing herself off the cliffs below a remote Irish castle.

Charles Fitzcarlton, Geraldine Frances...Silver...'my cousin Charles'.

Was there any connection, or was he allowing his intuition to play idiotic tricks on him? It was a fantastic and ridiculous assumption that Geraldine Frances Fitzcarlton, by all accounts a tragic, lonely woman who had killed herself rather than face life without her father, could possibly be the same woman he had heard swearing revenge and hatred against the man who had deceived her.

There was nothing in the tape to suggest that any relationship other than that of cousins had existed between Charles and Geraldine Frances...no hint that his intuition was right. The death of the Earl followed by the suicide of his daughter was tragic, yes, but these things happened...

And yet, why would a man as astute and intelligent as James Fitzcarlton was reputed to have been specifically tie up his estates and monies in such a way that *only* his daughter could inherit? Why would he draw up a will that deliberately bypassed his nephew, that deliberately excluded him from inheriting his wealth?

Why would he petition the Queen to have his titles passed on direct to his daughter?

It was common knowledge that Charles Fitzcarlton was obsessed with Rothwell and the earldom, that already, whenever he could, he anticipated his right to

use the title...that he refused to take the advice of his
accountants and close up Rothwell until such time as he
inherited enough money to run it.

Would a man like that, with a female cousin younger
than himself...a female cousin, moreover, whose father
intended that she should inherit everything ahead of him,
casually stand aside and allow that to happen?

Charles Fitzcarlton had married once for money...
Marriage to Geraldine Frances would have secured her
titles and her wealth...

Unless, of course, she had refused him...unless, of
course, she had married someone else... Then the only
way for him to inherit would be through her death.

His frown deepened. Silver had spoken specifically of
loving the man, and someone of Charles Fitzcarlton's
stamp would not make the mistake of allowing his prey
to remain available to any other fortune-hunter. Silver
had been a virgin.

It was ridiculous to assume that Geraldine Frances
Fitzcarlton and Silver Montaine were one and the same
person, and despite his attempts to check he uncovered
nothing to confirm his suspicions.

But they still remained, which meant that *if* she
was...she must have known about Charles's involvement with drugs. Had known and said nothing.

She wasn't a user herself; but then, neither was
Charles. As Jake drummed his fingers on the table he
told himself that he couldn't afford not to follow through
and check her out completely, and that his determination to put his suspicions to the test had nothing to
do with her personally. Nothing at all... And that he
had come to London purely because that was where Beth
had been murdered and because he was already convinced that her murder had been ordered by whoever
was in charge of Ortuga's London operation.

According to his informant, of all the pushers they
had managed to identify, Charles Fitzcarlton would be
the most likely to give way under pressure. He had more

to lose than any of the others, lived a much higher-profile life, had a public image to maintain which would make him vulnerable to the threat of his involvement with the drug scene being made public. He must also by now be fearing the reaction of his employers to the knowledge that he had been misappropriating their profits.

So why was he experiencing this reluctance to begin putting pressure on Charles? He could, after all, be completely wrong about the man's involvement with Silver. There was one very easy way for him to find out.

He stopped the tape, rewound it, and selected another. Each of them was carefully marked so that he could recognise them by touch. He inserted the new one into the machine and played it.

It hadn't been hard to track down Silver. He had known she was staying in London, and he had known the milieu in which she intended moving.

Quite why he had felt the necessity, the compulsion almost, to track her down, he still wasn't sure.

He told himself it was force of habit ... insurance ... common sense ... but no amount of reassuring himself that his behaviour was nothing more than an automatic reflex action totally banished the inner knowledge that he was making the classic mistake of allowing his emotions to reach out and colour his reactions.

He had come to London for one purpose and one alone, and that was to track down his wife's murderer. He switched off the tape abruptly, his mouth grim. His first step must be to make contact with Charles.

Within a couple of hours of Charles's departure, Silver herself had checked out of Blake's.

Having fulfilled her purpose in staying there, there was now no need for her to remain. Her Knightsbridge apartment was waiting to welcome her, as was the interior designer.

She studied Silver discreetly as she handed over the keys. She had been curious about this particular client, whose instructions had been so meticulous and exact.

The way a person chose to decorate and furnish their home normally gave away a great deal about their personality. This woman's instructions had been explicit . . . and yet, studying her, the designer discovered that she was not as she had imagined at all.

'I want the apartment to reflect the lifestyle of a woman who is essentially a hedonist . . . a sensualist,' she had instructed, and that was exactly what it did, subtly, discreetly, with no suggestion of vulgarity or ostentation . . . and yet this woman in her Chanel suit, her eyes cool and unreadable as she surveyed their work, was very different from what she had expected.

Silver dismissed her. She was pleased with the apartment. Its pastel colours and pretty chintzes were exactly what she had wanted. The rooms breathed warmth and perfume; they were rooms that belonged to a woman without in any way being over-feminine or fussy.

Everything Jake had taught her was reflected in this apartment, right down to the open fires that burned in the elegant grates.

Her agents had found her a housekeeper, a discreet and efficient woman in her late fifties who would live in the small staff flat attached to the apartment.

As Silver studied the deep, softly upholstered sofas, she tried to imagine Charles seated on one of them . . . Charles trying to make love to her . . .

She turned away, frowning at the way her body rejected the image.

In her bedroom was an antique French bed, lavishly draped with fabric . . . a large double bed with crisply laundered white sheets and pillows, not plain like the ones in Jake's chalet; these were trimmed with expensive handmade lace and scented with pot-pourri . . . She smiled drily to herself. It was a bed that Jake would hate sleeping in. Jake... Jake... why did she keep allowing him into her thoughts? He had no place there...

It was Charles who should be occupying her thoughts; Charles on whom she ought to be concentrating.

Today, in his eyes, she had seen that he was attracted to her, but she had angered him by refusing to have dinner with him.

Well, tonight at the reception she would discover which emotion had been the stronger. If he appeared at the reception...

Silver dressed for the reception with the same meticulous attention to detail she had accorded to every small part of her plans.

The dress she had chosen to wear came from Lacroix and could only be worn by a woman possessing equal amounts of beauty and self-possession.

In it she would be the cynosure of all eyes; if Charles wasn't at the reception then it wouldn't be long before he heard reports of her appearance there; to that end, the discreet work of her agents would ensure that when the event was written up in the gossip columns her name would feature there. And if Charles *was* there...

Well, Charles had always liked the kudos of squiring the kind of women whom other men looked at and desired.

As she checked her make-up in the mirror, she frowned. Only on one point had she deviated from her original plans, and as her attention was caught by the small bottle of perfume on her dressing-table she wondered a little at her own weakness in wearing it.

Jake's perfume, for Charles—a fitting gesture in so many ways... so why did she feel almost as though in choosing to wear Jake's perfume next to her skin she was somehow taking Jake with her into this new life in which he had no place?

* * *

Judiciously Silver timed her arrival at the reception just over halfway through the evening, late enough to cause a certain amount of interest, but not so late that her arrival looked obviously contrived.

She had visited the Embassy before on many occasions, normally attending similar events to this one with her father, but, she reflected grimly as she pretended to give her full attention to the man talking to her, in those days she had never received the kind of attention she was receiving tonight.

She had known before she left Switzerland that physically she was now a beautiful woman, but she had still not fully adjusted to the effect her new face had on others. Men who had once openly avoided conversation with her now stared obviously and admiringly at her, women who before had dismissed her patronisingly now studied her with narrowed, critical eyes.

Beauty brought its own problems, she recognised grimly, fending off the unwanted advances of yet another overweight middle-aged male.

Those whom she had employed to do a little discreet preliminary PR work on her behalf had done well. Her name was familiar to enough of the other guests for those who were not familiar with it to accept her on the strength of their knowledge.

To those who chose to ask her questions she answered simply that she was and always had been attached to England, and that, finding herself widowed—and, by implication, wealthy—she had decided to make her home in London.

It was hard sometimes to remember the image she was supposed to be projecting, to remember that she must not, as she wanted to, snub the advances of the men who were soon surrounding her, that she must remember that she was no longer Geraldine Frances but *Silver*, and that she must act accordingly; that she must flirt and pout and generally behave as though she were the seductive, sensuous, self-centred woman she had created especially for Charles. And all the time she was talking, smiling, laughing, she was also watching, discreetly surveying the room, wondering whether or not Charles would appear.

The group she had come with had long ago split off, and she had deliberately chosen not to have a specific escort for the evening. She spent a rather sardonically amusing few minutes chatting to the Ambassador, who, while far too urbane and worldly actually to flirt with her, still discreetly managed to make his admiration plain.

Was this the same man who had dismissed her with austere and obvious disgust when her father had originally introduced them? Fastidious and meticulous, he was an excellent ambassador, but, like all men, vulnerable through his vanity...

Like almost all men, she amended, remembering one man who had not had that vulnerability.

Not for the first time, she wondered what manner of man Jake had been before he had lost his sight. He had loved his wife...that much she knew, and wished that she didn't, and that moreover that specific bit of knowledge about him didn't cause her the sharp pang of emotion it did cause.

To anyone watching her, and there were many, Silver appeared relaxed and totally at ease. No one could have guessed at her tension...growing slowly as the evening advanced and Charles did not appear. This was only the opening move in the game, she reminded herself. There would be other occasions...other opportunities.

She had her back to the open double doors, but there was a mirror on the opposite wall facing her, through which she could see those entering and leaving the elegant reception-room.

Even so, she did not see Charles until he was several feet away from her, his blond head shining as bright as the gold paint gilding the plasterwork on the ceiling.

In evening clothes he looked magnificent, a god among lesser and mortal men; without the cruel harshness of daylight to highlight the signs of self-indulgence that marred his physical perfection, he looked very much as he had once been, and for one second out of time Silver was instantly transported back to the past, to the time when merely to look upon Charles's face had been enough to set her stomach churning and her heart pounding.

Perhaps something in her expression betrayed that weakness, because all of a sudden he smiled at her, a brilliant, triumphant smile that brought her abruptly back down to earth. The temptation to turn away from him and ignore him was overwhelming, but she suppressed it.

Humiliating him now in public would serve no good purpose. When she humiliated him she wanted that humiliation to be so complete, so all embracing that he would carry the scars of it with him for the rest of his life, just as she must carry hers.

As he came to her, a path seemed to open up in front of him... a testimony to his charisma... or to his arrogance, Silver thought cynically, watching the way others reacted to him.

How many people here knew that other Charles...the one that she knew so well? Some of the women, certainly... Charles, as she had discovered from her agents, had a voracious appetite when it came to changing his lovers... How many of them knew still yet another side to him...the one her father had discovered...the Charles whose greed had led him into the shadowy world of drugs and all that went with it?

It was no secret that a great many wealthy and bored socialites took drugs... Drugs that were supplied by men like Charles.

He had reached her now, holding out his hands to her... Automatically she placed hers in them and suffered the focus of everyone's curious attention as Charles lifted first one and then the other to his lips, kissing the blue-veined inner flesh of her wrists with openly sexual enjoyment.

A fierce shudder ran through her. She knew he had seen and felt it...saw the triumph leap into his eyes.

He thought she desired him. How wrong he was. Her shudder had been of revulsion.

Willing herself to remember the lessons so painfully learned, she smiled at him, and said archly, 'Charles, what a surprise!'

This was obviously territory with which he was familiar. He returned her smile and murmured confidently, 'A pleasant one, I hope...'

She was surprised how natural her laughter sounded, how natural and how sensual; several other people turned to look at them and Charles continued to hold her hand, obviously pleased by the attention they were getting, obviously enjoying being seen with her. Just for a moment she remembered with bitterness how he had once felt about her, and then she dismissed her own weakness, reminding herself of the high stakes she was playing for. She couldn't afford to make a mistake this early on in the game. It was important now that she lull Charles into a false sense of security, that she flatter and please him.

She moved slightly closer to him and replied, 'Very much so...'

She saw that he was pleased. How vain he was...how self-assured.

He rewarded her with the kind of smile that would have once dazzled her.

She added questioningly, 'I didn't realise you were invited to this reception. You didn't say...'

She wondered how he would respond, if perhaps it would have been wiser to say nothing, but he was still smiling at her.

'How could I *not* be here once I knew you were going to be?'

He was still holding her hand; he raised her wrist to his mouth a second time, deliberately lingering over the kiss he placed there. This time she was prepared. She laughed softly, breathlessly, as a woman aroused by his touch might. He had as good as admitted that he had come to the reception to see her. She watched the way he reacted to her response . . . saw how easily her pretend desire deceived him.

How right Jake had been. A man will always respond more to a beautiful woman who desires him than one who doesn't, he had told her, and she could see from the look on Charles's face how much it pleased him that she should seem vulnerable to him physically.

And then, while she was still looking at him, a flash of light exploded, startling her.

Glancing up, she saw a woman holding a camera and she frowned briefly in recognition, while Charles swore briefly under his breath, released her and strode over to where the woman was standing.

It was obvious that he was annoyed, and Silver thought cynically that she could imagine there would be any number of reasons why Charles would not want their photograph appearing in one of the gossip columns.

The woman didn't look particularly concerned. She was older than Silver, almost masculine-looking in some ways; very authoritative; very sure of herself. She was also alone. Silver had recognised her immediately. As well as covering society events, she did a great deal of freelance work in other fields. She had at one time done fashion photography.

Whatever she was now saying to Charles, it obviously didn't please him. He was looking as sulky and sullen as a small boy, Silver reflected, studying them surreptitiously. She was a little surprised at the woman's obvious control of the situation. She would have expected her to be a little more intimidated by Charles's maleness and good looks. It was several minutes before Charles returned, looking both angry and very on edge.

'An old friend?' Silver mocked, and was a little surprised by the sharpness of his response as he snapped,

'No. What makes you think that? She's a photographer. She works freelance for some of the Fleet Street rags... I've seen her around, but no, I don't know her...'

Silver shrugged, a little perplexed by his vehemence, and by the extent to which the incident had disturbed him.

She wondered if she dared risk taunting him a little more, flexing her claws, so to speak, and then decided that she did.

'Anyone would think you didn't want to be photographed with me,' she said softly, watching him.

For some reason her comment had the effect of easing his tension. He smiled at her, the easy, triumphant smile of the self-assured.

'Not at all,' he told her smoothly. 'In fact, I was thinking of *you*. Who on earth let that woman in here I have no idea...'

'I suppose she's only doing her job,' responded Silver absently. She had just remembered something—something that puzzled her.

Charles had claimed not to know the photographer, but Silver, who had recognised her, had just recalled that she had once seen Charles looking at a photograph of the woman in a magazine and had been told by him at the time that they had been at school together. So why was he now pretending he didn't know her?

She shrugged the question aside. What did it matter? Charles lied about everything, as she had good cause to know.

'What are you doing after this?' Charles was asking her, bending towards her so that he was almost breathing into her ear—an accident...or a deliberate ploy to make her aware of him?

She stepped back from him and said calmly, 'Nothing; I——'

'Let me take you somewhere for supper.'

When she raised her eyebrows, he added softly, 'Surely
you've realised that the only reason I'm here tonight is
to see you?'

It should have meant so much, should have gone so
far towards assuaging her old pain, but to her surprise
it meant nothing; less than nothing.

'This lunchtime you were with someone else,' she
pointed out coolly.

Charles shrugged, unfazed. 'A relationship which was
over long ago...'

'Your companion didn't seem to think so...'

Charles shrugged again, the look he gave her saying
smugly that it was hardly his fault if women made fools
of themselves over him.

'Have supper with me,' he repeated.

Everything was falling into place just the way she had
planned it. A quiet, intimate supper would give her the
opportunity to draw Charles even further into her net,
but the thought of spending more hours with him,
stroking his ego, flattering him, merely being with him
when already she was so bored with him that she was
amazed he couldn't see it, made her feel profoundly tired.

What she really wanted was to be alone so that she
could assimilate her progress so far. Her time in
Switzerland and the life she had lived before it had given
her a taste for solitude which must be the reason she was
feeling so eager now to be on her own.

'I'm afraid not,' she heard herself saying, and saw as
she looked at him that Charles was not pleased, and that
she had made a grave error. Refusing him once had been
one thing; refusing him a second time, and after he had
taken the trouble to attend the reception... But it was
too late to call back her refusal... Anger was glittering
in Charles's eyes. Anger and the same bitter resentment
that she had seen in those blue eyes before... it struck
her that for all his many affairs Charles was not a man
who liked her sex. Rather, he preferred to dominate
women, to hurt and destroy them... it hadn't just been

her, Geraldine Frances, he had hated. As she looked at him, half of her was tempted to let him go, to let him walk away from her, and she could even feel the first stirrings of an odd sense of relief that he might do so. Deliberately she forced it to one side. She could not afford to give in to such ridiculous emotionalism. She was being stupid... perverse... and why? Because being with Charles was making her face up to the realisation of how much she was physically dreading having to touch him... be touched by him.

But *why*? *Why*, when she had gone through the torture she had endured with Jake Fitton to prepare herself for just that purpose?

She could not afford this ridiculous emotional vulnerability... if she couldn't do it for her own sake, then she must do it for her father's.

Stifling her feelings, she said palliatively, 'I really am sorry, but I have an early morning meeting tomorrow with my financial advisers...' She smiled ruefully. 'I never realised that having money would be such a problem.'

Her smile invited Charles to share her amusement. 'Your late husband was a wealthy man?'

'Very wealthy,' Silver agreed, knowing that Charles had probably by now checked up on her, and that the information she had arranged to be carefully leaked concerning her background and her past would have included the fact that her husband had been a wealthy Swiss industrialist.

'He was a lot older than you?' Charles added.

'More of a father to me than a husband,' Silver agreed, smiling at him and then adding pettishly, 'It is such a bore having to attend these meetings. When Heini was alive I never had to bother, but now that I am responsible for his wealth...' She gave Charles a soft-eyed look and said, 'I cannot have supper with you tonight, for I am very tired. I moved into my new apartment only this afternoon. But perhaps if you were to invite me to dinner another night...'

She waited, half holding her breath, wondering how Charles would react.

He reacted much as Jake had suggested he would, flattered by her interest and made arrogant by his belief that he had regained the upper hand.

'I'd like to,' he told her. 'But I'm pretty fully booked for the rest of this week. Look, why don't you give me your telephone number, and I'll give you a ring?'

Calmly Silver did, knowing even as she gave it to him that her reactions were wrong. By rights she ought to be feeling nervous now, anxious to see if she had pushed him too far...if he would respond or simply lose interest. But instead all she was feeling was a tremendous surge of relief...of escape...as though she had succeeded in putting off something unpleasant and unwanted.

She left the reception before Charles, having made sure first that he had seen her receiving the flattery and attention of several other men.

Their interest amused her. It was as though they were flirting with someone else...as though it wasn't she who was receiving their compliments, and in a way it wasn't... It was her face that dazzled them...a set of perfect features at which they looked and saw nothing else.

Were all men like this...wanting only beauty in a woman...needing to see physical evidence of her perfection before they would allow themselves to be attracted to her?

Even her father, who had loved her dearly, had been vulnerable to beauty...

What was the matter with her? she mocked herself on her way home; her looks were simply the means to a specific end; they had not been created for her own pleasure...nor had they been created to enable her to fulfil a child's dream of perfect love...of high romance. A fairy-story in which she had been the frog hoping to be transformed into beauty by the eyes of love.

She paid for the taxi and went to the entrance of the block which housed her apartment, taking the lift to the second floor.

Her heels tapped sharply on the black and white lozenge-tiled floor of the foyer. The heavy scent of fresh flowers displayed there made her wrinkle her nose a little in rejection.

She dealt with the complex lock system and opened the door.

It was just gone eleven o'clock, and the last thing she felt like doing was going to bed, but the iron discipline she had instilled in herself warned her that her body was exhausted even if her mind wasn't.

Tomorrow there would be fresh reports for her to read on Charles; and she must find out from her agents if she was right about the connection between the photographer whose name she remembered as Helen Cartwright and Charles... She was sure she was.

By tomorrow Charles should have found out the extent of her supposed fortune; if he hadn't done so already... He was desperately in need of money; desperately. Her wealth should bring him back to her side, if nothing else, and yet as she stood tiredly in the hallway she was conscious of having done less with the evening than she might.

She need not have had supper with him, but she *could* have given him more encouragement; she *could* have allowed him to believe more than she had that she desired him. And in fact she *should* have done so... So why hadn't she?

It wasn't a question she wanted to answer.

She opened the drawing-room door and then froze.

The man seated on the chair opposite the door looked up towards her and smiled. 'No Charles?' he remarked sardonically, standing up.

'Jake!' She was too stunned to do anything more than gasp his name and stare at him in disbelief.

'I did warn you that it might not be as easy as you assumed, didn't I? That he...'

All at once anger rolled over her, catching her up in a heavy, crushing wave that crashed through her self-control.

'How *dare* you break into my apartment? How *dare* you? And if I had brought Charles back with me...'

'You wouldn't have found me here,' he told her drily, 'but you didn't, did you? I wonder why not...'

Now that she was over the first shock of seeing him, her brain was starting to function again. Several unpleasant facts were being assimilated as she stood and stared at him.

'What are you doing here, Jake?' she demanded coldly. How had he found her? And why? In Switzerland he had been as keen as she that once their business relationship was at an end, they never saw one another again... In Switzerland he had also seemed completely indifferent to her as a woman; and yet, during that last night they had spent together...

Her body went hot, her thoughts and memories shaming her, making brilliant colour sting her skin. It had all been an act...an act, that was all...that desire, that tenderness, that caring...they had meant nothing...nothing at all.

'You're wearing my perfume.'

Silver glared at him, wondering as she had wondered so often before why it was she found it so impossible to remember that he couldn't see her.

'I asked you a question,' she reminded him tersely, wishing she had the courage to threaten him with the police, but knowing that he would only laugh at her. She wanted the police here as little as he would, and he knew it.

'Surely it's obvious,' he told her, shrugging. 'I wanted to talk to you...'

'About what?'

She and Jake had already said all they could possibly have to say to one another. She had bought a specific office from him and, having paid for it... Her heart twisted sharply, an unsuspected pain that made her catch her breath. Unless, of course, he *was* going to try to blackmail her.

'About what?' she repeated, a hard edge creeping up under her voice.

For a moment she thought he wasn't going to reply, and then he said quietly, 'Why, about Geraldine Frances Fitzcarlton, Countess of Rothwell, of course.'

The words hit her like stones. How *could* he have found out? She had been so careful...so sure... *Too* sure, her brain mocked her. He *had* found out, and it was pointless wasting time wondering how. She had other, more pressing matters to worry about now.

She knew there was no point in denying it, her very silence had already betrayed her, and so she said bitterly, 'How much do you want, Jake? I take it that *is* what you're here for,' she demanded scornfully. 'To blackmail me into buying your silence, in the same way that I paid for the use of your body...'

He looked at her, that disconcerting, direct look that always threw her, because she knew he couldn't possibly see her.

Her taunt had failed to rouse him to anger...to any kind of response other than a certain thoughtfulness that made her wince inside for her own folly and how much she had already betrayed to him.

'You didn't buy my *body*,' he told her calmly. 'You bought my expertise, and if you feel you've been short-changed in any way you should have said so at the time. And I haven't come here to blackmail you...'

'No? Then why have you come?' Silver demanded trenchantly. 'Not for the pleasure of my company...'

There was another brief, telling pause. She had turned her back on him and now she wished desperately that she had not been so rash. With her back to him she

couldn't see him...couldn't judge how he was reacting...not that he ever allowed his face to give very
much away. Why was it, when he was so obviously dis-
advantaged, that she should always feel he had the edge
on her...that he was always one step ahead of her?

'No, not for that,' he agreed, and for some reason her
stomach plummeted downwards. 'I've come to talk to
you about your cousin Charles.'

Now she did turn round.

'Charles...what connection do you have with
Charles?'

His voice hard, he derided, 'You're not a fool, Silver,
whatever else you might be.' He didn't tell her how much
he knew about all that she was and all that she had been,
and that the knowledge had been like the opening of a
door into a hitherto unsuspected place. A door which
he had been very quick to close...and lock.

'Why didn't you tell me about your cousin's involvement with drugs? You *do* know he's a pusher, of
course...of course you do,' he mocked gently, answering
his own question. 'How could you not? You don't use
them, of course——'

He was almost speaking to himself, but Silver cut
across his soft, musing words, demanding flatly, 'What
are you trying to say? If you think I'm involved in any
way——' she broke off, angry with herself for trying to
justify her error. 'I didn't mention it because it wasn't
important...at least, not to me...'

He wondered if she knew how much she was betraying her upbringing with that cool, haughty little
voice, that upper-class arrogance that was so effective.

'No,' Jake agreed, less than pleasantly. 'Your own
feelings mattered far more. You'll forgive me, I'm sure,
if I tell you however that to me it *is* important. If, of
course, you are lying to me, and you deliberately suppressed your knowledge once you realised how important it might be to me... Why would you do that,
Silver? A female settling of some imagined score against
me?'

'No!' She had made the denial without even thinking of what she might be giving away, truth echoing through the vehemently uttered word.

Jake's mouth thinned.

'Odd, don't you think, that *you* should be so horrified at the thought that I might accuse you of seeking revenge for some imagined slight when you've already told me that revenge is exactly what you intend to exact from Charles?'

The words 'that's different' trembled on her tongue and were suppressed.

'Why didn't you tell me about Charles's involvement with the drugs scene?' Jake demanded hardily.

Silver shrugged, turning away from him, affecting a bored, careless tone of voice totally at variance with what she was feeling.

'Why should I?' she asked.

'Why indeed?' Jake agreed, and then warned softly, 'Has it occurred to you that your cousin might tell a different tale. If you *are* implicated...'

'I'm not,' Silver told him fiercely. 'And as for Charles...whatever he tells you, *if* he tells you anything, will be lies. Charles lies about everything. He even lied to me tonight about knowing Helen Cartwright,' she added cynically.

Jake frowned. Helen Cartwright. The name rang a bell. He repeated it questioningly, and Silver told him.

'She's a well-known freelance photographer. She and Charles were at school together; I'd forgotten for a moment. She photographed me with Charles tonight. He was furious...so furious, in fact, that he went over to her to object. They were talking for some time, but when I asked him if he knew her he denied it. It was only later that I remembered about their being at school together.' She gave a small shrug. 'You see, Charles is a congenital liar. He can't seem to help himself. There was no need for him to lie about Helen.'

Talking about Charles reminded her of her reluctance
to accept his supper invitation, and that in turn made
her angry and resentful of Jake, as though in some way
it was *his* fault that she couldn't will her emotions to
allow her to do what she knew must be done.

'Speaking of which,' Jake intervened, 'how come you
aren't with him now?'

Suspecting that he was in some way taunting her, Silver
retaliated quickly.

'I could have been... He wanted me to have supper
with him...'

'And you refused... Why?'

Silver tensed. 'Why not? It won't do any harm to keep
him guessing a little...'

'No... *if* that's why you refused him.' And then, suddenly and brutally, Jake came over to her, grasping hold
of her wrists. Not amorously, as Charles had done, but
grimly, as though he was about to shake her. And yet
there was something about the cool, sure touch of his
fingers against her skin that set her pulses racing in a
way that Charles's touch had not achieved.

'Face it, Silver, you didn't accept his invitation because you're scared... scared of discovering that you're
not as indifferent to him as you'd like to think. You're
scared of wanting him... of loving him...'

The accusation, so very different from what she had
expected and dreaded, stunned her. She almost laughed
with the relief of it, but just in time she stopped herself.

'And the reason you didn't tell me about his involvement with the drugs scene wasn't because you didn't
think it mattered, but because you wanted to protect
him.'

He was wrong, more wrong than he knew, and it
amazed her that a man she knew to be so intelligent
should make such an erroneous judgement.

The reason she hadn't told him had been because she
had been afraid, all right... afraid that if Charles *was*
by some mischance one of his targets, he would snatch

away her own chance of retribution before she was able
to fulfil her self-imposed task.

She wasn't going to tell him that, though...let him
think what he wished. He already knew far too much
about her. That he should have discovered who she
was...

He released her wrists and she stepped back from him,
rubbing them not because they ached but because the
sensation of his fingers circling them still lingered there,
imprinted on her flesh, causing unwanted *frissons* of
sensation, unwanted memories to flood her body.

She turned towards the door, and said huskily, 'Well,
now that you've said what you came to say, will you
please leave?'

He was looking at her again, the odd, direct look that
always had the power to unnerve her.

She ignored it and walked past him towards the door
that led to the bedroom, saying curtly, 'I'm tired, Jake.
I'm going to bed.'

As she walked through the door away from him she
heard the outer one closing. He had gone...she ex-
pelled a shaky sigh of relief.

The shock of coming back and discovering him here,
and, worse, the shock of her own unwanted and dangerous reaction to the sight of him...

She made up her mind that when next Charles asked
her out she would accept, and that moreover she would
actively encourage whatever advances he chose to make
to her.

Discarding the Lacroix dress as though it was something she had picked up from a car-boot sale, she went
into her bathroom.

She was desperately tired physically; her body ached
for sleep while her mind ran round and round in tiny,
tormented circles. She *had* to punish Charles. She *had*
to make him suffer...for her father's sake if nothing

else . . . and if, in the course of doing so, she herself suf-fered . . . She hardened her emotions against herself. *She* wasn't important, not in this.

CHAPTER TWENTY-ONE

JAKE waited ten minutes before letting himself back into the apartment, wondering as he did so *why* he was doing it. He already had the information he had come to get. Silver was not involved with her cousin in the drugs scene.

But she *was* concealing something from him, suppressing something.

His mouth hardened as he remembered her reaction to his accusation that she still desired Charles Fitzcarlton, and still loved him.

Did she really think he wouldn't have guessed? By rights he ought to be in his own flat working out how best to infiltrate Charles Fitzcarlton's life. He smiled grimly to himself; there was little point in asking for Silver's help there.

He found his way to the sofa and sat down on it... Why was he doing this? There was no point.

The shower stopped running. A door opened and then closed. Silver had gone to bed.

To dream about her dear cousin Charles.

Silver was dreaming, but not about Charles. She was dreaming about her father... a dream she had had over and over again since his death and since her own realisation that Charles had probably killed him. The dream was always the same.

The three of them were alone on horseback, the landscape around them barren, bare, hostile almost. As they rode, her father and his horse started to draw away from Charles and herself, and as she watched him a terrible presentiment came over her...a feeling of tremendous fear for her father.

She tried to call out to him to warn him, but could make no sound; the terror was all around her, pressing down on her like a thick grey cloud. She turned to Charles to beg for his help, but he too was riding away from her and towards her father.

At first she was pleased, relieved, and the pressure of her fear lifted. Charles would reach her father and then he would be safe from the unknown danger she could sense plaguing him.

But when Charles started to catch up with her father her relief suddenly evaporated; the landscape grew dark as though stained with her own growing horror; fear and pain mingled inside her; she spurred on her own horse, hatred staring at her from his eyes.

She saw his arm lift, the blade of a knife glittering malevolently in his hand.

She heard herself scream, but the sound didn't reach her father; Charles drew abreast of him and as she watched, helpless to stop him, Charles plunged his knife deep into her father's heart.

She woke up, her body slick with sweat, her heart pounding. She ought to be used to the nightmare by now, she had dreamed it so often, but each time the fear and horror was as fresh as though she had never experienced it before. She shivered in the darkness as her skin grew chilled. The sound of her own screams still seemed to echo round the room. She had been awake only seconds, and when her bedroom door opened abruptly she said the first name that came into her mind, whispering it through a throat scraped raw.

'No, not Charles,' a familiar male voice told her, and as she stared into the darkness she saw Jake walk cautiously into the room.

Habit made her reach for the bedside light and snap it on. Jake was fully dressed, his hair tousled and untidy.

The draining intensity of her nightmare left her no resources to react to him, and all she could manage was a weak, 'Jake...I thought you'd gone.'

'Why did you scream?' he asked her, ignoring the question in her voice. He had found his way over to the bed and was standing over her, staring down at her.

Oddly, in some confusing way she found his presence comforting; where she should have felt outrage and resentment, what she actually did feel was a sense of relief and security.

'A nightmare,' she told him unsteadily. 'I've had it before...'

Although Jake couldn't see her, he could hear the fear in her voice, and with it the dread and pain. Whatever she had been dreaming about had been no ordinary nightmare.

He sat down on the edge of her bed. He had been deeply asleep himself when he'd heard her scream. He hadn't intended to fall asleep. But, somewhere between mulling over what she had told him and wondering if it was worthwhile staying and trying to make her see the danger she could be in if she persisted in what she was doing, the exhaustion he had been fighting off for days had overcome him.

As he sat down, Silver automatically drew up her knees and sat up, wrapping her arms around them.

The hours of wakefulness and anguish that normally followed her nightmare were even worse than the nightmare itself; the guilt of feeling somehow through her dreams that she had been the one responsible for her father's death was almost impossible to bear. The long, dark hours of fruitless heart-searching were non-productive and painful. Finding Jake here was like finding the safety of a solid barrier between her and that hopeless heart-searching. She didn't stop to question why he was still in her apartment, nor what he might want from her, but said huskily, 'Stay with me, Jake.'

Stay *with* her? He felt his muscles tighten against the shock of it. She smelled of the perfume he had bought for her; it clung to her skin as though it loved it.

Stay with her...the words had been those of a frightened child; for an instant she had reminded him almost unbearably of Justin...of Beth...of all those people who were vulnerable and in need.

This woman in need? He must be going soft in the head. He got up abruptly, clumsily almost, and Silver, her mind still clouded by the horror of her dreams, reached out to him almost desperately, her fingers clutching at his arm as she scrambled to the edge of the bed.

Her silk nightdress, the nightdress she had chosen for the woman she had decided she must be, did little to conceal her body; her hair, normally so elegantly restrained, tumbled wildly around her face on to her shoulders; but she felt no constraint, no awareness of any particular intimacy. After all, Jake couldn't see her.

But he could smell her, taste her almost in the warmth of the scented air stirred up by their movements; and he could feel her, her body pressed up hard against his own as she shook his arm pleadingly.

Without doubt there was nothing in her anxiety that could be remotely described as provocative or sensual; and equally without doubt she was arousing him to the point where if he touched her now... He dared not even raise his arms to fend her off.

Instead all he could do was to use his voice, the voice she had heard issuing so many cool, dry, controlled commands over the days and nights she had spent with him.

'Let me go, Silver...'

It froze her immediately, and then she started to tremble, panic overwhelming her. If Jake walked away from her now...left her with her fears, with the memory of that dream...with the knowledge that Charles had

killed her father...that he might possibly also have tried
to kill her...that he would certainly have destroyed her
emotionally and mentally...

Her fear was like a dam threatening to burst its banks,
a wild panic she couldn't control, stronger than logic,
than sanity, stronger even than pride; it carried her with
it in the full force of its dangerous tide.

She shook so violently that Jake could feel the air
between them vibrate with her tremors.

Logic fought with compassion and compassion won.

'What is it?' he asked softly. 'What is it that makes
you so afraid?'

So he recognised her fear. Silver breathed more easily,
not questioning where she had gained the knowledge that
the fear would ensure that he wouldn't desert her.

'Is it Charles?' Jake pressed her angrily, waiting bitterly for her denial, but instead her body shook as though
it were gripped by a deathly fever. He could even hear
her teeth chattering together as she fought to control her
reaction.

Unable to stop himself, Jake reached for her hand,
monitoring the frantic pulse in her wrist.

'If you fear him, why pursue this vendetta against
him?' he asked her. 'He's a dangerous man...'

Silver jerked back from him. She didn't want to discuss
Charles...she didn't want Jake to start analysing her
motivation all over again. If he did...she felt so vulnerable that she was terrified she might actually tell him
the truth. Only she herself knew how great the temptation was to let him know...to let him lift the burden
of responsibility from her shoulders...to let him tell her
and convince her that it was not her fault that her father
was dead...that it was not necessary for her to avenge
that death.

The knowledge of her own weakness hit her like a
sledgehammer, stunning her, terrifying her. It was a
knowledge she didn't want...it weakened her too much.

'Put the past behind you, Silver. Let it die.'

The roughness in his voice startled her, it was unfamiliar, cloaking something that was almost tenderness.

'I can't,' she told him in despair. 'I can't... He...'

'He what?' Jake demanded angrily. 'Hurt you... betrayed you? Forget that—there'll be other men... other loves...'

'No...'

Both of them tensed.

'I don't want that,' she told him thickly, and her body slumped slightly as she withdrew from him. She had been a fool to think even for a moment that Jake might offer her comfort... compassion... caring. He was here for only one purpose, and that was to find out how much she knew about Charles's involvement with drugs... And, unlike her, Jake was able to remain aloof, withdrawn and remote... Unlike her, he could concentrate fully on his own goals.

'Go, then, if you must,' she told him tiredly. The fear was still there, lying in wait for her, and the moment he was gone it would rear up and threaten her, but she hadn't the spirit tonight to argue with him, to hold him at bay.

Something in her weary air of defeat reached out to him. If he had any sense at all, he would go right now, but illogically he heard himself saying, 'For what's left of the night it hardly seems worth it. I might as well stay here.'

Not for the first time, Silver was glad he couldn't see her face. She knew it must mirror her shock... and her relief.

He stared to move towards the door.

'I'll sleep in your spare room, though, if you don't mind; those settees of yours aren't long enough.'

'No... No, not there. I want you to stay here with me.'

The shock of it jolted through him. He tried to measure the silence to guess if it was all simply some fantastic, childish game of revenge, but her voice had held only fear and sincerity.

Even so...

'What as?' he questioned her coolly. 'A barrier against your nightmares or a substitute for your nightmare lover?'

So he had guessed her dreams had been about Charles. She shivered a little and then realised what he was saying.

'I don't want you to make love to me, Jake,' she told him angrily, and then, when he remained silent, she tilted her chin and added fiercely, 'And if I did, I'd tell you...not pretend to be afraid so that——'

'All right, you've made your point.' He sounded almost weary, and the tension eased out of her. 'Move over, then,' he told her laconically, when he reached the side of the bed.

Automatically she moved away from the side she knew he preferred, turning on to her side so that she wouldn't be facing him, but she couldn't relax totally until she heard him undress and felt the bed dip under his weight and knew that he was beside her.

As she snapped off the light, the feeling inside her was one of relief. Now that Jake was here she could go to sleep in safety, knowing that she wouldn't dream.

Only she couldn't. And not because her thoughts were full of Charles, either.

It was Jake himself who made it impossible for her to sleep. When she had told him that she didn't want his services as a lover she had meant it, but now, with the hard, warm weight of him lying against her back, with the knowledge imprinting itself on her body that he was naked, with the awareness of him which she seemed to have absorbed along with everything else he had taught her, she found it impossible to stop thinking about him. And her thoughts were not the ones she might have expected to have had either.

They were rebellious, erotic, and dangerous. And, while she knew that all she had to do was to move away from him to cease being so tormentingly aware of him, she didn't do it.

She had thought she was alone in her self-induced torment, until Jake said quietly, 'I'll acquit you of doing it deliberately, Silver, but will you please stop moving against me like that? I'm not made of stone, you know.'

She tensed immediately, her body absorbing what he was telling her with a curious and highly explosive pleasure. She *wanted* Jake to desire her. The knowledge shocked her, confused her and, once admitted, would not go away.

Heedlessly, wantonly, she turned over, absorbing the pleasurable heat of him against her breasts and belly as she pressed against his back, her hand on his arm as she said quickly, before she could lose her courage, 'Jake, I've changed my mind. I do want you to make love to me.'

He turned round, not to reach out to her, but to grip her arms and push her away, but she was being driven by a recklessness that refused to accept any check or rejection, as though once she had admitted to her own physical desire for him there was no longer any point in concealing either from him or from herself exactly how intense that desire was.

Before he could move away from her, her hands splayed out against his chest, her mouth open and hot as it eagerly caressed the hard column of his throat.

Ignoring the grim pressure on the fingers he had tightened round her skin, she closed the gap between them, her body against his at once both a caress and an invitation, her mouth inciting and cajoling.

It was as though all the skills he had fought so hard to teach her had suddenly taken on a life-force of their own, so that every muscle moved in liquid song to the ancient rhythm his own body recognised.

'Make love to me, Jake.'

She whispered the words into his mouth, biting into his bottom lip, letting the straps of her nightdress slide down her arms so that they brushed against his knuckles, just as her nearly exposed breasts brushed against his chest.

She felt no hesitation...no doubts...no shame.

If she was wanton, sensual and eager, well, then, she was only what he himself had taught her to be; the pleasure craved by her flesh was only the pleasure *he* had taught it to need.

It never once crossed her mind that tonight she could have been sharing her bed with Charles...that *Charles* could have been the recipient of all that she was now squandering on Jake...wasting on Jake, whose body lay rigid with rejection beneath her own, Jake, whose hands were bruising her skin, and whose mouth remained brutally closed against the soft invasion of her lips and tongue.

But she wasn't going to give up. After all, wasn't it Jake himself who had taught her so coldly and so skilfully exactly how to arouse desire in any man?

She kissed his throat again, circling the hard swell of muscle with her tongue, feeling him swallow, feeling his tension.

The top half of her body was lying across his, but when she lifted her pelvis to press herself caressingly against him his hands left her arms and descended to her hips holding her off.

Silver ignored his denial of her. Her mouth touched his chest, her tongue investigating the hard flatness of his nipple. No response, none at all, but she must have learned more from him than she had thought, because his tension told its own story, and she refused to be deterred. With each touch, each caress, her own desire was growing, feeding her determination to break through the barriers of his self-control, and make him feel the need that was possessing her.

So far he hadn't said a word, and the silence continued, cold, chilling, rejecting her as her hands and mouth moved over his body.

She knew quite well there were easier, quicker, more direct methods of arousing him than by the slow and delicate exploration of his flesh by her fingertips and mouth, but she was enjoying what she was doing, enjoying the challenge she had set herself, and enjoying, too, the subtlety of her slow assault on his senses.

When she reached his belly she stopped, sitting up in the darkness to say softly, 'I'm not going to give up, Jake. I'm quite prepared to start at your toes in the prescribed fashion and work my way up over every inch of you until...'

She felt him flinch, and into the darkness he said harshly, 'I don't know what the hell you think you're playing at, Silver, what possible pleasure you yourself——'

'Oh, I'm not playing,' she told him coolly, 'and as for pleasure...'

Before he could stop her she reached for his hand, placing it boldly over the hard swell of her bare breast and deliberately moving his hand against the hard pulse of her nipple.

'Why... why the hell are you doing this...?'

She released his hand and looked at him. 'I don't know,' she told him honestly. 'I only know that tonight I need you as a man...'

'As a substitute for——'

'Charles has never been my lover,' Silver pointed out to him drily. 'You have.' She leaned over him and begged softly, 'Please, Jake.'

His nostrils were full of the scent of her, his body tense from the effort of denying his reaction to her; there was nothing he wanted more than to roll her over and pin her to the mattress with the weight and heat of his body, while he punished her for each exquisite second of torture she had just inflicted on him by letting her feel the torment he himself had just endured.

Instead he sat up and said abruptly, 'No.'

She hadn't expected that. She had genuinely thought that he would give in. She had genuinely thought that he would desire her, she recognised bleakly. She had been a fool. Just because once, on one never-to-be-forgotten night he had held her, touched her, possessed her so thoroughly and so intimately that her body would never be free of its memories of him, it didn't mean that his flesh was as vulnerably responsive to her as hers was to him.

That knowledge pierced the bubble of self-confidence, of sureness that had buoyed her up and out of her normal caution.

With the sick realisation that he meant it and that he didn't want her came an equally sickening realisation of how much she had humiliated herself . . . how much she had abandoned herself.

Hot colour burned her skin, and to her horror her throat clogged with tears . . . Tears . . . Oh, God, that was all she needed. She sniffed quickly, choking them back, but not before one escaped and rolled down her face.

Jake heard the betraying sniff, and felt the dampness of her tears as they hit his skin.

'Oh, God, no . . . Don't cry . . .'

The moment his arms came round her her self-control shattered. She howled uncontrollably, beating at his chest with angry fists, demanding to be released.

'Isn't it enough that you've already rejected me?' she demanded between hiccups. 'You don't have to humiliate me like this as well. I'm not a child . . .'

'No,' Jake agreed drily, and the underlying note of humour in his voice made her tense and look up at him.

'I don't need you to tell me you're not a child, Silver,' he told her. 'My body is already getting that message across to me loud and clear.'

He felt her shudder and she thought she heard him say indistinctly, 'This is madness,' but the sensation of his mouth moving on her own completely destroyed her remaining ability to think.

For a second she hesitated, wary of further rejection, of further traps, but his tongue ran round her closed lips and the sensation of its moving against them caused her to moan softly and allow him to draw her down against the blissful hardness of his body, no longer cold and withdrawn from her, but pulsing with the same delirious heat that ached inside her own.

It was different this time from that last night they had spent together, because now her body knew the pleasure his could give it; knew it and welcomed it, eagerly accepting his touch, his possession.

He made love to her fiercely, demandingly, and her body gloried in its responsiveness to his, matching its every intensity and need; then he held her in silence while her body shuddered down from the peaks to which his had taken it.

'Now,' he told her, whispering the words against her mouth, 'You can start at my toes if you still want to.'

She still wanted to, and so, it seemed, did he.

When he left her in the clear, bright daylight of the early summer morning, a daylight he couldn't see as he silently retrieved his clothes, all the time aware of the sleeping warmth of her in the bed where he had left her, Jake wondered what madness had possessed him.

Even given that the urge to make love to her had been overwhelming, he should have resisted it. She was a complication he had no room for. He had done many things in his life that he had later regretted, but this was the first time he had knowingly made love with a woman who was using him because she couldn't have someone else.

She might not be involved with Charles Fitzcarlton's drug trafficking—in fact he knew now that she was not—but she had kept her awareness of Charles's involvement from him. Through her love for her cousin, she was vulnerable to him, and now *he* was vulnerable to him as well. There was nothing to stop her betraying him to her cousin, warning him . . .

He had things to do, and not very much time to do them in, and yet even so he lingered, breathing in the warm woman-scent of her, remembering how it had felt to hold her and touch her, recalling the generosity of her giving and his own dangerous responsiveness to the pleasure of it.

When Silver woke up she was alone. She was reaching out automatically to the other side of the bed when she realised what she was doing and why. She sat up abruptly, appalled by the way her body registered Jake's absence with aching regret.

What had happened to her? What was it about him that had made her react to him like that? A substitute for Charles, was what he had called himself when he'd refused her. She hoped that of the two of them she was the only one who knew how far off the mark that accusation was.

For days she waited, half hoping he would ring or call and half dreading it, and then, when he didn't, she forced herself to acknowledge that what she had done had been the ultimate folly and that it was something she would be wise to forget.

It was like trying to shut a door on a floodtide, and she thanked God that it was only her body that was so physically obsessed with him that it now yearned unceasingly for him.

It was Charles on whom she ought to be concentrating...Charles on whom all her attention should be focused. Charles with whom she would be accepting dinner engagements...Charles...

She kept on repeating his name in her head until she felt safe that her brain could echo to nothing else.

CHAPTER TWENTY-TWO

'SO TELL me... what brought you to London?'

Seated opposite Charles in the intimate setting of a very exclusive London restaurant, Silver forced herself to remember exactly why she was here.

'I've always loved it,' she told him, giving him a provocative smile. 'When my husband died I decided to come and live here.'

'Your husband was much older than you... such a marriage couldn't have been easy.'

Silver gave him a speculative smile.

'No marriage is easy. *You* must know that. You've been married yourself.'

She made it a statement and not a question, knowing that his vanity would be flattered by the knowledge that she had been interested enough in him to make some enquiries about him.

'A bad mistake... my marriage was a disaster. My wife... but I don't want to bore you with my problems. I'd much rather talk about you. You fascinate me, do you know that? You're not like any woman I've ever known.'

He was holding her hand, tracing the shape of her fingers with his nail. His touch repulsed her, so much so that she had to fight not to withdraw her hand from him. Panic seized her. If she felt like this when he was merely touching her hand, how was she going to manage when...?

A waiter came up to remove their plates, and Charles released her.

Thankfully she tucked her hands out of sight, fighting to conceal her tremor of revulsion. It was all so much harder than she had expected. She had thought that because she had once desired Charles, because she had been able to endure the ordeal of learning the lessons Jake had taught her, the physical intimacy she would share with Charles would be unimportant to her. But she had been wrong.

The restaurant he had brought her to was the kind of discreet establishment favoured by lovers. Nearly all the tables were occupied by couples. The atmosphere stifled her, choked her. She desperately wanted to escape to breathe clean, unperfumed air.

'Is something wrong?'

The sharp words halted her flood of panic. Charles was no fool. He knew her sex if he knew nothing else.

'I was just thinking about my husband,' she lied. 'Like yours, my marriage was not a happy one. I married him for all the wrong reasons.' She made a wry face. 'He was very rich, and I was very naïve...but, like you, I don't want to spoil a very pleasant evening by talking about the past.

'I understand you have a magnificent house in the country?'

'Rothwell,' Charles acknowledged. His voice almost purred over the name, and Silver wondered if he knew how much he was giving away.

'Is it as beautiful as I've been told?' she asked him.

He paused and then suggested, 'Why not come and see for yourself?'

She allowed herself to look hesitant.

'I'm having a small "do" there next weekend,' he told her, observing it. 'It's nothing special, just a few friends over for drinks and dinner.'

Silver smiled at him as she accepted his invitation, wondering how it would feel to be back at Rothwell—without her father—as a guest...

'We could travel down to Rothwell together early on Saturday. That will give me the chance to show you around before the others descend on us.'

He reached for her hand again and she let him take it.

'You're a very desirable woman, Silver, and right now I want very much to be alone with you.'

Odd to think how once those words would have thrilled her. Now they simply caused her to wonder if he really believed that she was ready to throw herself into his arms simply on the promise of spending the weekend at Rothwell. If so, he was going—— She stopped herself abruptly. She was allowing her own personal thoughts and feelings to intrude on what was simply a necessity to ensure that she had him completely within her power when she delivered the final blow. At this stage it was vitally important that she make him believe she desired him as much as he apparently desired her...

She hesitated, and then said softly, 'I think it might be very dangerous for me to be alone with you right now...'

'You think I'm dangerous?' he challenged, obviously liking the thought.

She smiled at him, a coquette's smile, all warm invitation and promise.

'Very dangerous,' she told him huskily, 'especially to me... you are a very, very handsome man, and it's a very long time since I have had the pleasure of such a man's company.'

She saw the way his eyes glittered and the betraying tension of his body.

'Perhaps if I were to give you my word that if I were alone with you I would behave as a perfect gentleman...'

She allowed herself to laugh, a mocking, caressing sound that made his hand tighten on hers.

'Ah, but I'm very much afraid *I* might not be able to act as a lady,' she told him teasingly, watching the hot glitter darken his eyes as he stared obviously and very pointedly from her face to her body.

'If we were on our own right now——' he began, and then broke off as the waiter interrupted him to say that there was a phone-call for him.

Predictably, he didn't ask for the phone to be brought to the table, but excused himself to go and answer it.

He was gone almost ten minutes, and when he came back he looked tense and withdrawn. Silver wondered to whom he had been talking, and about what.

For the rest of the evening he remained on edge, but once they were in the taxi on their way to her apartment he seemed to throw off his tension, sitting more close to her than Silver really liked, pressing his body purposely against hers as the cab lurched around a corner, his hand straying to her knee and from there to her thigh.

Much as she longed to brush it off, she couldn't. Not after the come-on she had been giving him over dinner.

She knew she had done it deliberately, committing herself because she was desperately afraid that, if she didn't, when she actually *was* alone with him she would panic and back off. And she couldn't afford to allow him to guess how she really felt about him.

The taxi stopped, and Charles got out and opened the door for her. She knew he would expect to be invited in. Her body cold and tight, she did so.

In her drawing-room she offered him a drink . . . he accepted and she poured it, marvelling at the steadiness of her hand.

'Nice place,' he commented, calculating the cost of the pretty room. He had already checked that she was as wealthy as rumour suggested. He would enjoy going to bed with her; she was his kind of woman . . . But not tonight . . . that damned phone-call . . . sweat beaded his skin suddenly, and he shifted uneasily from one foot to the other. It was easy enough to reassure himself that he had nothing to worry about . . . that he could soon convince them that he could repay the money he had borrowed... He looked calculatingly around the room a second time. A rich mistress... a rich wife...

'You're a very beautiful woman,' he told Silver huskily and truthfully. 'One of the most beautiful I've ever seen.'

She smiled back at him, wondering what he would say if she told him that he had once called her the *ugliest* woman he had ever seen.

He drained his glass and came towards her purposefully.

Silver knew what was going to happen. It was, after all, what she had planned would happen—what she wanted to happen—but that didn't stop the coldness invading the pit of her stomach when his arms came round her and his body moved close to her own.

This was *Charles*... Charles, whom she had once adored, worshipped... desired beyond anything else. Charles, who had made her ache and yearn, caused her sleepless nights and so many tears that she had thought she had cried them all away. And yet now, held in his arms, his body moving eagerly against her own, his lips against her throat, hot and demanding, his hand against her breast, all she felt was a deep inner revulsion, a sickness that chilled her blood and turned her body to stone.

'I want you...'

He must have mistaken her shudder for a tremor of excitement, because she could hear the thickening of his voice, feel the sexual tension of his body.

Oh, God, if he didn't let her go soon she was going to be sick, but his mouth was already crawling over her skin, seeking her lips, his hot, unsteady breath making her want to retch.

'Silver... Silver...' He moaned her name as his teeth savaged her bottom lip and his hands moved roughly against her breasts.

She endured it for as long as she could, before breaking free and saying sharply, 'No!'

For a moment he looked furious, and then he seemed to gather himself together, and as though it had been he and not she who had broken the embrace he said raggedly, 'I can't stay... I only wish I could.'

Her lip was bleeding a little where he had savaged it. She ached to touch it with her tongue, but dared not, in case he read in that small gesture an invitation to resume his lovemaking.

'Tomorrow night I'll take you to dinner, and then——'

'No...'

She had said it without even thinking, her body's revulsion expelling the denial before she could check it.

He looked surprised and frowned, and against every screaming protest from her flesh she forced herself to say softly, 'No...not tomorrow night. I'm afraid I already have an engagement, but perhaps lunch...?'

Lunch was safer...lunch would be easier. So she told herself while she waited for her nausea to subside and wondered painfully why it was that her body had chosen to betray her like this.

Without its support, she would still go on...still pursue her goal. She had to, she owed it to her father, but it was going to be so hard...so hard.

She went with him to the door, trying not to shudder while he embraced her, his tongue flicking over and over the small cut he had made as though he enjoyed the sensation of hurting her.

'I wish to God I didn't have to leave,' he whispered as he drew back from her...and, hearing the sincerity in his voice, but at that moment not caring why he had to leave just as long as he did so, Silver did not wonder, until he had actually gone, *what* it was that had made it so necessary for him to leave.

Whatever it was, she was thankful for it.

She had gone out tonight determined to let nothing
stand in the way of her fulfilling the target she had set
herself.

Tonight, if Charles had desired it, they would have
made love, and in doing so she would have shown her
commitment to her self-imposed goal. Tonight, no matter
how much her flesh had cringed and her body had cried
out against it, she and Charles would have become lovers,
and once they had...once they had there would have
been no going back...no change of heart...no shaming
weakness.

No childish desire for another man's hands, another
man's mouth, another man's body.

But Charles had left her, and only she knew how
grateful she was for that fact.

She was trembling as she stood under the shower,
washing every last trace of him off her skin. Her bed,
when she curled up in it, disconcertingly smelled of Jake,
even though she knew that her housekeeper had changed
the linen.

Whichever way she turned in the darkness, Jake
seemed to be there, his memory tormenting her. *Why*
had this happened to her... *why* was she suffering like
this, when she had suffered so desperately already? It
was so unfair...so unwanted, this feeling she had...so
unnecessary to everything she had planned for her life.
She didn't *want* to feel like this, and had she been able
to physically wrench her awareness of Jake out of her
consciousness she would have done so.

In Rothwell Square Charles stood to one side of his
desk, confronting the person waiting there for him, trying
to mask his unease.

'You're late,' he was told.

The contempt in the other man's voice angered him,
but he dared not show his anger. To the rest of the world
he might be the heir presumptive to one of the country's
premier earldoms, but to this man he was simply

someone much lower down the ladder of the organisation they both worked for. Charles hated that knowledge, but he had enough intelligence to hide his resentment.

'You're such a fool,' his visitor told him. 'Did you really think we wouldn't know what was going on?'

'I only borrowed the money,' Charles blustered. 'You'll get it back ...'

'When?' the other jeered. He had never liked Charles, resenting his upper-class confidence even while acknowledging that he was one of their best pushers. He could see that Charles was sweating; he was enjoying the other man's fear, but that wasn't why he was here.

'We want our money back, make no mistake about that. Other men have lost their lives for taking less than you've taken, Charles,' he warned. 'You didn't really think you'd get away with it, did you? The only reason you're still alive is because you're useful to us ... at the moment. I've got a message for you,' he added abruptly, satisfied by the fear and tension emanating from the other man. 'We're prepared to be lenient about the money ... to wait for payment, provided you agree to certain proposals ...'

Proposals ... what proposals? Beneath the swelling sense of relief easing his fear, Charles was still tense.

He had already agreed to make sure that Kilrayne remained empty and in his possession, so that the organisation could make full use of the facilities it offered, and now he wondered queasily how much more was going to be asked of him.

He had told himself that once the earldom was his officially, once he had no need of the income that dealing in drugs brought him, he was going to sever his connections with the organisation, but he was wondering if he would be allowed to do so. He comforted himself with the knowledge that once the money was repaid he could end his relationship with them. They were hardly in a position to blackmail him without risking exposure themselves. There were things he knew...

Seeing the smile, the man watching him tensed, wondering what had given rise to it. He preferred dealing with people who were properly awed by the authority his position within the organisation gave him.

'There's something we want you to do for us,' he said curtly.

'What?' Charles demanded. What he needed to do now was to concentrate on consolidating his position with Silver. A wealthy, sophisticated wife, young enough to give him sons, mature enough to realise that marriage need not necessarily involve fidelity. He sensed that, while she would be quite happy to have an affair with him, she might not necessarily want marriage. Charles had always enjoyed a challenge... His mind on Silver, he waited tensely to hear the other's demands.

'There's somebody we want to get to know a little better, and in private, if you know what I mean. This castle of yours in Ireland...Kilryan...'

'Kilrayne,' Charles corrected automatically.

The other man shrugged. 'Kilryan...Kilrayne...what does it matter? What does matter is that you make sure this guy goes there...'

'What guy?' Charles demanded.

'His name's Fitton...all you have to do is make sure that you get him out to your castle.'

Charles frowned. 'And how am I supposed to do that? I don't know him...'

'You will,' his companion told him quickly. 'You're having a dinner party this weekend.' He laughed at Charles's small start of surprise. 'Oh, there isn't much we don't know about our friends...and our enemies. You'll be having two extra guests. One of them you'll already know, and she'll be bringing with her as her partner this man Fitton. Your task will be to make sure you get him interested enough in this Irish castle to visit it...'

'And if I can't?' Charles demanded.

The way the other man smiled made him shiver.

'I'll do what I can,' he promised, and then couldn't resist asking, 'And the money...?'

'Still has to be paid,' he was told. 'This is just payment of interest, and nothing so very difficult really... Just a matter of inviting someone to visit you...'

In theory he was right. Charles wondered what manner of man this Fitton was, and what the organisation wanted with him, and then he told himself that it was none of his business, and that all he had to do was make sure the man went to Kilrayne. It shouldn't be too difficult. He hoped...

Charles waited until he was alone before giving way to his impotent frustration...

What was being asked of him wouldn't be too difficult to accomplish, but he disliked being put in a position where he was at the beck and call of others... He discovered that he was sweating heavily, and grimaced in disgust. Charles was a fastidious man; the first thing he always did whenever he had made love was to shower; he hated the smell of sex and feminine flesh clinging to him.

He glanced at his watch, wondering if it was too late to go back to Silver. His body burned and ached for release... the kind of release that came only through the kind of sexual violence he liked best.

Regretfully he decided that as yet it was too soon to demand that particular kind of pleasure from her... Later, perhaps...

Two miles away, in the discreetly anonymous surroundings of a busy wine bar, Charles's recent companion was talking to someone else.

'I've seen Fitzcarlton,' he announced as he sat down. 'He knows what he has to do.' He moved restlessly in his seat. 'I'm not so sure he's the right person to use.'

His companion stared coldly at him and told him, 'I am.'

His nerves crawled a little beneath the pressure of that cold stare, but he still said truculently, 'You were also sure that Fitton wasn't going to cause us any more trouble...' He shifted again in his seat. 'The man's blind, for God's sake... Why go to all this trouble? It would be the easiest thing in the world to simply arrange for him to have an accident...'

'Jake Fitton seems to have an irritating ability to avoid "accidents",' he was told. 'And I don't like the way he's surfaced here in London. As far as we can discover, he no longer has any connection with his old...employers...but I think we need to find out a good deal more about what he's doing before we arrange to dispose of him. We need to be sure that he isn't passing information on to anyone else.'

'We *know* what he's doing here.' For once he felt in control of the situation. His superior had been disturbed by Jake Fitton's arrival in London, disturbed and alarmed, to judge from the personal interest being taken in Fitton's activities. 'He's out to avenge his wife's death.'

'So we're told, but Jake Fitton is an extremely complex man. There might be more to what he's doing than we know.'

'You mean he could still be a threat to the organisation?' He was almost sneering... 'A blind man...what the hell can he do? He's a sitting target. One of our men could pick him off tomorrow if——'

'No.'

The sharp command silenced him.

'Before we do anything...anything at all, we need to find out exactly how much he knows and if he's passed that information to anyone, specifically his old friends in the anti-drugs squad. The reason we've had so much success here with our end of the business is because we've managed to remain anonymous...'

Because *you've* managed to remain anonymous, Charles's ex-companion wanted to say, but he didn't dare. He had never felt entirely at ease with his superior...had never felt that he was totally trusted.

Sometimes he thought that his superior's determination to maintain anonymity bordered on the obsessional, but there was no doubt that it worked.

The London end of the organisation was the envy of controllers in other parts of the world. He wasn't really sure how a man like Jake Fitton could threaten such supremacy. His own view was that his superior was overreacting to Fitton's sudden appearance in London.

They knew from their own agents what Fitton was after. Vengeance for his wife's death. He moved in his seat again.

The easiest way to get rid of Fitton was surely to drop a name that he could fasten on...someone unimportant and expendable within the organisation, on whom he could wreak his vengeance...either that or dispose of Fitton himself.

He said as much, watching the anger glitter in his superior's eyes as the latter said tersely, 'I've told you already why we can't kill Fitton. At least, not yet. And as for your other idea...whom do you suggest? Whose name do you suggest we put forward...your own?'

He paled and then suggested, 'We could ask South America for help.'

'No.'

He realised he had said the wrong thing.

'London is *my* territory, my responsibility. I'll deal with it...'

'But if Fitton is such a threat to the organisation, shouldn't they be warned...?'

'No. The first thing we need to do is to find out exactly how much Fitton knows, and whether he's passing on information to anyone else...'

'All this fuss over someone who can't even see...'

'Don't underestimate him,' the other warned him grimly.

His superior was standing up now and he followed suit, unable to resist saying blandly, 'As you did?'

The silent warning in the other's eyes quelled him, and he asked, 'What else do you want me to do?'

'Nothing. Fitzcarlton's been given his instructions...'

'Yes, and got off lightly, if you ask me. He owes us thousands...'

'Which will be repaid in due course. For now his co-operation is more important to us than the money. The organisation likes the idea of bringing in extra supplies via Ireland. For that we need Fitzcarlton's co-operation and his silence. His debt alone won't guarantee those, but if we can draw him in a little closer...

'And besides, we need him. We suspect that Fitton knows that Fitzcarlton is one of our pushers and therefore, for the moment at least, where Fitzcarlton goes, Fitton will follow.'

They were outside in the street now, both of them preparing to go in their different directions.

'So you don't want me to do anything...' he pressed.

'No. You can leave Fitton to me. I'll handle this in my own way.'

'I hope you're looking forward to this weekend as much as I am.' Charles's tone suggested that he already knew the answer. Silver gave him a slow smile, marvelling at the ease with which she was deceiving him.

Couldn't he see how much his touch revolted her...how much she dreaded his touching her? As she glanced out of the window of Charles's car she touched the small scar on her lip surreptitiously.

Over lunch he had had no opportunity to do anything other than make verbal love to her, and she had encouraged him, forcing herself to give him all the encouragement he needed.

Which wasn't much. Charles was making no secret of the fact that he was eager to be her lover, but it was too soon yet to be sure she had any real power over him. That would come later, after she had allowed him the intimacies of her body, after she had convinced him that she desired him as much as he desired her.

She wished she hadn't agreed to go to Rothwell with him. She was dreading the evening ahead. What if he had lied to her and it was only going to be the two of them? She shuddered inwardly. A weekend alone with Charles... Her flesh crawled at the thought.

But the presence of others at his formal dinner party wouldn't stop him from expecting her to share his bed. He had already hinted at as much, and she had not checked him.

How Jake would mock her if he knew what she was feeling. Jake... where was he now? What was he doing? Jake...Jake... Oh, God, she must find a way of shutting herself away from him, of forgetting that he had ever existed, that she had ever known him.

She was glad that Charles had elected to drive himself to Rothwell; that way at least she was sure of avoiding any intimacy with him.

It had been a shock at first to discover he was driving her father's Bentley. Somehow she had expected him to be driving something else, but the car had been only months old when her father had died, and besides...

It made her feel sick inside to realise how much Charles enjoyed handling his car... She wondered if he had actually physically enjoyed her father's death. The anger and pain inside her helped to subdue her physical nausea at the thought of him as her lover. She wished desperately that she could shut herself off from her own per-

sonal feelings, but the harder she tried the more
impossible it was.

The drive from London to Rothwell was so familiar
to her and brought back so many memories, especially
of her father. She clung hard to them, using them to
suppress her own personal feelings, to remind her of why
she was here with Charles.

How ironic it was that Jake should accuse her of still
loving Charles. She had thought she hated Charles, but
now she was discovering there was none of hatred's
warmth and fire in her feelings towards him. Loathing
was a more accurate description of his physical effect
on her, contempt and dislike came closer to describing
her emotional resentment of him. She could only marvel
that she had once actually loved him, and could only
blame her illusion on her youth and her ignorance of
what he really was.

Illuminatingly, she recognised how much of what she
now felt for him was because of all she had learned from
Jake. Unwittingly, he *had* revealed to her the difference
between a man's vices and his virtues.

Only one thing was keeping her with Charles now,
and that was her determination to make him pay for
killing her father.

She tensed as they approached Rothwell and then
turned in through the lodge gates. The drive was
sprinkled with weeds; there were gaps in the straight
double row of limes that edged the drive where the storm
of 1987 had torn up the trees by their roots and forever
destroyed the symmetry of their alignment.

Beyond the limes stretched the park, no longer as immaculate as she remembered. In fact, everywhere she
looked were signs that Charles could not afford to
maintain Rothwell to the same high standards as her
father had.

When Charles stopped the car, she got out shakily.
The sight of the familiar figure of her father's butler

almost made her betray herself. A greeting was on her lips before she remembered that he would not recognise her and that she could hardly acknowledge him by name.

Walking into the hallway brought an odd sensation of *déjà vu*... It was as though the air here held echoes of too many once familiar voices: her own, her aunt's, Charles's, and most of all her father's.

Nothing had changed, and yet everything had changed. Charles's obvious pride and arrogance in claiming ownership sickened her. Recklessly she wanted to challenge him there and then, to call down the wrath of heaven on his shoulders and accuse him of her father's death, but sanity stopped her.

'I'll get someone to take your stuff upstairs,' Charles told her, and her heart missed a beat. Tonight she would be sharing Charles's room, Charles's bed. The thought panicked her. To distract herself she asked him about the party.

'It's nothing special,' he told her carelessly. 'Just a few close friends. A fairly intimate dinner, but not as intimate as I would have liked.'

He came across the hall towards her.

'Why don't I cancel the whole thing, and then you and I——?'

'What about your friends?' she pouted up at him, stepping back from him. 'I was looking forward to meeting them, and you promised me you'd show me your house,' she reminded him. It would be hours yet before his other guests arrived. She had to keep him occupied, although what difference it could make if he made love to her before or after the party she had no real idea.

She was a coward, she derided herself as he showed her through rooms already familiar to her. A coward and a fool.

He would have taken her upstairs, but she stopped him. Already she felt dangerously vulnerable to the memories being here at Rothwell was reviving.

'I think perhaps now I should like to see the garden,' she told him, forcing herself not to shrink back as he came towards her and took her in his arms.

His mouth on hers was moist and hot, his hands hard through the protective barrier of her clothes.

'Not yet,' he told her thickly as his hand found her breast. His body moved against her, aroused and insistent. Fear and disgust formed a twin spear that pierced her self-control. She shook, and was amazed that he couldn't tell the difference between desire and distaste.

The door opened and the butler came in. Charles released her, cursing under his breath.

'Cook wanted to have a word with you about the arrangements for tonight...'

Discreetly Silver turned her back on them and walked over to the window.

'Oh, and there was a call for you... A Helen Cartwright...'

Silver waited until the butler had gone before saying lightly, 'Helen Cartwright—isn't that the photographer who was at the reception the other night?'

She wondered if Charles would deny knowing her again or pick up on the fact that she knew the woman's name, and met his wary look with an open smile.

'Yes,' he agreed tersely. 'She's been pestering me to let her photograph Rothwell for one of her rags... To get her off my back I've invited her here tonight...'

Silver allowed her eyebrows to lift slightly. 'That's very generous of you.'

He seemed not to hear the irony in her voice. 'She's been hounding me for weeks and it seemed a good way to get rid of her.'

'Who else is coming to dinner?' she asked him. 'Anyone I'm likely to know?'

He mentioned several names, some of them familiar to her. Charles appeared to have no really close friends, but instead a large circle of acquaintances.

The small scar on her lip throbbed from the roughness of his kiss.

'I'd better go,' he told her. 'But I won't be long.' He raised her hand to his mouth, making her skin crawl.

'I shall enjoy making love to you for the first time, here at Rothwell. The master bedroom has a wonderful Gothic ceiling...'

Her stomach twisted, resisting her control. She pulled away from him and walked over to the window.

'What a pity your grounds are so neglected...' She was gabbling, saying the first thing that came into her head, and inadvertently she had angered him.

'It isn't my fault,' he told her bitterly. 'My damned cousin...'

'Your cousin?' She turned towards him, wondering what he would say or do if she revealed herself to him now, but Charles hated discussing the fact that until Geraldine Frances was officially declared dead he could not legally call himself Rothwell's master, nor its earl, and he changed the subject hastily, drawing her attention to the gaps in the avenue of limes, telling her about the damage caused by the storm.

The first of Charles's guests arrived while he was conducting her through the portrait gallery.

The butler came to inform him of their arrival, and, following Charles back downstairs, Silver let out a shaky sigh of relief. Tonight she and Charles would be lovers, nothing was going to stop that. It was an inescapable fact... If she failed her father now...

Charles had invited ten other couples for dinner; when he entertained at Rothwell it was always people whom he had selected carefully. None of them ever included any of those members of society to whom he was supplying drugs; in the main they were older, sophisticated couples with cosmopolitan backgrounds, wealthy and reasonably respectable; guests who helped to preserve the illusion that he was a fitting successor to Rothwell.

Silver was talking with a group of them when the last pair arrived.

She saw them walk in through the double doors which had been designed by Robert Adam and which were as flawlessly impressive now as they had been the day they were installed.

The shock of seeing Jake framed in those doors drove everything else from her mind, even the fact that he was with another woman.

Fiercely, for one second, she hated him. He had followed her here... he was tormenting her... persecuting her... And then she focused on his companion and a dark, searing tide of emotion engulfed her, so intense and unsuspected that it took her breath away.

She was *jealous*, she acknowledged painfully, *jealous* of the fact that someone else was with Jake. *Jealous*... but how *could* that be? Jake meant nothing to her...

She saw Charles break away from his companions and walk to greet the newcomers.

And as she tried desperately to focus on something and hide the shock seeing Jake had given her, she realised that Jake's companion was Helen Cartwright.

Jake and Helen Cartwright... She frowned, not knowing why the sight of them together should disturb her so much. She had no right to feel jealous... no reason, either...

Watching him, half of her marvelled at the ease with which he moved, the confidence that allowed him to treat his blindness as though it didn't exist.

Helen Cartwright was not so confident, though; she was fussing round him, drawing first Charles and then everyone else's attention to his infirmity.

Knowing how much Jake would hate that, Silver waited for him to react. When he didn't, the ache inside her body intensified. How long had he known Helen Cartwright? *Why* hadn't he said anything about knowing her when she had mentioned her? But why should he...why should he tell *her* anything about his private life...his private thoughts?

Dinner was the worst kind of ordeal, a nightmare of shrill voices, of forcing herself to concentrate on Charles, on the others, when all the time her mind had only one focus. And Jake hadn't even spoken to her... But he must know she was there.

She was wearing his perfume and she wished violently and bitterly that she were not. Out of all the regrets she had in her life, she resented it deeply that her sharpest regret should be that he was here tonight to witness her ordeal.

After dinner the guests circulated, while Charles kept her by his side, one arm locked possessively around her waist. When he could, he touched her intimately and whispered to her that he couldn't wait for them to be alone.

She only escaped him when Helen Cartwright demanded an escorted tour of the house.

Free of him, she wandered into the library. This room had been so much a part of her father... If she sat here in his chair and closed her eyes she could almost imagine...

The touch of hands on her shoulders made her freeze and wrench herself away, unable to stop the denial bursting from her lips as she demanded rawly, 'Charles, please don't touch me.'

'I'm not Charles.'

She opened her eyes and whirled round. Jake was standing behind her.

'What are you doing in here?' she demanded huskily.

'I followed you.'

'Liar. How could you follow me? You can't...'

'See you...' he said mirthlessly. 'Maybe not, but I can smell you, my dear; you're wearing my scent...'

His scent... My God, if only he knew... She lay in bed at night, tormented by the pervasive muskiness that seemed to linger on her own skin... a scent that belonged to him alone and which seemed to have infiltrated her body and her bed, no matter what she did to try and rid herself of them.

'What are you doing here at Rothwell?' she demanded fiercely. 'If you're following me...'

'It wasn't you that brought me to Rothwell, Silver.'

She couldn't hide her shock and confusion from him. 'But——'

'I came with Helen Cartwright, as her—partner...' He felt the shock jolt through her, and added smoothly, 'At the dinner table, and not in bed...'

'Helen Cartwright.' Silver swallowed, hating herself for the relief she felt at discovering that Jake and Helen were not lovers. 'I didn't realise you knew her...'

'I didn't until quite recently, but it seems we have some mutual acquaintances.' Silver heard the irony in his voice, but couldn't understand the reason for it. 'We were both invited to the same party... we got talking... she mentioned that she was coming here, and asked me if I'd like to accompany her.'

There was something about his expression that jarred, something that rang warning bells in her mind, but she dismissed the feeling as irrational jealousy. She had no rights over Jake, if he wanted to be with someone else!

Jake, who could feel the emotions emanating from her, wondered how she would react if he told her the truth: that he suspected Helen Cartwright had deliberately fostered an acquaintance with him not because of any desire for him as a man, but for a different reason altogether.

He had never deceived himself. He had always known that the organisation would quickly discover his presence in London and the reason for it. Charles was involved with them—he knew it—and Helen Cartwright? He knew that he was probably placing himself in danger, but if that was the only way he was going to get closer to discovering Beth's murderer, then it was a risk he had to take.

Now, when he needed every ounce of self-control he possessed, finding Silver here at Rothwell was a complication he could do without.

Sensing that his thoughts were on something else, Silver bit her lip in vexation, and then made a small sound of pain as her teeth broke the skin Charles had savaged.

'What is it . . . what's wrong?'

He was too quick . . . too clever . . .

She winced and tried to jerk back as his hands framed her face, his thumb tracing her lips, finding the bruised flesh.

'You're playing with fire,' he warned her. 'Do you *really* know the kind of pleasures your cousin likes from his lovers?'

His words were savage . . . angry . . . beating down on her like blows.

'Let me go . . .'

She tried to twist free of him, but he wouldn't let her escape.

'I don't tell *you* how to run your life . . .'

'You little fool,' he told her mercilessly, ignoring her demand. 'Do you really think you're going to be able to go through with it? Is your pride really so important to you that you'll sacrifice yourself . . . your feelings . . . your body . . . ?'

'It isn't for me . . .' Silver cried out despairingly, and then tensed, but it was too late.

'No . . . then who is it for?'

It was too late now to lie to him. She could sense the purposefulness in him...the determination...the danger...

'My father—it's for my father...'

Unconsciously she had balled her hands into small fists as she made the tormented admission, and now she beat them against Jake's chest, as though she were drumming the words into him.

'Charles killed my father...I *know* he did...and I have to punish him for it...I have to.'

He caught hold of her hands and bound them easily behind her back, holding on to her when she struggled impotently against his imprisonment.

'Stop it,' he ordered pithily. 'What do you mean, he killed your father?'

She sagged in his hold, all the fight draining out of her. Until this moment she had not known how much she ached to share the burden of her knowledge with someone else.

'My father realized that Charles was involved with drugs...He...he told one of his agents to find out all he could about what Charles was doing. Charles discovered somehow or other that my father knew and that he would tell me. He killed him somehow while they were hunting. An accident, they said, but my father was a first-class rider... I *know* it wasn't an accident...I *know* that Charles killed him...'

She turned her head away from him and said in a low voice, 'I *know* that he destroyed my father, and he would have destroyed me too if I'd married him. And then he would have had Rothwell, just as he'd always wanted.'

There was silence and then Jake said emotionlessly, 'So it isn't because you still love him that you are pursuing this vendetta against him.'

'Love him?' She laughed wildly. 'Oh, God... I don't love him... I loathe him.' She gave a deep shudder. 'If it weren't for my father, do you think I'd be here like this ... with him?' She was beyond caring what she gave away now, driven by pain and fear into the trap of giving way to the relief of sharing her anguish with someone else.

She turned back to him and said huskily, 'I *have* to do it ... you of all people must understand that. For the sake of my father ... for the sake of Rothwell...'

'You don't have to go to bed with him to avenge your father.'

The words echoed hollowly through her.

Suddenly she felt light and empty, oddly dizzy... weightless and floating... She stared bemusedly up at him. His face seemed to be carved out of stone, all angles and planes, shadows on it she had not noticed before. She lifted her hand to touch the hard line of his lips and then let it drop as though she had been burned.

What was it about this man that bemused her so much ... that destroyed her determination and her willpower?

She didn't *have* to go to bed with Charles... The words seemed to reverberate through her. It was as though a huge weight had been lifted from her. Dimly she recognised the truth of what Jake was saying, and with it she recognised something else. Her determination to make herself suffer the ordeal of giving herself to Charles had been somehow connected with her own deep feeling of guilt over her father's death. It was as though she wanted to punish, not just Charles, but herself as well...

Confused and uncertain, she looked up at Jake, but he wasn't looking at her. He was frowning, his head turned towards the study door.

'They're coming back,' he told her abruptly, releasing her and stepping away from her so that when the door opened and Charles and Helen Cartwright came in they were standing yards apart.

Even so, Charles frowned suspiciously, while Helen Cartwright walked over to Jake and slipped her arm through his, saying chidingly, 'Jake, darling, how in the world did you find your way here? You really must be careful, you know. I'd hate anything to happen to you.'

Didn't she realise that Jake was a man and not a child? Silver wondered fiercely, stunned by Jake's acceptance of her chiding, fussing words.

'Silver... what on earth...?'

Charles was coming towards her. She looked at him and couldn't repress the shudder of distaste that convulsed her.

'I'm sorry, Charles,' she heard herself saying, her mind suddenly made up. 'But I'm afraid I can't stay after all; I must get back to London. I'll arrange for a taxi to pick me up, unless one of your other guests can give me a lift.' And without giving him the opportunity to argue with her she walked out of the room.

She didn't *need* to go to bed with Charles... Jake was right, she *didn't* need to. It was enough that she could simply reveal herself as who she really was. It was enough that she could deny him Rothwell. The rest... the rest was unimportant. To her father Rothwell and all that it stood for had mattered more than anything else. Rothwell was her sacred trust from him, and she had so nearly forgotten that in her desire to hurt Charles as he had hurt her. Charles was unimportant... that was what her father would have said. It was Rothwell that mattered. For too long she had allowed Rothwell to suffer at Charles's hands... it was time that Geraldine Frances came back to life and claimed what was rightfully her own.

From across the room she saw Charles watching her with baffled, angry eyes.

When he tried to persuade her to stay she refused to listen to him. All she wanted to do was to escape...from Rothwell, from Charles...and most of all from Jake and the way that seeing him with Helen Cartwright made her feel. She needed to be alone. To think...to plan...

CHAPTER TWENTY-THREE

IT TOOK Silver less than twenty-four hours to co-ordinate all the formalities that would enable her to reveal herself to the world as the person she really was, to be able to revert to her real identity as Geraldine Frances.

She intended to confront Charles with the information first. She wondered how he would react. With disbelief... with anger? Odd how she no longer really cared what his reaction was.

Resuming her own identity was simply something she had to do to protect Rothwell. Emotionally she felt nothing for Charles as a man; he was still her father's killer and she still had to make him pay for that killing, but the deep-seated need to make him suffer as she herself had once suffered had gone, burned away perhaps by its own intensity, even though she herself hadn't been able to see that until Jake...

Jake... She moved impatiently, angered by his possession of so many of her thoughts.

Without knowing why, she was anxious about him, a nagging, annoying feeling that wouldn't go away and which had nothing to do with the very different ache she experienced when she thought about how easily he had let her walk away from Rothwell, without making any attempt to get in touch with her.

What had she expected him to do? Follow her? Perhaps it was not what she had expected him to do, but she had to admit that it would have been wonderful to have him at her side as she left Charles.

No, this ache was not caused so much by the fact that she wanted him and missed him as by anxiety for him;

it was a deep-rooted, instinctive feminine ache she could neither analyse nor dismiss.

Where was he? What was he doing? Who was he with? Helen Cartwright?

Suddenly she wanted to be free of the past...of her obligations to it; she wanted to confront Charles with the truth to see justice done to her father's memory, so that she would be free to...to what? Run after Jake? She swallowed a mirthless laugh. Was she never going to learn...to break the pattern of loving hopelessly and impossibly?

Jake, Jake, Jake; he was all she could think of when by rights she ought to be thinking of Charles, concentrating on what she was going to tell him.

Irritated with herself, she picked up the telephone, and dialled the number of the Rothwell Square house. It was in the back of her mind that somehow or other she might be able to discover from Charles where Jake was. She was presuming that he had left the party with Helen Cartwright, and Helen Cartwright, if not precisely a friend of Charles's, was someone he knew. Inwardly she mocked herself for her own folly...for the lengths to which she was prepared to go. Stronger even than her need to confront Charles with the truth was her need to be with Jake... That was at least half the reason why she was telephoning Charles.

When there was no reply to her telephone-call she tried to contact Rothwell itself. To her astonishment she was told that Charles was in Ireland, at Castle Kilrayne.

Charles hated the castle. What was he doing there? Silver wondered as she replaced the receiver.

The staff at Rothwell had no idea when Charles was due to return and the impatience that now possessed her to have the whole thing over and done with wouldn't allow her to wait until he did.

Soon Rothwell would be hers again, and once it was…
Once it was…what then? She shivered a little. What
concerned her now was the present, and not the future.

She flew out to Shannon's International Airport with
a small case containing a change of clothes and a large
bundle of documents—photostats, of course; the orig-
inals were locked away in the vaults of her bankers. These
documents held the incontrovertible evidence that she
was Geraldine Frances. There were signed, dated state-
ments from her bankers, from her advisers…from those
whom she had admitted to the secrecy of her plans.

Charles held no power over her now. She had no fear
of him any longer. There were no vulnerabilities within
herself to him.

All she wanted now was to confront him with the truth,
to hear him admit that he had killed her father. And
then she would make him repeat that admission before
witnesses. Now she was the stronger of the two of them.
With the realisation that she no longer desired him, that
she was no longer held in thrall to him, had come the
knowledge that she was now at last free.

At Shannon she hired a car, and set out along the
familiar road that let to Kilrayne.

Ireland was enjoying a rare spell of good weather. At
the airport, American tourists had been marvelling at
the warmth and sunshine, and Geraldine Frances, who
had arrived at Shannon on many a summer's day to find
the airport wrapped in mist and the rain turning the earth
and sky an impenetrable, even grey, had smiled herself
at their pleasure, glad for them to be seeing this country
she loved so much in the true beauty of its summer greens
and blues.

She took the road that wound its way along the coast;
the Atlantic shimmered blue under the high arc of the
clear sky.

Where the road turned inland past the hauntingly
sombre rocky outcrops of the Burren, she automatically

slowed down. This bare expanse of limestone rock threw a powerful spell over whoever beheld it, and it had always fascinated her.

The valley which Castle Kilrayne guarded slumbered under the heat of the sun; beyond it the cliffs and headland on which the castle stood were stark and gaunt.

It had no fairy-tale prettiness, no gilded towers, no sleeping-beauty delicacy, this castle that was hers; it was no imitation French château, all airy towers and serene moat, nor did it possess the stalwart girth and squareness so beloved by a succession of British kings.

No, Kilrayne was an entity unto itself alone, a jumble of high, crumbling walls and towers that seemed to have been thrown up by some volcanic action of the earth and rock itself, rather than to have been constructed by man's hand. It had no symmetry, no stout, square towers or protective curtain wall, no moat or drawbridge, but reared up out of the rock to stare watchfully down across the land at its feet.

It was a place that stood in a no man's land between earth and sea; the rock of which it was built dropped sheerly down into the Atlantic, the water there so deep even at low tide that it was rumoured that during the Second World War a German submarine had surfaced there.

If it was true, which Silver doubted, there was no record of it in the family archives. She smiled to herself, remembering the hair-raising stories Bridie had told her about the castle's past.

From the landward side it was impossible to see the magnificent walkway that ran along the ocean-facing side of the castle, linking its twin towers.

There even the hard granite of the stone had not been proof against the Atlantic gales that battered it. The parapet was dangerously low, the walkway so unsafe in places that her father had banned its use.

She stopped off in the village, more out of habit than anything else. It hadn't changed at all during her lifetime, and her father swore it remained the same as it had been when he was a boy.

There was a small cluster of houses, very obviously built from stone 'borrowed' from the castle itself; one of them was the local store-cum-pub, and it was there that she stopped her car, ostensibly to buy a newspaper, but more for the pleasure of hearing the familiar soft accent, of knowing herself back in one of the few places she had actually felt welcomed and at home.

Here, in this remote part of Ireland, people were not judged on how they looked but what they were, and Geraldine Frances, poor, motherless child that she was, had been taken to their hearts with enthusiasm and love.

She wasn't recognised, of course. How could she be? Silver was stared at openly, her expensive clothes and sleek, elegant appearance assessed openly.

'You'll be wantin' the castle. American, are you, then?' one woman asked.

Silver shook her head, both amused and saddened that she should be so completely accepted as a stranger. But what had she expected—that somehow, because Castle Kilrayne was to her her true spiritual home, its inhabitants should immediately recognise her?

'Charles . . . Fitzcarlton is there, is he?' she enquired, only to find the woman frowning darkly at her.

'Aye, he's there all right,' she told her. 'Arrived yesterday, they did; it fair set Bridie in a rare lather . . . Not seen sight nor sound of him in over a twelve-month, and then he ups and arrives without a word of warning, demanding bedrooms for himself and his guests . . . demanding all manner of fancy food and complaining . . .' She gave a deprecating sniff. 'Sure, and where does he think poor Bridie is going to get fancy stuff from way out here? He's sent her off to Limerick this morning

with his driver and a shopping list as long as your arm...
And all that just to feed the three of them for a couple
of days...'

'The three of them?' Silver asked her curiously. For
some reason she had imagined Charles had come here
alone. The fact that he hadn't complicated things a little.
She could scarcely confront him with the truth while he
had guests.

It was so unlike Charles to come to Ireland in the first
place, and to bring two people with him... Guests? For
what purpose?

'Aye, there's a woman; some friend of his...'

Silver just managed to conceal her surprise. A
woman...

'Not his wife?' she suggested, watching as the woman's
face became grim.

'No, not her, poor soul. A wee useless bit of a thing
she was, and to be miscarrying her bairn like that...
And now he's put her from him and I don't doubt he's
looking round for someone else to provide him with an
heir. Aye, he'll want a man-child right enough. He won't
want to go the same way as his uncle, God preserve him.
A rare fine man was Lord James...'

Silver smiled at the bastardisation of her father's title.
Here in Kilrayne they had always referred affectionately
to him as 'Lord James'; she noticed they did not refer
in anything like the same way to Charles, who had never
been well liked. Not at Rothwell, and certainly not here
in Ireland.

'Aye, a hard-faced creature she is an' all, according
to Bridie... and as for the other poor soul that's come
with him...a blind man come to see the beauty of Castle
Kilrayne... why, it's a wonder——'

A blind man.

Silver knew she must have betrayed her surprise, because the woman broke off from what she had been
saying and looked at her.

A blind man... It could only be Jake; Silver had to suppress the urge to question her about what this blind man had looked like... what he had said... why he was here, but she knew that the woman was unlikely to have any answers. The probability was that she only knew of his arrival via the village grapevine, and that she had not even seen him herself.

Jake here at Kilrayne. But why? And then she knew. It must have something to do with Charles's involvement with the people Jake was trying to track down.

Surely he didn't think Charles was responsible for his wife's death? But no... Jake had told her that she had been killed on the instructions of the man who ran the organisation's London operation, and that man could not be Charles.

Charles wasn't intelligent enough to mastermind that kind of operation.

So why were Charles and Jake here? Had Jake perhaps threatened to expose Charles if he didn't co-operate with him and give him the information he needed? Had Charles brought him here to Kilrayne so that he could plead for clemency... so that they would have privacy... and secrecy? And who was this woman they had brought with them?

Was she with Jake, or was she with Charles?

Frowning slightly, Silver paid for her newspapers and got back in her car.

How like Charles to send Bridie to Limerick for food, when with a little forethought he could have telephoned ahead and she would have had time to get everything ready for their arrival.

As she drove in through the arched entrance of what had once been the castle's outer bailey, the old familiar sense of homecoming and peace enveloped her.

Warm sunlight bathed one side of the empty courtyard, the bulk of the castle throwing dense shadows along the other. Weeds were growing up through the

cobbles, adding to the castle's air of neglect and
desolation.

A solitary black cat emerged to inspect the new arrival, blinking green-eyed in the sunshine.

As Silver picked her way over the familiar cobbles,
heading for the kitchen door, her serenity was replaced
by a sharp sense of apprehension. She hadn't expected
to find Jake here ... she had expected to find Charles
alone. It was too late now to ask herself if she had been
over-impetuous and if she ought to have remained in
London to confront Charles on his return.

The kitchen was empty, its almost subterranean
vastness warmed by the familiar range, but for once the
air of the kitchen was not scented by one of Bridie's
mouth-watering concoctions.

Charles was a faddy eater; he had probably sent Bridie
to Limerick to buy flavourless battery-produced chicken
and equally tasteless sanitised vegetables, Silver reflected in disgust, remembering the delicious flavour of
Bridie's special stew, which more often than not had been
supplemented by the addition of a plump rabbit or two
caught in the woods beyond the castle.

As she made her way along the dark, uneven passage
that led from the kitchens to the castle's formal apart-
ments, Silver reflected that she should more properly
have made her way round to the main entrance instead
of walking in unannounced.

She expected to find Charles in her father's study, but
the door to that room stood open and the room itself
was empty.

In fact, the whole place had an air of desolation and
emptiness, she reflected, frowning a little as she walked
into the great hall, her heels echoing on the huge stone
slabs that formed the floor.

Beneath these slabs of stone were reputed to be secret
stairs that led down to what had once been the castle's

dungeons, and beyond them the passages cut through the solid rock out to the cliff-face.

Bridie had told her that these passages had been cut so that her ancestors could dispose of their prisoners by pushing them down the cliff-face and into the sea, but her father had laughed at this story and told her that it was far more likely that the passages had been cut for much more mundane purposes.

'Smuggling,' he had explained when she hadn't understood him.

Now the floor was sealed and the dungeons rendered inaccessible because of the danger they represented, but throughout the ground floor of the castle there were stones which echoed when one stood on them.

Sharp prisms of sunlight speared through the narrow, high windows into the great hall, highlighting motes of dust in the air and on the furniture.

There were no sounds to disturb its silence other than her own breathing. Charles, Jake and whomever it was they had brought with them—where were they?

Frowning, Silver acknowledged that they too might have gone into Limerick, although why Charles should take the trouble to come all the way to Castle Kilrayne and then spend his time in Limerick she had no idea.

She hesitated, wondering whether to wait for his return or to go back to England and confront him there. Common sense dictated the latter course, but in the end it was curiosity and not common sense that won. That, and the knowledge that if she stayed here she would see Jake.

Jake… What had he done to her? What had he turned her into? Almost automatically her footsteps led her towards the stairwell, and without realising it she started to climb them, taking the familiar route to her old rooms in the west-facing tower that looked out across the Atlantic.

Outside the door she hesitated, half reluctant to enter, remembering the scene of devastation she had left here. And then, taking a deep breath, she turned the handle, ready to confront the fears she had locked away.

The destruction she had wrought was gone; the room had been returned to order and neatness. Only someone knowledgeable about its history could know of the missing furniture...the absence of its silk hangings and wallpaper.

The French furniture, or what she had left of it, was gone; the room was virtually empty, only with a few odd items remaining.

As she looked round it she recognised that a part of her had died here in this room and that that part of her could never be resurrected... Nor, in many ways, did she wish it to be.

As she stepped out of the room and closed the door behind her she acknowledged that finally she was closing the door on the anguish of her past and that finally she was free of the cancer of misery and pain that loving Charles had caused her.

On the stairs she hesitated, glancing upwards. On such a clear blue day there would be a marvellous view of the ocean; there was enough of the old Geraldine Frances left within her to tempt her up there to brave the buffeting of the wind and to stare out across its vastness.

As she walked upwards, gripping the handrail, force of habit led her to remove her shoes. Further up where the stairs came out into the open and had no protection from the elements the deposits of wind-borne sea-salt often made them slippery and treacherous. Bare feet would be safer than high heels.

She was halfway up when she heard the muted sound of voices. Frowning, she quickened her step, muttering under her breath as she caught her elbow on the rough stone and grazed her skin... As she paused to inspect the graze she could hear the voices more clearly; she recognised Charles's angry hectoring tones, and then Jake's voice with its deep male resonance and its pleasurable cadences.

Jake and Charles, up here . . . but why? Charles must know how dangerous the walkway was, and for Jake, who, for all his awe-inspiring ability to deal with his blindness, was still blind . . .

She pictured the parapet, crumbling in places, unsafe to touch, and anxiously hastened her footsteps.

When she re-emerged into the sunshine, pushing her hair off her face as the wind caught hold of it, she saw that Charles and Jake were standing by the parapet of the other tower. Charles had his back to the inner wall, while Jake . . .

She caught her breath as she saw how vulnerable Jake was, wondering why on earth Charles didn't warn him of his danger.

She almost called out herself, and then realised that to do so might precipitate the very kind of accident she wanted to avoid.

Neither of them was aware of her presence, both of them concentrating on someone she could not see.

As she watched them she heard Jake saying flatly, 'So you admit it, then. *You* gave the order for Beth's death.'

He wasn't speaking to Charles, Silver realised, her heart thumping frantically as she realised what she had walked into.

'Not only did I give the orders, I executed them as well.'

Shock ran through Silver like a live current as she heard the gloating, amused words, and saw Helen Cartwright step out of the shadows of the tower towards Jake.

'Not that my admission will do you any good. What a fool you've been, Jake, allowing us to lure you here. Didn't it ever occur to you that we'd be watching you? You thought you could use Charles to lead you to me, but I was ten steps ahead of you all the way. You've disappointed me, Jake... I had hoped you would be less predictable, but it never even occurred to you that you might be looking for a woman and not a man, did it?'

'Not until recently.'

It was obvious that his answer displeased her. 'What do you mean?' she demanded sharply. 'You had no idea... you couldn't have had...'

'Not initially,' Jake agreed easily, while Silver marvelled at his calm and control. If he felt any fear, he wasn't betraying it. If he was aware of his danger he wasn't letting it affect him. Three steps backwards, maybe less; that was all it would take... She shuddered, aching to intervene, to step forward, but terrified that, if she did, Helen and Charles would send Jake plunging to his death before she could reach him.

'But quite recently someone said something to me that made me wonder a little——'

If she could just get a little closer to them... distract them for long enough for her to pull Jake to safety...

Without weighing the danger, she crouched down, hugging the inner wall of the walkway. She knew it so well that she could have walked it blindfolded... knew every stone... every crack in its masonry.

'Look, let's get it over with,' Charles interrupted. 'Why waste time delaying?'

'Poor Charles, you've never liked heights, have you?' Helen mocked him. 'What a pity, Jake, that we had to be on opposite sides. Together we could have been invincible... If you were to tell us who else knows about our operation we could reconsider the need to take your life.'

Jake remained silent.

'Come on,' Charles urged. 'We don't want Bridie coming back and finding us pushing him over the edge.'

'She won't!' Silver heard Helen snap irritably. 'For goodness' sake, Charles, you're more fussy than a woman.'

'I don't like this place; I never have.'

He glanced nervously over his shoulder, and Silver held her breath, flattening herself against the wall. Jake's head turned towards her, so that for a moment it was almost as though he was looking directly at her... as though he had seen her. She froze, faltering for a moment.

Charles still had his back to her; all she could see of Helen was her arm and the gun she held in her hand.

'Come on, Charles,' she heard her saying almost jovially. 'You can't expect him to make it completely easy for us and jump,' she chuckled. 'I'm afraid he's not as obliging as your cousin. Did she really commit suicide, by the way, or did you help her, the way you helped her father?'

'What...? How...? You can't prove...' Charles's shock almost matched her own, Silver recognised.

'My dear Charles, don't be a fool... I'm not threatening you. In fact, I admire you; I had no idea you could be so resourceful. But you did kill him, didn't you?'

'He was thrown from his horse...' Charles said sulkily. 'Everyone knows that.'

'And you were the only witness. Forgive me if I say that I find the convenience and neatness of his demise too extraordinarily beneficial from your point of view to accept that it was an accident. However, it isn't particularly important. You and I have other matters to discuss.' Silver heard her laugh. 'Ah, no... not the monies you owe us, my friend... although you will of course ultimately pay those back. It's very isolated here, isn't it? And I understand that no one properly knows how deep the sea is here. Almost a natural harbour for anyone wanting to bring a boat in close to the castle walls... but first we must dispose of our friend here. I'm almost disappointed in you, Jake... I never thought you would be so easy to fool. Such a tragic accident...a poor, blinded man foolish enough to come up here not knowing of his danger...

'So unfortunate...such a tragedy. And of course no one will really be surprised. After all, he won't be the first to fall to his death from here, will he? Your cousin, Charles...'

'Geraldine Frances committed suicide——'

'No, she didn't, Charles, she's standing right behind you,' Jake interrupted softly.

For a moment Charles froze, and then he swung round, his eyes bulging with fright and disbelief as Silver stepped out of the shadows and confronted him. Beyond Charles she could see Jake turning in the direction of Helen Cartwright, but she could not afford to pay attention to them, hoping Jake's resourcefulness would keep him safe as she concentrated instead on Charles and walked steadily towards him.

'You're not Geraldine Frances,' he started to babble, but as she stepped forward he stepped back...back towards the low parapet where Jake had just been standing.

'Yes, I am,' she told him softly. 'Did you really think I'd kill myself, Charles? How pleased you must have been... You'd got rid of my father and then I was gone as well, and you were free to take Rothwell. Only you couldn't, could you...not without my body as proof of my death? Only I'm not dead, you see...'

'You are...you have to be... Rothwell is mine... You can't be Geraldine Frances. You're lying to me.'

'No, I'm not... I *am* Geraldine Frances, and I can prove it...just as I can prove that you caused my father's death.'

It was a lie, but she saw the look of fear that crossed his face, and pressed home her advantage.

'Did you really think I'd let you marry me after I'd found out the truth...after I'd discovered you with someone else?'

'You're lying, it's all lies!'

The shock was beginning to wear off and he was staring at her with narrowed eyes.

Beyond them, there was a soft grunt of pain as Jake wrenched the gun from Helen Cartwright's hands.

As she doubled over and fell against the wall, she cried out angrily, 'Charles...the gun...' And Charles turned round, throwing his full weight against Jake, hurling him back against the parapet, the force of his fall causing a shower of stones to break free from the wall and crash down into the sea below.

As Jake fell he flung the gun out over the parapet. It glinted dully in the sun for a second before hurtling down on to the rocks below.

Charles grabbed Jake's arm, too late to retrieve the gun, and then kicked him savagely to the ground.

'Never mind about that...the wall...push him over...' Helen Cartwright commanded, staggering to her feet and going to help him.

As Helen moved Silver saw the crack that suddenly appeared in the wall and felt the movement of the walkway beneath her own feet as another crack opened along it.

She heard Helen scream as she tried to fling herself to safety, grabbing hold of Charles, but the whole parapet and the walkway were disintegrating, and as Silver looked on in horror the ground beneath Helen gave way.

She screamed as she fell, gripping hold of Charles. Angrily Charles turned his attention from Jake to the woman clinging to him, wrenching himself away from her so that she had nothing left to hold on to.

Silver heard her scream as she fell and felt the nausea rise up inside her... Whatever she had done, she did not deserve such a death... Silver shuddered.

She heard a grunt and focused on Jake and Charles. There was blood trickling from Jake's mouth; he was slumped against what was left of the wall, and Charles... Charles was trying to drag him towards the edge of the hole... Charles was going to kill him, she realised, and without even thinking about it she left her own position of safety by the inner wall and ran towards them, grabbing hold of Jake's arm, praying desperately that he wasn't unconscious and that he would be able to help her.

Across his inert body Charles snarled at her. This was the real Charles, she recognised, looking into the mask of hatred and fury he had turned towards her.

'You can't save him, and when he's gone...'

'You'll what—kill me?' She forced herself to laugh, although in reality she was sick with terror and shock. 'You'll never get away with it, Charles...'

'No? A blind man and an unknown woman fall to their deaths after a lovers' quarrel... and then, when they discover who you really are, Rothwell will finally be mine,' he told her gloatingly.

He was mad, quite mad, she was sure of it, but his physical strength far outstripped hers... and there was no one here to help her, only Jake... Jake, who was unconscious... Jake, whom Charles would kill if she didn't stop him.

'He's going to die,' Charles told her gloatingly. 'You're both going to die.' He laughed harshly, drunk on his own power. 'And then all this——' he got up, gesturing wildly with his arms '—will be mine.'

Numb with fear, Silver watched him, staring up at him as he stood facing the sun and laughing wildly, and then suddenly, as though the sunlight had blinded him,

he staggered and stepped to one side, reaching out for
the parapet . . .

The parapet that was no longer there!

Silver watched as he fell, saw the crazed fear in his
eyes as he looked at her one last time.

Even after his screams had ended and it was silent,
she remained where she was, crouched against Jake's
side, gripping his arm. It wasn't until pins and needles
burned her skin that she could bring herself to move,
carefully edging back from the crumbling masonry and
dragging Jake with her.

He must have been knocked unconscious when Charles
hit him, she recognised as she wiped the blood from his
mouth with the sleeve of her white silk shirt . . . An un-
natural calm had descended on her; she heard herself
talking to Jake as though he were conscious, and realised that her mind was trying to blot out the horror of
what she had seen.

She knew she ought to go downstairs and find someone
to help her with Jake, but it was a long time before her
shock cleared sufficiently for her to accept that if she
left him, if she ceased to crouch protectively over him,
Helen would not somehow reappear and push him to
his death.

Even when she knew that the fear was produced by
shock and reaction, she was still reluctant to leave him.
She touched his hair, her hand trembling, and then his
face. His skin felt hard and warm, deeply familiar . . . deeply loved.

A shudder wrenched through her. It wasn't Jake who
was blind; it was she.

How long had she loved him? From Switzerland . . . yes,
almost certainly. From even before he had touched
her . . . shown her . . . She shivered, conscious of so much
about herself which she had deliberately denied.

She hadn't been able to let Charles touch her because she loved Jake. Her mouth twisted. She hadn't changed at all...

What was it about her that made her inflict on herself the anguish of loving where her love could not be returned?

When she had left this place she had sworn, and believed it, that love was something that had no place in her life. Then she had been thinking of Charles, of the love she had thought she had had for him.

Now, once again, she must leave Castle Kilrayne, knowing that all that waited for her outside its gates was loneliness and pain.

She touched Jake's face again. He was breathing evenly and regularly. She reached for his wrist and felt his pulse and as she did so he moved his head and opened his eyes.

'Silver...'

'Yes. I'm here...'

'I know,' he told her drily. 'Where are the others?'

She told him briefly what had happened and then said, 'You ran a great risk tackling Helen Cartwright like that. How did you know where she was?'

'I heard some stones shift under her feet and knew that my only hope of escape—our only hope of escape—was to spring a surprise on them. I ran the risk of Charles overpowering you, but put faith in his shock when faced with a woman he'd thought safely out of the way.'

'Had you guessed, that Helen Cartwright...?'

'Only sort of... It was after you told me about Charles lying about knowing her that I started putting two and two together, and realised how well they made four.

'Her work enabled her to travel widely without suspicion; she had visited Colombia quite regularly, supposedly on photographic assignments.' He moved uneasily, wincing a little.

'Can you walk?' Silver asked him. 'It would be better if you could get back downstairs.'

She helped him as he got to his feet, accepting the hard weight of his body as he leaned against her for a moment.

'Why did you let them bring you here?' she demanded as they walked slowly back towards her own tower. 'You must have realised the danger...'

'I thought it was the only way to get the truth out of them. I didn't realise they were on to me and that they intended to kill me. Lucky for me that you turned up...' He said it drily, making her tense, wondering if he had somehow guessed how she felt about him.

'How did you know I was there?' she asked him. 'They didn't.'

'Your perfume...'

She stopped and stared at him. 'But I wasn't wearing any...'

'You don't need to,' he told her obscurely, and then winced again, distracting her, so that it wasn't until much later when he was comfortably installed in the bedroom that had been her father's, with Bridie fussing over him, that she remembered his comment and wondered a little at it.

The phone-call he had insisted on making to London would ensure Charles's and Helen's deaths received the minimum amount of publicity. The local doctor had announced that after twenty-four hours in bed Jake would be as good as new and, as she watched Bridie tending to him, Silver knew that she would always carry with her this memory of him wherever she went, lying on the high four-poster bed, in the room that the masters of Castle Kilrayne had always occupied.

It suited him somehow. She smiled grimly at the idiocy of her own thoughts... Even if he wanted her...even if he loved her...even if there were no past between them there could not be any future; she knew him well enough to know that.

And she knew that if she stayed she would forget her pride and her past, and ignore all the subtle inner voices that warned her against such folly, and she would tell him how she felt about him and beg him as she had once begged Charles.

It was her nature . . . her weakness, that for her loving another human being must always have this intensity . . . this absoluteness.

She was older now and wiser, and it wouldn't do to burden him with something that was not his fault, and so, when she was sure that he had everything he might need, she smiled at him and said goodnight, wondering if he guessed that what she was actually saying was goodbye, and then she walked away from him, grateful that he wouldn't see the tears that fell in silence from her eyes.

She spent six months travelling, visiting, re-establishing the friendships which had once been her father's, re-affirming her allegiance to the heritage he had left her.

She was once more Geraldine Frances, Countess of Rothwell, and to those who expressed astonishment at her changed appearance she said simply that she had grown tired of her old face and so had changed it for another.

The effects of her new face were predictable enough; men flocked round her, flirted with her, coaxed and flattered her, and then, once they realised that they were simply not getting through to her, they left her as they had found her: as alone as she had been in the days when she was alone through necessity rather than desire.

She accepted commiserations on her cousin's death and mentioned Jake to no one. If she had hoped that time and distance might dim the ache inside her she was forced to acknowledge that she had been wrong.

In November she was invited to spend Christmas and the New Year in Switzerland, but she turned down the invitation. Rothwell was where she would spend Christmas, and she would spent it there alone.

The staff welcomed her back with cautiousness, not sure how to treat this elegant, fine-drawn woman whose beauty was hauntingly perfect.

In the gallery she stood in front of the portrait of her father she had commissioned after Charles's death.

It was a good likeness of him. One day, too, her portrait would hang there; and after that those of her children... her sons...

Her sons. She had no wish to marry, no desire to share her life with any man who was not Jake, and to share it with him was an impossibility.

At first she had hoped that he might contact her, if only out of friendship and curiosity, but as the weeks and months passed she acknowledged that it was better that he did not do so, and she wondered grimly if he himself had recognised earlier what she had been so slow to see, and accepted that it was more than likely that he had.

On Christmas Eve she summoned the staff together in the library to give them their Christmas gifts, a custom started by her great grandfather, and then she told them that they might all have the rest of the holiday off.

She saw the looks they exchanged and wasn't surprised. It was an odd sort of person indeed who would spend the Christmas season completely alone, but her loneliness was less difficult to bear than other people's company.

After they had gone she returned to the library, and started going through the accumulated post.

She frowned as she opened one letter and saw the cheque it enclosed.

It was drawn on a bank in Chester and signed 'Jake Fitton', and it was for the exact amount of money she had paid him in Switzerland.

There was nothing else in the envelope, no letter, no message, and even though she went feverishly through the rest of the post several times there was nothing there to indicate why Jake had sent it or how he had come by the money.

While she was still frowning over it, she heard a car draw up outside.

One of the staff coming back for something they had forgotten.

She went to the door and walked across the hall. Outside, the car moved off and disappeared down the drive. Puzzled, she opened the front door. Jake was standing there, his face illuminated by the lights. As she stared at him in disbelief he said curtly, 'You're back, then? So obviously you've got my cheque?' and walked past her into the hall, leaving her to stare after him until the cold blast of air reminded her to shut the door. She wondered how he had known it was her and not Soames, the butler, but then she remembered that uncanny way he had of knowing her by her scent even when she wasn't wearing his perfume.

'Yes, I've got it, but——'

'Good...then that leaves only one small matter to be resolved...'

'One? But——'

'I don't have much time,' he told her briskly. 'I suggest we get it over with as quickly as we can. A month should take us almost to the end of January... I'm due to fly out to see Annie then...'

Silver was still staring at him, and as though he sensed her confusion he turned to her and asked softly, 'You do realise why I'm here, don't you?'

'No...no, I don't.'

'I should have thought it was obvious. I've returned the money you paid me...'

'Yes... How?'

'A generous accident of fate. My mother-in-law—my late mother-in-law, I should say—died unexpectedly four months ago. Since she hadn't made a will, I inherited everything...'

It took Silver several seconds to assimilate what he was telling her, and then, still unsure as to the purpose of his visit, she said tentatively, 'And you wanted to make sure I had received the cheque. Well, I have, and of course I would have acknowledged its receipt, but I've been away and I've only just returned.'

'I know...and it isn't acknowledgement of the cheque I'm here for, Silver.' He smiled at her and her heart started to thump. 'I've paid you back, and now it's your turn to repay me.'

'Repay you...but what...how——?'

'A month,' he told her softly, interrupting her. 'A month of your time, of your body in my bed, of——'

'No!' she told him stunned. 'I didn't buy you... I bought your expertise...your knowledge. You told me that. I can't repay those.'

'You can try,' he told her obliquely. 'Which is your room?' He was already heading for the stairs, and she followed him automatically, only catching up with him when he reached the top.

'Jake, this is madness!' she began. But he wasn't listening to her, and her heart was beginning to thump erratically; her mouth had gone dry, and her body was whispering all sorts of idiotic messages to her.

'Which is your room?' he persisted, and dizzily she told him, allowing him to draw her towards it.

It was a dream...a fantasy...it had to be, and yet there was nothing dreamlike about the way he undressed and then waited for her to come to him, smoothing his hands over her body, making her shudder in eager delight.

It had been so long since she had held him...touched him; she couldn't contain what she was feeling, crying out his name when he touched her, twisting frantically beneath him as he entered her, crying out to him how much she wanted him as the earth fell away beneath her.

He stopped then and she came crashing back to reality, vulnerable and afraid.

'At last. Say it again,' he commanded, and she shivered and shook her head, sickened and ashamed.

'Why?' she asked him, as the tears thickened in her throat and the pain knifed sharply inside her. 'Why are you doing this?'

'Why?' His voice was harsh, almost bitter. 'Perhaps because I'm sick of waiting for you to come to me, of aching for you at night, of wondering when the hell you're going to stop running and start living...'

'Waiting for me to come to you—but——?'

'Don't tell me you haven't wanted to,' he interrupted roughly. 'Don't try to pretend that you haven't wanted me...needed me. I might be blind, but I'm not stupid...you love me.'

He said it challengingly, almost desperately, and suddenly she knew.

'Yes,' she told him simply. 'I do.'

He reached out to shape her face, his touch almost anguished.

'You little fool,' he said roughly. 'Why did you go away like that?'

'I thought you didn't want me, and I knew if I stayed I'd end up begging you.'

'You, begging? You've got pride like the walls of that damned castle of yours...impenetrable...'

'Those walls crumbled,' she reminded him, and then, sliding her hands into his hair, said against his mouth, 'Jake...please love me. I love you so much.' She faltered and looked at him, drawing away. 'Or is all this to punish me, to——?'

He took hold of her and held her gently. 'No. I'm not a sadist. Hurting people doesn't give me any pleasure. I fought against loving you, yes...but I'd have fought against loving anyone.'

'Because of Beth?'

'Partly...it was my fault she died. If I hadn't married her... She was such a child...in many ways she reminded me of my brother Justin. She needed me...unlike you. You've never needed me, have you?'

She laughed. 'Is that what you think? I need you all the time, Jake, in more ways than you can possibly know; I need you so much that if you asked it of me I'd turn my back on Rothwell and walk away from it without a second thought.'

'Gloria's death has made me a wealthy man,' he told her obliquely. 'Wealthy enough to marry and settle down...to raise a family...'

Her heart was beating far too fast, and even as she tried to control her breathing she knew he was aware of what she was feeling. His thumb was on the pulse in her wrist, monitoring its frantic race.

'Would you care for a husband, Silver?'

'Only if that husband is you.'

She saw him reach for her through the blur of her tears. She found his mouth eagerly with her own, letting down all her barriers, letting him feel what the touch and taste of him was doing to her.

Later, when they were lying curled together in the middle of her bed, she whispered to him, 'In a way I'm glad that you've never seen me; this face I have now is beautiful, but it's only outward beauty...'

'I have seen you,' Jake contradicted her gently. 'I've seen the woman you are inside, and it's her that I love. A beautiful woman marrying a blind man; the Press will have a field day. They won't know that to us neither of

those things is important. It's you I love, Silver, not your
face, nor even your highly desirable body... It's you,
the woman, and I started loving her a long time ago in
a chalet in Switzerland, when I listened to the pain in
her voice and recognised its shadowing of my own pain,
when I realised that here was a woman who had suffered
as I had suffered; a woman who was real.

'Beauty is, after all, in the eye of the beholder, and
my eyes see the inner woman, not the outer.'

Silver waited a while, absorbing the wonder and the
promise of all that he was saying to her, and then, after
they had kissed, deliberately lightened their mood by
saying teasingly, 'My perfume... I never did find out
how you managed to get it into my room.'

He laughed. 'That was the easy bit... I simply used
a courier service. I dared not risk delivering it myself.'

'But you wanted me to know it was from you.'

'Yes,' he agreed. 'I suspect that even then I knew in
my heart of hearts how much I was committed to you.'

'You had the perfume specially blended...'

'I drove them mad. What I wanted was a perfume
that reminded me of the scent of your skin...of you...'

'I love it,' she told him. 'Even though I was furious
with you when I opened it.'

'But you wore it, all the same...'

'I told myself that I'd worn Charles's perfume with
you, so it was only fair that I wore yours with——' She
broke off and shuddered. 'Even now sometimes I can't
believe that it's over...you could so easily have died.'

'We both could, but we didn't. It's all in the past now,
and that's where it should stay.'

They were married three months later, and their eldest
son was born at Rothwell on the anniversary of the night
his parents had first celebrated their love there.

They had already decided that if he was a boy he was to be called James Justin Richard and, if a girl, simply Beth.

It had seemed a fitting tribute to the memories of those they had loved and whom they would always remember—with grace and with gratitude.